RADICAL LIES

RADICAL
LIES

RADICAL LIES

STEVEN SCULLI

Published by Wilkinson Publishing Pty Ltd
ACN 006 042 173
PO Box 24135, Melbourne, VIC 3001, Australia
Ph: +61 3 9654 5446
enquiries@wilkinsonpublishing.com.au
www.wilkinsonpublishing.com.au

Follow Wilkinson Publishing on social media.

WilkinsonPublishing
wilkinsonpublishinghouse
WPBooks

© Copyright Steven Sculli 2022

All rights reserved. No part of this publication may be reproduced, stored in a retrieval system or transmitted in any form by any means without the prior permission of the copyright owner. Enquiries should be made to the publisher.

Every effort has been made to ensure that this book is free from error or omissions. However, the Publisher, the Authors, the Editor or their respective employees or agents, shall not accept responsibility for injury, loss or damage occasioned to any person acting or refraining from action as a result of material in this book whether or not such injury, loss or damage is in any way due to any negligent act or omission, breach of duty or default on the part of the Publisher, the Authors, the Editor, or their respective employees or agents.

ISBN: 9781922810038
A catalogue record for this book is available from the National Library of Australia.

Editor: Sally Green
Design by WorkingType Studio
Printed and bound in Australia by Griffin Press

CHAPTER 1

PARKER, ARIZONA, FRIDAY 17 AUGUST

When Ishmael arrived at his rented apartment from the office on Friday evening he found a package on his doorstep. He tore it open and pulled out a customized roll of Velcro fastener. It had been ordered over a week ago from a manufacturer in Los Angeles, and he'd been waiting anxiously for this, the last piece of material he needed to complete his suicide bomb belt.

He raised a fist in the air. 'My soul longs for the moment when it will be united with yours in heaven. May the curse of God be upon all unbelievers,' he muttered softly.

After going inside and locking the door, he drew all the curtains and quickly set to work. First, he took off his sports jacket, tie and shirt and draped them neatly over the back of a chair. He then wrapped a strip of Velcro around his narrow torso and cut it accordingly. Next, using electric hair clippers, he shaved off the hooks and loops in the middle sections of the Velcro.

On the kitchen table he used a pastry roller to roll the blocks of C4 — plastic explosive — into thin sheets.

He sandwiched the C4 between the Velcro strips and then wired up the detonators and LED armed/disarmed indicators. For the power supply, he had chosen an ordinary mobile phone.

What looked like the little copper studs found on Levis were actually the triggering buttons for the detonators, any two of which, when pressed consecutively, would separate the top and bottom of his body, dispatching him and any bystanders to God. 'Always use two. Less chance of accidentally blowing yourself up before you are ready,' the munitions expert at the training camp had repeatedly stressed to all the budding combatants.

It was after eleven when fatigue and the drowsy effect of the soldering fumes finally set in. He knew the rule: if you become tired when working with explosives, it is time to call it a day.

CHAPTER 2

PARKER, ARIZONA, SATURDAY 18 AUGUST

By seven-forty the following morning, Ishmael had just finished securing the lethal band around his torso with duct tape, having gone through a number of rolls of tape and layers of skin trying to get the tension right. He chided himself for not having shaved his wildly matted stomach and chest hair.

Ishmael wriggled the lethal band around his waist so the two detonators were hanging above his right hip pocket, looped a leather belt around his jeans and tucked in the two buttons.

He put on two tight-fitting singlets, a loose-fitting shirt and tucked it in neatly. He swiveled his hips and touched his toes. Except for a little pinching around the hips, it did not feel cumbersome.

Ishmael studied himself in the full-length mirror. Apart from an ever so slight bulge at his waist, he looked okay. With a jacket on, the bulge would be unnoticeable. He was admiring his handiwork and intoning glory and praise to God when he was shocked out of his reverie by a loud knock on the front door.

'Scot, Jim here!' the voice called.

Ishmael's eyes shot to the clock on the wall. He had completely lost track of time. Panic stricken, he dashed into the bathroom, calling out in a controlled voice, 'Hang on Jim. Just getting out of the shower.'

He peeled off his shirt and two singlets in one swoop and dropped his pants. As he fumbled to get a grip on the duct tape, he noticed, to his horror, that the LED light was flashing on and off, indicating the belt was now armed. He studied one button, then the other. Why was the light flashing? What had gone wrong? Was it a faulty LED? He examined the detonation buttons more closely, lightly passing a finger over the pair. Neither had been pressed. All he could think was that one of them was defective. Which one? Why hadn't the LED picked up the problem when he had finished soldering the wires in the loop? Maybe a wire had broken away from a circuit while he was jiggling about. No, that couldn't be it. His soldering was impeccable.

He stared wide-eyed at the flashing LED. The only way to isolate the faulty button was to connect a third detonation button in the loop that would bridge the wiring and offset the defective detonation button. If he removed the belt before replacing it with an inactive button, the active button's impulse would detonate the belt. The detonation electronics were configured to automatically detonate the bomb belt if tampered with, just like a home security system.

It would take him at least ten minutes to fault-find and deactivate the system, longer still to remove the entire belt. He repeatedly cursed himself. 'Just like the Americans, stupid and hopeless.' He would just have to wear it. Ishmael knew it was a crazy thing to do, but he had no choice.

He hitched up his pants and slipped the two singlets and shirt back on and tucked himself in carefully. He went into the bedroom and sorted through his jackets. The day was going to be a scorcher, so he needed something light that he could keep on all day. He pulled out his linen jacket, donned it, checked himself in the mirror and patted himself. The care he had taken to make the belt fit like a second skin, even going to the trouble of evenly overlapping the duct tape, had been worth it in retrospect.

Back in the bathroom, he ran the cold water and splashed some on his face, dampening his neatly cropped hair. He sucked in a deep breath and let it out slowly. After a few moments he found himself, to his astonishment, quite composed and invigorated. 'God would be proud of my fidelity!' he thought.

Ishmael went into the kitchen, scooped up his holy book from the kitchen table, hastily opened it and read the first thing his eyes focused on, an inspiration from his God, he felt:

Be thou exalted, LORD, in thine own strength
He shall swallow them up in his wrath
The fire shall devour them that infest the Soul
Their sword shall enter into their own heart.

He closed it, kissed the cover and gingerly placed it in a drawer. He was feeling more relaxed and comfortable about wearing the belt, attributing this as proof of God's presence with him in his hour of need.

Just before he opened the front door, Ishmael raised his arms to his God in a gesture of defiance, closed his eyes and vowed never to be taken alive. Dropping his arms to his side, he had one last feel of the belt with the inside of his forearms, then he unhooked the security chain and opened the door.

Jim, wearing a flaming red shirt that fitted tightly around his heavy waistline, stood before Ishmael, punching out an SMS message. He looked up. 'Morning Scot. It's been a heck of a morning. You wouldn't want to know about it.'

Before Ishmael could say a word, Jim's phone rang. 'It's the wife. Meet you at the car.' He strolled off down the walkway talking into his cell phone.

Ishmael leant against the doorjamb and thought about trying to buy some time to get the belt off, but the feeling of wearing it was visceral. With every passing second he felt more alive, readier than ever before to die a good death for the sacred brotherhood. A surge of adrenaline pumped through him. The whole experience was surreal, empowering. He felt invincible.

Ishmael ducked back into the bathroom and checked himself one more time. Then he went into the kitchen, grabbed a matchbox, fished a couple of detonation buttons out of the drawer and placed them in the box. An opportunity to work on the problem might present itself during the day, he thought.

After locking the apartment, Ishmael went out to Jim's SUV and slid onto the front seat, acutely aware of the device around his body.

Jim cranked the engine. 'We've got a stack of things to do — pick up Joan's birthday cake, buy balloons, drinks and snacks. Robin's taken the birthday girl and Ayden out for the morning. Got to have everything ready by two o'clock sharp.'

Ishmael smiled modestly and said, 'I will do my best to help.'

'I'm sure you will,' Jim responded and reached over and clapped him on the shoulder. Ishmael stiffened. 'After the kids have finished partying, us oldsters are going to party until we drop.'

During the course of the morning's shopping, Ishmael found the presence of the belt on his body emotionally stabilizing, enabling him to focus his mind's eye on his God with a clarity he had never experienced before.

While Jim scooted around Walmart, pushing a shopping trolley brimming with party supplies, Ishmael purchased a pair of fingernail clippers and a roll of fine copper wire, and then ducked into the restroom. There, in a stall, he peeled back the duct tape to get at the circuit. He needed to replace the faulty button. Luckily, it was the first button, saving valuable time. As he trimmed off the ends of the copper wire, he considered taking off the belt, but decided against it. It was too much of a delicate operation to do in the confines of the toilet stall, and even if he did manage to take it off, he would have no place to put it.

Realizing that he had wound an excessive amount of tape around himself, he removed the excess to enable greater freedom of movement, and dumped it into the toilet. What would have been better, he figured, was to use a girdle and do away with the duct tape.

He flushed the toilet, but the tape being too stiff to flush, became stuck and water flowed over the top of the bowl onto his right shoe. He jumped back, nearly slipping in the puddle that was rapidly spreading. He hurriedly left the restroom.

He wandered through the shopping aisles looking for Jim and came upon the lingerie section. A mannequin wearing fishnet stockings and a lace-up corset caught his attention. He stopped to examine the display more closely. He pulled and tugged at the spandex fabric, inserting his hand in between it and the mannequin, feeling about, assessing the tension of the garment. Yes, he thought, if I wore one of these with the bra cups cut off I could ditch the duct tape.

'You want to get your hands down the real thing!' Jim called out.

Ishmael spun around, abashed, lost for words.

Another voice chimed in, 'Can I help you, sir?'

Ishmael turned around. A heavily built African American saleswoman, blonde extensions running down the front of her blue satin dress, was standing next to him.

'See ya at the checkout, Scot,' Jim said. Chuckling, he continued down another aisle.

'Just looking,' Ishmael said nervously. 'Do you have a size that would fit my ... my ...?'

'Oh, don't you be embarrassed, sir. Lots of menfolk buy these for their partners.' She leant over, straightened the corset on the mannequin and gazed down the aisle at the back of Jim. 'Love your friend's red shirt,' she said, winking at him.

Ishmael was insulted, believing that the woman was insinuating he had some type of immoral relationship with Jim. His mind already hot-wired by the bomb belt on his body, his programmed religious defenses leapt up in him. He stared contemptuously into her large, heavily painted eyes, and summoned up the fires of hell to consume the big black woman. His eyes moved to her lips, highlighted with purple lip gloss. She was talking to him but he was not listening. He followed the thick line of her neck, a heavy gold chain with an amulet hanging in the dark recess of her cleavage. Its shape and shiny texture suddenly looked familiar. It triggered an image of his departed mother wearing something similar.

Ishmael froze, his animosity towards the saleswoman abating. He shook his head at this image, turned slowly and walked away, listening to his right shoe squelching, leaving the saleswoman somewhat baffled.

CHAPTER 3

VIDAL JUNCTION, CALIFORNIA, SATURDAY 18 AUGUST

It was around lunchtime when they arrived in Jim's hometown, Vidal Junction, twenty-five miles across the Arizona and California state line.

'Every drop in that canal is vital,' Jim said as they turned off the old aqueduct road that ran parallel to the man-made river. 'In this heat the evaporation is phenomenal.'

'Why don't they pipe it?'

'As a matter of fact, that's on the drawing board. Let me know when you're through with drafting the plan for the number one hydrometer. I'll pull a few strings and get you on the team, if you like. We can use a bit of Canadian know-how.'

'Yes I'd like that,' Ishmael replied.

They drove on for about a quarter of a mile into a sparsely populated housing estate that went by the name of Desert Vistas. Jim, his wife Robin, their five-year-old daughter Joan and six-year-old adopted son Ayden lived in a two-story house. It had a gabled roof and a wrought-iron balustrade that ran around the first-floor veranda. Japanese lanterns and wooden chimes had been hung intermittently. The house, set back about thirty yards from the street, stood on a knoll.

By 2 pm, the decorations were up and the first guests had already arrived. Soon the house was alive with children running around, their squealing and laughter fuelled by raspberry lemonade.

Despite the air-conditioning being on full throttle, it wasn't keeping the house cool. The continual opening of outside doors by children running in and out was turning the house into an oven. He could feel the perspiration running down his legs.

Ishmael wandered around, mildly amused by the festivities. He wore a cone-shaped party hat, doing his best to fit in. In one hand, he held a paper cup filled with iced water and in the other, a party hooter. He watched intently as Joan tore open gifts presented to her by each guest.

Ishmael could not help casting his mind back to the modest birthday parties he had experienced as a boy in his hometown of Bikaner in India.

Jim's was a family of the kind Ishmael had once wanted, and he wondered where he would be now if the earthquake had not destroyed everything he called home and family. A deep longing for his family gnawed at him. Ishmael painfully realized that his actions would determine the fate of Jim's family. The children would be deprived of their father and Robin of her husband. Jim, along with the fathers of numerous other children who also were at the party, were destined to die.

Ishmael stood with his back against the far wall, watching little Joan blow out the candles on her birthday cake. He silently castigated himself for allowing such feelings for the soon-to-be fatherless children and bereaved wives. As soon as the cake was served, he was going to call a cab.

Just then, someone brushed up against him. He stiffened, turned and saw a frail, elderly woman clutching a walking frame standing next to him. It was Mrs. Rayner, Jim's mother. He moved aside to let her pass, but she remained stationary, peering fixedly over the top of her glasses at him. Her clouded grey eyes cleared and decades rolled off her face. Her expression seemed to Ishmael to indicate that she could see right into his soul. Mrs. Rayner's eyes contained no doubt as to what was on her mind. He felt naked. A chill ran down his spine.

Chapter 3 *Vidal Junction, California, Saturday 18 August*

'My dear, dear sweet boy, you really do not want to make these children suffer,' said Mrs. Rayner in a clear, resonant voice.

The color drained out of Ishmael's face. He groped for something to say. Mrs. Rayner slowly about-faced and shuffled off, leaning heavily on her walking frame. With a horrified expression on his face, he quickly looked around to see if anyone had overheard her comment, but she had brought no attention to him. Ishmael stood frozen against the wall. Was it meant to be a joke? No, he decided. It was too serious a remark to have been a joke. He needed to cross-examine the old woman and get to the bottom of this. He followed Mrs. Rayner into the kitchen, his eyes pinned on her spindly frame.

'Excuse me, Mrs. Rayner!' Ishmael called out.

He felt someone tapping him on the shoulder, he spun on his heels.

Robin gazed at him quizzically and half raised her eyebrows. 'Jim's mom is away with the pixies,' she said.

'Pixies?' Ishmael repeated.

'Dementia. She has lost all her marbles.'

'But she just said something and I may have given her the impression that I ignored her.'

'Forget about it. She's always muttering things. You get more sense out of some of these children than out of Grandma,' she joked.

Robin smiled broadly. She was an average-sized woman, rather pleasant to the eye. Her thick mane of auburn hair accentuated the few freckles that were speckled across her cheeks.

Ishmael smiled wanly. His concentration hovered between Robin and the old woman who was now making her way through the sliding glass doors to the back veranda. Rosasharn, Jim's younger sister, was steadying her with one arm, while cradling a red balloon full of water in the other.

Sucking in a deep breath, Ishmael pinched the bridge of his nose and said, 'Um, I'm not feeling the best, Robin. I have a splitting headache ...' he lied, hoping she would get the hint and leave him alone.

'Now, you just sit down there while I get you some aspirin.'

She led him to the kitchen table and pushed him down onto a chair. The sharp edge of the Velcro pinched the flesh around his hip. He clenched his teeth.

Ten minutes later, Ishmael found himself lying on top of a bed in one of the children's rooms staring up at a model airplane that hung from the ceiling. It would have all been so easy if he were a qualified pilot working for one of the American airline companies, he thought.

He propped himself on one elbow and looked out the window into the backyard. Mrs. Rayner was still under the lemon tree. From the angle of her head, she looked as if she was dozing. If there wasn't that group of mothers sitting around the outdoor table near her, he would have marched downstairs and confronted her.

Did he really imagine that she had been talking to him? No, he did not. Given his own experience of being left alone, how could he not feel empathy for the children of the fathers he worked with?

Mrs. Rayner had prophesied the consequences of his action on the children. Whether she was mad or not, he felt an urgent need to interrogate her. He lay down on his back and tried to relax. Maybe he would get a chance to talk to her when that mothers' meeting was over. He ran his thumb lightly over the two detonator buttons.

If the room were to be stormed by the people downstairs demanding an explanation of whatever the old woman had told them, he would be left with only one alternative. 'I will be silent before my accusers. Let them speak, then I will say my final prayer of entrance into the presence of God.' This was a sacred text that had been handed down from time immemorial to all the faithful who were ready to die for the God who had chosen them and promised to give them a new name, a name beyond reproach.

Chapter 3 *Vidal Junction, California, Saturday 18 August*

Ishmael folded his arms across his chest and arched his back. The tension caused by the belt around his torso drained away and he relaxed again.

Just ten or so minutes of solitude with his God in this cool oasis was all he needed, before going back downstairs and trailing the old hag's heels, until an opportunity presented itself to assess whether she was a threat.

Being in the midst of people whom he regarded as enemies gave Ishmael an eerie feeling that, ultimately, it did not matter whether the Colorado Aqueduct Plant was destroyed. He closed his eyes and prayed silently to God for guidance. He lost track of time and drifted off into a shallow sleep.

'Wake up, Scot. The big children's party is about to get under way.'

Ishmael rubbed his eyes and looked at the Mickey Mouse clock on the wall. It was five thirty. He had slept for over an hour.

He sat up in bed and gazed out the window. The bench under the lemon tree was empty. The thought that Mrs. Rayner might have already told others that he had evil intentions flashed through his mind. He rested his hand over the detonation buttons.

'Won't be a minute,' Ishmael said.

'See you downstairs,' Jim replied and shut the door.

After a trip to the bathroom, Ishmael joined the guests downstairs. Most of the children had gone. A dozen or so adults were milling around. He recognized some of the faces as workers from the plant.

He looked around to see if Jim's mother was still about and caught sight of her sitting alone in an armchair in the lounge room, watching television. This was his chance. He had to act fast, before anyone drew close enough to overhear their conversation.

He hesitated for a moment, uncertain what to say to her, then approached her as naturally as possible. If Mrs. Rayner gave even the slightest indication that she recognized him from their earlier encounter, then the old lady was not as mad as Robin had made her out to be.

'Scot, come and have a drink with us!' Percy Owens called out from across the room.

'I'll be over in a few minutes,' Ishmael replied.

'Hello, Mrs. Rayner. Anything good on the television?' Ishmael watched her reaction intently. Her expression was blank and her eyes remained unfocused as she stared at the television set.

'Mom, time to go home.'

He turned around.

'Sorry to startle you. I don't think we've been introduced. I'm Rosasharn, Jim's sister.'

Ishmael took her proffered hand and shook it gingerly. 'Pleased to meet you. Scot Fall. I work with your brother at the aqueduct plant.'

He glanced at the old woman, and then his eyes darted back to Rosasharn. He guessed her to be around her early twenties. She was just over five feet tall, a little plump in all the right places and a touch too awkward-looking to be called pretty, but she had a kind of simplicity about her. Her features were soft, her skin pale and clear, apart from a faint scar about the size of half a matchstick on her dimpled chin. Her long, lustrous, chestnut hair was tied back in a ponytail.

'Despite what Robin says, Mother is not as vacant as she looks.' She smiled wryly and turned her attention to her mother.

Rosasharn's contradiction of what Robin had told him puzzled him.

'Upsy daisy. Time to go, Mom.'

Rosasharn lifted her mother to her feet. Ishmael grabbed hold of her walking frame and placed it in front of Mrs. Rayner. He stared fixedly into her unfocused eyes.

Rosasharn smiled again at Ishmael as she escorted her mother out of the lounge room.

Chapter 3 *Vidal Junction, California, Saturday 18 August*

'Excuse me, would you be driving through Parker? I need a ride home.'

Rosasharn steadied her mother and faced Ishmael. She folded her arms, dropped her left hip and tilted her head slightly as she stared at Ishmael. Ishmael held her gaze. What struck him about her was that he could not help feeling there was more to this woman than just being a party girl. She had none of her brother's modesty or shyness and little of his restraint. During the course of the afternoon, she had caught his attention while he watched her play some of the birthday games and helped the mothers paint the children's faces. The children were all amused by her mad antics as she laughed and squealed along with them. Now, however, she was all serious, leaning forward slightly with her arms crossed, leaving no doubt about who was in charge. She had a strong presence, like someone who was always in control.

Ishmael cleared his throat, 'I came in with Jim this morning. Someone from maintenance was going to drive me home later, but I'm not feeling the best,' he said, half pleading.

Rosasharn straightened herself up and smoothed the front of her dress. It was a powder blue dress with yellow sunflowers printed around the hem that fell well below her knees. She scratched at a red paint spot and looked first at Ishmael and then at her mother, as if making a connection.

'As a matter of fact, yes, I am driving through Parker,' she said at last, 'but I need to drop Mom off at the Water's Edge Nursing Home. Then I'm off to Lake Havasu City. If you don't mind the detour, sure, you're welcome.'

'No, no, I do not mind the detour,' Ishmael said, sounding a little too eager. 'I really don't want to hold you up, but I would be most grateful if you would give me a couple of minutes while I say a few goodbyes.'

'Of course. See you out the front.'

Ishmael was saying his goodbyes when Percy Owens, the personnel manager from the Colorado Aqueduct, leant into him and said, 'You better be careful pard'ner. Rosasharn is single. I hear she's looking to hitch herself to a man. She's a tigress.'

'Her mother is leaving with us.'

'Then watch out for her mother.'

Percy and the people around him burst out laughing.

As Ishmael walked away from the group, Percy came up behind and caught him by the arm. Ishmael spun around and stared aghast at Percy, shaking his arm free of Percy's tight grip.

'Easy, Scot, didn't mean to startle you, my boy.'

'What? What is it, Percy?' he stuttered.

'Seriously, Rosasharn is sharp as a whip, woman with a damn lot to say. Working on a book of some religious sort. Also does a bit of freelance writing for the local papers on environmental issues. She is hell-bent against the billion-dollar upgrade of the aqueduct to increase capacity. Now, you be a good boy and have a go at getting her to tone down her rhetoric.'

'I'll see what I can do, Percy.'

'Talk to her about the snow, say as long as it keeps snowing in the Rockies — and when does it ever not snow?' — he rolled his eyes, 'the effect down river from the aqueduct is minimal.'

'Got it. Snow always falling, minimal effect.' Ishmael nodded.

Ishmael found Jim and Robin out the front of the house. Rosasharn was helping her mother into the back seat of her 1985 Oldsmobile.

'I was looking for you, Jim. Your sister's giving me a ride home,' Ishmael said.

'The sleep didn't do you much good?'

'No.'

'Too bad you're not staying, Scot. Anyway, thanks for your help.' Jim then turned to Rosasharn, who had finally managed to get Mrs. Rayner settled into the seat.

Chapter 3 *Vidal Junction, California, Saturday 18 August*

'Thanks ever so much, Rosesharn, for bringing Ma along.'

'It was nice that she could be here for Joan's party.'

Jim hugged her and said, 'I wish I could do more for her.'

'You've got Robin and the kids to worry about. I really don't mind taking the responsibility.'

'Well, thanks awfully, Rosasharn,' Robin said. 'It's a big relief for Jim that she has you to look after her.

Rosasharn smiled weakly and got in the car.

'You better make sure he gets home safe, you hear, Rosesharn?' Jim joked.

Ishmael got into the car and gazed at the house, then at Jim and his wife, and recalled what Akmid, his mentor, had prophesied. That he, Ishmael, had been chosen by God to go into the enemy's house, not through the back door, trying to steal in undetected, but to go in as would invited guests, to sit and drink at the his table, and while the he rejoices and feasts in honor of his guest, he would be destroyed, swiftly, by the hand of the all Powerful.

With a toot of the horn, they drove off, leaving Jim and Robin standing out the front of their house, waving them goodbye.

CHAPTER 4

VIDAL JUNCTION, CALIFORNIA, SATURDAY 18 AUGUST

Ishmael stared fixedly at the serrated peaks of the Whipple Mountain Range. He was at his wits' end of how to tactfully approach the elusive matter of determining if Mrs. Rayner was a threat. Robin and Rosasharn had told him conflicting stories. He didn't know who to believe. If he couldn't pry anything important out of the daughter then, once he knew the whereabouts of the nursing home, he would come back later that night. Screw on the silencer on his .38 super semi-automatic he purchased at Walmart and execute the old woman. By the time ballistics had traced the murder weapon back to him, he'd be in heaven.

'It's very kind of you to give me this lift,' Ishmael said, fiddling with the ashtray in the door.

'Glad to,' said Rosasharn.

'How long do you think it will take to get there?'

'It's usually about twenty minutes from Jim's, but in this traffic I reckon over an hour. All these cars with boat trailers that come out for the weekend, choke up the highway.'

Ishmael nodded agreeably. 'By the way, where is your mother's nursing home?'

'Between Earp and Big River. The place is by the Colorado River on a high bluff overlooking Deer Island. It's such a pretty place with the water and trees. Mom seems to be settled there.'

Chapter 4 *Vidal Junction, California, Saturday 18 August*

'That's nice.' Ishmael casually picked up the street directory from the dashboard and flipped it open to eastern California. He located Parker and traced the road back to Big River.

'Can't spot it. There's Big River.'

Rosasharn reached out and stabbed in the general vicinity with her finger. Her hand brushed along Ishmael's torso. Ishmael stiffened.

As Rosasharn wove in and out of the traffic, a thought started niggling at Ishmael. The more he considered it, the more probable it seemed that Rosasharn's mother might utter another comment in reference to his mission. 'Despite what Robin says, Mother is not as vacant as she looks.' That's what Rosasharn had told him back at Jim's. Any remark from Mrs. Rayner would arouse suspicion and lead to some serious questioning by Rosasharn.

What if he couldn't explain away whatever the old lady alleged about him? Ishmael reasoned that Rosasharn would, in all probability, talk to Jim. On Monday morning, Jim would take him aside and demand an explanation. Did Jim agree with his wife or his sister regarding their mother's mental health? He didn't know. If he failed to discredit Jim's mother's accusations against him, he would bet that, by mid-morning, he would most likely find himself sitting across Percy Owens's desk getting quizzed over contentious matters that had been brought to Percy's attention.

Ishmael tried to think what Percy might say. Maybe he would just laugh and slap him on the back and tell him not to lose any sleep over whatever the mad old woman had said. Knowing Percy, he would notify the authorities behind his back.

The consequences were getting serious. Everything could be put into jeopardy by the old hag sitting behind him.

As these thoughts whirled around in Ishmael's head, making him feel more and more out of control, he felt like reaching over and strangling the old lady.

'No, no!' he said and stomped his foot.

Rosasharn looked at him askance, 'Are you all right?'

Ishmael frowned. 'Yes, fine. Sorry. Just thinking out loud,' he said.

If the old woman talked, he would have to eliminate the daughter as well. Slowly, he turned and faced Rosasharn, narrowed his eyes and nodded imperceptibly.

In the wake of this option, an impasse came to mind. Disposing of the bodies would not be the problem here. By the time they were discovered, their bones would have been picked clean by buzzards and bleached by the sun. No, the problem was that by being the last one to be seen with the two missing women, the police would be on his doorstep before he had dispatched himself to heaven.

A cold, damp sweat enveloped his body. He dreaded the prospect, and the cost of the old woman opening her toothless trap. He cranked down the window. Hot, stifling air blew into his face, leaving him gasping hoarsely.

'Are you sure you're all right?' Rosasharn quizzed.

'It's just that it's been a long day ... all those children. I'm not used to kids.'

'Is the air-con too much?'

'I shouldn't have it blasting in my face.' He wound up the window and repositioned the vents a little lower.

'Yell out if you want to stop.'

Vexed and exhausted over what to do if the mother talked, he slouched in the car seat. The Velcro dug into him. He could feel a cloud of melancholy sweeping over him.

Ishmael reproached himself for asking Rosasharn for a lift home. If the old lady spilled the beans, he'd have to abort his mission. Then what?

Chapter 4 *Vidal Junction, California, Saturday 18 August*

The holy leaders of the Global Azad Front would hold an inquiry and the truth would come out. The failed mission in America had all stemmed from feeling sorry for the soon-to-be fatherless children of the Americans. Maybe he could tell them a few forgivable lies to hide his weakness. Werter von Stumpf, his religious mentor, would stand by him and quote wise, compassionate counsel from the holy book in his defense.

If by the grace of God, he was pardoned in the eyes of the leaders of the Azad Front, he still had to contend with Canaan. His lifelong friend would see through it all and not be fooled. Canaan would accuse him of being a coward, telling him the same old thing that he should have abandoned a religion that had been hijacked by mad men.

'All is not lost,' he heard himself say aloud as a flash of inspiration came to him.

'What's not lost?' Rosasharn asked.

'Just thinking aloud again, things about work. You put a lot of effort into a project and then it gets shelved,' Ishmael replied edgily. 'Then out of the ruins some of it gets back onto the drawing board.'

'I'm happy for you.'

Ishmael straightened himself. All he needed to transport himself into the wonderful presence of God was around his waist. Unfortunately, by killing two mere women, his death in the service of God would not be a celebrated good death. In the light of this he was comforted by the prospect of his most holy act at least gaining the attention of the world's media once the pieces were put together by the authorities. His apartment would be searched, bombs and plans to blow up a vital American utility discovered.

The Global Azad Front would be poised to claim responsibility and post on the Internet his inspirational video that had been shot during his final days at the training camp. It was a video about heralding in the new millennium of freedom fighters. He was dressed in a graduation gown with a mortarboard rakishly tipped on his head, brandishing a sword in one hand and clutching a rolled diploma with the other. He stood defiantly in front of a couple of dozen masked combatants wearing headbands scripted with inspired verses and holding up AK47s as they chanted, 'Death to the enemies of God.' He felt so proud of himself, being the first of a new generation of cultured, sophisticated freedom fighters, and overjoyed that the days of barbarous uneducated fighters recruited from the rural poor and refugees would be no more.

Suddenly, he wondered whether his inspirational video would even be released. Being the first to marshal in the new era of cultured and sophisticated freedom fighters, surely the world would look upon his martyrdom as a farce in light of him ending it all on a desert highway with two women.

Ishmael's eyes lit up at the sight of a petrol tanker coming over the rise from the opposite direction. He prayed that the force of the bomb belt exploding would send the car careening out of control into one of them. The carnage would be guaranteed, crediting him with more dead Americans.

'If this is how God has predestined my exit from this world, so be it,' he said to himself. Hope welled again in Ishmael's breast. Yes, the video would be released after a little bit of editing. Akmid and Werter von Stumpf would see to that. The pair would certainly be able to turn his meagre martyrdom into a grand one. Detonating now definitely had the potential to incite just as much terror as blowing up an American utility.

They had travelled no more than another couple of hundred yards when Ishmael was overcome with an eerie sensation; he could feel the old lady's eyes boring into the back of his head. He twisted around and gazed into the eyes of the elderly woman. A bolt of glaring white light shot through his brain. Mrs. Rayner's eyes expressed intelligence and insight. She seemed to be reading him like a book.

Chapter 4 *Vidal Junction, California, Saturday 18 August*

Rosasharn glanced at Ishmael, applied her foot to the brake, tilted the rear-view mirror and brought her mother into view. 'Oh no, that's what's troubling the poor guy. Mom's at it again,' she exclaimed. 'Mom, stop it!' she shouted.

Mrs. Rayner snapped out of the present, her eyes dilated and became unfocused. Rosasharn turned to Ishmael and said, 'I'm so sorry, Scot. Mother is playing her mind games again.' Turning her full attention to the driving, she floored the accelerator and tried to hide her amusement. 'I have a feeling I know what Mom was about to say,' she said to herself and giggled.

Oblivious to the levity Rosasharn was trying to contain, Ishmael's paranoia escalated. Can she read my mind too? Yes, she can. She will tell Jim. The mission is lost. She will ruin everything. Canaan will have his way with me. No one will see the video.

Ishmael unsnapped the seatbelt, slid his hand inside the waistband of his jeans and located the detonation buttons. He tightened his grip and sucked in a deep breath, exhaled and pressed one button. The belt was armed. It was as if the detonation switch was hot-wired to his brain.

Ishmael silently recited the holy prayer of martyrdom:

The asylum of the Faith, strengthened by heaven, aided against enemies,
The arm of the victorious government, the lamp of the resplendent teaching,
Perpetuate the prosperity of them that offer their mortal lives in service of thee.

In his mind's eye he saw heaven open and his two guardian angels descend to earth. Now they were hovering above the car, their angelic smiles beaming on him, their arms outstretched, ready to descend to pick up his bleeding and bruised soul and carry it off to the resplendent presence of God. The martyrs of this holy faith would return to the God of Heaven and Earth who had chosen them.

He started to pray aloud in the ancient Arabic dialect that the prayer was originally inscribed in, the text of which was found carved into the base of a sandstone cliff in the Wadi Musa (Valley of Moses):

Aid me to plunge the sword of the Almighty into the vile heart, to silence the mind of him whom God doth judge as the corrupters, the usurpers of the promise to the first-born son of Ibrahim.

Rosasharn cocked her head towards Ishmael. 'Why are you praying, Scot?' Trying her hardest to keep her eyes on the road, they were drawn down to his crotch. At the sight of his hand down his jeans she burst into such a loud, ringing fit of laughter that she found it difficult to drive. In between her gasps she said, 'I'm pulling up into this gas station.' Rosasharn swerved the car into the driveway.

Just as Ishmael was about to recite the final line of the prayer, his index finger poised over the second detonation button, the front wheel clipped the curb. Ishmael bounced, hitting his head on the roof and catapulting across the split bench seat, ending up with his head on her lap.

The bump on the head and the sudden cessation of movement jolted Ishmael out of his trance, breaking the rhythm of his praying. He relaxed his right hand just enough to not press down on the second detonator. He lay for a moment with his head across Rosasharn's thighs, staring up at her breasts. The heavy fragrance of her perfume filled his nostrils.

Rosasharn pulled up and cut the engine. She was almost in hysterics. Tears streamed down her cheeks.

Ishmael grimaced, straightening himself up. 'Why are you laughing?!' Ishmael yelled.

Chapter 4 *Vidal Junction, California, Saturday 18 August*

'I'm sorry, really sorry,' Rosasharn blurted in between fits of laughter.

Finally regaining her composure she faced her mother. 'Mom, you all right?'

As Ishmael became more aware of his surroundings, a Greyhound bus parked next to a petrol pump seized his attention. He flung open the door.

'Stop! Don't go! Let me explain!' he heard Rosasharn call above the din of impulses in his brain. Ishmael stepped out of the car and marched towards the bus. He lifted his eyes to the sky, searching for his guardian angels. Silently, he implored the Almighty to immediately order them back and swore on his mother's grave that fear had not tainted his heart, laying all blame on Rosasharn's bad driving, for mocking and making him lose his concentration. From the corner of his eye he saw two motorcycle cops coast into the service station. He quickened his pace.

'By the time that laughing, crazy girl attracts their attention, no doubt to single me out unjustly as a terrorist, I will be on board a bus full of Americans. A more profitable target than two women,' he muttered to himself.

The heat was unbearable. The short walk from the car to the Greyhound bus left Ishmael breathless. As he neared the bus door, he composed himself.

Joining the queue, he calmly climbed aboard. A quick scan showed the bus to be full. The faces all looked vaguely familiar, like those he had encountered a few weeks ago when traveling on a Greyhound bus — Mexicans, Blacks, Asians — except for a group at the back of the bus, a large, rowdy Jewish family. The mother was scolding the three young boys wearing skullcaps.

Making his way down the aisle, Ishmael spotted an empty seat in front of a large, blotchy-faced woman occupying two seats. She looked up from the magazine she was reading, twiddled the ends of her headscarf and eyed Ishmael warningly as he eased himself into the seat.

Ishmael glanced down the aisle. The driver was now behind the wheel. Ishmael began to recite the holy prayer of martyrdom. His right hand located the detonator that was yet to be activated. His heart pounded in his chest, almost bursting. His breath came in spurts.

Ishmael reached the final stanza. His inhibition vanquished, he envisioned his guardian angels hovering above the bus:

Direct thy holy vessels of destruction, their inclinations to every evil thing against the enemies of the most holy faith. God be praised. Be glorified. Be magnified....

He pressed the button, fully expecting to feel nothing. He knew that the speed of the shockwave would sever all the nerves to his brain before his body could register any pain. He closed his eyes tightly. Suddenly, there was a shudder that was followed by a loud noise. His eyes sprang open. The bus was moving. He was alive. The bomb hadn't exploded. What had gone wrong? He pressed the button again and again. Nothing.

'What you doin' sittin' in my nephew's seat?' the fat lady blurted. She poked her hand through the gap in the seats and prodded Ishmael in the arm. 'Hey you, mister, what you doin' sittin' in that seat? It belongs to Dennis.'

His attention fixed on setting off the bomb, Ishmael was oblivious to the fat lady.

Infuriated over being ignored, she called out at the top of her voice, as if summoning a dog, for the driver to stop the bus.

An elderly Texan wearing a white Stetson with a Star of David embroidered on the front, sitting behind the driver, tapped him on the shoulder and said, 'Hey, captain, lard ass is a-hollering for you to stop.'

Chapter 4 *Vidal Junction, California, Saturday 18 August*

'What is it this time? She get herself stuck in the privy again? Goddamn son of a bitch.' The driver cursed and stopped the bus with a jerk, causing the passengers to jolt forward.

The fat woman stood up, gave Ishmael a cursory glance and started down the aisle for the driver. Due to her width, she had to turn sideways and shimmy along it. The hem of her tent-like dress became caught up, causing it to ride up almost to miniskirt level, revealing her large, cellulite-ridden, varicose-veined legs. Jeers and fat jokes were bandied around. Barging her way to the front, she reached forward and knocked the Stetson off the Texan. Grabbing the driver by the arm, she shrieked in his ear, 'Hey driver! Driver, are you listening? There's a man sittin' in Dennis's seat. You gotta check his ticket. He's in the wrong seat.'

Ishmael leapt out of his seat. 'That's it. Go and lock myself in the toilet and strip it off until it discharges automatically.' He dashed to the toilet, but it was occupied. He pounded on it with his fists. Looking down the aisle, all Ishmael could see was the back of the fat lady. From his vantage point at the back of the bus he reconnoitered the area, ducking down between the Jewish couple to peer out the window.

'Who do you think you are? What sort of way is this to behave?' the woman rebuked him and then muttered something in Yiddish to her husband.

Ishmael's blood froze. He half expected to see a regiment of law enforcement officers pointing machine guns at the bus, to hear a voice talking into a megaphone, calling out for him to give himself up, but to his utter surprise all looked normal. He spotted Rosasharn, arms crossed, standing beside her car, looking towards the bus. He located the motorcycle cops. They were standing next to their motorcycles, eating ice cream.

He heard the latch click and little Dennis, looking pale and drawn, stepped out of the cubicle. Ishmael ducked in, locked the door behind him. He undid his belt buckle and was about to drop his pants when it suddenly occurred to him that Rosasharn did not have a clue what he was up to. If she had, she would have flagged the two policemen by now. He recalled the final moments in the car, which seemed like an eternity ago. 'Yes,' he punched the air. She was not onto him. Everything was not lost.

He hitched up his pants and tucked in his shirt. As he stepped out he was confronted by the gruff driver, who stood with his arms akimbo, demanding to see a ticket. Next thing he knew, he was being escorted off the bus by the scruff of his neck.

Ishmael was about to step onto the concrete when the bus driver gave him a helping shove with the side of his boot.

'Next time, buy a goddamned ticket!' hollered the driver.

Ishmael fell awkwardly, landing heavily on his side. As he hit the ground the aluminum bracket that held the circuits on his bomb-belt buckled. It partially cut the insulation on the wires that were connected to one of the faulty buttons. A slight jolt or movement the wrong way and Ishmael would not even have time to say his prayer.

The doors slammed shut and the bus drove away. Dazed, he picked himself up and scanned the sky, trying to spot his guardian angels. They would have seen what happened. He was ready. He had done everything right — the prayer, the sequence. Surely the angels would report all this to the Almighty. In what little comfort there was to be had, Ishmael consoled himself with the knowledge that it was a technical problem. In no way, either in heaven or on Earth, could it be regarded as an aspersion on his fidelity to the call of martyrdom.

'Hey, Scot. You don't really want to catch a bus home, do you?'

Startled, he turned and saw Rosasharn with her head cocked out the car window. Their eyes locked for a moment.

'You look like you've been to hell and back. Aren't you hot in that jacket?'

Ishmael smiled wanly. His face glistened in a sheen of perspiration. I nearly went to heaven, he thought to himself, on the verge of tears. He looked down at his shoes and swallowed his tears.

'Looks like you've worked out that it was the wrong bus. It would've taken you to Vegas.' Rosasharn paused and looked at her watch. 'If you want a bus that'll get you into Parker there's one that comes through here in about an hour or so.' Rosasharn revved the car slightly. 'I guess I owe you more than an apology. Please get in and I'll explain,' she said, her tone contrite.

Ishmael shuffled on the spot and raised his head. His eyes were brimming with unshed tears. So much had happened in the last five minutes that he was having trouble catching up to where he was now. He couldn't let her go without sorting out the issue about her mother. He got in the car. As he sat down he felt a slight jab on his side. He ignored it. He reached for the door and slammed it shut.

'Easy on the hinges. Now, pull yourself together,' Rosasharn said slowly.

'What are you going to explain?' Ishmael grumbled.

Rosasharn reversed into a parking bay, put the car in neutral, left the engine running and turned up the AC. The motorcycle cops, who had mounted their bikes, rolled slowly past them. Ishmael eyed them menacingly.

'Scot, I should have told you.'

'What?'

'About my mother.' Rosasharn paused for a moment. 'That's if you hadn't already figured it out.'

'Figured what out?' Ishmael placed both hands on his lap, took a deep breath and sucked in his stomach slightly to ease the tension on his torso. He felt the jab when he exhaled. Again he ignored it.

Rosasharn brushed the hair from her eyes. 'Look, Scot, I'd already guessed that Mom said something to you at Jim's. That's why you were in the lounge room with her.'

Though Ishmael found Rosasharn's gaze disconcerting, his face remained impassive. He turned back to glance at Mrs. Rayner. There went that jab again, its seriousness still not registering.

'Whatever was going on between you and Mom, it's really none of my business.'

'So why are you making it your business now?' Ishmael retorted.

Rosasharn shrugged, unbuckled her seatbelt and pushed her seat back. She twisted around, propped herself on her knees and faced her mother. Ishmael stared at her pale thighs as her dress crawled up around her thick waist.

Rosasharn gingerly brushed her mother's cheek with the back of her hand. Mrs. Rayner's eyes flickered.

Rosasharn faced Ishmael. 'When I heard you praying in Arabic. It was Arabic, wasn't it?' She paused and repeated a snippet.

'Yes, it was.' Ishmael willed himself to relax.

Rosasharn continued trying to pronounce the words.

'Silence. It is not right for a woman to speak those words.'

Rosasharn stopped, looked at him, a bemused expression on her face. 'Yes, I am aware of your religious lore, the division of women's petitions and men's petitions to God.'

'Good.' Ishmael nodded approvingly. 'How is it that you know Arabic?'

'I studied Middle Eastern history at Arizona State, got a fair knowledge of the language.'

'Have you no respect for a man when he prays?'

'Oh, let up on me, Scot. Honestly, I wasn't laughing at you for praying,' Rosasharn said, her voice full of sincerity. 'I'll start from the beginning, just to put everything in perspective.'

'Yes.' Ishmael crossed his arms.

Chapter 4 *Vidal Junction, California, Saturday 18 August*

'Well this thing with Mom has been happening.'

'What do you mean, "this thing"?' Ishmael snapped.

'Whoa, prosecutor, you're badgering the defendant. Hear me out. If I'm guilty, then you can sentence me to the scaffold for mocking your piety.'

He motioned her to continue.

'Mom blurts out what people are thinking. She can mind read,' Rosasharn tapped the side of her head.

'Mind reads!' Ishmael exclaimed.

'I'll give you an example. Mom came right out and said in front of a doctor, with one of his nurses present, that he ...' She stopped in mid-sentence, bit her lower lip and continued. 'This doctor was supposed to be focused on Mom, not on me, and Mom told him so. Later, the nurse pulled me aside and applauded Mom for her frankness and said it was about time that womanizing, walking stethoscope was shamed. And listen to this. She wanted to parade a couple of other sleazy quacks in front of Mom in the hope of embarrassing them, too. I said to this nurse that Mom's condition isn't something she can turn on at will. She just drops the bomb on whoever is there at the time.'

'So, you are accusing me of being immoral?' he said defensively.

'No! I am not.' She bored her finger into the cracked vinyl of the headrest. 'Look, Scot, I understand, so let's just drop it and get Mom home.'

'Understand what?'

'It's really none of my business.' Rosasharn shook her head, clenching her teeth.

'I am now ordering you to make it your business.'

'Okay, buster, you asked for it,' Rosasharn replied and burst out laughing again. She took several moments to quiet down before she continued. 'I look over at Mom, see that all-too-familiar expression on her face. Oh no, please don't, Mom, I say to myself and with you next to me getting all religious, with your hand ...' She stopped in mid-sentence, glanced down at the crutch of his pants and made a concerted effort not to giggle. 'Gee, Scot, a girl can't help putting two and two together. I just wanted to save you the embarrassment.' She sighed. 'Your God answered your prayer because I stopped her. Hey, isn't that neat?' She gave him an angelic smile.

'Wouldn't it have occurred to you that I am a man of faith?' He held his right hand over his heart. 'I am required to pray many times a day,' he said proudly.

'As a matter of fact, I wasn't told you were a man of faith. Maybe you should have announced that you were going to get on your knees, and I should have let Mom say whatever she was going to say. I'm sure it would have been something juicy, or then again ...' She paused, narrowed her eyes and said ominously, 'Maybe she was going to voice out loud some dark purpose of yours. Mom sometimes picks up on what lurks in the unconscious.'

Ishmael's head jerked back as if his face had been slapped.

'Hmm ... That reminds me of this time when Mom and I were standing in line at the bank. Mom turned around to this creepy-looking guy who was behind us. He was all fidgety, reeked of B.O. and beer. You know what Mom said to him?'

Ishmael averted her scrutinizing gaze and looked towards the highway.

'Mom told him that it was not right to steal other people's money. Straightaway this guy about-faced and marched straight out the door, not once looking back. Whether he was going to fraudulently withdraw money or hold up the place, I can't say.' She leaned back onto the steering wheel and pulled down the hem of her dress. 'Mom was definitely going to say something. I felt it was my responsibility to spare you the embarrassment.'

'Maybe she was going to say something about you,' Ishmael said accusingly.

Rosasharn rubbed her chin, giggled and then nodded agreeably. 'Okay, I give in. Maybe I was having some erotic private thoughts to myself.'

Victory shone in Ishmael's eyes.

'I'm so sorry, Scot. Please, forgive me for laughing at you,' Rosasharn said, more coquettish then serious. 'For the mere fact that you were praying to be delivered from temptation says a lot about a man in my books.'

'All right, I accept your apology and I believe that you weren't ridiculing my faith,' Ishmael said begrudgingly.

Rosasharn faced her mother and waggled her index finger. 'Mom, you're going to have to learn to hold your tongue when I'm around.' She looked at her watch. 'It's almost six, Mom. Have to get you tucked in for the night and your medication down. So,' she said to Ishmael, 'you have heard me out. Do you still want to catch the bus home?'

'You can drive me.'

Rosasharn put the car into gear, eased onto the highway. The traffic had slowed to a crawl.

Ishmael reached over his shoulder for the buckle. Again he felt something biting into his side. Probably the abrasive edges of the Velcro, he thought.

As they edged their way in the traffic, a gleaming black SUV convertible cut in front of them causing Rosasharn to brake abruptly.

The shrill voices of three scantily dressed girls singing the Eagles' 'Peaceful Easy Feeling' assaulted them both. The trio was standing up in the back, hanging onto the roll-bar with one hand, longneck beer bottles in the other. Their short summer dresses were blowing in the wind. Two of them were singing into their beer bottles as if they were microphones.

Ishmael stared a little longer than he would have liked at one of the girls who was wearing a G-string. He tore his eyes away from her gyrating pelvis, bowed his head and dangled his arms between his knees. He fantasized about taking Rosasharn then and there, showing her that he was a real man. If it were not for the holy equipment he had on, he would have made a pass at her.

'Has your mother informed the police of the things she has detected in people's thoughts?' Ishmael said, breaking the uncomfortable silence between them.

'Who's going to believe a senile old woman? Even when she was well she didn't go around informing the authorities of would-be criminals and frustrated perverts.' She shot him a quick glance. 'It wasn't her style.'

'What about repeating what she has said?'

'I haven't heard her say anything more about the guy in the bank, or the doctor, and he still regularly goes into her room to read her medical chart. He does get a bit jumpy when I'm there.'

Ishmael let out a sigh of relief. Instantly realizing what he had done, he pretended to sneeze.

Rosasharn took her eyes off the road and looked at him quizzically.

Ishmael cleared his throat. 'You say your mother always had this ability?' He resolved to keep focused on anything but his mission, in case Mrs. Rayner homed in on his frequency again.

'Ever since I can remember. Mom was always intuitive. Not like any other mothers I knew. Being way older than all the other moms, she could have passed for my grandma.'

'How old was she when she had you?'

'Forty-four. She's almost seventy.'

'And your dad?'

'He was nine years younger than Mom.'

'Don't get me wrong. Mom wasn't your crackpot soothsayer. This woman back there,' she indicated with her thumb, 'had an extraordinary talent. Spent years running a salon, chatting to her clients about their lives. She had the knack of saying the right thing at the right time, something that seemed to make a difference or strike a chord. Now she

Chapter 4 Vidal Junction, California, Saturday 18 August

says it at the wrong time.' She giggled to herself and continued. 'Eventually, she closed her shop and moved to Sedona to run a psychic healing practice. It was like she went from cutting hair on heads to reading what went on inside them.'

'What about fortune-telling and things like that?'

'She dabbled in the supernatural. So did a lot of the women who came to get their hair done. When I was helping Mom out in the salon, I'd listen to them talk about apparitions and the strange things that happened during séances.'

Ishmael listened, a slight smirk on his face.

'Did your father have any extraordinary ability?'

'The only extraordinary thing about him was that he was into the Mormon faith real big-time.'

'So you are of the Mormon faith?'

'No. I didn't get into religion, or, I should say, the serious historical study of it, until later. Yeah, sure, I attended church meetings and did the church social thing.'

She lowered her voice, cupped her mouth and, leaning towards him, said in a conspiratorial tone, 'This is between you and me. Some Mormons adhere to their divine right of having multiple wives. A few still believe they are above the law of the land. Let me tell you there were some promiscuous goings-on in the Big River Temple of Mormons.'

Ishmael faced her and said authoritatively, 'It is something they copied from our holy book. In those days it was necessary for a man to have many wives.'

'Some men still feel the necessity these days, and not just to help out around the farm. Anyway, isn't that supposed to be biblical times?'

'That's what my wise teacher used to say.'

'Whatever. Each to their own,' Rosasharn said, rolling her eyes.

Rosasharn thumped the dashboard with the heel of her hand. 'Shit, look at that temperature gauge. It's skyrocketing. Damn radiator is thirsty. There's a bottle of water in the back. Grab it, please.'

Ishmael poked his head between the seats and as he twisted around, the sharp corner of the aluminum bracket jabbed into his side. 'Ouch!' Ishmael yelped.

'You okay?' Rosasharn inquired, concerned.

'I think I pulled a muscle when you hit that curve,' Ishmael griped.

'Should've been wearing your seatbelt.'

He rummaged through the empty beer cans, chocolate wrappers and crumpled newspapers on the floor and scattered over the seat beside Mrs. Rayner. 'Can't find any bottle.'

'Keep searching. There's a slow leak in the system. I can drive for a week before I have to add water, but when this Oldsmobile is crawling in traffic it's a bitch.'

'Found it.' He pulled a plastic bottle out from under the driver's seat and held it up. 'It's empty.'

'Hell's teeth.' Rosasharn sighed.

'You should've filled it back at that gas station,' Ishmael said.

'Yeah!'

They crawled along for a little longer until they came to a standstill.

'I'm going to have to turn off the AC. Sitting in this jam is cranking up the temp big-time. I can hack it. Mom's the worry.'

'How about stopping and letting it cool down?' Ishmael fingered the air vent.

'Still need water,' Rosasharn insisted.

'Hail a passing car?'

'This is America. No one gets involved.'

'Look, there's a farm way over there.' Ishmael stared at a lone outcrop of buildings perched on a hillside, shimmering in the distance.

'From memory the access route was back a few miles. It sort of does a horseshoe and runs along the aqueduct.'

'Pull up. You can jump the fence and get to it on foot,' Ishmael suggested. In her absence he wanted to fix the problem with his belt.

'That's about a mile and a half away, so three miles there and back. It'll take me at least half an hour, and by the time I find a tap …' A wry grin crossed her face. 'Hey, what about you?'

'I couldn't do it any quicker.'

'I'm tempted to cruise down the emergency lane. With the speed up I'll get good air flow over the radiator and we can keep the air on. It's about two miles to the Big River turnpike. There's a gas station just before it. I figure having an old woman in the car suffering from the heat is an emergency,' Rosasharn said.

'Do what you must.'

Rosasharn flicked on the hazards, pulled off the blacktop into the emergency lane.

'Scot, keep your eye out for cops.'

'Okay.'

About half a mile along the emergency lane they encountered a police cruiser in front of a bright yellow Hummer.

'Stop! Police. Now! Now,' Ishmael commanded.

Rosasharn attempted to cut in front of the car behind the Hummer. The driver began honking its horn, staccato fashion, and narrowed the gap between his car and the Hummer.

'Get your hand off that blasted horn, you asshole,' Rosasharn growled. She swung back into the emergency lane, attempting to get in behind the horn honker, but the lane had come to a sudden standstill.

'They've seen us. The police officer's got his head out the window looking back at us. Now he's waving to us!' Ishmael cried out. 'Why didn't you listen to me?'

'It was that idiot with the horn that got the cops' attention. Damn him,' Rosasharn sighed. 'Anyway, what's your problem?'

Ishmael squinted at the copper-faced officer. Was this the same officer who was in the Navajo police car that investigated the trouble he had caused at Warm Springs Bar and Grill at Tuba City a few weeks back? Ishmael couldn't tell these American Indians apart. They all looked the same — big, bronzed, and eagle-beaked, he said to himself.

The officer was waving at them. Rosasharn pulled up alongside the police cruiser and lowered her window.

To Ishmael's relief, he was obscured from the officer's view by Rosasharn and the door pillar. He shifted back into his seat. There goes that pain again. A notion that something apart from the defective detonators was seriously wrong with his bomb belt assailed him.

'What's your reason for driving in the emergency lane, lady?'

'I have an overheating engine and a very sick old lady in the rear. We really need some water for the radiator so we can run the AC. The heat is affecting her badly. I would say that's an emergency. You agree?' Rosasharn said.

The officer gave her a slight nod.

'Do you have any water to spare? Enough to get us to the gas station at the turnpike?' Her big, pleading eyes were full of sincerity.

'Sure, we have some water. Pull over beside that billboard,' he pointed, 'and I'll see what I can do.'

Rosasharn pulled away from the cruiser. 'I think we got on his good side.'

Ishmael stared at her, wide-eyed.

Jokingly, Rosasharn asked, 'You in trouble with the Indian law? Did you not lose enough money at their casino?'

'No, no, nothing like that.'

'So, what's the problem?'

Chapter 4 *Vidal Junction, California, Saturday 18 August*

'I was touring around the Navajo reservation and I ...' Ishmael paused, trying to think of something to say. 'I scratched a car as I was parking in front of the Warm Springs Bar and Grill at Tuba City. I couldn't find the owner, so I left my name and number with the bartender. I'm worried maybe some eyewitness reported me to the police.'

She cocked an eyebrow at him. 'Should have left your name and number on the windscreen,' she said.

'Yes, I should have.'

'Hey, chill out. They're not Navajo. They're from the Havasu Police Department.'

Ishmael recalled the days after his trip to the Grand Canyon with Canaan, when he had decided to visit the Navajo reservation.

CHAPTER 5

TUBA CITY, NAVAJO RESERVATION, SATURDAY 4 AUGUST

Tuba City's surrounds were littered with old mobile homes amidst ramshackle barns and rusted-out machinery half-hidden among weeds and dry vegetation. He saw signs of life — chickens, dogs, goats — and Native Americans digging in small garden plots, the rich green vegetation a stark contrast to the dry, dusty, flat landscape. Are these the people I have come to destroy he repeatedly asked himself as he slowly cruised into the town center.

The main street was lined with adobe houses and steep-roofed wooden buildings. Apart from the ubiquitous convenience and fast-food stores there were signs of Indian culture — tipi-shaped buildings, shops selling souvenirs, trinkets, traditional medicines and clothing.

Ishmael pulled up alongside two chopped-down Harleys in front of a Western-style saloon called the Warm Springs Bar and Grill and went inside for a bite to eat. The place was dark and cool. Charlie Rich — 'Behind Closed Doors' — was playing on the jukebox. The pine panelled walls were decorated with black-and-white photographs of warriors and great leaders dating back to the nineteenth century.

Other than the bartender and two heavily built bikers who were feeding the slot machines, there was no one else in the bar. The bikers looked as if they belonged to some tribal motorcycle gang. Each man wore moccasins and a beaded vest; their jet-black hair, which hung in tresses,

Chapter 5 Tuba City, Navajo Reservation, Saturday 4 August

were tasseled with feathers and their thick, dark arms were emblazoned with tattoos depicting bears and wolves, corncobs, arrowheads and tomahawks dripping with blood.

Ishmael gravitated to the images on the wall. He walked up and down, engrossed in the pictures. There was a picture of Falling Tree, just like the one in his motel room. Next to it was one of an Indian holding a rifle across his chest, kneeling down on one knee. It was the famous Apache chief Geronimo. It appalled him how these images were degraded by being displayed in such a place. It was disrespectful, unholy. The brooding and somber faces of the Indian leaders had a hypnotic effect on him. They seemed to emerge from the walls. His anger started building. He looked around the bar. The sight of row upon row of bottles of alcohol and the line of slot machines infuriated him.

'They were great leaders of our people, but the white man's ways destroyed everything we once were!' the wizened Navajo bartender called out to Ishmael.

Ishmael grimaced and stared belligerently at the bartender. The man wore a single, white-tipped eagle feather at the end of a braid of silver-white hair on the back of his head.

Ishmael rubbed his temples, bowed his head. He questioned why he was working himself up over a bunch of pictures of men hanging on the wall. He looked up at the bartender again, who was pouring a glass of beer, and felt nothing but contempt for him.

'You are Indian. Why join forces with the enemy?' he shouted out across the room.

One of the bikers nudged his partner and nodded in Ishmael's direction.

The bartender finished pouring the beer, looked up and squinted over to where Ishmael was standing. 'Hey, young fellow, we got to survive. Can't beat 'em, join 'em,' he chuckled. He bent down, grabbed a tray of clean glasses and placed them on the counter. Under his breath he muttered, 'Damned outsiders. Who the hell they think they are? Been watching too many Hollywood westerns.'

Ishmael's face contorted with rage. The flickering red neon of the Budweiser sign hanging behind the bar blurred in his vision.

'What a poor excuse: if you can't beat them, join them,' he shouted as he stormed over to the bar and grabbed the old man by the shirt and pulled him over the counter.

'You are guilty of the continual destruction of your people by using the images of your great warriors as tourist attractions,' he shouted into the bartender's face, 'Have you no respect for your great leaders, old brother?'

Ishmael was distracted by something whooshing past his head. A beer bottle smashed on the opposite wall. He looked to the side and saw the two bikers bearing down on him. He let go of the bartender and bolted for the door, knocking over chairs and tables. The bikers hurled curses and abuses at him but gave up their pursuit as Ishmael burst through the batwing door. The bartender straightened his shirt and rang the Navajo Reservation Sheriff's Office to report the incident.

Ishmael jumped into his car and sped out of Tuba City. As he raced around a bend about half a mile out of town, the car started fishtailing. He lost control and ran off the road into a ditch. He tried desperately to reverse back onto the road, but the back wheels kept spinning on the spot. Ishmael slumped over the steering wheel.

He was stunned by his outburst, yet somehow, those faces in the pictures got inside of him, stirring him to take a stand for them. How could he not feel any empathy for the leaders of a people that had once fought the enemies of the sacred brotherhood?

He got out of the car to assess the damage. The car had a flat front tire. No damage to the body.

'That was cool driving, mister.'

Ishmael spun around and saw three young boys standing by the roadside.

'We watched ya come over the hill,' said one of them.

The youngest of them grabbed hold of an imaginary steering wheel, jerked at it to and fro, kicked up some dust with his bare feet, took a few steps forward, pivoted and threw himself to the ground. His two companions laughed and jumped on him. They kicked, punched, screamed and tore at each other's clothes.

Ishmael leant on his car, his arms crossed. The boys picked themselves off the ground and dusted themselves.

'I need to get the car back on the road, boys. How about some help?'

The youngest of the three looked up at him, smiled a gap-tooth grin and replied, 'I know someone down the road with a truck. He might come and help.' He paused, looked down at his dusty bare feet and then looked up.

'My name is Clancy, that's Roy and he's my big brother Ernie.' The three assembled themselves and stood side by side, their swarthy, round faces beaming with pride. 'We're all born to the Deep Canyon clan and for the Ironwood people.'

'My name is Scot.' Ishmael pulled his wallet from his back pocket and handed Clancy a five-dollar note.

'That is for you. Go and find him. Tell him I will pay $100 if he comes right away to get my car back on the road.' Then, turning to the other boys, who were now standing at ease, he forced a smile and said, 'You two want to earn some money?'

'Sure do,' they said in unison.

'I'll give you five dollars each if you help me change the tire.'

The boys were tightening the lugs when a clapped-out Ford F100 rumbled over the hill and pulled up adjacent to his car. Ishmael handed each of his two helpers their five dollars. Before he could thank them they darted off, waving their money in the air.

A short, heavy-set man of about sixty stepped out of the cabin. His face was dark and deeply lined. He had high cheekbones and his broad, eagle-beaked nose was slightly turned up at the end. He was dressed in denim overalls and wore a black felt hat decorated with a silver and turquoise band and a turkey feather. Behind each ear hung tightly braided ropes of hair, the end of each tied with a red ribbon, Sioux-style.

The man walked over to Ishmael's car. Glancing at him, he grunted an acknowledgement and got to work. In about ten minutes, the car was back on the road. The man dropped to his knees and, after inspecting underneath the front of the car, stood up, dusted his knees and shook his head. 'You won't be able to drive. Front end's busted and steering shaft is just about broke.'

'Can you get it fixed?' Ishmael asked with despair.

'Not this late in the day. Have to order parts from Flag. You'll be on your way lunchtime tomorrow, if you're lucky.'

Ishmael sighed and kicked the tire.

A vehicle came over the rise and pulled up behind Ishmael's car.

Ishmael stared wide-eyed at the Navajo tribal police cruiser, he swallowed dryly and glanced at the Indian man who, in turn, gave him a conspiratorial grin.

The patrolman wound down the passenger window and called the Indian man over to his car. They talked briefly, after which the police car did a reckless U-turn and sped back over the rise. The spinning back tires sent a hail of stones cascading over the back of Ishmael's car.

The Indian man stared at the trail of drifting dust for a moment, then turned and walked towards Ishmael.

Ishmael stood next to his car. He didn't know what to make of the police car's sudden disappearance. He noted a slight gleam in the Indian's deep-set eyes.

Ishmael threw his arms up in the air in resignation.

Chapter 5 *Tuba City, Navajo Reservation, Saturday 4 August*

'There was an incident at the bar back there. I may have offended one of your people,' Ishmael said.

The Indian man grinned. 'The Navajo people run this reservation and all that is in Tuba. A Navajo is who you offended. I am from the Hopi nation. On this land, as far as the eye can see and beyond, my people are the minority.'

Ishmael gave him a puzzled look. 'I am sorry, but I don't understand.'

'Our so-called reservation lies in the canyons of the first, second and third mesas, thirty miles east of Tuba City.' He pointed to the line of red mesas rising in the distance.

Ishmael squinted towards the horizon shimmering under the noonday sun.

'On paper, it is written that here, where we stand, belongs to the Navajo. In blood and truth it belongs to the Hopi.' He stamped his foot, bowed his head, and said solemnly, 'Navajo men have been lobbying Washington to extend the boundaries of their nation. The Hopi reservation is being squeezed by the Navajo reservation.'

Ishmael nodded thoughtfully.

'I am Old Smoke, born to the Rocks People and for the Spring Water clan.' He extended his hand.

Ishmael shook his hand. 'Scot Fall.'

'My father was a great Skin walker. I am also.'

'Mr. Old Smoke, forgive me for being ignorant, but what is a Skin walker?'

'First, we take care of your car, then we talk.'

They left Ishmael's car by the side of the road and made their way to a repair yard located on the other side of Tuba City. They drove past the Warm Springs Bar and Grill. The Navajo tribal police cruiser was parked in front, next to the motorcycles. Ishmael sank low in his seat. Old Smoke gave him a sidelong glance, grabbed hold of his beaded necklace which had some type of bone attached, pointed it at the police car, and mumbled an incantation in his native tongue.

Ishmael waited in the truck while Old Smoke got out and talked to a mechanic who was working under a hoist.

'My friend will organize the towing of your car and have it ready for you tomorrow afternoon,' Old Smoke said as he got back in the truck.

Ishmael took $200 out of his wallet and offered it to him.

'Take it. You helped a lot.'

Old Smoke graciously accepted the money, folded the notes neatly and slid them into his shirt pocket.

'I have to find a place to stay for the night. Can you recommend anywhere? Preferably somewhere out of town.'

'You can stay at my place.'

'I don't want to put you out. You've done enough for me already,' Ishmael protested.

'It's no trouble. I have to come into Tuba tomorrow.'

CHAPTER 6

TUBA CITY, NAVAJO RESERVATION, SATURDAY 4 AUGUST

Back at the Navajo tribal police station in Tuba City, Chief Archie Rosedale had just finished talking over the two-way radio to Deputy Billy Apple, the officer who had been assigned to investigate the Warm Springs Bar and Grill call. He lumbered into his office, threw his clipboard on his desk, unstrapped his tooled leather gun belt, draped it over the coat hanger and slumped his three-hundred-pound bulk into his swivel chair, which creaked under the strain. He sat still for a few moments, wheezing for breath.

Rosedale was a full-blood Hopi who could trace his ancestry from the time when, according to their Kachina religion's Genesis-like account of creation, his tribe emerged from the underworld.

Chief Rosedale was not happy about an outsider on the reservation creating extra work for his men. He was puzzled by the incident, and wondered why some irate tourist would get worked up over a few pictures hanging on the wall.

When Deputy Billy Apple radioed him what he had seen — Old Smoke helping the man who tried to assault the bartender — he quickly judged that Old Smoke must have been behind the incident, and assumed that he was conducting one of his incantations using an outsider to intimidate the locals.

A lot of the old people were steeped in superstition. They held belief in witchcraft and the supernatural. Old Smoke held some authority, so much so that Chief Rosedale believed Old Smoke undermined his own authority and that of all the other reservation police agencies. The old folk tended to go to Old Smoke to resolve their problems, some of which were matters that should have been reported to, and resolved by, the reservation police — sheep and cattle rustling, domestic violence, substance abuse — and worse still, consulted the old charlatan on medical matters.

Rosedale felt that Old Smoke gave the reservation's invalids and terminally ill false hope. How could they believe that a prayer danced over buried nail clippings, tufts of human hair and clothing that were surreptitiously taken from friend or foe; performed on some lonely outcrop of rocks on a mesa could reverse the corrosive properties of cancer cells? People would ring his office in the morning complaining that they had woken up with a bad haircut; irate women phoned complaining that their freshly polished fingernails had been clipped while asleep.

Old Smoke was also renowned for being a were-animal, supposedly owning a wardrobe of animal pelts and skins that he used to change himself into. Some complained to Chief Rosedale that Old Smoke had been vexing and spooking them, disturbing the wildlife on his nightly frolics while disguised as a were-animal.

Despite repeated warnings from himself, his deputies and sheriffs of other tribal police agencies to cease these practices, Old Smoke persisted. In particular, he continued with his Supreme Spiritual Council meeting ritual with the great warriors and leaders of all the Indian nations scattered across the American continent. This contentious ritual had created a lot of talk across the two reservations and beyond.

Archie pushed himself away from his desk, swung his right foot onto the desktop and rasped at the multiple folds of skin under his chin. He leant over, picked up his clipboard and read the notes he had jotted down while talking to his deputy. Then he picked up the telephone receiver and punched in the number to the radio dispatcher.

'Avalon, have a patrol car pick up those two Muscarlero bikers who were at the Warm Springs Bar, and while you're doing that, order me a dozen beef burritos, four extra large serves of spicy potato wedges and a two-liter bottle of Mountain Dew.' He paused. 'No, make that Diet Pepsi and tell Esposito to go easy on the sour cream.'

CHAPTER 7

CHILCHINBITO CANYON, NAVAJO RESERVATION, SATURDAY 4 AUGUST

Old Smoke's ranch was located in a shallow arroyo bordering the craggy bluffs of Chilchinbito Canyon, about an hour's drive north-east of Tuba City. The ranch consisted of a few old weather-tortured sheds, a horse corral and a single tipi made from buffalo skins pitched under a cluster of juniper trees. The only comfort of modern life to be seen was an aluminum trailer home parked under a row of gnarled cottonwoods.

Old Smoke took Ishmael into the canyon and showed him a way of life that was a stark contradiction to the world's typical view of America. By sunset, Ishmael had convalesced, refreshed by the simple activities that Old Smoke had assigned him. Stripped down to his waist, barefoot, his skin baking under the hot sun, he hauled buckets of water from the well, topping up the scarred old bathtubs used by the horses, goats and chickens for drinking troughs. He watered the melons, beans and corn, hand fed Zuni and Salina, the two appaloosa mares, stacked bales of hay, gathered chicken eggs and reset the rabbit traps.

He felt as if he were in his natural element. He reminisced about when he was a boy living on the edge of the Thar Desert, in the sun-drenched state of Rajasthan. For a living, he had carried water from sunrise until sunset in a pair of camel-leather pouches from one of the scarce wells located five miles outside of the town. He sold the water for a few copper coins, or exchanged it for rice with those who were unable to travel the five miles to collect it. A week would not pass when he would bring water to those who could pay for it no longer, at times even stubbornly declining what little money they had to offer him for his troubles. He would urge them to use it for other, more pressing needs.

Young Ishmael had not only brought the much-needed water to the frail, incapacitated, terminally ill and those eroded by leprosy; he also brought cheerfulness that was much welcomed in their suffering.

That evening, under a cloudless sky, and to the resonance of yammering coyotes deep in the canyon, the two men spent the evening in front of the campfire.

Ishmael sat on a milk crate, hunched over, his elbows resting on his knees, watching Old Smoke expertly prepare the rabbits. Old Smoke bit off a chunk of skin from the rabbit's neck, spat it into the fire then, gripping the two hind legs with one hand, he plunged the thumb of his other hand in the bleeding hole and peeled off the skin. He grabbed a knife, slit the animal's belly, scraped out the intestines and tossed the offal to a wildcat stalking around the campfire.

Ishmael tore at the meat, drank hot coffee from a tin cup and questioned Old Smoke about the Native American peoples and their connection with the land.

'The great leaders of all the Indian nations saw the mistake of swapping land for useless objects with the white settlers. Losing the connection to the land was the downfall of all the Indian nations. The white man gave my people alcohol, which they drank until they saw the Earth and Heaven in one vision, and they said the Great Spirit had come down to them. Then, they gave up their land for the firewater and guns.'

Old Smoke got to talking about the Louisiana Purchase.

'Fifteen million dollars is all they paid for everything west of the

Mississippi,' he said. 'Napoleon was so desperate to finance his war with England that he decided to sell it to the Americans. We, the original peoples of this land, did not have a say in our destiny.' He held up his hand and counted off the number of times his homeland had fallen under different ownership. 'First the French, then the Spanish, then the British, then the French again, and finally, the Americans.'

Ishmael was fascinated with the history that Old Smoke was recounting. In his soul he understood these original peoples from the land called America. After all, hadn't his own country, India, been under British occupation?

Old Smoke picked up a stone and rolled it in his palm. 'Before the stones were hard, we were in this land. The Europeans came after the stones hardened,' Old Smoke said mournfully.

'Yes, I understand,' Ishmael murmured. He sipped his coffee and sniffed the wood smoke.

'We have our reservations and we have autonomy in the way we govern them. You see, we are not part of the state of Arizona, we are a nation within a nation. Only full-blood Indians can enjoy all the benefits of the reservation. Not that there are any benefits, but living and dying here does instill one with dignity, knowing that we are a nation unto ourselves, exclusively, and that the white man can never dispossess us of what little we have left. Now we fight among ourselves over ownership.'

Old Smoke gazed up at the ridges of the canyon silhouetted against the rising moon. 'Billy Apple, the patrolman that pulled up today, accused me of using you to stir trouble in Tuba City.'

Ishmael gave Old Smoke a puzzled look.

'Apple and his brothers who live on the other side of the canyon have been trying to run me off the reservation. They look for any excuse to put pressure on me.'

'Why is that?' questioned Ishmael.

'Water. This side of the canyon has an abundance of underground water.' He motioned towards the well. 'They have to truck theirs in ...'

They talked late into the night, Ishmael somewhat regretful that he was able only to talk about a fictitious identity. That night, he had trouble getting to sleep as one question coursed through his mind. 'Am I supposed to hate Native Americans too?'

CHAPTER 8

TUBA CITY, NAVAJO RESERVATION, SUNDAY 5 AUGUST

The following day, Ishmael and Old Smoke drove back to Tuba City. Ishmael so much wanted to stay at Chilchinbito. Hanging out with Old Smoke had awakened a part of his being that he had not connected with for a very long time. He thought about the earthiness and simplicity of a life without any of the trappings of modernity, of one's heritage and connection to a land owned by one's ancestors since time immemorial, a land that had nourished and supplied all needs, material and spiritual.

By the time they arrived, Ishmael's car had already been repaired.

'Old Smoke, thanks for all that you have done for me.' Ishmael extended his hand from the car window.

'You are welcome any time at Chilchinbito,' Old Smoke said as he cupped both hands over Ishmael's.

Ishmael was ten miles from the Navajo reservation boundary when he stopped for prayers. The road in front of him and behind was clear of traffic. As he was stepping into his car after relieving himself by the roadside, he saw a police car parked a little way behind his. The officer was standing in front of his vehicle, looking through binoculars that seemed to be pointed directly at him.

He held his breath. As he slowly pulled away, the police car remained stationary. In his rear-view mirror he saw the officer move around to

Chapter 8 *Tuba City, Navajo Reservation, Sunday 5 August*

the driver's side of his car, lean in and grab what he assumed was a radio mike and talked into it.

Ishmael drove towards Flagstaff, his head spinning around all the events of the past twenty-four hours. He experienced an ungodly feeling of being alienated from his religion. He repeated aloud, almost yelling at himself, that he was just tired and wasn't thinking straight.

CHAPTER 9

BIG RIVER, ARIZONA, SATURDAY 18 AUGUST

Rosasharn stopped alongside the billboard and turned off the engine. She leant across the back seat, wound down the side window and unbuttoned her mother's collar. A hot wind whistled through interior of the car. The patrol cruiser pulled up behind her.

Ishmael felt as if he were being dipped into a vat of boiling oil.

'Don't get out until the cop says you can. Cops around these parts shoot first, and then offer you help,' Rosasharn teased.

Ishmael ignored her. He unbuckled his seatbelt and stepped out of the car. He rolled his shoulders and arched his back.

'Sir, you must remain in the vehicle.'

He turned himself about and saw the patrolman, whose mirrored shades caught the low afternoon sun, making his eyes look like two headlights on high beam. Ishmael blinked and squinted. The big, copper-faced officer stood in front foot forward position.

Ishmael threw his hands in the air. 'Yes, yes, I'll get back in.' He jumped back in the car. 'Ouch,' he grunted as the metal stabbed into him.

'What's the problem, Scot?'

'Nothing. Just that muscle again,' Ishmael groaned.

'You poor thing. Where does it hurt?' She reached out to touch his back.

'Don't touch, please. I am okay,' he assured her. 'The police.' He pointed to the patrolman, who was now standing beside Rosasharn's door.

The patrolman squatted beside Rosasharn's door, slipped off his shades and eyed Ishmael.

'Need water ... mad old lady ... AC has to work,' Ishmael stammered nervously. He picked up the empty plastic bottle and waved it.

'Hey jerk wad, that's my mother. Don't call her a mad old lady,' Rosasharn hissed at him, then turned her attention to the policemen.

'So, your mom doesn't like the heat,' the patrolman said as he looked into the car, checking out everything. He nodded to Mrs. Rayner, who sat there comatose.

'We not only need water for the AC, but Mom's two hours overdue in taking her medication. We need to get her to the Water's Edge Nursing Home over by Deer Island.'

'Has he also been without his medication?' He nodded towards Ishmael, then winked at her and slipped on his shades.

'I think he needs a lobotomy. Been partying at my niece's birthday. The kids and the heat have got to him.'

Ishmael dabbed his sweating brow with his sleeve. 'Don't worry about me. I'm doing fine.' He forced a smile.

'Can I see your driver's license please, ma'am?'

'Sure.' Rosasharn reached around the back of the seat, grabbed her bag, pulled out her purse and handed the police officer her license.

The patrolman studied it for a moment and then handed it back to her. 'I'll tell you what, Miss. Seeing as you do have a kind of emergency and that you drive an Oldsmobile 1985 Cutlass Supreme, one of the nice ones... Not ashamed to say I drive one myself.'

'Used to be my daddy's,' Rosasharn replied and smiled proudly.

'I bet your daddy looked after it a lot better than you do.'

Rosasharn pursed her lips and shrugged.

'This time I'm going to overlook the fact that you have one busted brake light and a cracked windshield.' He reached around the roof pillar and tapped on it, then leant back and assessed the front tire. 'Hmm. I won't mention that this front tire is looking a little too smooth.'

'I've been meaning to get them fixed.' Rosasharn twirled the end of a strand of hair.

The officer turned his attention to Ishmael. 'Sir, you go and ask my partner to fill that bottle. Honey, you open up the hood and we'll see what I can do.' His knees popped as he hefted himself up, rubbed his lower back and swaggered to the front of the car.

Ishmael eased himself out of the car and scurried over to the police cruiser. He held up the empty bottle and waved it at the officer behind the wheel talking on his cell phone. Ishmael stood there for what seemed like an eternity, baking in the heat. Looking down the slope he noticed a clump of saltbushes that ran along behind a barbed-wire fence adjacent to where they had stopped. They looked like they would provide good cover. Maybe if he got a chance he could wander down there and get behind them to spend a few minutes shifting that sharp edge away from his hip.

Finally, the officer, unhurried, got out of the car and strolled around to the rear of the cruiser and removed a canister of water from the back. While Ishmael held the bottle, the officer filled it, all the while preoccupied with who he was talking to on his phone.

The bottle filled, Ishmael went back to the car. The patrolman was under the bonnet, and Rosasharn stood next to him, pointing at a leaking water hose. Ishmael gazed into the greasy engine bay and said, 'Here's the water.'

Rosasharn lifted her head. 'Scot, why don't you take off your jacket. It's making me feel hotter.' She fanned herself with her hand.

The patrolman looked up. 'I'll get that jacket off him. I just might take him down to the station for a strip search.' He smiled broadly at Rosasharn.

'That might not be a bad idea,' Rosasharn crossed her arms and stared at Ishmael.

Chapter 9 *Big River, Arizona, Saturday 18 August*

Speechless, he only managed a shrug. He handed the bottle to the patrolman and dabbed his sweating forehead with his sleeve.

A cattle truck slowly rolled along past them. The fetid smell of dung and urine and the sound of moaning cows instantly transported Ishmael back to his childhood trauma.

Rosasharn turned towards the truck. A horn protruding from between the slats seized her attention. She gave it a cursory glance and then looked over at Ishmael, who, at the same time, looked at Rosasharn. Their eyes locked for a few moments. Simultaneously, they turned away.

After pouring a little water onto the radiator cap to cool it down, the patrolman slowly released the pressure.

Unaided, Mrs. Rayner painstakingly stepped out of the car, hobbled to the front and sidled up to Ishmael.

Just as Ishmael was about to slip away to get behind the bushes he felt something brush up against his back. He spun around and to his astonishment found himself looking into Mrs. Rayner's clear, expressive eyes. Aghast, Ishmael jumped backwards and collided with the patrolman then hastily shuffled forward and knocked into Mrs. Rayner. She tottered, about to fall. The patrolman shoved Ishmael out of his way, doubled over and scooped up the little old woman in his arms.

Ishmael stumbled backwards down the slope with his arms flailing. He just managed to pull himself up before he ran into a barbed-wire fence.

He stood rigid, holding in the excruciating agony radiating from his side.

Rosasharn stood aghast, arms akimbo. A short blast of the police siren snapped everyone to attention. The cruiser pulled out from behind Rosasharn's car and stopped just forward of it. The window came down. 'Jerry, put down the lovely bride and get in. Accident up the road.'

The patrolman gingerly placed Mrs. Rayner back on her feet and faced

Rosasharn. 'Make sure he gets his medication,' he said, pointing towards Ishmael. 'And make sure you fix your car.'

'I will, and hey, thanks,' Rosasharn said. She darted around to her mother's side and embraced her.

As the patrolman hopped into the cruiser, he shot Ishmael a suspicious glance. He shut the door and the cruiser sped off down the emergency lane, lights flashing, siren wailing.

'If Mom had hit the ground she could've broken her hip or something, you fucking idiot!' Rosasharn yelled.

'I'm sorry. I wasn't thinking. I ... I ... didn't see your mother standing there.'

'Yeah, right!' she shouted and then turned her attention to her mother.

Seizing the opportunity to get behind the bushes, Ishmael turned around. As he was about to get on his haunches to crawl under the fence, a clear mental image of the wiring and aluminum bracket assailed him. Lots of little colored wires must have also been exposed. Alarm bells tolled. Providence had brought him back to where he had left off in the car with Rosasharn and her mother. He wondered if his guardian angels had retired for the day. Two trips to Earth and each time they had left empty-handed.

He estimated that Rosasharn and her mother were about thirty feet away. He was severely tempted to make a dash for them, to tackle the pair like a football player. How close was a wire to being severed? It was possible the bomb might go off before he tackled them. Whether they were killed or seriously injured depended on how close he managed to get to them. And what if the belt didn't go off? Where would that leave him? He hated to think what next. It would have been better had it gone off when he bumped into the police officer.

Ishmael sighed deeply as the opportunity to tackle the pair slipped away. Rosasharn had helped her mother back into the car and was standing at the front of the car.

Chapter 9 *Big River, Arizona, Saturday 18 August*

Ishmael despaired of entering paradise with no dead Americans to credit his name. Not even Akmid would be able to salvage his reputation, and Werter von Stumpf would be at a loss to find something in the holy book that could dignify so pitiful an exit from the world. Worse still, once Canaan joined him in the afterlife, he would be hounded for the rest of eternity about his shameful death for a stupid, religious, ill-fated cause.

Ishmael's despondency, his weariness of the road he was on, was starting to overwhelm him. He reached for a fence post, steadied himself, closed his eyes and swayed. What was happening to him? Where was his strength and conviction to stand tall in the face of adversity? With defeat staring him in the face he started to believe that God had abandoned him. He gazed into the sky and recited a much-loved prayer:

Consider, O God, the reproach of Thy holy martyrs;
How I do bear in my bosom the reproach of all the mighty people;
Wherewith Thine enemies have reproached, O God;
Wherewith they have reproached the footsteps of Thine anointed.

He gasped at what he deemed to be an omen. A pair of buzzards were flying low, their ugly heads craned towards him. 'God has sent his blessed scavengers to feed on the carcasses of the Americans.' How the prophecy was to be fulfilled eluded him for just a moment. Then he heard the blast of a truck horn and looked towards the highway. He slapped his forehead and the dark cloud over him was suddenly gone. Praise and heartfelt gratitude to God welled up in his breast. An honorable way out had been revealed.

'Yes, wait by the roadside until a petrol tanker comes by, then throw myself under the trailer wheels. The force of the bomb will rip the tanker apart and rain down fire!'

Ishmael again summoned his guardian angels, knowing he would not let them leave empty-handed a third time. He carefully put one foot forward, then the other. The pain in his side was excruciating. He doggedly persevered.

Ishmael had progressed about fifteen feet. His confidence that the bomb was stable enough for him to make it to the roadside grew with every delicate step. After a few more steps, convinced that the bomb was secure now, he found himself struggling with the temptation to go back and get behind the bush. Knowing that he had to crawl under the fence, and that this would without a doubt add more precarious tension around his waist, he overcame the temptation and edged closer to the side of the road.

He was almost to the roadside. Rosasharn, he observed, was bent over the engine. Now, as his eyes swept the highway, he spotted a petrol tanker creeping over the rise, between a line of passenger vehicles. Something prompted him to look at the fence. The impulse came upon him with such accelerated force that he found himself almost spinning around. His eyes fastened on a breach that he had failed to notice, a short distance from where he stood. He turned to look at the tanker. He was buffeted between the temptation to go back behind the bushes or be obedient to God's revelation.

'Rosasharn, I am going behind the bushes to pray.'

'Fine, do what the fuck you want, loser,' She shot him a cursory glance. 'Just hurry up,' and continued to pour water into the radiator.

Ishmael cautiously made his way back down the slope.

Rosasharn twisted the cap on the radiator and looked down the slope. She caught a glimpse of the side of him as he disappeared behind the bushes. She shut the bonnet and got back in the car, faced her mother and said, 'That clumsy, sexually frustrated clod has at least the sense to get behind the bush to pray. Hey, Mom, can you just imagine what a crusty redneck going by in a pickup truck might do if he happened to catch sight of Scot by the roadside on his haunches? He wouldn't think twice about pulling up, grabbing his rifle from his gun rack and filling Scot's cute little ass full of lead.' She burst out laughing. Finally recovering herself she said, 'Mom, if he heard me laughing this time, he'd be wanting to hitch back to Parker. No bus stops around here.'

Mrs. Rayner stared at her daughter, expressionless.

Finally secluded behind the bushes, Ishmael took off his jacket, shirt and singlet, and dropped his trousers. He shivered as the hot wind whipped around his damp body. He peeled off the duct tape and stuck an end on a branch. Then he sucked in his stomach so as to minimize the pressure of the metal on the wires and began to slowly rotate the belt around his torso. Despite the pain, which so numbed his mid-section, he did not feel the sharp metal edge cutting into his skin. Blood seeped out along the hem of the belt onto his white underwear. He persevered until he slid the belt into place. Then he relaxed his stomach and pried open the Velcro and stared into the opening.

The aluminum bracket that the circuit board was attached to had cut into the insulation of several of the wires. Miraculously, none of the wires had been severed. He slid his hand in between the Velcro. As he applied pressure to the bracket, his fingers slipped.

'Ouch!'

He pulled out his hand, sucked his thumb and spat out a mouth full of blood. He was about to dip in a second time, but the blood oozing from his wound barred him. Everything would become slippery; if he lost his grip, his hand could bump into a wire and pull it away from a circuit. He attempted with his other hand but could not accurately clamp his thumb and index finger around the shaft. He tried using his little finger and thumb, but the way his hand fitted in the narrow pocket meant he would have to twist his wrist into an awkward position in order to exert the pressure he needed to bend the metal. This would force open the pocket and that, too, would put extra tension on the wiring, again creating the potential for a wire to come away from a circuit. Whether he rotated the belt to his right or to his left, he would still have to use his little finger. It was just the way it was, a job for his left hand.

He groaned aloud. 'Why am I still alive? Why?' He cursed the faulty detonators. He cursed the farmer who had neglected to fix the broken fence. And finally, he cursed himself with all his heart.

Mouth agape, he stared at his outstretched arm caked with dried streaks of blood, at the blood oozing from the wound, and the flies hovering around it. He would just have to make his way back to the roadside.

The duct tape flapped in a gust of wind. Ishmael stared wide-eyed at the tape. He tore off a strip with his teeth and wrapped it around his bloody thumb.

He slid in his hand. This time, he was able to successfully twist back the shard of aluminum. Utilizing the duct tape once more, he ripped off thin strips with his teeth and re-insulated the exposed copper wires, after which he rotated the belt back into its original position and secured it with the duct tape. Then he dressed himself. As he made his way back to the car, he pulled the tape off his thumb and let the blood ooze freely. Better to let Rosasharn see it. He would tell her he had fallen over and cut himself on a sharp rock.

Rosasharn found a clean rag in the boot to wrap his thumb in. Ishmael apologized profusely for his carelessness. Rosasharn told him that made them even.

A couple of miles up the road, they encountered the police cruiser again. The black SUV convertible was stationary in the right lane. One

Chapter 9 *Big River, Arizona, Saturday 18 August*

of the members of the teen-singing trio they'd seen earlier was splayed out on the road. Her distraught girlfriends were gathered around her. The patrolman was crouched on the highway cradling the girl's head.

'Oh, the poor thing. Hope she's not seriously hurt,' Rosasharn exclaimed.

Ishmael silently praised God for punishing the teenage American whore for going around like uncovered meat left out for the cat, tempting the righteous into lecherous acts.

CHAPTER 10

DEER ISLAND, ARIZONA, SATURDAY 18 AUGUST

The sun had gone down when they reached the Water's Edge Nursing Home. Rosasharn escorted her mother inside while Ishmael waited in the car. Exhausted, he could hardly wait to get home and take off the bomb belt. The pain that had wracked his body had ebbed and all he felt was a dull throbbing around his mid-section.

On the way, they had stopped at the gas station at the Big River Turnpike where, while Rosasharn topped up the radiator, Ishmael had gone into the restroom to bandage up his thumb and freshen up. The attendant gave him gauze from the first-aid kit. With Mrs Rayner out of the picture, Ishmael was visibly more relaxed. Finally he could stop counting colored balloons and was well-nigh satisfied that he would not have to take the issue with the old lady any further.

CHAPTER 11

BIG RIVER, ARIZONA, SATURDAY 18 AUGUST

They were driving down Rio Vista Drive, the main road through Big River, when Rosasharn braked heavily and exclaimed, 'Oh, I just have to see this!'

She double parked in front of a narrow shop sandwiched between a storefront Baptist church and the courthouse plaza.

'See what?'

'This gift shop. It was boarded up for weeks. Looks like they're officially opened for business now. Been dying to check it out.'

'Have you?' Ishmael said.

'It was Mom's old hair salon. Boy, they've totally revamped the place. The woman who originally bought the business from Mom, only remodeled a little of the interior. You could still see it was the salon.' Rosasharn leant over the steering wheel to get a better look. 'Nothing left but memories. I practically grew up in that place.' She sighed, paused and then continued. 'See where all those shelves are?' She pointed.

Ishmael stared disinterestedly into the shop.

'The wall behind the counter used to be all mirrored. The basins ran along the adjacent wall. In the far corner there used to be an overstuffed leather couch. After school I'd prop myself on it with my books and pencils and do my homework. When I'd finished I'd help out until Mom had to close up shop. Yeah, it was kind of okay during school, but during the holidays, I hated it.'

'Why?'

'Well, to cut a long and sad story short, Jim hung out with Dad and I got to hang out with Mom.'

'Girls are supposed to be with their mothers.'

Rosasharn eyed him narrowly. 'You sound just like my dad,' she said.

Realizing that he had hit a raw nerve, Ishmael urged her to continue.

'I never really connected with Dad. Hauling livestock from Tucson to Bozeman twice a week, he was hardly ever around. Holidays were the only time to spend with Dad. Jim, of course, was always the one to get to travel with him. When Dad wasn't driving he was a part-time rodeo clown. I'd beg him to take me along, but he rarely did. The times I did go, I had to sit all by myself in the stand while Jim got to help out with his clown make-up and hang out with all the good-looking cowboys.' She paused and stared down at the paint spots on her dress and scratched at a yellow paint drop.

Ishmael raised his eyebrows, looked at his watch and tapped on the glass.

Rosasharn continued. 'The one lousy time I was allowed to put Dad's face paint on him I decided to paint hearts instead of boring diamonds around his eyes.' Her voice rose slightly. 'I wouldn't let him look in the mirror until I had finished. When I was done, he took one look at himself and flew off the handle. He didn't have time to scrub them off and slap on the boring diamonds, so he went out into the arena with hearts painted around his eyes.'

'Hearts or diamonds, what's the difference?' Ishmael said.

'What's the difference? It's who got the credit for them. That's what pissed me off. A few weeks later there's a picture in the local paper of Dad in his clown suit, hearts around his eyes, shaking hands with the mayor of Amarillo beside a hospital bed with his son in it.'

'What did he do to get in the paper?'

'They did a hero story on him, about how he saved the mayor's son from being stomped on by a raging bull after being hurled off. Dad single-handedly staved off the beast and dragged the unconscious boy to safety.'

'Wow, that's really brave.'

'Yeah, Dad was so selfless in the arena, but heartless when it came to me. I told everyone that the heart shapes were my idea. Dad said it was Jim's idea and accused me of lying.'

'Didn't Jim tell your dad he got it wrong?'

'Jim stuck up for me, but Dad insisted that Jim had forgotten. You see, Scot, it wasn't just about hearts and diamonds or who painted them first. It was about Jim always getting the credit.'

'Oh, I see.'

'Hey, don't get me wrong. I love my brother to death, but in Dad's eyes Jim could do no wrong. Everything I did Jim could do better, according to Dad. Even school reports. No matter how well I did, Jim's report card was always better, which it was. He was a straight A student.'

'Jim's one very smart guy.'

'I'm not saying he's not. I just didn't like being compared with him. When you grow up with a lot of negativity and hear your dad saying stuff like I'd never amount to anything more than sweeping hair clippings, it eats away at your confidence.'

'Didn't your mother support you?'

'She did, in her own nice, motherly way, but she would always end her support with.' She mimicked her mother, ' "Well, sweetie, you've always got the salon to fall back on if schooling doesn't work out." I knew in her heart she wanted me to join her in the salon. So I'd laugh off whatever Dad said and make out I never took him seriously. Deep down I really thought Dad was right and that I was going to spend the rest of my working life inside those four walls. In the end I had no choice but to go to university.'

Rosasharn sank down in the car seat and stared into the shop. After a few moments, she straightened herself up and said, 'Let's go. This place is depressing me.' She put the car in drive.

'How was the decision made for you?' Ishmael asked.

'When I finished high school Mom signed me up at the Julia Dandy Academy of Hair and Beauty in Kansas City. At the same time I also enrolled at Arizona State to major in environmental science. I can honestly say I couldn't make up my mind between Julia Dandy's and ASU.'

'Decisions,' Ishmael said. 'Life is full of them.'

'It was a Monday. I had three weeks to decide. A hot, dusty gale was blowing across the state like they get over in the Oklahoma dust bowl. They're real unusual around these parts. I was in the salon sweeping up the dust that was getting in from everywhere when this old-fashioned car, a British job, the one with the little silver lady at the end of the hood ...'

'Rolls Royce.' Ishmael recalled Akmid's 1980 Silver Shadow that Canaan and he used to drive around Munich on the weekends.

'Yes, that's it. Anyway this Rolls Royce pulled up in front of the shop, backfiring and bunny hopping. The driver got out. He was wearing a monkey suit and had a whopping waxed moustache with the ends all curled up and hair slicked back. He opened the back door and this woman gets out and comes into the salon.'

'What sort of fancy dress was the lady in?' Ishmael said wondrously.

'Fancy dress! What do you mean?'

'You said the driver was wearing a monkey suit. So what costume did the lady have on?'

'You're playing games with me, aren't you?'

Ishmael laughed nervously. 'Yes I am, ha, ha.'

'I didn't mean a hairy monkey suit. The driver was dressed like a

Chapter 11 *Big River, Arizona, Saturday 18 August*

bellhop boy. He had on a brocaded suit. Lots of silver threads and flowery patterns all down the lapels and cuffs.'

'Ahh yes, go on.' Realizing that he'd taken it literally he was slightly embarrassed at his naivety. Akmid had categorically told him time and time again: 'If you're not sure of what is being discussed, my dear boy, do not guess. Silence never betrays ignorance.'

Rosasharn brushed a strand of hair from her eye and continued, 'You want to know what this lady was wearing? I'll tell you. She was wearing a diaphanous shawl over a bolero and a narrow, crimson velvet skirt, a little too high for my liking, but I have to admit she had great legs for a woman of her years. She wasn't old or young, kind of timeless looking. She walked erect and held herself as if she were royalty.'

'That sounds like fancy dress to me.'

'Around these parts on a late Monday afternoon, I'll pay that one. So, in she came. Mom was tallying up the day's receipts. She stared at Mom, and Mom stared back for what seemed to be a long time. I swear something passed between them, some kind of recognition. Don't know any other way to explain it. Mom dropped what she was doing, went over to her, escorted her to a chair and started washing her hair, which was odd because I always did the washing. I didn't think too much of it at the time, just swept a little more dust and left. Told Mom I was going to the movies and that I'd be home late. Three days later the woman comes in again, and the same thing happened as the first time.'

'Did the driver come in to get his hair cut?'

'No! He stayed outside, pacing the sidewalk and puffing on these horrid fat cigars. It was like his head was on fire. So I grabbed a magazine and pulled up a chair near the washbasin. This woman never once said so much as hello to me. I pretended I was reading, but I had my ears pricked up, listening to them talk. Mom and her spoke real low, almost whispering. Every now and then I'd catch a word or half a sentence. She had an odd accent that was hard to make out. It wasn't American, it was like ... hmm, I don't really know. Could have been Hungarian or Russian. She called herself an intergalactic medium and I heard her say that she had had a vision that Mom was a chosen one. What for I didn't have a clue. I sat there listening a little longer when Justin, this guy I was dating came into the salon and asked me if I'd like to go and watch him play football, so I went. I wish I'd stayed. I had completely forgotten about her two visits to the salon.

'Thursday the following week, Mom announced that she was going away that weekend to stay with Zara at her sanctuary in Roswell, New Mexico on the Pecos River. What so surprised us was that Mom never closed on the weekend. It was her busiest time.

'I recalled that I'd heard Zara call herself an intergalactic medium and put two and two together. Can you believe it? Roswell of all places, where that UFO was supposed to have crashed in 1947?'

'UFO? Wow!' he exclaimed. He had heard of the term but for the life of him could not recall what it stood for.

'At first I never could believe that stuff. At the time I was reading *Chariots of the Gods*. It got me wondering. Anyway, that's beside the point.'

'Yes, hard to believe that stuff.' Ishmael nodded agreeably a little too enthusiastically.

Rosasharn took her eyes off the road and looked at him. 'Dad hit the roof, absolutely forbade Mom to have anything to do with that conjurer and the members of her intergalactic cult. Friday night before closing Dad came into the salon and threatened to leave Mom if she went to Zara's sanctuary. I was in the storeroom and didn't come out until he left.'

'Did your dad know you were there, in the storeroom?'

'He knew I helped out every Friday night. I heard Mom tell him she was going through a rebirth, and that she interpreted Dad's threat as some sort of a sign. Yeah, right. A sign that their marriage had hit the skids. It had been written on the wall for about two and a half years. Mom told Dad that if he had heard the calling to leave, then leave he must. Dad left the salon in such a rage, vowing never to come back. He slammed the door so hard that the front windows were still rattling when he roared down the street in his truck, blasting the horn. I regret it to this very day for not stepping out to see him, because I never saw him again. Mom closed the shop and went off to Roswell.'

'Just like that?'

'Yep, just like that. I was so fucking angry at Mom.'

'Why?' Ishmael asked.

'For letting Dad walk out on her. I just lost it. I stomped out of the storeroom, glared at Mom and was about to ...' Rosasharn stopped in mid-sentence and rubbed the back of her neck. 'Oh, my neck hurts when I get worked up. I don't know what I was about to do. I felt like I just wanted to punch her, knock some sense into her, and I'm not a violent person.'

'Did you say anything?'

'I said nothing, just left. I caught up with Jim at the library and told him what was going down.'

'Did he get upset?'

'No. He said I was reading too much into it and it would work itself out. Then he buried his head back into the book he was studying. So I went to a bar and got drunk and ended up spending the weekend in a hotel room in Vegas with a bunch of strangers. I got back on Monday night. When I walked in the door Jim and Mom were sitting at the kitchen table just about to start dinner. I sat down. Dead silence, no one's talking. I just played with my food, didn't feel like eating.

'Finally, Mom broke the ice and announced that she was selling up and moving to Sedona to take over Zara's mental healing practice. Jim and I were shell-shocked. On Tuesday Jim got a letter from Dad asking him to come and live with him in Indianapolis.

'Did Jim go?' Ishmael stared out the windscreen, wishing for the ride to end. He didn't really care about her life and family problems. He just wanted to get home to attend to his wounds and have a hot bath.

'By eight that evening Jim had his haversack across his back and was clutching a one-way Greyhound ticket in his hand. Kissed me and Mom goodbye and he was gone. That was it. Everybody went their separate ways. Not having the salon to work in, I was free and guiltless to go and study. I moved to Phoenix and rented an apartment down the road from ASU.

'I got stuck into my studies and used to go and see Mom on my breaks. She was starting to make a name for herself in Sedona as a counselor. It was as if she had blossomed from being a small-town nobody into a somebody. People from all over the country came to see her.

'After Mom felt they had connected, she would just encourage them to do what they thought was best. She never gave specific advice about what action to take. Once she helped a serial killer who was wanted in six states to turn himself in by her gentle handling of the matter.'

'She must have really gotten to him,' Ishmael said, astonished.

'Mom really worked out what he was all about,' she said slowly. 'You're one of the converted, having witnessed Mom in action, three times in one day.'

Ishmael squirmed in his seat. 'Did you ever see the Zara lady?' he said.

'Mom would occasionally go to see Zara at her sanctuary, but I never saw her again. I made some inquiries about her in Sedona when I was visiting Mom. Only a handful of people knew of her and they were all reluctant to talk about her. A few days later I was talking to Mom on the phone and learned that Zara had sold her property on the Pecos River and was moving to Europe. The last I heard was that she was living in Belarus.'

Chapter 11 Big River, Arizona, Saturday 18 August

'Did you hear any word from your father?'

'Every week Mom used to get a letter from Dad with the same quote from the Old Testament. Nothing else in it, not even a hello or how're you going, just the same verse written in a thick black marker pen. Mom just stopped opening them and stuffed them in a drawer.'

'What was the verse?'

'It was from the Book of Isaiah:

And when they shall say unto you, Seek unto them that have familiar spirits, and unto wizards that peep, and that mutter: should not a people seek unto their God? For the living to the dead.

'Twelve months or so passed and we got word that Dad had died. I was devastated. For all that he put me through I still believed we would connect again someday.'

'That's so sad,' Ishmael said, his empathy genuine.

Rosasharn wiped a tear from her eye. 'Sorry, Scot. I get so worked up over what might have been.' She paused, dried her eyes on her sleeve. 'I don't even know why I'm telling you all this.' She accelerated and overtook a couple of cars.

'You don't have to go on if it's too painful. I understand.'

'I've started telling you, so I just better get on with it. Besides, you've taken such an interest in wanting to know about Mom.' She reached out and gently squeezed Ishmael's arm. 'These days no one ever asks me about her. Some still blame her so-called evil ways for Dad leaving. After the funeral, Mom sank herself into her newfound vocation. Jim by then was at Harvard. I went back to my apartment in Phoenix. Then, over a holiday weekend I went to Mom's and sorted out a lot of issues about her and Dad, the rumors that were flying around at the funeral. Don't want to go into that.' She shook her head.

'No, no, you don't have to,' Ishmael quickly responded.

'The morning I was leaving Mom's I asked if I could have Dad's letters. I took them home and sorted them by date, read and re-read every single one of them over and over again. Heck, they were all the same, but in the course of going over them I started to notice and appreciate all the little nuances in his handwriting, the way the "z" in "wizard" always fell way below all the other letters. Some looked as if they'd been written more hurriedly, others were neater. Oh, I don't know. It sounds silly, doesn't it?'

'I don't think so.'

'When I look back I can see that I was compelled, driven.' Her voice rose. 'Putting it bluntly, I became obsessed with seeking out a deeper connection with the meaning. It had never bothered me in the past. So, I took up the challenge that Dad had wanted Mom to take, which is how I interpreted his motivation, though I guess I'll never know for sure. In a nutshell, I started seeking God. Not in a religious sense. I'd done the church thing growing up. I just wanted to do it my way. Just like the Sinatra song, though I liked Elvis's version better. It came more from the heart.'

Ishmael knew the song. Akmid was a big fan and had all Sinatra's records and movies.

'During those turbulent months after the funeral I lost all interest in my course and was seriously considering dropping out of ASU to enroll at Julia Dandy's and open up a salon.'

'And sweep up hair clippings for the rest of your life,' Ishmael joked.

'No! To order someone else to do it.' She paused and continued. 'Well, with this awakening I was going to approach my quest from a historical and archaeological perspective and combine it with theological studies. So I ditched my current course. I'm not saying I learnt my way, but it's a journey. Three years later Mom had a stroke. I put my studies on hold and moved to Lake Hasavu to be near her.'

'That was very unselfish and noble of you, Rosasharn,' Ishmael said sincerely.

'Thanks. You sometimes need to hear that said.' Rosasharn nodded appreciatively. 'You're not such a whacko after all,' she quipped.

'How did your dad die?'

'It happened at a rodeo show in Amarillo. He was clowning around in front of a bull pen. The chute hadn't been properly secured. The cowboy had just mounted this monster of an animal and as he was slipping into his stirrups the beast reared on its hind legs against the unsecured chute. The bull burst into the arena and flung off the rider like a rag doll. Dad got clipped by the door. As he was regaining his balance, he turned around just as the bull jerked up his head. Its horn impaled him, pierced his heart and lung. The coroner determined he was killed instantly.'

Ishmael's jaw dropped, his face ashen.

'Hey, are you okay, Scot?'

'Yes, I'm, okay,' he croaked.

'Daddy was so funny, not like a lot of mean-spirited rodeo clowns.' Rosasharn sighed. 'I was going to go up and see him that weekend he died. As much as I kicked myself for not going, I am so glad now I didn't. If I had, I would have witnessed the whole thing.' Her eyes brimmed with tears. 'Daddy should have retired ages ago. He was the oldest clown on the circuit. A younger clown would've seen it coming and jumped away.'

'I am sorry, really sorry,' Ishmael said again. He felt like telling her the story of how his mother had died at the expense of a Hindu god that had chosen to live and move in the image and likeness of a brindled cow. Ishmael wanted to overlook everything he did not like about her, a thought he found troubling.

CHAPTER 12

PARKER, ARIZONA, SATURDAY 18 AUGUST

When they finally arrived in Parker, Ishmael directed Rosasharn to where he was staying. She pulled up in his driveway. Ishmael opened his door to get out, paused and said, 'I am sorry again for being careless around your mother.'

'Please, Scot, you don't have to explain.' She put the car into park, draped her arm over the back of the passenger seat and faced him. 'She didn't fall, thanks to that officer. As far as I'm concerned it's over.'

Ishmael nodded and gave her a subdued smile.

'Being around my Mom is like being in the presence of the thought police. Between the three of us, the matter is over. Let's shake hands on it. No harm meant, no harm done,' Rosasharn said and stretched out her hand to him.

They shook hands and she held his a little longer than he expected.

'Hey, Scot, there's one more thing.'

'Yes?'

'Please don't mention anything to Jim about laughing at you when you were praying.'

Ishmael's eyes lit up. 'I won't if you don't tell him I accidentally bumped into your mother.'

'It's a deal.'

They sighed simultaneously. Rosasharn giggled and Ishmael chuckled.

'How's your head?' She reached out and ruffled his hair.

'It's fine.'

Chapter 12 *Parker, Arizona, Saturday 18 August*

Ishmael stepped gingerly out of the car. With stiff limbs he walked towards his front door. Rosasharn rolled down her window, called out to him and waved him back.

'Hey, it was good talking to you. You're a good listener. I really ...' a tiny pause before she continued, 'having someone to pour out all those memories into, after seeing what had happened to Mother's old shop was a tonic. I would've brooded over it well into the night.'

Ishmael stood there, overcome by her sincerity.

'Scot, I'm going to Sedona tomorrow. Would you like to come along?' she said, almost pleading.

'Yes,' said Ishmael without thinking.

'Great. It's a date.' She smiled. 'Pick you up around nine.'

Ishmael nodded, unsure what he was getting himself into.

'Give me your number just in case I'm running late.'

She wrote it on the back of her hand. 'Scot, do you mind if I ask you one more thing? And please, don't take it the wrong way.'

'Go ahead.' He gazed over at his front door and then back at Rosasharn.

'You remember when that cattle truck went by and I looked over at you?' She stopped. The words seemed to get caught in her throat. 'Ah, it doesn't matter. Get yourself inside and treat yourself to a hot bath. You look like you're going to collapse.'

Ishmael stared at her, wide-eyed. 'Yes, I think I'd better.'

'See ya tomorrow.'

Rosasharn gave him a quick wave and sped off.

Ishmael slammed the door behind him, tore off all his clothes and stared at the blinking LED. He peeled off the duct tape, grimaced as it tore at his skin, scrunched it into a tight ball and threw it at the wall, where it stuck. He turned up the AC to full and went into the kitchen and fished all the detonation buttons he could find out of the drawer and set to work. Before connecting any of them, he ran an electrical signal through the remaining buttons and discovered that two of the six were faulty. He savagely cursed the Aryan Brotherhood biker that had supplied them.

Using a basic multimeter, he analyzed all the electrical circuits on the belt. After assuring himself that all was in order, he was able to loosen the belt and let it hang on his hips, his relief was instant. The interminable twitching of his lower back muscles ceased.

He went into the bathroom and viewed himself in the mirror. His lower torso was deeply lined and red raw. A thin cut resembling a cat scratch ran all around his midriff. Gazing at his reflection, he noticed dark shadows under his eyes and how pale he looked.

Mrs. Rayner's words kept coming back to him: 'You do not really want to make those children suffer.' It was as if her words were his own inner voice, imploring his consciousness, questioning his actions.

As he pondered further what Mrs. Rayner had said to him, her humane and compassionate undertones began to metamorphose into the long-forgotten last words of his mother. 'They are the Hindu god's likeness, they are a holy thing and they must live too. If I should die, remember me whenever you see a holy cow and be good and kind.'

It was more than he could bear. He clenched his fists and pounded his distraught reflection in the bathroom mirror, the mirror cracked. 'Why?!' he cried out. 'Why is the God of my life prolonging this agony?'

He hitched up his bomb belt and stomped into the kitchen, sat at the table and cradled his head in the crook of his arm, struggling to purge all the bad thoughts that stalked him, repeating to himself that what the old woman had said did not have any correlation with his mother's dying words. He rose in rebellion, vigorously denying that he would ever lower himself to feel sorry for the orphaned American children. It was the devil's subtle attempt to beguile him from fulfilling God's will. He drew consolation by quoting holy verses aloud to himself.

Chapter 12 *Parker, Arizona, Saturday 18 August*

His thoughts turned to Rosasharn, her laughter that mocked him, and he wondered whether her apology was sincere. Or was it that she was trying to mask the fact that she had humiliated him and accused him of being a sinner when he was being a saint, hired by God to destroy the enemies of the sacred brotherhood?

He wished that the belt had gone off when he had collided with the police officer. Then the officer, Rosasharn and her mother would be in their place with the damned of the world, and when he stood before God, receiving his reward for dying a good death, he would be the one laughing at them.

Ishmael lifted himself up and rocked back and forth in the chair. Anguish melted into elation. 'I pressed the buttons. I truly pressed both buttons,' he repeated aloud, over and over. His mind returned to the Greyhound bus episode and slotted everything that had happened before into perspective. It had served to drive him to go all the way, to stand alone with his God, to rush into His embrace. Had it not been for a technical problem he would have been there now.

Rehashing all the reasons to end it all on a desert highway, he was shocked when he came to the conclusion that his motivation was to save face with Canaan, a thought that pierced his ballooning ego. He sat at the kitchen table for a very long time, the suicide belt half coiled beside him.

He wished he could find the inspiration to go forward as he had the first time Canaan had tried coercing him into abandoning his call of martyrdom. That was back in 2004, when Canaan was in Rome planning a terrorist attack and Ishmael was studying at the University of Munich.

CHAPTER 13

ROME, ITALY, APRIL, 2004

It was just after seven p.m. when Canaan, disguised as a Franciscan monk, trailed behind a dozen or so people into Saint Augustine Cappella in the city of Rome. A hand grenade wired up to an alarm clock was concealed under his cloak. Father Rudolph Ipswich stood clutching a walking frame in the ornate marbled vestibule, cordially greeting all the visitors. Father Ipswich, in his prime, had been earmarked as a future pope. He had worked across South America in various church offices and held the post of Archbishop of Argentina from 1980 to 1995.

Canaan knelt in front of the frail old priest who held out his hand to be kissed. Canaan responded accordingly. Slowly rising to his feet, Canaan shot him a piercing glance and noted the flinch in the priest's watery grey eyes.

After stealthily placing the bomb under the wooden bench in the confessional, the alarm set to the hour when the priest would be in the closet, Canaan left the church. He disrobed under a bridge and flung the robe into the Tiber River and went back to his hotel room at the Albergo Medicea in Via Della Vitta where he religiously stayed whenever he was in Rome.

Father Ipswich belonged to a clandestine ring, the Multi-Denominational Pedophile Priesthood, that had banded together to perpetuate, in ecumenical unity, a way of life that had for centuries been outwardly condemned by the Church. However, ecclesiastical doctrinal platform

Chapter 13 Rome, Italy, April, 2004

states that all sin has the sanctity of forgiveness by the shedding of the blood of the lamb on the accursed cross. Only sin against the Holy Ghost was beyond forgiveness and prevented one's entry into the presence of the Most High.

At eight twenty-five that evening, Father Ipswich would be the fifteenth priest to be dispatched to hell. Away from his professional terror duties, Canaan had mounted his own private terror campaign for the extermination of all men who preyed on children.

It was ten past eight. He tuned the radio on the bedside table to the BBC World Service for the newsflash of the church bombing. The broadcaster was reading an editorial from the *Wall Street Journal*.

'When the Soviet Union was waging war in Afghanistan,' the broadcaster read, 'the CIA set up training camps and recruited mercenary combatants to fight against the Soviets...'

Canaan sat upright. He recognized some of these names. According to this broadcaster, most of the leaders of the Global Azad Front had once allied themselves with the Americans.

Canaan's interest in the broadcast grew with every word. It so absorbed him that he forgot about the bomb.

His gut feeling about the new religious world order, advocated by mad men as a farce, was now confirmed. If Canaan had any wish other than to exterminate all the pedophiles on Earth, it was to rid the Earth of all religion.

He had to enlighten Ishmael on what he had just learnt. The broadcast was interrupted by a newsflash: a bomb had been detonated in the heart of Rome.

CHAPTER 14

SALZBURG, AUSTRIA, MAY, 2004

Ishmael was studying in his second year at the University of Munich. Canaan secretly arranged to meet Ishmael in Salzburg on Mount Mönchsberg, along the northern road at a park bench that overlooked the township. Canaan was incognito, dressed as a tramp.

It was mid-morning when Ishmael arrived in Salzburg. To Ishmael, the immaculately preserved medieval town nestled up against the craggy cliff face of Mönchsberg Mountain with the foreboding fortress of Hohensalzburg glowering down was reminiscent of his hometown Bikenar, in Rajasthani. The location of the fort reminded him of how Junagarh Fort loomed over the old Sanskrit town. Though the climate was the exact opposite, with customs and people worlds apart and most structures neglected, it did make him feel a little homesick.

Ishmael spotted a figure lying on a park bench with a newspaper over his head and half dozen or so beer cans around him. They had arranged a signal. Ishmael was to walk past the park bench, kick an empty beer can and then walk over to the lookout terrace.

Ishmael looked around to see if anybody was nearby. Apart from two old men playing a game of chess on a life-sized chess board a little way down the path, there was no one else. One of the men was sitting in an electric wheelchair, circling the perimeter of the board.

Ishmael followed the plan. As he gazed across the valley, he heard Canaan speaking to him in Hindi.

Chapter 14 *Salzburg, Austria, May, 2004*

'Ishmael, I felt your presence even before you kicked the can.' Canaan grinned broadly. 'I cannot tell you how happy I am to see you.'

Ishmael grinned too. 'I smelt your presence about two hundred yards back down the road,' Ishmael replied in Hindi. He stared at Canaan. His worn-out clothes, a fake wispy beard and a wig of greasy, matted hair looked so real that had it not been for Canaan's sharp blue, boyish eyes, he wouldn't have recognized his friend.

'I tell you a truth. It is tolerable when it's your own sweat and urine. You should try working with some of the fools at the training camp who do not know the meaning of a wash,' Canaan replied wryly.

'Do not say such things. They are a pure clean brotherhood.'

Canaan pulled from the inside of his coat a transcript of the BBC radio program he had heard in Rome and handed it to Ishmael.

'What is this?'

'Read it, my friend,' said Canaan, his voice stern. He trudged back to the bench and lay down.

Ishmael propped himself against the railing. After reading a few paragraphs, he dismissed it as a pack of lies, screwed up the sheaves of paper, threw them over the terrace and marched over to the park bench. Stiffbacked, he stood looking at the ragged, still figure stretched out before him, hands folded on his chest.

'So, my good friend?' said Canaan eagerly.

'It is all misinformation to discredit those who have been appointed by God to lead His people,' Ishmael retorted.

'It appears that God first appointed the Americans to inspire His leaders with money.'

'God's ways are just. He will punish those who speak such lies against his chosen ones.' Ishmael sat down at the end of the bench.

'God's chosen ones were chosen by the Americans first, then, when the Americans spat them out, your imageless God comes along and scrapes them up.' Canaan paused and then said mockingly, 'Get your logic right, my friend.'

'No, no, I do not want to hear it.' Ishmael grimaced. He cupped his ears and started murmuring an intercession to God: 'God the Splendid Almighty ruler of all, please forgive Canaan, be gracious, merciful, blot out his transgressions against the sacred brotherhood, enlighten his soul, show him your omnipotent glory …'

Canaan raised himself up, grabbed Ishmael's hand and wrenched it from his ear. 'Shut the fuck up!' he yelled in English. 'My friend, I did not make it up. The whole world knows about it. The CIA admits that it …'

Ishmael continued with his prayer of intercession.

'Have you not learnt at your university that one day China will be stronger and richer than America? Your duplicitous leaders will once again be back on the American side, fighting the rice people,' Canaan scoffed. He threw down Ishmael's limp hand and gazed at the side of Ishmael's head rocking back and forth with eyes shut tight. Canaan slumped forward, holding his head between his knees and trying to swallow back his tears.

Ishmael, satisfied that his prayer had appeased God's wrath against Canaan, put his arm around Canaan's shoulder.

'I am tired of waiting, so tired,' sighed Canaan. 'I am scared of losing you, my brother. Please, I beg you, leave all of Akmid's plans behind. I will leave the Azad Front. Let us be done with terrorism and make our own way to America and die for our cause,' he pleaded.

'No, I cannot, Canaan. You must understand that we are chosen, you and I. You must have patience,' Ishmael said softly.

'Patience, you say. It has been years.' Canaan dried his eyes on his ragged shirt sleeve.

'Yes, I know, but look how far we have come. If it was not for Akmid being led by God to find us, heaven knows where we would be today. We would still be in the Uttar Pradesh Juvenile Prison.'

Chapter 14 *Salzburg, Austria, May, 2004*

'The camel-lipped man is led by Hitler, you fool.'

'We are not to make fun of Akmid's big dropping bottom lip. Anyway, Hitler was led by God to kill the greedy Jew people. God bless Hitler.' Ishmael raised both hands into the air.

'Where are those papers I gave you? Did you read the bits from the *Wall Street Journal*?'

'The wind blew them out of my hands before I could finish. Besides, there is nothing to explain.' He paused and looked down at his shoes. 'The mysteries of God cannot be explained by the logic of men,' Ishmael said, matter-of-fact. 'Only the prophet knows the mysteries of God.'

Canaan threw his arms into the air. 'All right! It is our story that is important, and that is not a mystery of God.' He jabbed a finger into Ishmael's arm. 'Can you not understand?' Canaan said forcefully. 'Do you not remember that we agreed to pretend to be carpet worshippers? So I could kill the American priest who was going to visit the prison prayer room. And the only way we could be in the room was to pretend to become good and faithful believers. We were fortunate that, at the time, Akmid came to the prison to recruit young men for his revolutionary terrorist training method. He needed two pretenders as much as we needed him to get us out of prison before we rotted in there.

Ishmael faced Canaan, ecstatic. 'Yes, yes, I did pretend, but God, all merciful, has forgiven my pretending. So there.' Ishmael folded his arms.

Canaan shook his head in disbelief. 'I am afraid you have taken it too far. You are becoming like one of them.'

'I have not taken it far enough.'

The idea of an omnipresent, omniscient and omnipotent god had been the underlying platform on which Ishmael had built his newfound religion. This was in stark contrast to the Hindu ways — the pantheon of gods that were constantly at war with each other — in which Ishmael had grown up, along with his lowly status as an Anglo-Indian. It was once Canaan who had filled his mother's place in his life. Now it was God, because God was a god above all gods. Canaan also occupied a place, but it was now secondary.

'Look what has happened to our holy brothers around the world.'

'Our holy brothers, my bum,' Canaan mocked. 'I have no brothers except you.'

Ishmael continued. 'They are all being oppressed by American imperialism, but we are the chosen ones who will turn the tide on the great evil nation.'

'I do not care about the holy brothers or Akmid's plan for us. All I care about is dying together,' Canaan lamented.

A sparrow perched on the edge of a rubbish bin, pecking at a bread crust, caught Canaan's attention. He reached down, picked up a rock and threw it at the bird. In an instant, the bird was on the grass flapping its broken wing. Canaan pulled a cigarette lighter from his pocket and rushed over to set the broken bird on fire. Just as Canaan flicked the lighter, the broken bird died. Canaan kicked it in a rage of frustration, then stomped back to the bench.

He stood over Ishmael. 'Your allegiance is to me, to die for my cause! It is not to die for your faith!' Canaan hissed into Ishmael's ear. He grabbed Ishmael by the shoulders and shook him violently.

Ishmael pried himself loose. 'But so much has happened. We have to go beyond our personal desires.'

'We have our truth and our experience to inspire us,' Canaan snapped.

'I beg you, accept me for who I am and what I feel. For so long it has always been your way for me. Now it is time for me to have my way, which is in God's hands.'

Canaan slumped down on the bench. He was disgusted with the pompous expression on Ishmael's face. He had seen the same thing in the eyes of the mules when he had strapped suicide bomb belts around them and sent them off with an oral benediction, punctuated with a silent curse from the devil. In more recent times, he had begun to hope they would get caught and killed by the authorities. Indeed, he was sorely tempted to tip off the authorities; however, being the planner, the responsibility of things going wrong would fall upon his shoulders. Nevertheless, it had given him great satisfaction to destroy the reputations of other planners.

'If I go now to America and kill Reverend Jonathon Duvall and then jump into the fire of death, where would that leave you? When your time comes, could you jump into the fire without me?' Canaan demanded sharply, 'Quick, answer truthfully.'

Ishmael stared wide-eyed at Canaan and shook his head violently. He got up and walked over to the terrace.

'Answer my question!' Canaan shouted.

Ishmael stared across the valley. The sun had begun dipping towards the horizon. Salzburg was engulfed in shadows. In the glint of the sun, the river looked like a stripe of fire.

Canaan came up behind him, demanding an answer. Ishmael turned around and looked Canaan squarely in the eyes.

'I will answer your question if you agree to answer mine,' Ishmael said.

'What is your question?'

'If I die for my faith before your time comes, could you jump into the fire without me?'

Ishmael noted the flicker of frustration in Canaan's eyes and a faint quiver on his bottom lip.

'Stalemate!' one of the old men playing chess called out to his partner.

Canaan and Ishmael looked at each other in surprise, then towards the old men. The invalid in the wheelchair was tearing around the chess board, knocking over all the pieces in an apparent rage.

Without another word, their meeting ended.

Apart from his disappointment that Ishmael was not going with him to America, Canaan remained confident that, no matter how much Ishmael immersed himself in religion, he, Canaan, held the key to Ishmael's exit from the world of the living.

CHAPTER 15

PARKER, ARIZONA, SATURDAY 18 AUGUST

Ishmael booted up his laptop, did a Google search and found the number of the *Mark Twain*, the Mississippi riverboat Ishmael knew that Canaan was staying on.

He felt a strong urge to log onto one of the radical chat rooms. Whenever he felt the whole world was pressing down on him, he often consoled himself by conversing with like-minded people and disaffected youth. On these sites, they would egg each other on, mouth off sadistic rhetoric, and vow to perform deadly deeds against their enemies. Some bragged about being members of this group or that, but it didn't much matter to Ishmael if they were telling the truth or not. He judged that as long as their hearts were in the right place, God would open a way to perform their most holy desires against His enemies. On numerous occasions, Akmid had reprimanded and warned him to stay off these sites. 'You never know who you could be chatting with, dear boy. Maybe a law enforcement official perhaps.' Remembering Akmid's warning, Ishmael reluctantly decided against logging on.

He grabbed the landline from the bedside table and dialed. A cheery receptionist answered and put him through to Canaan's room.

After three rings he heard Canaan's voice. 'Hello, hello. Who is this? Hello?'

Ishmael listened, somewhat comforted by the familiar voice on the other end of the phone. Frozen, he was unable to utter a word. He did not have a clue where to begin. No, that was wrong. He knew exactly where to begin from. The very first day he set foot on this accursed land they call America.

'Hello, hello,' Canaan repeated. 'Who is this?'

Lost in a morass of fear and guilt, tears rolled down Ishmael's cheeks. He let out a blood-curdling wail. As he stood up, the room began to spin. He stumbled into the bathroom and ran his head under the shower. The cold water left him gasping for breath. He toweled himself dry, went back into the bedroom and fell into bed.

The cold water gave him only temporary relief. Soon he was back in a torment so intense that he almost blacked out. Ishmael struggled to let go of the day's events.

Lying there in the depths of despondency, he caught the faint musky scent of Rosasharn's perfume on his jacket, bunched up next to the pillow. The scent was like a breath of heaven, giving him the respite he so needed. As he held the jacket to his face, taking it all in, thinking about the moments after he had hit his head on the roof and come to rest with his head on her lap, staring up at her heaving breasts. Eventually, Ishmael peacefully drifted off to sleep in anticipation of spending the next day with Rosasharn.

CHAPTER 16

PARKER, ARIZONA, SUNDAY 19 AUGUST

Ishmael awoke just before dawn, reached over and flicked on the bedside lamp and picked up his holy book. He gazed at his crumpled jacket lying on the floor, and was overcome with the temptation to pick it up, hold it to his nose and savor the last faint wisp of Rosasharn's perfume. He stretched over the edge of the bed to grab it while holding onto the holy book with the other hand. As he leaned over he lost his balance and dropped the book. It tumbled over the side of the bed. The frustration and anguish of the previous night flared up in him. 'No!' he yelled at himself. Aghast, he lurched over and gingerly picked it up and clasped it tightly to his bare chest, bowed his head, and closed his eyes. He implored God to forgive his foolish ways and pleaded with Him to remove any further obstacles that Satan might have up his sleeve to divert him from his holy mission. He flipped the holy book open and recited aloud verses to himself.

Uninspired, Ishmael placed the holy book on the bedside table and checked his watch. It was close to eight. He hauled himself out of bed and had a quick shower, dressed, and took a few painkillers that Doctor Abdullah had prescribed to him for his tumor, which was unusually painful this morning.

Twelve months ago, Ishmael had noticed a growth under his left armpit. He was diagnosed by a doctor in Montreal who had advised him that the small lump was benign, but if left untreated could metastasize and be fatal. Over the past few weeks it had become quite inflamed. At the training camp, he received minor treatment for it from the camp doctor. He assured Ishmael that the tumor would not be a problem in the afterlife. A few pounds of plastic explosive around his waist would blow it permanently off his immortal soul with no morbid side effects for the rest of eternity.

He retrieved the bomb belt from the corner of the room went into the kitchen, placed it on the table and made himself some coffee and toast. He was inspecting the wiring on his bomb belt when the phone rang. He reached over to answer it but hesitated. 'Maybe it's Canaan trying to work out who had called him. What will I say? 'I will deny it,' he exclaimed aloud and snatched up the receiver.

'Hello.'

'Scot.'

'Who's this?' he snapped.

'Rosasharn.'

'Oh, it's you.'

'I'm at Water's Edge. Mom didn't have a very good night last night. I had to go in and talk to her doctor early this morning. All is okay now though,' she said, sighing. 'I'm running a little late. Be there in about hour and half.'

'Maybe you should spend the day with her. We can go to Sedona another time,' he said, unable to hide the disappointment in his voice.

'No, there's not much else I can do here. They pumped her full of some powerful sleeping pills. She'll be zonked out for the day.'

'That's good.'

'That my mum's zonked out?'

'Absolutely not. Just that our day trip to Sedona isn't cancelled.'

'I'm happy, too. See ya soon.'

Ishmael hung up, relieved that it wasn't Canaan. He leant back in his

Chapter 16 *Parker, Arizona, Sunday 19 August*

chair, clasped his hands behind his head and wondered what Canaan had been up to since arriving in America.

CHAPTER 17

SAN FRANCISCO, CALIFORNIA, WEDNESDAY 1 AUGUST

Canaan's plane landed at McLaren International Airport in San Francisco the same day that Ishmael arrived at LAX. Canaan nonchalantly pushed his passport with his entry document between the pages across the checkpoint counter. The customs officer thumbed through it and read Canaan's particulars.

Age: twenty-three years. Name: Paul South. Address: Alberta, Canada. Occupation: sales representative for Locust International, a Canadian agricultural machinery manufacturer.

Like Ishmael's, Canaan's new identity was unassailable. He was, to all intents and purposes, the adopted son of Joseph and Hilda South who took him home with them from a sordid Calcutta orphanage.

The customs officer studied the passport photo, cross-referenced it on his computer terminal and stared at Canaan. Canaan had a neatly trimmed beard and shoulder-length hair that was severely tied back in a ponytail. The customs officer gave Canaan a curt nod and stamped his travel documents.

Canaan, knowing that his journey was drawing to a close, was buoyed by an exhilaration of extraordinary intensity, the likes of which he had experienced only when he had wiped a pedophile off the face of the earth. Interpol and other European law enforcement agencies had been hampered in their investigations by the lack of witnesses coming forth with information on the 'vigilante serial killer', which is how Canaan had been dubbed by the world's media.

Within an hour of passing through customs, Canaan picked up his new blue Ford Taurus he'd ordered a week before, drove to a nearby tire dealer and purchased two spares, then to the First National Bank on the corner of Jefferson and Hyde.

He parked his car in one of the parking bays adjacent to Fisherman's Wharf, rummaged through his bag for the ID he needed to access the safety deposit box and noted the time — three-thirty. Everything was running to schedule. He had to leave San Francisco in time to be in Sacramento by seven-thirty. From there he would travel on to Flagstaff to meet up with Ishmael.

Canaan walked into the sandstone art deco building with purpose and showed his ID to the desk clerk. A security guard led him to the seventh floor where his safe deposit box was stored. As soon as the security guard left, Canaan removed the envelope. It was an electric moment, supercharged with feelings of hope, but also despair that the information held in the envelope of Reverend Jonathon Duvall's whereabouts was going to be unfruitful. Knowing that Akmid would have kept his end of the bargain to locate Reverend Jonathon Duvall once Ishmael was finally qualified — both religiously and academically — and employed at a vital American utility, he dismissed his negative thoughts.

Everything Canaan had done since his mother's death was for the fulfillment of the promise he made to her the day she died. Over the years, he had seriously considered the alternative, of cutting a deal with American Homeland Security, convinced that Duvall's life would be a fair price to pay for the wealth of information he had.

Even if it entailed turning himself in and having Ishmael arrested and extradited to the United States, he would have done it in exchange for

Duvall's miserable life. He would tell the world how he had fooled the leaders of the Global Azad Front into believing he was one of them, and snatch the glory by declaring the deeds that he had done had absolutely nothing to do with advancing their ill-fated cause, thus making them a mockery in the eyes of all.

Canaan expected that Ishmael and he would be tried. It would be a quick trial, no wasting precious time in Guantanamo Bay and making lawyers rich. They would plead guilty and be sentenced to death immediately. He couldn't help picturing how this last scene in his life on Earth would play out: the three of them in a room, Ishmael and himself with their wrists and ankles shackled to a wooden chair, electrodes attached to their bodies, a damp sponge on their heads. Duvall all bundled the same way. After gladly witnessing Duvall being zapped into eternal damnation, then it would be their turn to be zapped into heaven, where he expected to meet up with his mother.

The instant he was in his car he ripped open the envelope. He spent a moment memorizing the address. Just knowing Duvall's exact whereabouts was sufficient tonic to quash his anxiety. He knew that the Jack Folsom Southern Baptist Revival Crusader's headquarters was in Baton Rouge and believed Duvall to be residing somewhere in that riverfront city. However, this information gave the name of a Mississippi riverboat, the *Mark Twain*.

Deep within, Canaan felt the dislodgement of his life's burden. Calm blanketed him. Tears brimmed in his eyes and rolled down his cheeks. For the first time since that horrible day so long ago, the resonance of his mother's screams perpetually sounding in his head abated. He stared at the sheaf of papers for a long time, then, as he became aware of the world around him, he was finally able to get a grip on himself.

CHAPTER 18

SACRAMENTO, CALIFORNIA, WEDNESDAY 1 AUGUST

Canaan's next port of call was Sacramento, where he was to make contact with a member of an outlaw biker gang with strong links to the Aryan Brotherhood, who specialized in recovering unexploded bombs from military test sites. Akmid had sourced the supplier through a colleague from his former association, the Nazi Socialist Party.

The pick-up did not go as quickly as Canaan would have liked. The transfer of $75,000 from a dormant World War II account held at a Swiss bank into Canaan's Cayman Island bank account had not been credited. The money was to be transferred into the biker gang's account at the same bank.

It was just after ten p.m. when the money finally came through and he had divided and packed ten pounds of C4 — a plastic explosive — and fifty pounds of RDX — Research Department Explosive — in the inner tubes of the two spare tires. Flagstaff was 700 miles away. He had planned to get a couple of hundred miles out of the way before bunking down for the night, but jet lag and the stress of the long delay had exhausted him. He rang the Flag and left a message for Ishmael that he would arrive early on Friday morning.

He pulled in at a roadside motel just out of town. Before taking his room, he stopped at a 24-hour department store and bought a half a dozen sets of bed linen, a dozen towels, five bars of soap, rubber gloves, industrial strength cleaning fluids and a suitcase to pack them in.

He had learned that if you want anything cleaned thoroughly you have do it yourself and shut up about the bed linen.

CHAPTER 19

EL PASO, TEXAS, SATURDAY 4 AUGUST

By sunset, Canaan had travelled as far as El Paso, desperately in need of a comfortable night's rest after sleeping in the car the previous night. He checked into the Hotel Sonora. He checked into the Hotel Sonora. It was a small, run-down establishment on the edge of town. After sanitizing the bathroom and changing the bed linen, he freshened up and ventured across the road from his hotel to the Rio Grande Cantina for a bite to eat.

Canaan wandered inside. The place was jam-packed with a diverse mixture of people. Asians, Hispanics, cowboys, college boys, bikers and businessmen were standing around the bar and seated at tables. The oppressive, low ceiling was supported by fluorescent green walls covered with posters of bull fighting and exotic Mexican resorts. A purple neon sign of a cowboy on a bucking bronco pulsated on the wall behind the battle-worn mahogany bar. Scarred porcelain spittoons flanked either side. The bar was on a raised platform that overlooked a cockfighting ring. The pit was railed and enclosed with chicken wire.

On the far side of the room in a cordoned-off area, between an elevated bandstand and a bank of slot machines, was a line of cages holding that evening's fighting birds.

A blinking red neon sign that hung over the back wall grabbed Canaan's attention. It read: 'Fight to the death'. The sign's sentiment intrigued him.

Canaan crossed the dance floor to get a closer look at the contenders, even though that part of the room was strictly off limits to anybody not directly connected to the birds. No one seemed to take notice, despite the fact that owners were all around him talking quietly to their contacts and shoring up the gambling odds.

Canaan peered into the cages, intently eyeing the birds. He was mildly amused by their flamboyant appearance. Some were decorated with bows and ribbons, others, their heads held high, were strutting around their cages with tiny spurs of steel attached to their legs. He could not help noticing the peculiar light in the small, dotted eyes of the birds. The longer he stared into them, the more the nuances of their expressions became vivid to him.

Some had a glimmer of confidence and pride, others clouds of fear or weakness. Intuitively, he knew who would live or die. Sport and other entertainment had never interested Canaan, but this was one of the rare times in his life when he was going to give himself the liberty to become one of the spectators in the crowd.

After dinner, he stood under the arched doorway of the lobby separating the dining room and the bar, and surveyed the scene. Close to the fighting pit he spotted a vacant chair at a table where two men sat.

Canaan went up to the table and placed both hands on the back of the empty chair. 'Is this chair taken?'

A middle-aged, heavy-set man wearing a cowboy hat, rhinestone shirt and a thick square-cut black beard streaked with grey stared up at Canaan and grinned. He took a hit from his shot glass, chased it down with a mug of beer, and slowly turned to his companion. 'Monsignor, will we let him have the pleasure of our company?'

The padre dipped the tip of his cigar in his glass of Masco, took a long draw and, with his attention fixed on a bawdy bunch of college students joking and sparring among themselves over by the slot machines, answered

Chapter 19 El Paso, Texas, Saturday 4 August

in a strong Mexican accent, 'I do not see why not. He looks like a decent enough young fella.'

The priest had jet-black hair that was oiled sleek against his skull, accentuating his broad, sloping forehead. The skin on his face was mottled with scar tissue. His sunken eyes and hollow jaw gave him a rather cadaverous appearance.

The big man doffed his hat and stretched out his hand to Canaan. 'Rowan J. Nash. This here is Padre Juan Enrico.'

Canaan accepted his hand. 'Paul South.'

'Where you from?' Nash asked, pumping Canaan's hand.

'Alberta, Canada,' Canaan replied as he sat down.

'I hear it's a right pretty place, snow and all that.'

'It is,' Canaan said.

Padre Enrico faced Canaan. 'So what brings you down south, South?'

Canaan gave the padre a cold stare.

Padre Enrico held Canaan's stare, grabbed the bottle of Masco, topped up his glass and gulped it down.

'If you not want the pleasure of my company, just say so,' Canaan said sharply.

'My holy friend here didn't mean to be rude.' Nash gave Padre Enrico a heavy slap on the back. The padre gave him a cruel sneer.

'You have not answered the question, amigo.' The padre pointed his cigar at Canaan.

'I'm a sales rep for Locust International, an agricultural machinery manufacturer,' replied Canaan flatly.

'Farming machinery is very, very profitable business to be in,' Padre Enrico said.

Nash called out to a passing waiter to bring a glass. He leant across the table towards the padre and whispered to him. Then he turned his attention to Canaan. 'Padre here is collecting money for his parish across the border.'

Canaan shrugged, a blank expression on his face.

The two men stared at Canaan. Padre snuffed out his cigar stub and lit another. Nash drummed his fingers on the edge of the table.

An uproar of mocking laughter from a group of bikers standing at the bar seized the trio's attention. A drunk, conservatively dressed businessman was belly up on the floor. As the man slowly picked himself up, Nash faced Canaan and cleared his throat. 'You're new in these parts, so let me explain the way things work around here, friend.'

'Explain what?' Canaan leant back on his chair and crossed his arms.

'People sitting ringside are here for a piece of the action.' Nash motioned to the tables around them where bets were being offered and taken. 'When you take a chair, it is a custom that you place a wager. You've been here for about two minutes and have failed to indicate to the good padre and yours truly that you're either a high roller or just a happy-go-lucky sales rep throwing a bit of money around just for fun.'

'I see. No money on the table, no ringside chair,' replied Canaan, nodding his head.

'We will forgive your ignorance, muchacho,' Padre Enrico said in a softer tone.

Nash pulled out a book of betting slips from his shirt pocket and placed it on the table.

Canaan stared at the betting book and then toward the cages. 'Just give me a few minutes, gentlemen.'

'You have eleven minutes before the next round starts,' said Padre Enrico tapping his watch. 'If you come back and find someone in your seat, please *señor*, I ask you not to bother us anymore.'

Chapter 19 El Paso, Texas, Saturday 4 August

A waiter arrived at the table and placed a glass on it. Canaan stood up and went over to the holding pens to refresh his memory.

Before too long Canaan strutted smugly back to the table and sat down. He dug into his shirt pocket, pulled out his wallet and counted out one thousand dollars in $100 bills. '$200 on each of these numbers: two, five, seven, ten and thirteen.'

'You seem very sure of yourself, Mr. South,' Padre Enrico said. He sucked hard on his cigar and blew a cloud of smoke in Canaan's direction. Canaan waved his hand in protest.

'I am sorry *señor*, that you do not appreciate cigarillo smoke,' said Padre Enrico. He flashed a patronizing smile that displayed a gold front tooth that caught the light, then puffed another cloud in Canaan's direction.

'So,' Nash said as he jotted down the numbers on the betting slip, 'you reckon they're the winners?'

'No, the losers,' Canaan said forcefully.

'A strange way to bet, *amigo*. Why you not bet on who will win?'

Canaan smiled thinly and said, 'Losers are easier to spot. Especially when two of them are staring you in the face.'

'What are you talking about?' Nash questioned gruffly.

'Betting on who dies first.' Canaan paused, and drew a long, deep breath. 'It's just the way I see things.' The threat of violence that radiated off Canaan was palpable.

The padre and Nash exchanged a quick glance and stared at Canaan incredulously.

'Don't know what kind of a game you're playing,' Nash said flatly. 'But we'll take your bet any way you want.' Nash filled out the betting slip, tore out the carbon copy, placed it on the table and pocketed Canaan's money.

Canaan leant back in his chair and said, 'My friends, you misunderstand my actions. I don't want your money. It means nothing to me.'

'It means a lot to the little motherless and fatherless children across the border, *amigo*,' said Padre Enrico solemnly. He scooped a wooden rosary from his jacket pocket, twirled it around his hand and dropped his head, clasped his hands under his chin and mumbled a prayer in Spanish.

Canaan eyeballed the silver crucifix dangling between the padre's forearms and tried unsuccessfully to suppress the raw emotion erupting from deep in his soul.

The bell rang. The crowd cheered with excitement. Two handlers walked into the middle of the pit holding the contenders in a firm grip. As the gap closed between them, the cocks eyed one another intently. The handlers narrowed the distance between the birds close enough to peck at one another and have their anger flare up for a few moments, then they were let loose. They rose into the air, spurs and beaks slashing feathers and flesh. Blood began to flow. The crowd roared as the feathered enemies clashed.

A minute and a half into the first bout and it was over. The din of the crowd came to an abrupt halt as one of the cocks succumbed. For a fraction of a second there was silence, almost as if the crowd was paying its respects to the lifeless, crumpled ball of feathers being picked up off the floor by its grieving owner.

With the first fight over, another two cocks were getting acquainted with one another.

People were getting up from their tables and crowding around the railing that encircled the ring, obscuring Canaan's view. He stood up and squeezed his way to the front railing.

Nash tapped Padre Enrico on the shoulder and motioned him to follow.

CHAPTER 20

EL PASO, TEXAS, SATURDAY 4 AUGUST

At the rear of the Rio Grande Cantina's dining room was an alcove where special agent for Internal Revenue Service Salvador Emanuel Menendez, alias Padre Enrico, and special agent for the FBI Uriah Stuyvesant, alias Rowan J. Nash, would often retreat.

Uriah Stuyvesant flung open the sash window that overlooked the street. A fire truck whizzed past, its sirens blaring, momentarily masking the roar of the crowd in the saloon. Salvador Emanuel Menendez reached for a stool, positioned it against the wall and propped himself on it. A gilt-framed portrait of Pancho Villa hung above him.

Salvador sighed and rubbed his eyes. 'Stale sweat, testosterone, smoke and blood. I am fucking sick of it.' The padre's thick Mexican accent was gone.

'You're not complaining about the Masco.' Uriah smiled wryly.

'So what do you make of this Paul South?'

'Real hard to say, Sal,' replied Uriah. He craned his head out of the open window to breathe in some fresh air.

'Someone who says he hasn't got a clue about house rules, goes and inspects the roosters, throws a grand on the table, bets on the losers and says he is not interested in taking the money has got my brain working overtime,' said Uriah.

'Betting on which cock dies and that being just the way he sees things ... Gee, Uriah, I don't know. I swear he was referring to us.'

'I picked up the same vibes. Loaded with innuendo, buddy boy.'

'Did you get a good look at his eyes? Something about them makes me uneasy,' said Salvador.

'You should have seen the gleam in them when he stared at your crucifix while you had your head bowed over the rosary. Looked like one possessed by a legion of demons.'

'A lot of people have got a beef with God's anointed,' said Sal.

'If you ask me the man's got a beef with life itself. Period. This dude is some kind of a psychopath. Maybe a killer for hire.'

'You think so?'

'If ever I saw one, he sure fits the bill,' replied Uriah, stroking his beard with the back of his hand. 'I've sent enough of them up the river and fried their piss-ant brains on old sparky to be able to tell them apart from every other type of miscreant.'

'Sounds like you're the expert,' Sal said, eyeing off a black-haired Mexican beauty wearing a short skirt that rode up her thighs as she swung her legs under a table. The girl's attention was fixed on the brightly dressed man bedecked in chunky bracelets and rings who was sitting across from her, talking into a cell phone. Sal nudged Uriah in the stomach and pointed towards the girl.

'Real nice.' Uriah nodded, let out a lustful groan and then said, 'You see, Sal, these types are natural-born killers, like a wild animal with no thought for their prey. All they want is to satisfy their gastric juices.'

'Is that a fact? I've got a few juices I need satisfying,' Sal said, his eyes fixed on the girl's long legs.

'Sure is, pardner.'

'Hey, assuming that he is a hired gun, you know what I can't understand?'

'What?'

'Hired guns are ghosts. They do their job and disappear. So why has this guy come right out in the open and implied that we're his next meal?'

'Got a gut feeling he's probably working for the Malatestas and I bet my sweet ass the turkey brain is making a statement.'

'About what?'

'Do I have to spell it out to ya? Letting us know that the game's over.' Uriah gritted his teeth.

Sal nodded thoughtfully. 'You're kidding me.' He cocked his head and looked up at Uriah. 'You really believe he's part of a grease balls' set-up?'

'The Malatestas have a lot a people on their payroll.'

'So you figure they were tipped off?'

'Look, to tell you the truth, I got a hunch that the powers that be in the FBI have set up this whole undercover operation of ours to weed out who's been tipping off the Malatestas.'

'What? The IRS is just being used for the Feds' own ends?'

'Every government department has been used in some way or another by the FBI ever since Hoover was running the show. You know that.'

'So here I am, ruining my health for the past six weeks, all the while thinking we're going to hit pay dirt.' Salvador was indignant.

'It's just a hunch. Hey, I could be wrong and this could be just plain old, up-front undercover work.' Uriah stared down at his silver-capped leather boots and polished the tips on the back of his jeans. 'Don't stress. I'm only saying ... I'm probably wrong,' Uriah said, trying to sound upbeat.

'It's our last night in this hellhole. What a perfect goodbye present from the low-life of Louisiana.' Salvador grimaced.

A horn blew to signal the end of the round of fighting.

'The slaughter's over, your holiness,' said Uriah. 'Let's go bury the dead.'

Between the rounds, Canaan picked up on a bit of small talk about how great some of the cock trainers were. The Azad Front's leaders ought to abandon their ineffective religious instruction and incorporate some of these cock-training techniques. It would vastly improve their retention rate Canaan reasoned, and chuckled to himself. Even if he tried, he could not put a number to the amount of men he had strapped bombs onto and sent off on their deadly missions, only to learn later that they had reneged on their commitment to die a good death, and were never seen or heard of again.

Now, as he sat down again wondering where his gambling companions had got to, he saw Padre Enrico coming towards him, twirling his rosary beads.

Padre Enrico gave Canaan a curt nod. Canaan nodded back. The padre sat down and filled his glass, draining the bottle of Masco. He turned the empty bottle upside down and shook the worm into the neck, held the bottle to his mouth, sucked out the leathery grub, chewed and swallowed. Canaan placed his betting slip on the table. Padre Enrico picked it up and crosschecked the numbers against those on the winning board hanging over the fighting pit.

'Mr. South, you are a very, very lucky gringo. You picked straight losers, which, in your case, are the winners.'

'Beginner's luck, I suppose,' Canaan replied indifferently.

Nash arrived back at the table. He sat down, topped up his shot glass and knocked back his drink.

'We will not be taking back much money for the hungry children at the mission. Mr. South has been extremely lucky,' Padre Enrico said mournfully.

Nash snatched the betting slip out of the padre's hand.

'Remember, Mr. South put his money on the losers,' Padre Enrico said.

Nash tallied the numbers. 'We'd better pay the man,' he replied. Out of his shirt pocket he pulled a thick roll of bills, counted out two thousand dollars and placed the money on the table.

Canaan noted the suspicious look in Nash's eyes. 'Look, gentlemen, I am not a gambling man. I'll take back my $1000 and you keep yours.'

Chapter 20   *El Paso, Texas, Saturday 4 August*

'In all my years collecting money for the orphans, I have not come across anyone as generous as you. I will petition the holy Jesus and Father of all mercy to bless you,' the padre said. He made a sign of the cross and dangled the rosary beads in front of Canaan's face, mumbling a prayer in Spanish.

Canaan glowered at the padre. He slammed both his hands on the table and bowed his head. All this talk of orphans and their school and of Jesus ignited painful feelings. He quickly composed himself, drew in a deep breath, held it for moment and exhaled slowly, then looking steadily at the two men he gave them a curt nod, reached out and picked up his money, got up and walked out.

Hastily, Uriah got up and went over to the dining room window. Salvador followed him. They watched Canaan go into the hotel across the road.

'He's a weird guy, not taking the money. Either he has a hell of lot of it or, like you said, is making a statement.' Sal stared up at the portrait of Pancho Villa. 'Would you say, Pancho, that our little charade was curtains from the start?'

'This guy's straight out of a comic book,' Uriah said. He turned to face Sal. 'Of all the people we've come across in the six weeks we've been here, this one just pops up out of the blue. A grand isn't chicken shit to walk away from, it's got to mean something.'

'Whatever. I figure he's the one we should maybe focus on,' Sal remarked with a doleful look of certainty. 'I'll get someone from the El Paso branch to look into the guy, maybe put a tag on him.'

'We don't know for sure if this South is connected with the grease balls,' Uriah said as he tapped on the windowsill. 'By the time the IRS talks to the Bureau and all the bullshit red tape has been cut through, South will have done a disappearing act.'

Looking at Uriah as if he already guessed what his partner was going to say next, Salvador said, 'No. No, don't. It ain't worth it.'

'Listen Sal, before you start churning out the paperwork, I want to know which coop this pigeon's flying back to. If the Bureau has sent us on a wild goose chase, yours truly is going to find out.'

'Hell, you can do what you like. After midnight I'm defrocked, through with wearing these fuckin' priest's clothes and ruining my health.' He pried his finger into his collar and pulled it away from his skin. 'How they wear these over-starched chokers is a miracle.'

'It's all about imitating the suffering of Christ.' Uriah slapped Salvador on the back and forced a smile. 'Trust me, Sal. I am not asking you to go out on a limb.'

'You start your vacation tomorrow. You don't want to be working on your own time. Let someone else do the chase. Hey, what about that resort down along the Gulf you been dreaming about?'

'I never made any reservations.'

'You don't need a reservation. You just front up. Spend the first few days working on your report then kick back on the beach and watch the pretty girls get an even suntan.'

Uriah reached up and straightened the portrait of Pancho Villa. 'Sal, I would love nothing more than to let someone else do the chase, but who the hell is going latch onto him with what we've got? Think about it for a moment.'

'Someone like you.'

'Precisely. It's in my blood, and when it starts coursing through my veins over some douche bag I ...'

'Yeah, yeah, tell it to your quack,' Sal said, cutting him off. 'If this ends up being a goodbye message from the Malatesta brothers, we'll just send them a thank you card.' He looked at his watch and tapped on the glass. 'At five a.m. I'm on the redeye to Oklahoma City to give evidence in the Sarafini case.'

CHAPTER 21

EL PASO, TEXAS, SATURDAY 4 AUGUST

Salvador and Uriah kept a watch on the Hotel Sonora from their hired van parked a little way down the road from the hotel.

'So he got lucky on the fights and donated all his winnings to charity,' Salvador said as he adjusted his seat in a horizontal position, trying to get comfortable. 'What else am I going to write about? That he gave you high blood pressure? And besides, whether he's been sent by the Malatestas or not doesn't enlighten us on our brief.'

'To find out who's washing the Malatesta money,' Uriah cut in. 'Look Sal, I'll play it this way. I promise that, for whatever it's worth, by midmorning I will personally give it over to the locals.'

'Honestly, Uriah, what's there to give? Think about it.'

'Nothing yet. Hell, what the fuck am I making promises to you for?' Uriah cranked down the window and leant his elbow out.

'Okay, let's say he's some kind of a button man. You've got a feeling. Your blood's boiling over him. You're the expert. You read all the books.'

'I never said I read books. I just ... just forget it,' Uriah insisted as a bout of coughing seized him. He wheezed for breath, pulled out his Ventolin dispenser and held it to his mouth.

'You all right?' Sal asked, concerned.

Uriah nodded as he drew in a few puffs. As the tightening in his chest eased, he let out a sonorous sigh.

'If this guy's not connected, he ain't our problem. So why are we making it our problem? I could be in my hotel room getting a couple of hours' sleep.'

'Sal, I'm not holding you prisoner. Your hotel is only a couple of blocks from here. It's a beautiful warm night for a stroll. If you don't want to walk I'll drive you.' Uriah started the van.

'Cut the engine, and just hear me out.' Salvador adjusted his seat again, rolled up his sweater and put it behind his neck. 'If someone from the Bureau has tipped them off...'

Uriah tapped his fingers on the steering wheel and hummed along with an Alan Jackson song playing on the radio about buying his girlfriend tall trees and all the water in the seas.

CHAPTER 22

EL PASO, TEXAS, SUNDAY 5 AUGUST

It was just after one in the morning when Uriah spotted Canaan come out through the hotel's doors and walk in the opposite direction. 'Here's our man,' he said, shaking Salvador awake.

Uriah started the van and crept along, lights off and keeping well behind Canaan. They had gone no more than two blocks when they saw Canaan go into a service station. Uriah turned on the lights, drove past the station, dropped a U-turn and pulled up on the opposite side of the road.

Canaan came out of the gas station carrying a couple of shopping bags and headed back towards the hotel. About halfway between the hotel and the service station, Canaan disappeared down an alleyway.

'I'm gonna find out what that weasel is up to. Presumably he's making a rendezvous.' Uriah paused for effect. 'Someone who may be of interest to us.'

'Could be,' Sal said.

Uriah got out of the driver's seat and ducked into the back of the van. He pulled off his boots, slipped on some sneakers and a ragged-looking overcoat.

He got a bottle of water out of the cooler and drenched his beard.

'Hand me my piece out of the glove compartment,' Uriah said as he slapped on a baseball cap. 'While I'm checking him out, you get your ass into the gas station, find out what he bought, then call my cell.'

Sal drew a silver flask from his breast pocket, took a couple of gulps and offered it to Uriah.

'No,' Uriah replied as he loaded the chamber with bullets.

Uriah climbed out of the van, looking for all the world like a tramp. The course his life had taken since his wife left him, it was a wonder to him that he hadn't already wound up on the streets. He was a little way down the alleyway when his cell phone vibrated.

'Hey, dude, what gives?'

'He bought three cans of pet food, a Zippo, and a canister of petrol.'

'Maybe whoever he's meeting has a dog with him,' Uriah said.

'Or fancies that kind of food and he's going to cook it,' Sal replied.

'Stand by. I'm going to move in on him.'

Uriah took his Colt Python .357 Magnum with a four-inch barrel out of his overcoat pocket and cocked the trigger. In his best Dirty Harry imitation, he said, 'The question you gotta ask yourself is: Do you feel lucky, punk?'

Uriah deliberately unsteady on his feet, walked down the alley, keeping close to the fence, for about a hundred yards to where another alley crossed. He crept up to it and peered around the corner. In the distance he could see the shadowy outline of a figure illuminated by a bank of floodlights aimed at an adjacent wall. Uriah slipped his gun back into his overcoat and lifted his cell phone to his ear.

'Sal, are you there?'

'You all right, man?'

'Don't stress.'

'How far up the alley are you?'

'About a hundred yards at a crossing with another alley. South is a little way down from me to my right. He's on his haunches dumping pet food onto the cobblestones, rhythmically flicking the Zippo. Every time it sparks up it lights up his face and he sure looks pissed off about something.'

Chapter 22 El Paso, Texas, Sunday 5 August

'What you think he's up to?'

'That's what I'm gonna find out. Get the van over to the north side of the block and cover the entrance to the lane.'

Uriah went forward a few more steps and tripped over a coil of fencing wire, knocking over some trash cans.

The sound of tumbling trash cans took Canaan by surprise. He leapt up onto his feet and stealthily made his way towards the noise.

Warning bells tolled in Uriah's head as he found himself on the ground looking up at Paul South, standing over him holding the canister of petrol and flicking the Zippo lighter.

'Hey, buddy, whasha doin',' Uriah said, pretending to be drunk. 'Ya gotta drink for me?'

Canaan's eyes flashed as he stared down at the sprawled figure. Something alive to burn, he said to himself.

Uriah levered himself into a sitting position, slipped his hand into his overcoat pocket, singing aloud now to mask Salvador's tinny voice squawking from his cell phone.

'I will buy you tall, tall, tall glasses of beer and all the water in the seas. I'm a fool, fool ...'

Salvador turned left at the first crossing and skidded to a halt just a few feet from where Uriah was lying. In the fraction of a second it took for Uriah to stare, shocked, at the headlights coming right at him, Canaan darted off.

It was around three in the morning when Uriah dropped Salvador off at the airport. The pair had been at loggerheads since the alley incident, blaming each other for the stuff-up and debating what Paul South was really up to. In the end, they agreed to disagree.

After dropping Sal off, Uriah went back to his hotel, packed, showered, and then delivered the van to the El Paso FBI office. He picked up his own car and went back to the Hotel Grande. He jotted down all the cars in the hotel's parking lot, rang the Bureau and matched Paul South's name registered to a blue Ford Taurus.

He then called the National Crime Information Centre in Washington DC and ran Paul South's name, along with his plate numbers. Ten minutes later he got a call back. Uriah listened and thanked the cheery girl on the other end of the line and clicked off the phone. Just what he expected: the information confirmed South's identity as a farm machinery salesman. It was squeaky clean. Way too clean. Not even an unpaid parking fine. Uriah knew that if his suspicions were correct, South would have multiple identities at his disposal, complete with legitimate drivers' licenses, social security numbers, credit cards, maybe even a wife and family somewhere to go with each one.

He positioned his car in a spot adjacent to the Taurus, fished out an empty beer bottle from the back floor of his car and placed it behind the front wheel of the Taurus. Then he reclined his seat and got some shut-eye.

Just on sunrise Uriah was startled out of his shallow sleep by the sound of crunching glass. Through the back window of his car he observed Paul South drive off.

If Paul South were to bump into Uriah on the street, he wouldn't recognize the FBI man as the bum he'd found in the laneway wearing a shabby overcoat and sneakers, nor as Nash, the cowboy he'd met at the cantina. Gone were the cowboy hat, the Western clothes, the square-cut beard and the high, silver-capped leather boots. He was just Uriah now, a plain, unassuming, affable looking, clean-shaven man with a round, jowly, humorous face, wearing khaki slacks and a loose cotton Hawaiian shirt.

Uriah was still running with his gut feeling that South was some

Chapter 22 *El Paso, Texas, Sunday 5 August*

extraordinary type of button man, the likes of which he had rarely encountered, the kind who didn't kill for money or sport, who weren't even natural-born killers. Winning five straight cockfighting bouts and then not taking the winnings just to prove a point simply didn't make any sense. One thing Uriah was sure of, though, was that Paul South was no philanthropist. El Paso was home to a dozen or so people who were on the Malatesta brothers' payroll. Some of them were also on the Bureau's watch list. Uriah hoped he might get lucky enough to join the dots between these people to the extent that they might lead him to the Malatestas, and confirm his notion that the brothers had been tipped off about their undercover work in the Rio Grande Cantina.

Uriah cruised well behind Canaan's car, with his elbow slung out the window of his dark green 1967 Mustang coupe, sipping from a longneck beer bottle. A couple of weeks back, he had dropped a new engine into his only prized possession.

Initially, Uriah had planned to fly back to Laredo, his hometown, to check out if his old shotgun shack was still standing. During his stint in El Paso, a category three hurricane had hit Brownsville and Corpus Christi and reports said it had come as far inland as Laredo. With a bit of luck, it might have only ripped off a few sheets of corrugated iron from the roof, blown down a fence or two and, if he was as lucky as South had been on the bantam cockfights, the mailbox crammed with long-overdue bills would've been uprooted and finally laid to rest with its contents scattered over the Mexican border. Whatever needed fixing he figured wouldn't take more than a day or two. Then he was going to fly up to Oklahoma City to meet up with Sal, write the report on the El Paso assignment, and tie up a few loose ends. Finally, he would get back to El Paso and drive his beloved Mustang home.

CHAPTER 23

SONORA, TEXAS, SUNDAY 5 AUGUST

As the two cars notched up the miles and the smoking oil refineries and high-tech industrial parks of El Paso had long since sunk into the horizon behind them, Uriah gave up the idea that South was going to see someone in El Paso.

South's spiel about being a sales rep for Locust International was starting to wear thin in Uriah's mind. Not once had South ventured off the blacktop down an unpaved road to knock on a barn door, or honk his car horn to get the attention of some lone rancher plowing a field with a prehistoric tractor, whether to sell or chat about updating farm machinery.

They had even passed by one of the conglomerate's huge sales yards. Surely, even if he wasn't visiting the denizens of the lone star state, South would have dropped in at least to talk shop to the local reps. South's whole front of supposedly being a man who deals with people who earn a living from working off the land, was out of character with the ponytail, and his sleek city clothes also just did not cut it with Uriah.

Yeah, sure, South had the bronzed complexion, but more from birth. Uriah figured him to be of some oriental, East Asian origin maybe. The color of his skin was about the only thing he had in common with a Texan who spent most of his waking hours without a roof over his head, but that's where it stopped.

During the long drive across the flat, dusty landscape of east Texas,

Chapter 23 *Sonora, Texas, Sunday 5 August*

drawing closer and closer to San Antonio, Uriah's thoughts turned to his five-year-old son from his first marriage who lived with his mother. It had been ... good God, he grimaced, and squeezed the steering wheel, his knuckles turning white. Was it three or four months? He couldn't remember. Well, however goddamn long it had been, it was way too long since he last saw him.

CHAPTER 24

SAN ANTONIO, TEXAS, SUNDAY 5 AUGUST

It was late afternoon when Uriah lost sight of South's car on the I-10 turnpike at the edge of the outer suburbs of San Antonio. 'Where the hell did he go?' Uriah cursed and thumped the steering wheel, frustrated at letting his mind wander. He poked his head out the window, looking back, forward and sideways. All those years of covert surveillance work with the Bureau had taught him to not dwell on personal issues when on the job. It makes you sloppy.

Uriah wove in between cars, cutting in front and forcing them to give way. The traffic was getting heavier. With no sign of the blue Taurus after about half a mile, a fit of wheezing and coughing overcame him, making it hard for him to drive. He pulled over, grabbed his Ventolin, puffed, and cursed the god that his saintly mother taught him to worship for giving him a pair of defective lungs.

After a few moments he was breathing painlessly again. He eased back onto the road and continued lane hopping, searching for the blue Taurus. He had gone no more than a mile when the traffic came to a standstill. He was no stranger to the time it took to cross the sprawling metropolis, especially at this hour of the day. Having been stationed in San Antonio about five years ago, Uriah knew all the byways and highways.

Uriah decided to go for a long shot. He would try to pick up South's trail on the chance that his quarry was still on I-10. Uriah headed south on I-37 towards Floresville, aiming to circumnavigate San Antonio's inner

Chapter 24 *San Antonio, Texas, Sunday 5 August*

city and pick South up when he rejoined the I-10, hopefully in front of him, around Seguin.

Uriah called Sergeant Mulligan on his cell phone. Sergeant Jed Mulligan worked in the sheriff's department in San Antonio, and was a good friend of Uriah's from his rookie days with the Texas State Troopers.

'Jed, it's Stuyvesant.'

'Stuyvesant, you fat-ass son of a bitch. How ya doin?'

'Good, good. Yourself?'

'Up to my hairy armpits in paperwork.' Mulligan sighed, then said, sounding more upbeat, 'And counting the days down to my fiftieth birthday bash.'

'Nice to hear you got something to look forward to.'

'You're not calling me up to tell me you can't make it, are you? If you are, I'm gonna be mighty peeved off.'

'No way, Jed. Wouldn't miss it for the world.'

'So how's everything on your side of the fence?'

'Tell you the truth, Jed, my back is killing me. The new engine in the Mustang is running like a dream, but the whine in the diff is driving me crazy.'

'Sounds like you're having fun.' Jed chuckled.

'Fun? I should have been home hours ago checking out if the shotgun shack is still standing after that hurricane.'

'The man in the sky passed a mighty wind between his holy cheeks.'

'Oh yeah. Tell me about it. Brownsville is going to change its name to Pancakeville.'

'So, what's on your mind, friend?'

'Malatesta,' Uriah said in an exhausted tone.

'I hope you're not bringing that lowlife to SA.' Jed's tone dropped and Uriah sensed he'd hit a nerve.

'Look, Jed, I don't have much time. Can you get your people to keep an eye out for a blue Ford Taurus, California plates 7QIZ304?'

'Want us to pull him over for you?'

'No. I've been following him since El Paso. I lost him in traffic at Castle Hill. I've got a hunch he's heading southeast, maybe to Orleans, so I'm betting he's still on I-10.'

'You sound pretty pumped, Uriah. This guy kill someone?'

'Not sure, Jed. You know what it's like. You get a gut feeling about some meltdown. You know they're up to no good.'

'I'll be in touch if we spot your man, Uriah. And hey, don't forget. The theme for my fiftieth is the Civil War. You gotta get dressed up.'

'I bought just the outfit.'

Uriah turned onto I-10 at Seguin. It took him just under an hour to go around the city. With still no word from Mulligan, he assumed that if South were heading along I-10 he would now be in front of him. He pulled over into the emergency lane, got out, opened his bonnet and waited. He scoped the streaming traffic for the blue Taurus from under the hood. There was no sign of South and Uriah steadily grew impatient.

At 6.15 p.m., after a forty minute wait and no word from Mulligan, he decided to give up the chase. For now the most he could do was write up a suspect report and pass on what little he knew about Paul South to someone else in the Bureau, who would, in all probability, fail to read it and put it in the not-very-important basket, which, over time, would get emptied into the trash can. Yet Uriah instinctively felt that any man with the vacuous interior and malevolent disposition of Paul South should be in a padded cell or reposed on old sparky.

For now, the Malatesta connection was history. With reluctance, Uriah had to admit that it had been a long shot from the start. Now, it being day one of his vacation, there was nowhere he needed to be

Chapter 24 *San Antonio, Texas, Sunday 5 August*

but back home to check out the hurricane damage. The detour to San Antonio had not taken him too far out of his way, but having driven all day, he did not fancy driving a further 140 miles so he decided to bed down in a hotel, aiming to get an early start in the morning.

He hopped into his car and merged into the traffic flow.

CHAPTER 25

SAN ANTONIO, TEXAS, MONDAY 6 AUGUST

It was a little after one. Uriah had been dozing on and off. The long drive had taken its toll on his lower back. He grabbed a bottle of beer from the fridge, flicked on the TV and scanned through the channels, finally settling on the local news.

A reporter was covering a story live from downtown where an arsonist had burnt alive four cats and two dogs in an alleyway. The fire department had just extinguished the fire and police were on the scene.

'So that's what the fuck that pyromaniac was up to with the pet food and the can of gas.'

In a matter of minutes he was dressed and on his way to the crime scene.

He pulled up opposite a patrol car that was parked across the entrance to the alleyway. Two uniformed police officers were in their car drinking coffee. Uriah stepped out of his car and approached them, flashing his badge.

'Golly gosh, the FBI is on the scene,' said one of the cops as he dunked a donut.

Uriah rested his elbows on the window and peered in. The two-way was squawking and he could smell marijuana.

He cleared his throat. 'I'm looking for my dog.' He paused and waited for a reaction. 'By the way, fellas, did you happen to catch the firefly?'

'Did you hear something, Captain?' said the one behind the wheel.

'Some insect.'

Chapter 25 *San Antonio, Texas, Monday 6 August*

'Yeah, a firefly,' the captain said and chuckled.

Uriah gave up on them, assuming they knew nothing and that even if they did they wouldn't talk.

'Thanks, gentlemen. You've been most helpful.' Uriah backed away, whistled, and hollered out in his best Yosemite Sam impression. 'Belvedere, oh Belvedere! Where are you, boy?! Come out, come out, wherever you are, you flea-bitten mutt!'

'Stay behind the yellow tape,' one of the uniforms called out.

Uriah marched up the alley and stepped over the yellow tape. He pulled out his pocket torch and scanned the area. The whole scene was straight out of a Stephen King novel. It looked as if the unfortunate animals had been hogtied before being set alight. Blackened flesh around one of the heads had peeled away from the creature's teeth. From the shape of its snout Uriah guessed it must have been one of the cats. He shook his head in disbelief. His intuition about Paul South was confirmed.

When South had stood over him in the alley, with the flint of his Zippo bursting like heat lightning and the reek of the fuel can he was gripping, the murderous intent in South's eyes had been unmistakable. The moral vacuity radiating from his whole being had been palpable. It was as if South and death had made a pact. What was it he lacked? Uriah asked himself. A mother, a sister, a pet dog? What on God's blessed Earth had killed his soul?

Outside of the taped-off zone Uriah spotted a couple of burnt-out cans. He went over and took a closer look. Apart from their blackened exterior they showed no signs of wear and tear. He removed his handkerchief from his trouser pocket and lifted one of the cans to his nose — it smelt fresh. He placed it back in the position he found it and went back to his car. Smoke was wafting out of the police car window. The officers' glazed eyes under their drooping eyelids watched as he swaggered past, wagging his finger and scolding his imaginary dog.

Uriah drove around the surrounding blocks until he found the closest convenience store. He went inside and had a word with the attendant. Uriah gave the man a brief description of Paul South and asked if any dog or cat food had been sold recently to a man fitting that description, but the attendant's response was much too vague to be of any use. He scoured the pet food section. Out of the six brands the store stocked he matched up two that were similar in size and had the same corrugated markings as the ones he had found in the alley: Happy Dog Chowder and Cool Cat Surprise with real Mouse chunks. He was positive that, even if that's what they had been fed, the cat didn't feel so cool or the dog so happy after their last supper.

Uriah was hopeful that if Paul South was Mr. Incendiary, then what happened here could be a repetition of last night's episode in El Paso. He drove around the nearby streets for almost an hour, combing nine hotel car parks before spotting Paul South's blue Taurus at the Texakana Motel.

Uriah positioned his car much the way he had the previous night, and waited for the firefly to emerge. He rubbed his tired eyes, dreading the prospect of another night cramped in his car.

CHAPTER 26

LAKE CHARLES, LOUISIANA, MONDAY 6 AUGUST

Uriah spent another six grueling hours behind the wheel, tailing Paul South. As they approached Houston he dreaded the possibility of losing him again in traffic, but South stayed in his sights and they had just now crossed the Louisiana state line.

He wanted to nail this walking incinerator. The only thing he loathed more than cruelty to animals was child abusers.

Wherever South was driving to, Uriah was sticking to him like a bloodhound. Twenty years in law enforcement had taught him you rarely got a second chance once the fish got off the hook. Now that he had South again in his sights, Uriah was determined to reel him in.

Twenty-five miles from Lake Charles, South stopped at a gas station. Uriah pulled over into the concealed driveway of a plumbing store a couple of hundred yards beyond and waited for the Taurus to get in front of him again.

Uriah eased himself from the driver's seat. He was looking forward to stretching his legs, but the stop was short-lived; the Taurus sped past him.

'That was a quick pit stop,' he grumbled, and jumped back in his car. Before he could hop into a lane, he had to give way to a couple of school buses and an SUV, one of which was playing a thumping hip-hop tune that rattled Uriah's windshield. He gunned the engine to overtake the SUV and slip in between the buses.

Uriah's cell phone rang.

'Hello.'

'Uriah? Sal here.'

'Howdy doody, pardner. You have a good flight?'

'Plane was cancelled so I took one via Tulsa. I arrive in Tulsa, then that gets diverted to Atlanta, so I had to kill another two hours in transit before the next to Oklahoma City. Happens every time I fly out of that shithole.'

'Maybe things would have been different on 9/11 if those terrorists had flown out of El Paso,' said Uriah.

'Yes,' Salvador sighed.

There was a moment's silence as each recalled where they had been on that fateful and macabre morning.

Uriah recounted the events of the past twenty-four hours.

'You would have been barbecued if I hadn't come along,' Salvador said.

'Don't forget I had my hand on my gun,' Uriah snapped.

'You had your hand on your dick.' Salvador burst into a maniacal laughter.

'That's what I love about you, Sal. You laugh at your own jokes.'

'We gotta get him off the streets, or else he's gonna put all the dog catchers out of business,' said Sal.

'I've got the boys from research combing the files for a match on what little I've got on him.'

'Those kinda people learn to play with matches real early. He's probably done time. Tell your people to try looking into juvenile detention centers, places like that.'

'Yeah, thanks for the advice,' Uriah said sarcastically.

'Tell me, is he a Malatesta connection? Gotta get cracking on my report.'

'Benny the Baby is a convicted pyromaniac. Maybe the two of them became matchbox buddies in some institution.'

'Maybe.'

Chapter 26 Lake Charles, Louisiana, Monday 6 August

'Hang loose on South, Sally boy. I'm still on his ass and Orleans is still another two hundred miles away. Anything could happen.'

CHAPTER 27

PARKER, ARIZONA, SUNDAY 19 AUGUST

The sound of the doorbell brought Ishmael back to reality. He looked at the clock on the wall. It was nine-thirty exactly. He gulped down his cold cup of coffee, grabbed the belt and stashed it in the bedroom wardrobe, turned on the answering machine and went to the front door. He felt his heart leap at the sight of Rosasharn.

'Good morning, Scot. Ready to go?' she said cheerfully, anticipation in her voice.

Rosasharn wanted to drive, but Ishmael insisted they take his car. After yesterday's debacle, he wanted to be in a more reliable vehicle. Ishmael backed his car out of the parking space and Rosasharn drove hers in.

Ishmael watched Rosasharn stroll over. She was carrying a small box of books. Her step had a slight bounce to it, almost a skip. Her hair was swept back in two loose ponytails. She was wearing a pale blue windcheater with 'Arizona State University' stencilled in bold lettering across the front and candy-striped capri pants that she wore unfashionably high on her waist. She had a kind of simplicity about her, an almost girlish manner.

'I have to drop these off to a friend in Prescott. It's on our way,' Rosasharn said as she placed the box on the back seat.

'Did you plan this trip before we met, or because of what happened yesterday?' Ishmael said as he put the car in drive.

'Yes and no.'

Chapter 27 *Parker, Arizona, Sunday 19 August*

'I don't get it,' Ishmael said gravely.

'Oh, don't be so serious, Scot. Yes, I did plan to go and no it wasn't because of what happened yesterday.' She paused. 'I wanted the company, so I invited you to come along, but I didn't expect you to drive.' She wagged her finger at him and giggled.

'Thank you for the invitation, Rosasharn,' Ishmael said graciously.

The moment he had set eyes on her, all his worries had seemed to vanish. Rosasharn radiated such light and buoyancy that the atmosphere around her felt unaffected. What struck him was that he did not feel inferior being around her: a woman apparently free of pretensions, unlike most of the girls he had dated from his workplace in Canada.

He felt surrounded by joy and life, which seemed to emanate not only from her but also from everything around them, feelings so beyond his experience that he did not know how to make sense of them. He attributed it all to God's way of caring for him, of giving him refuge, even if temporarily. Women from America are not, it seemed, all bad. Ishmael believed — wanted to believe — that Rosasharn was an exception to the rule.

They stopped for fuel on the outskirts of Parker. Rosasharn insisted on paying; she would not take no for an answer. Twenty minutes later they were crossing the craggy terrain of Black Peak Mountain.

'Look at those gigantic boulders. It's an awesome sight,' Rosasharn said, pointing to the rocks perched precariously on the edge of the cliffs. 'You don't realize how much you miss when you're behind the wheel.'

'Yes. You can only focus on what's ahead of you. I caught a bus from LA to Flagstaff and sat in the back seat and watched the world go by.'

'That's magnificent country coming into Flag from the west. The forested plateau region is just divine. It's like being in a plane, soaring through green clouds.'

'An interesting way to describe it,' Ishmael said.

A pickup truck, piled high with bales of hay, pulled out from a side road, causing him to back off a bit. Stalks of loose, dry straw blew all around them.

'Now we're driving through a straw storm,' Ishmael said. 'I always wondered how much gets blown off.'

'I've thought about that myself. Driving across the country it'll be noticeable, but down the road, maybe not.'

'That's it, Rosasharn,' he said excitedly.

'That's what, Scot?'

'Looking for the good in your life, when things go haywire.'

'I understand perfectly. Hey, what's another word for good?' Rosasharn said.

'Is it a trick question?'

'It might be.'

'Let me see.' Ishmael considered the question for a few moments. 'I give in.'

'Subtract one "o" and you get "God".'

'If you spell it backwards you get "dog".'

'Yes, but that's not synonymous. You can say God is good, good is God. But God is a dog and dog is God? I don't think so.'

'I suppose,' he said half-heartedly.

'Now take the first chapter of Genesis. The writer points out that the creation was completed without the appearance of evil. It ends with the verse, "And God saw all He had made, and lo and behold it was very good". So anything that is good, *truthfully* good, cannot exclude anybody or anything.'

'That's very deep, Rosasharn,' he said in a flat tone. 'I don't want to talk about religion.' He gunned the engine and overtook the pickup truck and its wake of straw. What little he understood of it he vehemently disagreed. God was good and bad at the same time, good to the sacred brotherhood, the true sons of Ibrahim, and full of wrath and contempt to the immoral brotherhood, the illegitimate sons of Ibrahim.

Rosasharn glanced at him and arched her eyebrows.

An icy silence ensued between them for a couple of miles.

Ishmael was strangely aware that he was mad at himself for having snubbed her last comment. He felt tongue-tied and wondered how he was going to restore the vibrancy he had been feeling before Rosasharn's attempt to draw him into a conversation about religion.

Rosasharn removed a packet of Oreos from her carry bag and ripped it open.

'Would you like some?' She popped two biscuits into her mouth.

The crunching of biscuits snapped Ishmael out of his gloom. 'No thanks. Had a big breakfast.' He patted his stomach.

'More for me,' she said and stuck out her biscuit-coated tongue at him and giggled.

Ishmael forced a smile, somewhat relieved that Rosasharn had taken the initiative to clear the air. *If only I had some bubblegum, I'd show her*, he said to himself.

'So, tell me about yourself.'

Ishmael rattled off the details of his fictitious life, the well-rehearsed story he had been telling anyone who had questioned him on the subject, that his father was a British national and had met his mother, who was an Indian national, while he was working for a German pharmaceutical company in Bombay. When Ishmael was twelve, they moved to Munich where his father took up a position teaching chemistry at the university, and how he came to study hydro engineering at the University of Munich.

Rosasharn listened, from time to time slotting in questions such as where he spent his summer vacations. Missolonghi, he told her. She asked him if he was a fan of Byron. He replied that he never could get into poetry. She asked him if he had any brothers or sisters. A younger brother named Joey, he replied, who died in a tragic house fire while staying at a friend's house. She offered him her deepest sympathy. Did he have any relatives in Bombay? No, he replied, his mother was an orphan, brought up in a Catholic girls' convent. What about on his father's side? Only an uncle who lived on the island of Jura in the Hebrides.

'So tell me, how did you convert? I'm assuming that your parents were not of the faith.' She twisted an Oreo apart and scraped off the cream with her front bottom teeth.

Ishmael shot her a glance and swallowed dryly a few times. 'Ah, you don't want to hear about that,' he said.

'Sure I do.' She popped another Oreo into her mouth.

Ishmael adjusted the side mirror and pretended to concentrate intensely on his driving. He wanted to get off the subject.

In everyday life, Ishmael was supposed to give the impression that he did not adhere to the strict practices of the faith. Even the fabricated events that led up to his religious conversion had been tactfully connived by Akmid and von Stumpf to be inoffensive. Ishmael had complained to Akmid about them, desiring something a little more dignified, but Akmid was adamant that Ishmael stick with it. 'What with a lot of young people in this day and age converting because of radicalism, your spiel is absolutely unobjectionable, my dear boy.' All these things were very contentious issues in the eyes of those in charge at the Azad Front.

They crossed Granite Pass and began their descent into the picturesque valley that separates the Buckskin and Harquahala Mountains.

'You're riding the brakes, Scot. Can't you smell them?'

Ishmael sniffed the air. 'Yes, so I am.'

'Use your gears to slow down and the brakes only when you really have to. Here we go. Try it on this bend,' Rosasharn said encouragingly.

'What do you mean, "use the gears"?'

'You use the gears in a descending order to slow down.' She traced a reverse 'H' in the air with her index finger.

'You mean negative gearing?' Ishmael said, trying to sound serious, but he burst out laughing.

Rosasharn laughed with him. 'Hey, that's a neat way of putting it. Negative gearing.'

'You wouldn't be an accountant of some sort, would you?' Ishmael said.

'Me? An accountant? No. I'm just a little old Midwestern gal who handles insurance claims,' she said in a Texan drawl. 'Now, have a go on this bend. You can do it.'

Ishmael kept overworking the brakes.

Rosasharn wound her window. 'Wind yours down, for fucks sake.'

Ishmael obeyed.

'You're going to have to learn how to work those gears backwards,' she said forcefully.

'Are you serious?'

'Yes. By the time we get back tonight you'll need new brakes and probably new brake drums too. There's a stretch of straight road around the next bend. It goes for a couple of miles. Good place to get your confidence up.'

Ishmael begrudgingly followed her instructions. From third to second gear he changed too quickly and was slow on the clutch, causing the car to stall.

The driver of a car towing a mobile home blew his horn as he came to a screeching halt behind them. Ishmael got the car going and pulled over into the emergency lane.

Rosasharn leant over and pressed the heel of her palm hard on the horn. 'For the life of me, I do not understand why these old farts don't bunk up in motels.'

For a few moments Ishmael's face was buried in her hair. He moaned.

Rosasharn tilted her head so that the nape of her neck was against his chin. She craned her head and faced Ishmael. Their cheeks were almost touching.

'Now don't you be intimidated by those grumpy oldsters. You're gonna do just fine, honey.'

Their eyes locked and each was conscious of their closeness. Ishmael was about to kiss her but hesitated and the moment was lost. He leant back on the headrest as she resumed her sitting position.

'Scot, you just have to trust me.'

'Okay, I will trust you,' Ishmael said sheepishly.

'Let's get moving.'

He started the car, checked his mirrors and pulled out onto the road. As they approached the next hairpin bend in third gear he applied the brakes and then shifted down into second.

'A little too fast on the gear change. Here, I'll help you out. You work the clutch. I'll do the gear change.'

'I don't think that's a good idea. It's a steep drop. Those barriers look like they couldn't hold a feather back.'

'Confidence, *mon ami*,' she said and placed her right hand over his on the gearshift. Ishmael shuddered at her touch.

'Relax, don't be scared,' Rosasharn said soothingly.

After a dozen or so bends, Rosasharn took her hand away from his and watched him carefully.

Ishmael wanted her to keep her hand cupped over his. His heart was fluttering, longing for more human touch.

They reached the bottom of Palomosa Mountain Range. The cars and trucks that had been forced to trail behind overtook them when the road expanded into a two-lane highway. As they sped past, some tooted their horns, waving their fists out the window.

'That was nice going on those last couple of hairpin bends.'

Chapter 27 Parker, Arizona, Sunday 19 August

'That traffic behind us didn't think so.' Ishmael frowned.

'They can all go and get wrecked.' She patted him gingerly on the shoulder. 'Navigating these mountains takes plenty of practice. I've been travelling them for years.'

'I am used to driving in deserts and flat country,' said Ishmael. An image of himself driving a clapped-out Bedford truck along the Pakistani and Indian border loaded with coconuts embedded with hand grenades flashed in his head. Exchanging this image for a more recent, local one, he asked, 'Have you ever been up to the northeast corner of Arizona?'

'Yes. There's a Navajo reservation in that neck of the woods,' she said. 'I've been up to the Checkerboard Reservation but not the Navajo.'

'I was touring around those not so long ago. I met a Hopi Indian called Old Smoke in Tuba City. He showed me around and put me up for a night.'

'Was that when you scratched that parked car?'

'Yes,' Ishmael replied, grinding his teeth.

'You could get lost in that wilderness.'

'That's the place I'd choose if I wanted to disappear from the face of the earth,' Ishmael said, nodding. He cursed himself for mentioning Tuba City.

'If I wanted to disappear from the face of the earth, guess where I would go.'

'The North Pole.'

'No. Too cold.'

'Where?'

'I'd go to Australia and live among the kangaroos and koalas. I love the way those kangaroos hop around the place, and those little bears are so cute and cuddly.' She crossed her arms and made like she was hugging one.

'Australia, that's a big country.'

'Sure is. It's a continent, I think the oldest on the earth. Hey, talk about old. I bet you didn't know that these roads are old as the hills. The Pueblo Indians used them long before white settlement.'

'Is that a fact?' Ishmael recalled the pictures of the Indian chiefs in the saloon bar in Tuba City and wondered if those men had travelled these very same roads at a time when they were just narrow passes.

CHAPTER 28

PRESCOTT, ARIZONA, SUNDAY 19 AUGUST

By twelve, they got as far as Prescott and onto Montezuma Street, Prescott's main thoroughfare.

'People certainly love their alcohol here. I've never seen so many bars and saloons in one place. There's one on just about every corner,' Ishmael said.

'They call it Whiskey Row,' Rosasharn replied. 'Back in the old days this was just a trading post and a stopover for cowboys who worked along the Chisholm Trail. Bar hopping went on every night. During the mining boom there was over forty of them.'

'It's a fitting name,' Ishmael sniggered, not bothering to hide his disdain.

'That's right,' Rosasharn said coolly, 'Your kind don't drink alcohol.'

'Nor do many Christians,' Ishmael replied indignantly.

Rosasharn directed Ishmael to her friend's house where she was to drop off the box of books, but no one was home.

'Let's go buy a card. I want to write her a note,' Rosasharn said as she hopped back in the car.

'I got some paper and a pen.'

'No, it won't do. A card and maybe some chocolates. Yes, Bridget would like that.'

They stopped at a convenience store a couple of blocks away. Ishmael waited in the car while Rosasharn went inside.

When Rosasharn got back to the car with her purchases, Ishmael had his head bowed. She stared curiously at him through the front window for a few moments.

When she opened the door he snapped to attention and pretended to yawn, unaware that she had observed him praying.

'More munchies for the last leg of our journey. Sedona is just sixty miles away,' Rosasharn said as she hopped in. She tore open a large packet of salt and vinegar crisps with her mouth, and shoveled a handful in. Then she opened the two-liter bottle of Dr. Pepper and drank from it. She let out a burp and squealed with delight at herself. 'Excuse me,' she said.

'Did you get the strawberry bubblegum?'

Rosasharn dipped her hand into the bag and handed the packet over.

Ishmael unwrapped a couple of cubes and popped them into his mouth. He offered her one, but she waved him off with one hand while continuing to grab crisps with the other. Rosasharn smiled as she watched him mash down on the gum just as unashamedly as herself. Ishmael attempted to blow a bubble. The gum flew out of his mouth, landing on the dashboard. He picked it up and dropped it into the ashtray.

'You're blowing too hard. Keep your lips tight and do this with your tongue.' She leaned over and pursed her lips only inches from his face and played the tip of her tongue against her upper lip, back and forth.

Ishmael could smell the salt and vinegar on her breath. He leant in slightly towards her and tilted his head to the side. They exchanged intimate glances. Rosasharn threw her head back, reached up and gingerly pinched both his lips together. 'Now, let me see the tip of your tongue.'

He went cross-eyed trying to stare down at her fingers. His attempt sounded like a flatulent discharge.

She sat back in her seat and giggled. 'After I finish this bag of crisps I'll show you how it's done.'

Chapter 28 Prescott, Arizona, Sunday 19 August

'I have a friend in Munich who has the best set of lips for blowing the biggest bubbles.' He popped another piece of gum into his mouth.

Rosasharn stared longingly at him. Ishmael half averted her eyes.

They dropped off the books, along with the card and chocolates. A couple of miles up the road, they came to the turn-off to Sedona.

'Here's the road to Sedona, the most significant New Age center in the southwest, possibly in the entire country,' Rosasharn said.

'What do people do there?'

Rosasharn explained the New Age movement and their objective to transform the world into a better place to live.

'Why can't these people pray to their crystals at home?'

'Mom used to say that doing it in Sedona is about the feeling of the whole surrounding area, of being there. It's a land thing, the exquisitely sculptured red rocks, the Mars-like landscape. It's all out of this world. It gives one the impression that you're on another planet having a rarefied, life-transforming experience,' she said.

Ishmael drummed his fingers on the steering wheel. 'It sounds like a godless experience to me, looking for meaning in mindless rocks.'

CHAPTER 29

MOUNT MINGUS, ARIZONA, SUNDAY 19 AUGUST

As they approached Mount Mingus towering above the Prescott Valley, Ishmael was the first to break the comfortable silence that had settled between them.

'Percy Owens mentioned to me when I was leaving Jim's that you write articles for the local papers.'

'And what else did Percy mention?' Rosasharn smiled. Her eyes were deadly serious.

'Said you were writing a book.'

'Yes, I am. So, what did he say about my columns in the papers?'

'Nothing much. Just that you write them.'

'Old lanky wouldn't have ordered you to tell me to consider toning down my opposition to the upgrade of the aqueduct, would he?'

'Yes.'

'Well, consider it considered.' She brushed a strand of hair back from her face.

'Okay.' Ishmael shrugged.

Rosasharn gave him a slightly puzzled look.

'What's your book about?'

'It's a commentary on, and synthesis of the greatest political and religious events in the past three thousand years.'

'What made you start something like that?'

Rosasharn glanced down at her sweater and traced her finger around the letter 'A'. 'About two months after Dad died, I began to compile notes

Chapter 29 *Mount Mingus, Arizona, Sunday 19 August*

on historical and religious events that I'd come across in my studies that inspired me to explore more deeply. I was aiming to get a scholarship to the Middle East to do research on these notes after I finished my degree. Over time the notes gathered their own momentum. Tell you the truth, I never planned to write a book. In the end I never got my scholarship, but I've kept going with the book anyway.'

'Is it finished?'

'Not yet.' She sighed. 'It's like this. I complete a chapter on some momentous event and while I'm revising it I always seem to pick up on some minor loose thread about some battle led by so-and-so or some reigning monarch who gets advice from a little old nobody who, down the track, influences some obscure figure which ends up leading me to some meaningful event that was originally not on my radar, and it just goes on and on. Lo and behold, before I know it, I'm splicing in another chapter. It's sitting in a heap of handwritten notes and printout paper in a corner of my wardrobe, growing and growing, like a noxious weed.'

'Sounds like you're writing an encyclopedia.'

'Tell me about it.'

'How come you didn't get your scholarship?'

Rosasharn shifted her seat as far back as it would go and drew her knees to her chest. 'As I explained yesterday, some of it had to do with not being able to finish my course, you know, because of Mom. Even if I'd finished it I wouldn't have got the scholarship anyway. My grades were way down. Lecturers hated me.'

'What do you mean?' Ishmael glanced at her. 'Please remove your shoes from the seat.'

'Sorry, Scot, I wasn't thinking.' She placed her feet back on the floor and brushed the seat. 'At college they nicknamed me "The Giggling Agitator",' she said, stretching the word.

'What on Earth did you do to earn such a nickname?'

'Look, Scot, I'm a serious person, maybe too extreme at times, and at other times I'm extreme the other way. I joke and giggle at the most inappropriate times just to get a kick out of the effect it has on people.'

'So, you got a kick out of laughing at me yesterday,' he said tersely.

'Heck no,' Rosasharn said firmly. 'I told you I laughed about the predicament we were in. Now is that clear?'

'Yes.'

'You see, you and most of the human race never know where I'm going to come from next. I debate and argue with teachers, administrators, anyone and everyone, expose their biases against the East and towards the West. It drives me fucking insane that in our so-called institutions of learning there are so many narrow-minded people drilling their biases into the uneducated.'

'So, you see yourself as a victim?' he said.

'No!' she said emphatically. 'Never have and never will. I'm a radical reformer who challenged the system in my own limited way and in the process practically alienated myself from the career I had chosen.' Rosasharn's voice rose in exasperation.

'Why didn't you go to Europe to study?'

'Because I'm too committed to Mom. I feel she needs me, even though, after everything she's put the family through, anyone would wonder why I bother.'

'Yes, family does influence your decisions. Either you want to get as far away as possible or stay as near as possible.' Deep down, Ishmael could not help but feel sorry for her because she'd given up an education to look after her mother.

'Absolutely. You changed your religion,' she paused just for moment, and then said jokingly, 'because of your domineering mother.'

'Ma was not,' he retorted. 'What about your mom?' He wasn't angry with Rosasharn for what she said, but with Akmid for making him tell such a ridiculous story.

'Sorry, Scot, I shouldn't have said that.' Her smile was rueful. 'If I had my time again I'd be studying at the University of Jerusalem, the city where it all began.' She pressed her forehead to the windscreen, looking up at the huge granite rocks on the side of the mountain.

He shifted into a higher gear and accelerated a little too quickly as they approached the hairpin bend. The car lost traction, but he was quick to correct it.

Rosasharn jerked back, adjusted her seat forward. 'It's the extreme factions that keep the majority of religious people at loggerheads. What do you think?'

'How many ways can you look at an elephant?' he said.

'Elephant? I don't get it.'

'It's a metaphor. Three hundred and sixty degrees in a circle. Three hundred and sixty opinions on the one subject. What you people call extremist might be just another way of approaching an understanding of Truth.' Ishmael kneaded the steering wheel with his thumbs.

'You're saying that extreme radicalized religious groups are part of the whole?'

'Yes and no. Someone will write about it and the future will be the judge.'

'I see,' Rosasharn said. 'Extreme comes from the desire to achieve at any cost.'

'I know what it means.' Ishmael frowned.

Rosasharn buried her chin in her shoulder, trumpeted like an elephant and waved her arm like a trunk. 'I haven't done that in years,' she said excitedly.

Ishmael chuckled nervously.

'For the sake of this discussion, let's forget about the extreme religious factions. You know that it's all about Jerusalem.'

'Yes.' He raised his voice. 'It is all about Jerusalem for us, not for anyone else,' he said passionately.

Rosasharn gave him a smug grin. 'Are you saying that Jerusalem belongs solely to your faith?'

'I don't really care who it belongs to,' he replied, the passion drained from his voice.

They had reached the crest of the mountain and were beginning the descent. He was deeply troubled by where this conversation was heading and he knew that Rosasharn knew it. Taking into account all that he had said and done yesterday, and today, he was concerned about how much he had revealed to her. In an attempt to divert her he started purposely overworking the brakes.

'This mountain is steeper than the other one. These bends are much more difficult.'

'Pull over and I'll drive, if you've forgotten to negative gear. At this rate we won't be in Sedona until Christmas. Let's try to get there before the snow has settled.' Her sarcasm went over Ishmael's head.

He pulled over and they got out of the car to change sides. They stretched their limbs in the sunlight that had just broken through the cloud cover, drenching the valley below in brilliant light. Rosasharn leant on the fender, crossed her arms and eyed the summit.

Ishmael wandered a little way from the car. He stood with his back against a tree trunk and looked down at the cascading treetops. Little birds flitted and dived in and out of the canopy. He felt something crawling across the back of his neck. He brushed it off. A column of ants marching up the tree seized his attention. He crushed a dozen or so ants with his thumb, all the while deriving a cruel, boyish pleasure, then he made his way back to the car. As he approached, he looked at

Chapter 29 *Mount Mingus, Arizona, Sunday 19 August*

Rosasharn. She was twirling one of her ponytails around her finger and staring straight at him. He felt awkward, belittled by her calculating gaze, measured and found wanting.

Rosasharn settled into the driver's seat. Ishmael opened the passenger car door and just stood there, bemused. Barely able to find his voice, he said, 'Rosasharn, why don't you go on without me? Take the car. I'll hitch back to Parker.'

Rosasharn looked at him, surprised. 'Are you fucking crazy? Why would you want to do a thing like that?' she shouted.

'I'm confused.'

'Confused? Sure. A long walk back to Parker would certainly clear that screwed-up head of yours.' She paused, covered her mouth for a moment. 'Oh, did I say that? I'm so sorry,' she said, coquettishly pulling on her ponytails.

Ishmael got in the car, grimaced and motioned her to drive on. Rosasharn adjusted the seat, reached for her drink and took a long swallow from the bottle. She pointed to the bag of crisps on the floor. Ishmael handed them to her and she took a handful and shoveled them into her mouth.

'You really enjoy pigging out, don't you?'

She swallowed, brushed some flakes off the side of her mouth with the back of her hand, took another long drink, belched and said, 'I'm not normally like this. It's just when I get tense and anxious about things, like before going into exams, waiting for grades, you know, stuff like that.'

Ishmael nodded.

'So, what's your fucking hang-up about talking religion? You made no secret of it yesterday.'

Ishmael pretended he hadn't heard her. He stared down at his thumb. It was flecked with pieces of insect. He brushed it on the side of the seat.

The interstate through that area resembled two coiled snakes — bends every couple of hundred yards. They screeched down the mountain so fast that, several times, Ishmael felt that she was going to drive them right off the edge. He gazed out the window and tried to focus on the painted yellow line on the shoulder of the road as it blurred past. He sank lower into the seat. All he wanted was to get on his knees and pour out all his troubles to the God of his life. There was a pocket-sized holy book in the glove box he thought about grabbing, and to hell with her reaction.

They raced down the thickly wooded slopes of Mount Mingus. Rosasharn cast a glance at Ishmael.

'Hey, it's all right, Scot.'

'Those pads are burning,' Ishmael said, sniffing the air. 'You're not changing the gears as you made me do.'

Rosasharn grinned. 'Sometimes you have to use your brakes.' She slowed down, reached over and put her hand on his shoulder. He cupped her hand before she had time to draw it back.

Rosasharn slowly slipped her hand from under his and placed it on the gear shift. 'I have no great secret to reveal, no mystery to tell you about, Scot. All I'm asking is for a chance to share with you a bit of history and what I have learnt from it.'

Ishmael wriggled in his seat and groped for something to say, but nothing came to him. He folded his arms and resolved not to react to whatever she was going to say.

CHAPTER 30

BIG CHINO WASH VERDE, ARIZONA, SUNDAY 19 AUGUST

They came to a bridge that crossed Big Chino Wash Verde River. Rosasharn turned off onto the landing, pulled up and cut the engine.

'Why are we stopping?'

'Cool the brakes.'

Apart from a young couple making out on the levee, there was no one else. Big black thunderheads were now rolling over the mountain and darkening the whole sky. Heat lightning flickered in the distance.

'Before I get onto talking about Jerusalem, allow me to give you a clue where I'm coming from. Faithful believers are supposed to surrender to the will of God. I can't surrender to something I don't fully understand. I am not religious. I mean, not in a conventional way. What I'm trying to say is that I kind of ...' she shrugged, 'I think it's because I envy people with a childlike acceptance of faith. Faith was not an outcome of my religious instruction and I know that if you don't have that, there's a pretty big void to fill. For some people, at least. You know that, don't you?'

Ishmael thought for a moment, imagining how he would be without his faith. He laughed out loud and said, 'I would just have to learn how to live without it.'

'Okay,' she said, resolute. 'Where was I? Jerusalem and why it is important? It's where the great religions of the world converge. I'm assuming that you don't know some of what I am going to tell you. Just ask if you want me to clarify anything.'

'There is not much that I do not know about the greatest holy site in the world,' Ishmael said aloud as if talking to himself.

He stared straight ahead, unblinking.

'Jerusalem is important to the Jews because of the Wailing Wall, which is all that remains of the original temple built by King Solomon. The Jews believe that until they rebuild the temple of Solomon in Jerusalem, there will be no second coming of the messiah. The extreme Zionists are hell-bent on destroying the religious structures that are most important to other faiths.

'The truth is one.' Ishmael cranked down the window and leant his elbow on the rim. 'Whoever the facts belong to is the one who is correct.'

'That is absolutely right. The truth is one,' Rosasharn said emphatically, raising her voice.'

'All cannot be right,' Ishmael snapped. He glared at her and slammed his hand three times on the dashboard. He cleared his throat and spat contemptuously out of the window.

'And all cannot be wrong,' Rosasharn replied just as heatedly, and pressed the heel of her palm on the horn three times. 'Scot, my standpoint is that of an outsider,' Rosasharn said earnestly. 'That was the problem I faced in school. I could not possibly take sides. All religious faiths can be taken as divisions of the whole of truth. Truth must be universal. If you plunge into the depths of any of the inspired writings. Wisdom and Truth inevitably descends into your heart.'

Tight-lipped, Ishmael stared at her blankly.

'Let me put it this way. What is the common factor in Christianity, Judaism and your religion?'

'There is no common denominator. We're not dealing with mathematics!' Ishmael shouted at her.

Chapter 30 *Big Chino Wash Verde, Arizona, Sunday 19 August*

'Abraham,' she said doggedly, 'he's the patriarchal figure in the world's three faiths.'

'What does that mean?' he snapped.

'Patriarchal. A man who is the head of a family. Abraham is symbolically the father of the world's monotheistic regions.'

'He is only the father of the sacred brotherhood, not of anyone else.' Aloud, Ishmael repeated it over and over, like a mantra, then stopped abruptly and stared out the windscreen, unblinking, focused on some distant place, his Adam's apple working up and down.

Rosasharn gaped at the expression on Ishmael's face. She unlatched the door and continued. 'Abraham, or Ibrahim as you people refer to him, started it all for the people who believe in one God.'

The word 'Ibrahim' ruptured a raw nerve in Ishmael. He balled his hands into fists.

Voices of men now came to him, men steeped in an absolute hatred of life, in an objectified image of what they understood America to be. The voices were getting louder and angrier. He wanted to murder them all. Ishmael hunched his shoulders, buried his chin in his chest, clapped his hands over his ears and squeezed his eyes shut.

The sun broke through the cloud cover and speared a narrow ray of light through the windscreen. The interior of the car was illuminated by a peculiar iridescent radiance. The intensity pierced Ishmael's eyelids in great splashes of white, orange and red. He clamped his palms over his eyes. Still the glare penetrated, suffusing his entire body, reaching the depths of his soul, chasing away all the darkness in him.

Rosasharn spoke more loudly and boldly. 'Abraham was the first man in the history of the world to identify with one universal god.'

Her voice sounded to him like a thundering multitude drowning out the voices of the angry men in his head.

Ishmael felt as if the Earth was falling. He thrashed in his seat.

Terrified, he opened his eyes, squinting, trying to focus, but everything was awash in the blinding light. He felt himself spiraling upward and then, abruptly, he came to a stop and found himself hovering above a whitewashed, windowless room.

An American flag with all the stars burnt out was strung up on a wall. It was the interview room at the Uttar Pradesh Juvenile Prison. The three figures sitting around a table came into view — Akmid, leaning forward in his chair with a bemused grin on his face, pointing a cigar stub at Canaan. Canaan was sitting across the table from Akmid, expressionless, clutching a gold cigarette lighter with a swastika engraved on it. Sitting next to Canaan, Ishmael saw himself, slumped in a chair, head bowed, fingering the links of a chain shackled to his bleeding ankles.

As if in a lucid dream, the subconscious association of the moment and poignant feeling came flooding back to him.

At the time, he had appealed to God in voiceless desire, groping like a baby, wanting to extricate himself from Akmid's judgment of being an unfaithful believer, trying to undermine his first faltering steps in his new-found religion at a time when he was struggling between the militant radicalized teachings of the caustic Rupna Shahpura, the head jailer, and the benevolent guidance of the venerable Chirag Chowringhee.

Something stirred inside him. Above the din, he heard a still, small voice say, 'Fear not, Ishmael, for from the first day that thou didst set thine heart to understand, and to chasten thyself before thy God, thy words were heard, and I am come for thy words.'

Ishmael was hurled back to the present by the wailing of sirens coming towards them. A fire engine, blue lights flashing, sped over the bridge, followed by two highway patrol cars. The atmosphere between them had become so rarefied that they were awe-struck. Both of them felt that something ineffable had intervened.

Chapter 30 *Big Chino Wash Verde, Arizona, Sunday 19 August*

Rosasharn did not experience the extraordinary light in any such way, but was overcome by a burning sensation in the middle of her forehead. She pressed her palm against the spot and frowned. The discomfort, which lasted just for an instant, left her feeling light-headed and giddy; and even more compelled to go on. What stunned her was that the passion and all her initial motivation had melted away. As she spoke, she felt an authority and power not her own.

Rosasharn narrated the Old Testament story of Abraham in the Book of Genesis, word for word, as if reading from the book. She was amazed at herself because she only vaguely knew the story.

Her tone and inflections were like the voice of an angel to Ishmael. The words Rosasharn recited spoke exclusively to his heart, healing all the wrong. He was crying unashamedly.

> 'Then, Abraham gave up the ghost and died in a good old age, an old man, full of years, and was gathered unto his people, and his sons, Isaac and Ishmael, buried him.'

Ishmael dabbed his eyes with the sleeve of his shirt.

Rosasharn gave an inspired exegesis on the two sons of Abraham. Ishmael listened keenly, without comment, nodding agreeably to all she said.

'There never was any rivalry between the two brothers. It was the enmity between Hagar and Sarah vying for their offspring that caused the supposed separation of Ishmael and Isaac, Abraham's first two sons. God in the beginning said to Abraham that he would make his seed as the dust of the Earth.

'Literally interpreted, the sacred writings seem to be biased towards either son. Both declare that Abraham's seed was to bless their respective sons whom they consider as the firstborn.

'In the eternal divine scheme of things, did it really matter which womb brought forth a son first? That the progeny of this firstborn could inherit the earth? Or who was the legitimate wife of the first man to break rank with the pagan past? Even which son was offered for sacrifice?

'Abraham's beliefs about a god who is appeased by human sacrifice were being sundered. He marched up the mountain to sacrifice his son, be it Ishmael or Isaac. Can you imagine the uncountable human sacrifices that had been already laid on the altars of some abhorrent deity dictated by misguided priest craft?

'A new order in the primeval heart of universal humanity was being revealed. It was a breaking away from ancient Sumerian culture where human life was only regarded as a pawn in the hands of the gods of destruction, fertility, harvest, etc. who were perpetually in conflict with each other. Abraham let himself be led by the God who revealed himself not after the pattern of mortal life but as one, all-encompassing being.

'This new idea of one universal, benevolent God was gaining ground in Abraham's consciousness and finally culminates in him not going ahead with the grisly deed. The literal interpretation is fraught with contradictions. If they really mattered in the divine scheme we are all ultimately doomed ...' Her voice tapered off and she sighed heavily.

Ishmael sat upright. What Rosasharn said was a revelation.

They were both transfixed, lost in their own thoughts. Rosasharn stepped out of the car and went over to the river and stood beside the levee. She gazed at the reflection of gnarled cottonwoods in the stream. She was awe-struck over what she had just told Ishmael, how it had just poured out of her.

She leisurely strolled along the levee and picked some wild flowers from the bank, plucking the petals one by one, dropping them into the water and watching them float downstream. After some time she went back to the car.

Chapter 30 *Big Chino Wash Verde, Arizona, Sunday 19 August*

'Shall we drive on to Sedona?' Rosasharn said.

'Yes, I want to see it,' Ishmael replied, gazing at Rosasharn wondrously.

Rosasharn smiled at him. 'There's a lot I want to show you there.' She started the car and began to drive across the bridge. In the middle, she stopped and said, 'Give me a quarter.'

Ishmael reached into his pocket, grabbed a few coins from which he selected a quarter and gave it to her. Rosasharn took a quarter out of her purse and gave it to him.

'Open your window.' She opened hers. 'Make a wish and throw the quarter into the river. Don't forget to close your eyes and don't tell me what your wish is.'

Ishmael nodded, closed his eyes and threw his coin over the railing. Rosasharn did the same.

'Maybe one day we will share what we wished for,' she said.

CHAPTER 31

PARKER, ARIZONA, SUNDAY 19 AUGUST

They arrived back in Parker just after ten o'clock, having stopped at a diner along the way.

'I had an interesting day, Rosasharn. Thank you,' Ishmael said as he pulled up alongside Rosasharn's car.

'I did too, Scot.'

'Today I felt like St Paul on the road to Damascus,' he said, biting his lower lip. At the Jack Folsom Mission School, Ishmael had played the part of a high priest's cup bearer in a play adapted from the Book of Acts. No other story could fit his experience of that day more precisely.

Rosasharn smiled at him and nodded thoughtfully. 'So I must have been Ananias.' She paused and said, half serious, 'Well, Scot, you'd better be careful of the high priests for defecting to the Christians. The Jews are waiting at the gate to kill you.'

She collected her things, opened the car door and got out. Ishmael walked her to her car. As she was stepping in, she faced him. 'I know you've been filled up with dogma, believing someone else's interpretation of the Truth. One must not be scared to reason it out and discover it for oneself. The battle is within you. This is holy war or whatever you want to call it'. She kissed him on the cheek, got into her own car and drove off.

Ishmael entered his apartment. He went into the bedroom, threw himself on the bed and stared at the ceiling fan, his thoughts diametrically

Chapter 31 *Parker, Arizona, Sunday 19 August*

opposite to what they had been when he had got out of bed that morning.

Everything that had gone into making him who he was supposed to be, strangely seemed to belong to a life other than his. More than ever, he so much wanted to live out his life on earth, to grow old and decrepit, to the very last moment until his body would carry his soul no longer.

What struck him about Rosasharn now, looking back at those precious moments with her in the car when they were parked by the river, was the expression of her eyes. They were soft, serene, and truthful while she expounded the foundation story of the world's three great faiths.

'We are all Ibrahim's seed. It does not matter which womb it was planted in, Hagar's or Sarah's. God sent down His angel and stopped Ibrahim from murdering his son,' Ishmael repeated allowed to himself.

Ishmael turned over onto his stomach, buried his head in the pillow and tried to make sense of the turbulent events of the weekend. Suddenly, everything became clear to him. God had sent his guardian angel not to take his soul to heaven, but to foil all his attempts to kill innocent American people, and himself in the process. The form of that angel was Rosasharn.

Having lost his family in the earthquake, now he was going to lose a woman that he was beginning to grow awfully fond of, a woman who was God's messenger. He clenched his fists and pounded the mattress.

CHAPTER 32

PARKER, ARIZONA, MONDAY 20 AUGUST

Ishmael woke at sunrise after a restless and disturbed night, still dressed in his clothes. He had a vague recollection of a horrible dream. In it his whole body was wrapped in razor wire and he was being escorted by a column of giant soldier ants. With each step he was forced to take, the wire became tighter and tighter. Leading the column was Canaan. A herd of Texas longhorns encircled the march, and every so often one would make a charge at the column. As it thundered towards them, Ishmael welcomed it, but just as the steer was about to breach the column, Canaan would hurl a coconut at it, which exploded on impact. Splintered bones and entrails rained down on the giant soldier ants. On the horizon, like a setting sun, was a hologram image of Rosasharn's face. The image stared straight at him, exuding hope and encouragement.

Recalling his nightmare, the path before him became clear. He hauled himself out of bed, showered, dressed and then quickly set to work dismantling the pipe bombs. As he snipped at wires and circuits, Rosasharn's poignant words kept coming back to him: 'The battle is within you. This is the holy war.'

By nine Ishmael had dismantled all the pipe bombs and was sitting at the kitchen table drinking coffee, staring at the phone when he should have been at his office. He took a sip of coffee and sighed, unsure why he was being prompted to put into effect the contingency plan that had been devised if, for some unforeseen reason, he had to postpone what he

Chapter 32 *Parker, Arizona, Monday 20 August*

now considered as his abominable unholy act. He found himself picking up the phone.

'Percy Owens.'

'Good morning, Percy. It's Scot Fall.'

'Scot, how're you doing?'

'I am fine.'

'You get up to any no good on Saturday night?' His voice was full of mischievous humor.

'We dropped Rosasharn's mother at Big River, then she drove me home.'

'Did you invite her in?'

'No.'

'So you had it off with her in the back seat of your car, you desperate devil.'

'No Sex, she just left me out the front and drove off.'

'What about Sunday?'

'Spent the whole day working on some reports.'

'So, what can I do for you, my boy?'

'Got word from my aunt in Toronto late last night that my uncle suffered a massive heart attack and he's in a coma.'

'Oh my, that's unfortunate, Scot. I'm sorry to hear it. How bad is it?'

'My aunt said it was pretty serious. The doctor doesn't know if he's going to make it. I told her I'd try to get up there ASAP.'

'I hope he makes it.' Percy paused. 'You're aware that the reworked draft plan for the number one hydrometer is due at the end of this week?' he said firmly.

'Yes, I am. Ninety per cent of my work is complete. I just need some figures from the geological department to finalize it. Have you heard from Bernie when they'll have that data for us?'

'Damned geological department. Those assholes are always dragging their feet,' Percy grumbled.

'I can probably finish most of the work with the simulation software, but for really accurate results you know we'll need the real numbers,' said Ishmael.

'Hold the line. I'll give Bernie a call and find out just how long they're going to be.'

After a few moments he came back to Ishmael.

'You there, Scot?'

'Yes, Percy.'

'Take the whole week, Scot,' Percy said. Then he paused, leaving Ishmael to wonder what he was thinking. Would he change his mind? But after a few seconds, Percy said, 'Oh, fuck it, Scot, take two weeks if your uncle doesn't make it. Comfort your aunt after the funeral. That Bernie is a real prick. You know he'll probably take even longer now he knows that I'm onto him.'

'Thanks very much, Percy.'

'Think nothing of it.'

'Would you put me through to Jim's office, please?'

Ishmael explained to Jim about his uncle's heart attack and said he'd catch up with him in a couple of weeks.

Ishmael hung up and paced up and down the hall.

For the life of him he could not understand just why he had bothered to put the first stage of the contingency plan into effect. He just felt it was the right thing to do. The bridge had been burnt and there was no going back.

Having notified his workplace, the second stage was to inform a doctor, recently qualified and deeply indebted to Akmid, who ran a practice in Toronto. Once the call came from him, the doctor was required to commit a prearranged patient of his into a private hospital in Toronto under the name of Matthew Fall. Minimal and unlikely as the chance of an inquiry from someone at the Colorado Aqueduct

Chapter 32 *Parker, Arizona, Monday 20 August*

reaching this far was, the scheme was devised on the remote chance that it might.

Ishmael's thoughts turned to Akmid, Werter von Stumpf, to the leaders and combatants of the Global Azad Front, and he was astonished to realize that he felt no animosity towards them. These were men whose paths had not been crossed by the absolute Truth, so the struggle with themselves had not begun. It would eventually, Ishmael believed, and when it did, they would all be reformed. 'The battle is within yourself. This is the holy war.' He said it aloud and raised both his arms in the air to a God who he now saw as filled with compassion and mercy to all mankind. How could he have so unjustly accused the millions of Isaac's descendants of being usurpers worthy of death?

Standing in the hallway with arms stretched out above him, he became aware of the absence of pain. That morning he hadn't taken any painkillers for the cancerous lump under his armpit. He unbuttoned his shirt, felt around and, to his utter amazement, found that the swelling was gone. He darted into the bathroom and checked himself in the mirror. He pinched and kneaded the spot. Still no pain. Apart from a slight discoloration, there was nothing to be felt.

Ishmael clearly understood that his release from hatred and abandonment of violent radicalized doctrines had brought on the physical healing. Now more than ever he wanted to thank Rosasharn for the way she had expressed the Truth. He remembered a quote that the religious instructors at the missionary school were fond of repeating, something Jesus had said: 'Ye shall know the truth, and the truth shall make you free.'

Everyone, Ishmael thought, is in need of spiritual healing and all one's physical problems will disappear. He dropped to his knees, bowed his head and offered a prayer of gratitude for the miracle that God had worked.

Buoyed by his manifold blessings, Ishmael picked himself up off the bathroom floor and went into the kitchen, bagged up all the circuits and wiring, bundled the RDX and C4 back into the spare tire and placed it all in the boot of his car, with the exception of the bomb belt which he had kept intact.

After packing his belongings and tidying up the apartment, he spread his road map on the kitchen table. Using the scale on the map, he worked out that Baton Rouge was roughly two thousand miles from Parker. He decided to drive to Phoenix, then take Interstate 10 all the way to Baton Rouge. With an overnight stop in San Antonio, he should be in Baton Rouge by Wednesday, plenty of time before the meeting scheduled for Saturday. He considered for a moment whether to spend another day in Parker but decided against it. Rosasharn was too close and he could not trust himself. The way he was feeling, he would probably tell her everything.

Gazing at the map, his eyes drifted to the northeast corner of Arizona. Chilchinbito Canyon jumped out at him and he was overcome by a strong desire to see this part of Arizona, the place that had evoked so many childhood memories.

Studying the map further, he concluded that going there would only delay him by a day. Instead of Wednesday, he would get to Baton Rouge by Thursday. He made a spur-of-the-moment decision to go see Old Smoke.

From Parker, he headed north to Kingman. Driving through Lake Havasu City, where Rosasharn lived, he went through a mighty struggle to stop himself from going to find her. Seeing her would only complicate things. As he drove past the public library, he thought he saw her green Oldsmobile parked out the front, but he kept driving. In a short time, Lake Havasu City was miles behind him and with it the temptation to find Rosasharn.

CHAPTER 33

CHILCHINBITO CANYON, NAVAJO RESERVATION, MONDAY 20 AUGUST

Black Mesa's spectacular burnt-orange sculptures mesmerized Ishmael as he drove deeper into the Navajo reservation. During the course of the long drive, Ishmael ventured off the black top onto rutted dirt tracks lined with starving vegetation, tumbleweeds blowing. He drove as far as the tracks would take him — into the rock-strewn valleys where he stopped the car, slumped himself against the steering wheel and seriously contemplated disappearing into the maze of canyons and deep arroyos. On two occasions, he got out of the car and roamed aimlessly under the savage sun, gun in hand, trigger cocked, playing the past twenty-four hours over in his head. All he wanted was to live out his life, but the facts stood sharply before him. He knew he was already dead.

The sun had almost dipped behind the ramparts of Chilchinbito Canyon. It cast long spiked shadows over Old Smoke's property. Ishmael drove down the access route. As he came over the rise he spotted Old Smoke's truck and could make out Old Smoke hunched over a campfire.

Ishmael flashed his high beams. Old Smoke, recognizing Ishmael's car, waved and motioned him in. Ishmael pulled up next to the truck and walked over to Old Smoke.

'Just in time for supper, Scot,' Old Smoke said, fanning the fire. A jack rabbit, impaled on an iron rod, lay across it.

'I hope I'm not imposing.'

'You are always welcome here.'

'I need a place to stay for a night.'

'Sleep in the trailer.'

'Thanks.' Ishmael crouched on his haunches.

Old Smoke opened the ice chest, stabbed at something and lifted out a dead rattlesnake. He brought it up to his mouth and made like he was going to chomp down on it.

'I've never eaten snake.'

'Good for the soul. We eat after supper,' Old Smoke said as he carefully coiled the snake back into the ice chest.

Ishmael smiled thinly.

'Little Bird Double Head told me the full story of what happened at Warm Springs Bar and Grill,' Old Smoke said as he rotated the jack rabbit, sprinkling it with salt and pepper.

'Who?'

'The bartender.'

'Oh, him.'

'Little Bird Double Head heeded your protest. Removed the pictures of the great leaders of the Indian nations.'

'I really didn't mean to hurt or upset Little Bird Double Head. Honest.'

'What you did inspired a good thing in Tuba City. The bones of great men lie buried in this place. Thank you,' he said motioning towards the canyon.

'It just …' Ishmael hesitated, 'seemed so wrong.'

'It was wrong,' Old Smoke said, his voice grave.

The jack rabbit was starting to blacken. Old Smoke took hold of the iron rod and slid the carcass off onto a platter and dismembered it with his hands, throwing half of it onto a tin plate which he handed to Ishmael.

Chapter 33 *Chilchinbito Canyon, Navajo Reservation, Monday 20 August*

'I had a vision of you coming back.'

'You really mean that?'

Old Smoke nodded.

'What sort of vision?'

'Eat first, then we will go to the sacred place where my father's bones lie buried.'

They ate in silence. The sky over the canyon had turned inky blue. Ishmael felt at peace with himself. He was in the right place and in the right company.

They heard a car approaching.

'Sounds like we got company,' Old Smoke said.

CHAPTER 34

BATON ROUGE, LOUISIANA, MONDAY 6 AUGUST

Canaan crossed the state line into Louisiana. The state flag flying high by the roadside seized his attention. The flag reminded him of his days when he was a ward of the state at the Jack Folsom mission school in India. The same flag had been draped alongside the American flag above the entrance to the dormitories. The pelican brooding over its young was a shocking reminder of his sleepless nights when the Americans had rallied around his bed at two in the morning petitioning Jesus to save his soul by their 'laying on of hands'. The paddling and praying ordeal had been downright humiliating, as they had often shamelessly groped his private parts.

He stopped at a convenience store and bought a Baton Rouge street directory to find his way to the Jack Folsom Memorial Temple. It was located on the Airline Highway in the suburb of Sunnybrook.

By mid-afternoon, Canaan had crossed the Mississippi River into east Baton Rouge.

He slowed as he came off the ramp of the Earl K. Long Bridge and shot a glance upriver. A couple of riverboats were paddling upstream, white plumes billowing from their funnels. Maybe Duvall was on one of them. From what he knew, Duvall was running an evangelical ministry on the *Mark Twain* Riverboat Hotel.

With every passing mile he reveled in the prospect of finally fulfilling his promise to his mother. The interminable waiting was soon to be over.

Canaan parked in front of the Jack Folsom Southern Baptist Revival

Chapter 34 Baton Rouge, Louisiana, Monday 6 August

Crusaders Temple. It was an imposing gaudy structure. More than half of the exterior of the temple was stained glass, depicting Old and New Testament stories. Mounted on top of the soaring spire was an enormous crucifix tangled in razor wire, shimmering in the sunlight.

In the middle of the manicured green lawns was a bronze statue of Jack Folsom, also of epic proportions. Paths lined with palm trees spiraled out from the statue in all directions. Groves of cedar, pecan and willow trees bordered the grounds.

Canaan got out of his car and walked over to the molten image. The inscription read: 'The One, the Very Reverend Jack Folsom 1825—1892.'

Canaan gazed up at the giant, boyish-looking Folsom. The left arm was raised, a finger pointing up, the right arm outstretched holding a Bible. Canaan bowed his head. The usual torments of his existence raged within him. After a few moments he looked over towards the temple and his eyes lit up. Exhilaration and power surged through him. Then and there he decided that not only did Duvall have an appointment with the devil, but so did the abominable structure.

He took a stroll around the grounds to have a closer look at the building, plotting its demolition. Apart from a few gardeners tending the grounds, he saw no one else.

He concluded that nothing short of three hundred pounds of RDX going off in a van parked in front of the main entrance could do serious damage to the miserable structure. He toyed with the idea of going back to Sacramento to buy more RDX, but no he decided, he had to be more creative.

Staring up at the towering cross entangled in razor wire, an idea came to life. He pictured it crashing down across the entrance at the end of a Sunday service, shards of razor wire raining on the crowd milling around the entrance. He was sure he could execute this plan with his limited supply of RDX.

As Canaan drove out of the grounds and onto the Airline Highway, he looked back at the temple and noticed, for the first time, the placard that read: 'The Southern Mormon and Latter Day Saints Tabernacle.'

Canaan pulled up and read the sign again and checked the address in the street directory.

He swung the car back into the grounds and drove down the maze of avenues looking for one of the gardeners he had seen earlier. He spotted one on a ladder, cutting dead wood off a pecan tree.

'Excuse me, sir,' Canaan said tapping on the side of the ladder.

The gardener looked down at him, 'Boy! Get your arms around that limb and pull down on it. If that damn limb swings my way, I'll be taking the express way down.'

Canaan positioned himself under the branch. Stretching his arms, he just managed to wrap his hands around it. As the gardener sawed, Canaan pulled down.

'Pull harder. Use your weight, boy. Dat's it.' The gardener yelled, 'Timber!' as the branch cracked, peeling a wide strip of bark from the trunk. Canaan jumped back as the branch landed.

The gardener dropped his saw and climbed down the ladder. He was a tall, sinewy African American in his early fifties dressed in bib overalls and a bowler hat. The thick, corded muscles of his upper arms bulged from his short-sleeved shirt.

'Thank ya, much obliged,' the gardener said graciously.

'It was nothing,' Canaan replied.

The gardener's face glistened with sweat. He pulled a rag from his back pocket and mopped his brow. 'Ain't ya hot boy, in that long-sleeve sweatshirt? You're rugged up like ya was at the North Pole.'

'No.'

The gardener smacked his lips and nodded. 'Throw up your arms.'

Canaan stared at the gardener, expressionless, and raised his arms.

Chapter 34 Baton Rouge, Louisiana, Monday 6 August

'Dat's amazing. Ya armpits are as dry as a bone. If you get sent down to hell the devil's gonna have to do something about the heating,' he said, flashing a big toothy smile.

Canaan furrowed his brow. The satirical insinuation ran deep into his soul.

'Boy, I wanna know your secret of staying so cool, cos I'm gonna get down there before you. You know what I'm saying?' said the gardener, gravely meeting Canaan's eyes.

Canaan gazed into the man's huge, glassy brown eyes that expressed the sadness of the ages and, for a moment, was back in the sea port of Surat, staring into the pain-filled eyes of Captain Seasalt. From the chambers of his memory he heard the old captain's gravelly voice. 'Just look around you, son. You see these men?' He pointed with a half-filled bottle of cheap wine. 'Look at them. What do you see? I'll tell you what you see. Dead men. Life on the sea has drowned their souls. The salt preserves their carcasses. If they stayed on land too long, they would decompose.'

The gardener picked up the saw. 'The whole damn country got an appointment with the devil.' He held up the saw to his neck and motioned as if he were going to hack into it. Canaan grinned broadly at his gesture.

'Sometimes I say I'm gonna give me a close shave, but the Lord already done started his punishment. Ya see this here?' He pointed with the end of the saw to a patch of flaky white skin on his left cheek.

'Dat's what ya call a pig-men-tay-shun, something or other. I can't remember the name. My doc says if I live another ten years I gonna become a white man.'

'You'd better stop letting the white man get under your skin. You know what I'm saying?' Canaan said, mimicking his accent.

The gardener laughed heartily and said, 'Ya all right, boy.'

'Is this the Jack Folsom Southern Baptist Revival Crusaders Temple?' Canaan asked.

'It was,' the gardener replied as he folded up the ladder.

Canaan looked over towards the bronze statue and then at the gardener.

The gardener cocked his head and stood arms akimbo. 'Does that statue bother you, boy? Hey, let me tell ya this. Jack Folsom was a good man, but when he died a lot a bad peoples come along, peoples sayin' they was appointed by the Lord, done destroyed his reputation.'

'Sir, I didn't ask for a history lesson. If you know where the Jack Folsom Southern Baptist Revival Crusaders Temple is, could you please tell me?'

'You see that steeple just over the rise?' Canaan looked in the direction the gardener was pointing with his saw. 'That there's the original Jack Folsom Crusaders Temple.'

'How do I get to it?'

'What you want there, boy?'

Canaan gazed towards the spire towering above a canopy of live oaks. 'I'm interested in old architecture.'

'If you don't want to tell me, just say so, son.'

'I don't.'

'Good. Don't care for anybody who bullshits. A track behind them oaks leads to it.' He pointed. 'Follow it until you come to a footbridge that crosses the bayou and go right for about a quarter mile.'

'Thanks,' Canaan said and strode off towards the temple.

'Hey, boy!' the gardener called. 'Watch out! Place is crawling with gators!'

Canaan followed the narrow, winding trail through the cypress pines and live oaks. Spanish moss draped over the branches, billowing like nylon curtains as gusts of wind blew in from the gulf. Thick, low-hanging clouds were assembling for a mid-afternoon downpour.

Chapter 34 *Baton Rouge, Louisiana, Monday 6 August*

Canaan picked up his pace, hoping to find shelter before the rain started. He arrived at the footbridge, crossed the bayou and headed right. The road was rutted and full of potholes. Fallen trees that had been struck by lightning lay across it. As he got closer, he noticed a huge, gaping hole in the wooden steeple's side. Finally he reached the clearing where the church stood. On a bent, rusted placard, faded wording read: 'The One, the Very Reverend Jack Folsom Memorial Temple'.

The church looked as if it had been abandoned for decades. One corner of the roof had caved in, its splintered and cracked exterior was covered in vines and Spanish moss, and the smell of rotting timber hung heavy in the air. To the side of the building was a graveyard. A bunch of freshly cut flowers in a vase at the base of a shining marble crypt grabbed his attention. He read the inscription: 'Here lies The One. Very Reverend Jack Folsom, 1825—1892'. He kicked the vase, shattering it against the marble, and headed back to question the gardener.

Canaan stood under the tree where he had talked to the gardener, scanning the grounds for him. The sun had disappeared behind the clouds. Lightning forked and thunder rumbled. He spotted a figure in the doorway of a shed at the end of a gravel path and strolled over. As he got closer he recognized the gardener, sitting on a petrol drum playing a guitar and singing:

Me and my daddy can pick a bale of cotton
Me and my daddy can pick a bale a day...

Canaan stood in front of him, listening. The gardener's eyes were tightly closed. His left heel beat against the side of the petrol drum.

Me and my brother can pick a bale of cotton
Me and my brother can pick a bale a day.

Me and my brother can pick a bale of cotton
Me and my brother can pick a bale a day.
Oh, Lordy, pick a bale of cotton.
Oh, Lordy, pick a bale a day.

The gardener's deep, husky baritone punctuated with lisps dueled with the buzz and rattle of the strings slapping against the frets.

Jump down turn around pick a bale of cotton.
Got to jump down turn around pick a bale a day.

The gardener's rhythm and intonations infected Canaan's soul. He found himself swaying and tapping his foot. The urge to turn around and run from the music's toxic influence was overwhelming, but the magnetic effect held him captive. It challenged his hatred, his hurt and the unspeakable loss of his mother's love. It was a balm, a tonic, a comfort. Only one other time in his life did music have such an effect on him. It was in the lobby of the Albergo Medicea motel in Rome, listening to the owner; Silvia Spaccanapoli singing with Claudio Villa's a rendition of 'Mamma' that was playing on her cassette player.

Me and my mother can pick a bale of cotton.
Me and my mother can pick a bale a day.

The words 'Me and my mother' forced him to his knees. Canaan's private orchestra — his mother's shrill screams — joined with the singing. Tears rolled down his cheeks. The horrendous ordeal of that long-ago night was now vivid before him as he witnessed his mother being sacrificed, not to the chanting dirges of Hindu priests but to a genre of music that expressed the hardship of a race of people because of the color of their skin.

Me and my mother can pick a bale of cotton.
Me and my mother can pick a bale a day.
Oh Lordy ...

Gonna jump down turn around pick a bit of cotton.
Gonna jump down turn around pick a bale a day.

175

CHAPTER 35

BIKANER, RAJASTHAN, INDIA, APRIL 1994

At twelve years of age Canaan Ahab was severed from all that he held dear. His father, Salathiel, a wealthy and successful travelling merchant who sold household wares to people in the hundreds of little villages scattered throughout the province, was found murdered and robbed six miles south of his village. At the time Canaan's father was the chieftain of a secret society dedicated to preserving and continuing ancient Hindu religious rites and ceremonies outlawed by British colonisation.

Though classed as a Vaishya, the position elevated Salathiel to the status of a Brahmin, which meant that upon his death, he would be buried in accordance with the ancient customs of Hindu law. As a consequence, his wife Jeya would be immolated on her husband's funeral pyre.

Immediately after being informed of her husband's death, Canaan's mother packed all she would need, grabbed her only son Canaan and, holding him for life itself, dashed off to the railway station, unaware that her husband's disciples were stealthily observing her every movement.

Her neighbours saw Jeya and Canaan leave but made no attempt to stop her, nor to help her. To interfere would evoke a curse from Agni, the Hindu god of fire who, as superstition had it, would take the soul of one of their kin as punishment for interfering.

Five of Salathiel's disciples boarded the train on which Jeya and Canaan were passengers. As it happened the train had come to a halt because of an obstruction on the tracks. Under cover of the din of people

Chapter 35 *Bikaner, Rajasthan, India, April 1994*

boarding and disembarking to see what had happened, Jeya and Canaan were dragged off the train and taken to a stone hovel where they were held captive for three days.

Jeya was fourteen years of age when her father gave her to the unscrupulous shylock Salathiel as payment for a long-outstanding debt. Jeya was forced into wedlock with him and her father was in debt again, this time over the dowry payment.

Living in relative luxury, certainly in contrast to the impoverished masses around her, Jeya felt little comfort in her ill-matched union with Salathiel. Learning of her husband's fanatical association with the secret Hindu society, Jeya fostered a fear that one day she would have to fulfill her role as a suttee, which seemed imminent as Salathiel was forty-three years her senior.

Jeya's terror was exacerbated tenfold after giving birth to her firstborn, a son, whom she named Canaan, which meant 'promised land — heaven'. From early childhood, Canaan's mother drilled into him that the two of them should always be together, and that wherever she went, he would surely follow.

The first two days of captivity were bedlam for Canaan. Jeya held on to him for hours at a time, hiccupping dry sobs, her voice hoarse and her hands red from pounding on the door, pleading with the guard to let them go. During these outbursts, Canaan would squeeze himself into a corner, cup his hands over his ears and press his eyes closed as he struggled to shut out the scene before him. When he could bear it no longer, he left his corner and joined his mother, prancing and rearing like a caged wildcat.

On the third morning of their captivity, the hovel was awash with rays of sunlight piercing through the holes in the thatched roof. Canaan awoke expecting a repetition of the previous days' ordeal. To his surprise, he found his mother staring down at him, stroking his cheek, a beatific smile on her face.

'Has someone come to help us?' Canaan asked excitedly.

'Why do we need help? We have everything we need. Look.' She pointed to the pot of steaming hot food on a tray left beside the door.

'But ... but ... what about ...?' Canaan stammered, alarm replacing his short-lived joy.

'Shhh,' Jeya whispered as she embraced and gently rocked him.

Canaan tried to wriggle free. 'But Mama, we have to escape. It has been three days.'

'Let us eat first, my love. By tonight we will truly be free,' she said, and kissed him on the forehead.

As they crouched over their meal of steamed curried vegetables and boiled rice, Canaan, who had barely touched his bowl, watched his mother eat her first meal in days. Canaan shuddered as he stared into his mother's unfocused eyes. Canaan felt a detachment from his mother the likes of which he had never experienced before.

Jeya explained to Canaan what was to happen, and the importance of his role in it. She told him she would never be happy in the afterlife if he were not there with her and, without her, he could not possibly be happy in this life on earth.

'No. No, I will not let you do it,' Canaan said defiantly. He retreated to a corner and squatted down, drawing his knees to his chest and bowing his head.

Jeya kneeled beside him. 'Dearest, you must promise to follow your dear mother.'

'Why must we go to the afterlife? I want to stay in this life.' he whimpered.

'You will follow your dear mother,' Jeya gently insisted.

'No, no, I will not let you do it,' Canaan argued vehemently.

Over the course of the day, Jeya incessantly appealed to the boy's extreme attachment to her, and his fear of being alone she had instilled

Chapter 35 *Bikaner, Rajasthan, India, April 1994*

in him. Jeya persisted until Canaan finally promised to follow her.

At sunset five members of the order came to get her. The fortitude she had displayed throughout that day disappeared. Jeya had woken up to reality, as if from a dream.

Jeya became hysterical, running from wall to wall, bouncing off each surface, screaming that she did not want to be burnt. Canaan, who had solemnly promised to follow his mother's destiny, was again thrown into confusion. Unsure of what to do, he glared at the men standing at the door, two of them holding ropes.

The men pounced on his mother, pinned her to the floor and began to tie her up. Jeya, who had not slept for three days, seemed then to implode, giving up all vestiges of resistance. She swivelled her head, trying to get a glimpse of Canaan, weakly calling to him, 'The promise, Canaan, my child, do not forget the promise! Follow me, follow me!'

Canaan tugged the men's dhotis, pleading with them to tie him up with his mother. He managed to slip between the ropes as they were being curled around his listless mother who kept reiterating her plea, her voice growing weaker.

They swatted at Canaan and called out, 'Get that boy out of the way!' Canaan dodged the blows, then hurled himself back into the melee of hands, bodies and ropes. One of the men stood up, and with a venomous look, hissed a vile curse before giving Canaan a mighty push that set him reeling into the stone wall, knocking him out cold.

When Canaan regained consciousness his mother was gone. He was insensible to the gash on the back of his head. The back of his shirt was soaked in blood. His mother's voice, exhorting him to follow her, reverberated in his head.

He leapt to the door. It was unlocked. He stepped out and ran a few hundred yards this way and then that way. He turned back to where the hovel was and paused, he listened to the distant clattering of a train.

The sun had just set and a purple haze enshrouded the valley. A light breeze carried the faint scent of wood smoke to where he stood. Instinctively, he went upwind and came to a path he'd tracked moments before. Canaan ran through the dense underbrush, sniffing like a bloodhound. He raced up and down inclines, stopping at irregular intervals to breathe in the air for traces of wood smoke. He reached the top of a hill and saw an orange glow and a column of smoke rising in the distance.

He finally came to a clearing where a huge fire was being stoked by people he had never seen before. Their faces glowed orange atop their shadowy satanic forms. Under cover of the long grass, Canaan crept closer and watched as his mother was prepared for her entry into the next world.

Five scantily dressed young girls encircled her, showering her with petals. A man stood on a chair holding a silver jug from which he poured oil over her. Countless others stood nearby, chanting.

To Canaan's astonishment, his mother, who had a serene expression, seemed to be staring in his direction. There was an unsettling feeling of communion between them.

He became engrossed in how beautiful she looked with her oily long black raven hair plastered over her shoulders, bare breasts glistening in the firelight, her body covered with petals. He could hear her voice calling out to him. 'The promise, Canaan, my child! Follow me, follow me!'

Her call resonated in his head, growing louder. Her voice was calm, assuring that all would be well when they had both passed through the vestibule of flames. From that moment, all fears of following his mother into the fire were swept away by her siren's whisper.

The rites of preparation drew to a close. A sinewy old man wearing a loin cloth picked up a handful of Canaan's father's clothes and threw them into the fire.

Jeya, now with her wrists and ankles bound with bailing wire, was

Chapter 35 *Bikaner, Rajasthan, India, April 1994*

picked up by four pallbearers. They slowly marched towards the fire with her body raised high above their heads. The rhythmic chanting swelled to a crescendo as they hurled Jeya like a log into the flames.

Canaan's heart lurched with alarm. He sharply sucked in his breath and darted out from the long grass towards the fire, arms outstretched. A gust of wind blew flames in his direction, as if to welcome him. Canaan slid to an abrupt stop a few feet from the embers. The fierce intensity of the heat pushed him back.

In the midst of the leaping flames, he could just make out the twisting figure that was his mother. Her ear-piercing shrieks shattered the chanting.

Canaan felt himself being dragged away. He thrashed about, trying to wrench himself free of the hold, shouting that he had to follow his mother. The acrid smell of burning flesh dug into his nostrils. Canaan went limp and stared trance-like at the black smoke column billowing into the dusk like a falling tower.

A farmer had seen the fire from the hilltop and guessed that a suttee was taking place. He had sent his son into the village to inform the chief of police, who soon arrived with his officers. Those present quickly abandoned the ceremony. Let loose, a delirious Canaan staggered towards the smoldering ashes. "I'm coming, Mother!" A police officer scooped him up. Canaan kicked and thrashed, pleading with the officer to let him die.

Canaan was the prosecutor's prime witness against those charged with his mother's death. After the weeklong trial, he was put into the custody of the Rajasthani Children's Welfare, which in turn committed the boy to the care of the Jack Folsom Mission School, established in 1984 in the city of Bikaner by the Jack Folsom Southern Baptist Revival Crusaders of Louisiana.

CHAPTER 36

BATON ROUGE, LOUISIANA, MONDAY 6 AUGUST

Me and my mother
Me and my mother
Me and my mother ...

The gardener sang on and on. Thunder clapped overhead and hard rain began to pelt on the tin roof.

The rain cooled the hot air. Canaan experienced a strange feeling of refreshment and calm. The gardener concluded his song with a gut-wrenching moan. He lifted his head, opened his eyes and stared at Canaan. Canaan stared back unblinking, clothing drenched, still on his knees.

The gardener leant his guitar against the wall just inside the doorjamb. He grabbed a can of cola from an ice chest that stood on the ground alongside him and held it against his sweating brow.

'Did ya find it, boy?'

Canaan sniffled and wiped his nose with the palm of his hand. 'It's an abandoned ruin,' he replied.

'Dat's all there's left.' The gardener rubbed the white patch on his cheek, stared wanly at the flakes of skin on his palm, sucked in a deep breath and then blew them off. 'You see, this big mother was built in 1983.' He motioned towards the edifice. 'I tell you, boy, it was built on sand. Before then, things had been going just fine. Then, about ten or so years back, there was a murder and all sorts of evil happening. Church

Chapter 36 Baton Rouge, Louisiana, Monday 6 August

leaders went to jail, one committed suicide, members left in droves. This here building and land went up for sale. The Mormons bought it and I got myself a job.'

Canaan stood up. 'Why did they leave the statue up?'

'I done told you, boy. Jack Folsom was a good man.' The gardener threw the can of cola back into the ice chest, got up, went to the workbench and pulled out a tattered, clothbound booklet from a drawer. 'If you want to know, read this.'

'Can't you tell me?' Canaan pleaded.

'Telling and reading is two different things, boy. I ain't giving you a history lesson, 'cause you said you don't want one.' The gardener held it out to him. Canaan hesitated. 'Take it, boy.' He dropped it on the bench, picked up his guitar, sat down.

'What's with the number one before Jack Folsom's name?'

'The One,' the gardener corrected him. 'You want to know, read.'

Canaan stepped into the shed, snatched the booklet and went back to his car.

Canaan threw the booklet onto the front seat, opened the trunk, stripped down to his waist, and put on a dry shirt and sweater. The afternoon sun had just burst through the clouds. He gazed up at the statue, then at its shadow on the asphalt where steam was rising from the ground.

He glanced again at the booklet on the front seat and looked up at the statue with the arm outstretched to him, holding the Bible, imploring him to read. He got into his car and drove out of the grounds. He pulled up on the verge a little way up the road, picked up the booklet, turned to the first page and began to read.

On the front page was a handwritten note: 'In memory of Conway Lascelles, a journalist of impeccable integrity whose only crime was to tell the truth, which cost him his life. 1987.'

CHAPTER 52

ARKANSAS, 1800S

*The true story of Jack Folsom's life,
as written by Willy Bill Appaloosa.*

*From The Book of Psalms:
'Who will bring me into the strong city?
Who will lead me into Edom?'
When a child is born his people inquire of the Lord and discuss
with one another if this is he whom the Lord had appointed to lead
his people — 'the One.'*

When the Lord chose His new leader by a vision, a miracle, a calling out, the young boy from that day on would be referred to as 'The One' and become the spiritual leader of those among whom he lived. His family and friends would pamper him above all the other children. The One would be taught to read scripture and to understand the responsibility of being The One. He would be given the privilege of sitting next to the elders of the church on Sunday. Every day of his life and wherever he went, the people would refer to him as 'the boy who was The One'.

When Jack Folsom was born in 1825 in the small backwater town of Riversville, Arkansas, three miles north of the Louisiana border, nobody enquired of the Lord or consulted one another if he was going to be

Chapter 52 *Arkansas, 1800s*

The One, not even his mother, who brought shame on her kinfolk and her new son because she had given birth to him out of wedlock. Their kind may have been considered white trash, but it was just as possible for white trash to have The One as much as it was for blacks, mulattos and Cajuns. The choosing was up to the Lord and who would dare question the good Lord when He chose The One to lead His people out of the darkness into the light? From when time began to when time will end, the Lord's way will never change.

At the age of twenty-two Jack Folsom was a strapping, handsome young man, tall and lean, with eyes as clear as a summer's day. Not a hint of falsity could be found in his character. Love of God, fellow man, country and family were expressed in every lineament of his honest and upright countenance. He knew his place as God's very own chosen messenger and was true to his calling and behaved himself accordingly.

It came to be that, the older he grew, the more Jack became everybody's One, uniting the various strands of people in the town. People from all around the county and beyond came on Sunday mornings too, to hear Jack preach the scriptures in his own peculiar way. From across the river in Mississippi and as far as Tennessee they came; Indians from the reservations in Oklahoma came. Some of the people wanted to keep him for themselves. They said it wasn't right that blacks, Cajuns and dagoes claimed him as being their One. But to Jack, it didn't matter what color they were or where they were from — all were welcomed when Jack Folsom was preaching. Even with all the race problems the people had in those days on account of slavery, the north wanting to change things and the south resisting and eventually going to war, well, the people who went to hear him preach were willing, for one hour, to put aside their differences. Black and white, quadroon and mulatto sat next each other and, if there was nowhere to sit, Indians and Cajuns stood side by side.

In 1858, at the age thirty-three, Jack heard the Lord calling him to go off into the world's remotest corners to proclaim the gospel of his son Jesus Christ.

Jack slung his grip over his shoulder, said his goodbyes to his people and got a ride with a sinewy old farmer who was bringing a wagonload of rattlesnake watermelons to Vicksburg. Over two hundred watermelons were piled ten feet high on a cart drawn by six mules and an ox.

A couple of miles outside of Vicksburg the creaking old Pittsburgh wagon broke an axle, causing it to lose its load of watermelons and Jack had to make the rest of his way on foot. As he strolled into Vicksburg, a glorious city sitting on high, sunbaked bluffs above the Mississippi River, he paid homage at the statue of Reverend Newt Vick, who founded the city in 1808. Then, without a minute to spare, he ran for the paddleboat, the *Memphis Queen*. It had just cast off and was ten or so feet from the wharf when the pilot, one Horace Bixby, who, in 1856, met a young man by the name of Samuel Longhorn Clemens — Mark Twain — and persuaded him to join his trade, saw Jack making his dash.

Bixby smoothly eased the boat back, closing the gap between boat and shore, thereby enabling Jack to jump aboard.

This being Jack's first time on a Mississippi paddleboat, the goings-on caught him unawares. Jack felt that it was his solemn duty – he being The One – to thunder the Lord's wrath whenever he saw the devil having his way with the children of Israel. All the devil asks is to be let alone, but Jack would always see to it that the devil was never going to be let alone. It was plain to Jack that he had a job to do before the boat docked at New Orleans. Jack unpacked his Bible from his grip.

Jack, reading aloud from his Bible, ambled past a gang of ragtag Missouri trappers sitting at a table in the lower deck saloon. They were playing cards, gnawing on hardtack and swigging jugs of alcohol.

One of the trappers spat a wad of tobacco onto Jack's boot. Jack

Chapter 52 *Arkansas, 1800s*

looked down, then turned his eyes to heaven and said, 'Forgive them, Father, for they know not what they do.' The ringleader blew his nose on the palm of his hand and slapped Jack on the back.

The gang burst into a roar of laughter, jumped out of their seats, and brought him down to the floor.

While three trappers held Jack in submission, the ringleader grabbed a bottle of whisky and started trickling the liquid down his throat. Between gurgles and gulps, Jack called out for help. The piano player rolled his fingers along the keyboard, playing 'Amazing Grace' in a rich, triple time rhythm. Girls grabbed their men and danced a reel around the trappers holding Jack down. Everyone in the bar jeered and laughed at the pitiful sight of the preacher man being forced to consume the devil's potion. Before the song ended the ringleader had poured a good portion of whiskey down Jack's unwilling throat.

When the alcohol had the desired effect on Jack they picked him up and carried him to the stern, where they loaded the drunken preacher man in a skiff and cast him off.

Before too long the skiff became snagged on a branch stuck in the mud, the motion of the water making him violently ill and he threw up then passed out.

Jack woke up the following afternoon with a head as heavy as Mississippi mud, vaguely recalling what had happened. He managed to free the skiff from the tree branch and, using a piece of broken limb as his paddle, was able to get himself to shore. Disoriented, he staggered along the levee.

Night was beginning to envelope the Mississippi valley when he came across a cotton plantation. A wooden sign nailed to a pine tree, written in English, read: 'The Bombay Plantation. Owner and Proprietor: Jonney A Rumanujan." An arrow pointed down a track. He followed it until he came across a shotgun shack. A Negro eating an apple sat in a rocking chair on the porch.

'Excuse me, sir, where might I find the owner of the plantation?!' Jack called out.

The Negro stared wide-eyed at Jack and shook his head in disbelief. He pointed up the road.

'Thank you. Much obliged, my good man,' Jack said and doffed his hat.

A skinny, bony woman with wiry hair came out onto the porch from where she emptied a bucket of dishwater over the garden.

'Willy Bill, watcha you got dat smile on your face for?' she scowled.

'You never believe it, Sassafras. Some white man comes up from the river. He done called me sir,' Willy Bill replied proudly.

'If da master hears you talkin like dat ya better start sayin ya prayers, cos he gonna send ya to your maker,' Sassafras snarled. 'Now get your fat ass over to the river before it gets too dark.' Sassafras threw the bucket at him, turned around and marched back into the shack.

Jack staggered up the track, where it met a broad gravel road lined with oak trees. As he approached the big house he noticed strange little statues of animals and multilimbed beings, some with elephant heads, at the base of each oak. Each statue bore an inscription. He bent down to try to read the inscriptions, but they were in foreign lettering. One thing was certain: the people who owned this plantation were not God-fearing folk.

He drew closer to the stately antebellum house, apart from two slaves chopping wood there was no one about.

He knocked on the door. An elderly woman of dark complexion answered the door. She was wrapped in a colourful silk cloth. Her silver hair was pulled back into a bun. She wore a small silver ring through her nose and in the middle of her forehead was pasted a red dot.

'What can I be doing for you, mister?'

Jack took off his crumpled hat and held it to his chest.

'Excuse me, ma'am, I'm in need of a place to stay for the night. I promise I'll be gone before sunrise.'

'I am very, very sorry. You must be going away very quickly. This evening we must...' Her eyes brimmed with tears. 'I have lost my son and we are preparing for his burial,' she moaned.

Jack immediately offered his condolences. He asked for a Bible so he could say a few words for the departed soul, but his offer was declined.

Jack retraced his steps back to the river. The last faint glow of daylight was dimming in the western sky. Up ahead he saw a light burning and remembered the shack.

Jack knocked on the splintered old door. A voice shouted from inside, 'Who's there?!'

'The Reverend Jack Folsom from Riversville, Arkansas!'

The door creaked open and there stood the towering frame of Willy Bill, staring in amazement.

'Sassafras, de white gentlemens who called me sir is at da door.'

Sassafras stomped to the door, pushed Willy Bill aside and glared at Jack. 'What you want we ain't got. Best you leave us be.' She pulled Willy Bill into the shack and slammed the door on Jack.

A few moments latter Willy Bill burst through the door, ignoring Sassafras's incessant pleas to come back and have nothing to do with that white trash outside.

An hour later Jack and Willy Bill were sitting around a campfire, eating pinto beans and drinking black coffee out of tin cans. Willy Bill had made a bed out of cotton sacks in the barn for him and on the morrow was going to get Jack a ride to Morgan City.

Willy Bill looked at Jack with his big brown eyes wide open. His bottom lip quivered. 'Mr Jack, you done me good, calling me sir. That mean woman Sassafras done cuss you for it, calling you white trash, but I know'd it ain't so.'

Jack smiled. 'You think nothing of it, Willy Bill. We are equal in

God's eyes.' Jack reached over and patted him on the knee.

Willy Bill grabbed his hand and shook it vigorously. 'Da Lord bless you, Mr Jack,' he said as his huge, glossy brown eyes brimmed with tears. 'Da Lord bless you. I is never been spoken to with respect.'

By and by Jack told Willy Bill of his plight and finally got around to talking about matters concerning the people who owned the Bombay plantation.

'Mr Jack, them's mighty strange people, but them's good people in their own ways too,' said Willy Bill. He tossed a dry cottonwood branch onto the fire. The leaves fizzled and sparks shot into the air.

'I don't understand why they didn't want a blessing on the dead,' Jack said.

'Dere's some tings I ought not to talk about. Please don't make me, Mr Jack.'

He lowered his eyes and stared into the fire.

Jack pressed him further, but Willy Bill was closed up as tight as a bear trap.

'Well, Willy Bill, if you're not going to tell me, it looks like I'm going to have to march right on back to the house and find out for myself.'

'No, no, Mr Jack, you mustn't.'

'Sorry, Willy Bill. Being the Lord's humble servant I have to find out. Feelings have been running through my soul that something dreadful is going to happen. The way those two Negroes were stacking wood, it was like they was preparing to welcome the devil,' Jack said gravely.

'You gotta promise, Mr Jack, you gotta not tell a soul I tol' you, cos Master Rumanujan owns my hide,' he whispered, peering over his shoulder. 'It's best we talk quietly. You never can tell who's a listening.'

Willy Bill told Jack all about his master's Hindu ways and how the wife of their departed son was going to be thrown into her husband's funeral pyre.

Chapter 52 *Arkansas, 1800s*

Jack listened, his countenance growing darker. 'Being a man of God I have a duty to go back at once.'

'Please, Mr Jack, please. You is by yourself an' they ain't gonna take kindly to you interfering.'

'I am not by myself. The good Lord is with me.'

Jack stood up and finished the rest of his coffee and marched back to the house. Willy Bill dropped to his knees and prayed to the Lord to send a legion of angels to Jack's aid.

Willy Bill did not get to sleep that night and Jack never came back. At sunrise, with still no sign of Jack, Willy Bill decided to go tell Jack's people at Riversville.

Willy Bill made the journey in three days. He found the church elders and told them what had occurred at the plantation, but they did not believe his story and he was turned over to the sheriff as a runaway slave and sent back to the Bombay Plantation.

Jack Folsom was never seen again, but the memory of him did not die and his people believed that their One would come back some day.

Over time, what Willy Bill told the church elders became distorted and fancy came to take precedence over fact. A story about of Jack travelling to India and healing multitudes of Indians along the shores of the Ganges River became a focal point of his legacy and legend.

In 1876 a group of people who still believed that Jack Folsom would return, moved to Baton Rouge, where a church was dedicated and officially named the Jack Folsom Southern Baptist Revival Crusaders Temple. Slowly, the church grew and prospered.

The elders claimed that Jack Folsom returned and lived there the remaining years of his life and, when he died of old age, was buried in the church graveyard.

By Willy Bill Appaloosa

CHAPTER 38

BATON ROUGE, LOUISIANA, MONDAY 6 AUGUST

Canaan threw the booklet onto the front seat. He started the car, dropped a U-turn and drove through the twin arches of the Southern Mormon and Latter Day Saints Tabernacle. A crowd of people was gathered around the front entrance and the sound of a church organ floated on the thick, humid air. He gazed up at the razor wire, then back to the crowd below it. Canaan half smiled to himself and said, 'You are all spared.'

He pulled up beside the statue, wound down his window and stared up at it as if seeing it for the first time. Lights had been turned on around the base, illuminating the statue's outline against the early dusk sky. The bronze figure before him now evoked feelings alien to the black and white world he lived in. What had happened at the New Bombay plantation in Natchez, Louisiana had thrown him off balance. Jack Folsom lost his life trying to prevent the very same thing that had happened to his mother.

An early model Buick pulled up alongside Canaan's car. The driver's window wound down.

'I reckon you read that book, boy. I done told you he was a good man,' the gardener said, grinning.

Canaan nodded and forced a smile. He picked up the booklet from the passenger seat, stepped out of his car and held it out to the gardener.

'You keep it as a souvenir of the man, lest ye forget. You know what I'm saying?' the gardener said. He rubbed his chin with the back of his

Chapter 38 *Baton Rouge, Louisiana, Monday 6 August*

hand and said, 'Let me introduce myself. I'm Ezra Willy Bill Appaloosa Junior at your service.

Canaan gave him a puzzled look.

'Yes, Willy Bill was my grand pappy. Boy, I'm strapped for time. Got to get to a show. Five miles up the Airline Highway turn left at the Piggly Wiggly store, drive behind it and you'll see a trailer on a vacant lot. Only one there. You're welcome to come and talk.' He paused, and then said as an afterthought, 'Come hear some more Mississippi delta blues at Terraplane Bar on Lee Drive, a block down of Bayou Duplantier.'

Ezra put his car into gear and slowly drove off. He hadn't gone more than a few yards when he stopped and reversed back to where Canaan stood. Ezra stuck his hand out of the window and pointed to a green Mustang parked in front of the main entrance.

'Some other folks are asking questions too.' He winked at Canaan and drove away.

Canaan looked over to where Ezra had pointed, but he registered nothing. The man in the dark green Mustang hunched down low and buried his head in his newspaper.

That evening after listening to Ezra singing the blues at the Terraplane Bar, Canaan spent the night at a hotel a couple of miles up the road from the Southern Mormon and Latter Day Saints Tabernacle. The haunting melody of Ezra's song kept playing in his head. It subdued his craving to incinerate some living thing.

CHAPTER 39

LAKE HAVASU CITY, ARIZONA, MONDAY 20 AUGUST

Monday was Rosasharn's rostered day off. She'd been awake since dawn, lying in bed going over all that happened on the drive to Sedona, in particular, to what took place when she and Scot were parked beside the Big Chino Wash Verde River. Now, looking back on it, her intuition told her something inexplicable intervened between them, and that she had been a mouthpiece for an authority higher than herself.

The why of it all baffled her, however she did know that Scot was a changed man. In light of what had happened, she felt a little guilty for writing off Scot's religious conversion as farcical. So what if he'd had a hard time growing up? Hadn't she? It really is none of my business to judge, she thought. But why was he so reserved about not wanting to talk about religion? It just seemed odd that during the drive from her brother's house on Saturday night, he had been so open to talk about his religion, even to the extent of going behind a bush to pray.

What he'd said about feeling like being on the road to Damascus was deadly serious. Clearly, he understood the profound context in which he had put it. Rosasharn had to admit that things got a bit rough between them at Big Chino Wash Verde. All she wanted to do was to give him a bit of a history lesson, ingrain his faith with facts. Just thinking about it gave her goose bumps.

So much still did not make sense. Rosasharn wished she could stay

Chapter 39 *Lake Havasu City, Arizona, Monday 20 August*

in bed all day and think things through. She looked at the clock on the bedside table. It was nearly nine. She reached over and picked up a scrap of paper beside the clock. On it was written the Arabic words she overheard Scot muttering. While he was on the Greyhound bus, she jotted them down and attempted to translate them into English while she waited. On Saturday night, when she arrived home, she did a Google search. Having no correct spellings, the only response she received was 'No matches found'. She made some notes about the sectarian division of the sexes in a number of religions for her book and wanted to add the prayer to her notes.

Just what is it here that is forbidden for a woman to repeat?

It was a strange-sounding dialect. Picturing his overexcited state, she doubled over with laughter. Finally recovering herself, she said, 'Let's have another go at translating them.'

She bounced out of bed, threw on a bathrobe and went into the spare room to look for her Arabic dictionary and a couple of other reference books. Once she'd found them, she sat down with a pen and a legal pad and spent some time writing, trying to add to what she already had. All in all, she managed to string together four disjointed sentences and a few snippets. She made herself a cup of coffee and propped herself back up in bed.

Thumbing through the dictionary, she repeated the words, over and over, positive she was pronouncing them correctly, but the spelling eluded her. There appeared to be no definition for them in her dictionary. She figured they must be from an ancient Middle Eastern dialect, having done some research on the subject for one of her assignments.

After a few more fruitless attempts in the other reference books, she tossed them all aside and tried to figure out another way of solving the problem.

'That's it! I'll call Professor Rand.' She gathered up her books and piled them on the bedside table, finished her coffee, and looked up Professor Rand's number in her address book and dialed.

'Hello, Professor, it's Rosasharn.'

'Rose of Sharon. Good to hear your voice. How you been keeping, my girl?'

'Fine.'

'Don't tell me you called to take up the job offer in our research department here at Stanford?'

'No, I would love to take it, but, you know, with Mom in the nursing home, I want to live close by. Moving to San Fran ... well, I wouldn't be able to see her as often and I'd worry.'

'I do understand, Rose of Sharon. How I wish I'd spent more time with my folks. Should have stayed on the farm and ...' His voice tapered off. 'Rose of Sharon, you are a rare breed. These days not many daughters put their parents' welfare first.'

'For me, it's the right thing to do,' she said, twirling her hair with her finger.

'Of course, of course it is, my dear girl. As long as I am head of this department, there is always a position waiting for you.' He pounded his desk lightly.

'I really appreciate it, but don't hold it open for me. If you find someone with more talent, fill it.'

'That's always been your problem, Rose of Sharon. You put others first.' When Rosasharn didn't reply, he continued. 'What can I do for you?'

'I'm doing some research into ancient Arabic prayers. Can you give me the titles of some books that would be useful? I'm trying to find the meaning and context of a few words.'

Professor Rand referred her to a text. Allowing his curiosity to get the better of him, he asked her what the words were. Rosasharn read and spelt them. He scribbled the words on the corner of his desk blotter.

Chapter 39 *Lake Havasu City, Arizona, Monday 20 August*

'Is that a giggle I hear, Madam Rose of Sharon?' he said in his sternest classroom voice.

'No, no, Professor Rand. This is very, very serious.'

'Ok, my lovely, let me know if you get stuck.'

'Thanks a million, Professor. I'll tell you the whole story some other time.'

She hung up the phone and quickly dressed, scooped up her car keys from the table and hurried off to the library.

As she closed the front door, she seriously questioned why she felt such an urgency to learn the meaning of the words of the prayer. She could not quite put her finger on it, but felt something was compelling her to unravel the meaning. She touched her forehead and felt that burning sensation again.

Rosasharn didn't have much luck at the Lake Havasu City Public Library; however, the librarian, who located a copy of the book Rosasharn requested at the Phoenix Public Library, arranged to have it delivered by Federal Express.

Rosasharn spent the rest of the morning shopping and paying bills. She arrived back at her apartment just as the FedEx truck pulled up. She signed for the parcel, went inside and tore open the box. 'Great. Just what the professor ordered.' She went into the lounge room, kicked off her shoes and made herself comfortable on the couch.

Rosasharn finally put the fragmented words and sentences into context and traced back their origin. There was a reference to the prayer being found carved into a cliff face in the Wadi Musa. She slapped herself on the forehead, thinking how dumb she was for not checking a book she'd come across that morning that was packed full of information about archaeological findings at Wadi Musa.

Repeatedly she crosschecked, looking up variations of the words in the hope that they might mean something else, but no matter which way she spelt them, they all led back to the same place: the prayer of holy war.

Rosasharn sat rigid on the couch. She could not believe what she was reading. 'There must be some mistake,' she said aloud. 'This cannot be. Scot was reciting the prayer of holy war. Surely it was not the prayer of preparation for war?'

She went and got her book on Wadi Musa and flipped through the index and found several references to the prayer. 'That's why he didn't want me to repeat any of it!' she exclaimed. She thumbed through the corresponding pages until she came across a picture of the towering sandstone cliff face and, on the opposite page, the English translation of the full text of the prayer.

> *The asylum of the Faith, strengthened by heaven, aided against enemies,*
> *The arm of the victorious government, the lamp of the resplendent religion,*
> *Perpetuate the prosperity of them that offer their mortal lives in service of thee.*
> *Aid me to plunge the sword of God into the vile heart, to silence the mind of him whom God doth judge as the corrupters, the usurpers of the promise to the first-born son of Ibrahim.*
> *Direct thy Holy vessels of destruction, their inclination to every evil thing against the enemies of God.*

Halfway through the second verse she could taste the bile rising in her throat. Unable to hold it down, she ran to the bathroom.

She washed her face, brushed her teeth and threw herself on the couch. Maybelline her pet cat jumped up onto the couch and sniffed her bare arm. She prodded the side of Rosasharn's stomach a few times before finally settling at her thigh.

Chapter 39 Lake Havasu City, Arizona, Monday 20 August

'Oh, Maybelline, tell me it isn't so.' Rosasharn sighed as she stroked the top of her cat's head.

Rosasharn struggled to recollect her thoughts, methodically reviewing the events of the past two days, commencing from the moment she first set eyes on Scot Fall at Jim's.

During the party, she recalled vaguely noticing Scot a couple of times standing nervously among the guests, then in those few moments while she was at the kitchen sink, filling the balloon with water overhearing Robin telling him that her mother was away with the pixies. Rosasharn considered all the questions he had asked about her mother, especially whether she went to the police.

The police! She gasped. Maybelline lifted her head up and meowed. Rosasharn reached over and fondled Maybelline's ear. Yes! This would explain why he nearly jumped out of his pants when Mom stood next to him while the patrolman was pouring water into the radiator.

From the sketchy details she could recall, it was unquestionably a knee-jerk reaction. Could it have been because of the patrolman's proximity to him? Maybe that was it. She recalled the expression on Scot's face when he thought the patrolman was jesting about hauling him up to the station for a strip search. She reasoned that he must have been wearing something under his shirt at Jim's, something that, during the drive, he was trying to conceal. That would explain all that squirming and shifting in his seat, objecting to having his back rubbed and refusing to take his jacket off. Yesterday, during the drive to Sedona, he was more comfortable and didn't complain about his back at all.

She could not help surmising with growing horror that if he was reciting the prayer of holy war, logic would point to him having some kind of destructive device and, believing that her mother was going to expose him, decided to what ...? Surely not to blow himself up?

This was probably the reason for the prayer, the thing he was wearing. That's why he had unbuckled his safety belt and dipped his hand down his jeans so he could get at that thing.

Everything had become defused by her misinterpretation of what her mother had been going to say. She had believed that it was all about sexual innuendo and he was playing along, albeit reluctantly. Something more motivated him than an abundance of testosterone clamoring for release, she now realized. Yes, it all seemed so extreme.

It occurred to her that her mother must have been trying to help Scot. She wished that her mother was her old self, though she knew that, even if she were, her mother would not divulge the knowledge derived from her ministrations with her clients, not even to her daughter. There were people Mrs. Rayner considered to be beyond help, people determined to exact their revenge, cases she refused to give assistance to because she knew they were not looking for help, but for justification. Mom must have perceived the evil intent in him but, as in the days of her practice, she would only use that perception to try to awaken the individual to his moral responsibilities.

Rosasharn knew that, when it came to matters of the psyche, her mother was still alert.

'If Scot was looking for a way out of his radicalized religious ideology then I have to trust Mom's intuition and try to help him,' she said aloud.

Everything was now starting to make sense. The last thing they talked about was St Paul's journey to Damascus. St Paul was on his way to Damascus to persecute the Christians, she mused. 'You could classify St Paul as a terrorist.'

Rosasharn picked up Maybelline and put her on the floor. She got out her Bible and read the account of the story in the Book of Acts.

Rosasharn closed her Bible. She was convinced that Scot was a deradicalized terrorist. The significance of what had happened at Big Chino Wash Verde was even more phenomenal than she first thought.

Chapter 39 *Lake Havasu City, Arizona, Monday 20 August*

In retrospect, she could clearly see that she had been the catalyst for Scot's reformation. She had unwittingly crossed swords with a terrorist and won through divine intervention.

After they had left Big Chino Wash Verde, she felt as if she were with a different person. By late afternoon, and coming back from Sedona, Scot was not the man she had picked up that morning or driven home the previous night.

She had to see him before she reported him to the authorities. If he had changed, he deserved to go forward. Then, her momentary joy for him crumbled. If he ever came to trial, he would be found guilty of conspiracy to commit a terrorist act against the United States. What was he going through? She decided to ring him at the aqueduct plant.

'Put me through to Scot Fall please.'

'I am sorry, but Scot is not in and won't be for the next two weeks.'

'Is he still in town?'

'Had to fly up to Toronto because of a family emergency,' the receptionist replied.

Rosasharn hung up the phone. Scot hadn't said anything to her about family in Toronto. In fact he told her he had only an uncle who lived on the island of Jura in the Hebrides. He had lied about everything, even about his conversion.

She wracked her brain over everything Scot had told her, searching for a clue. She remembered him mentioning that he had been to Tuba City and stayed with an Indian called Old Smoke. That's it. He's headed for the wilderness, to a solitary place. It's where one goes to sit in sackcloth and ashes after a deep religious experience. She decided to go to Tuba City, though once she arrived, where to go from there was anybody's guess.

Rosasharn picked up her car keys and purse. As she was about to shut the front door she went into her bedroom. From under the mattress she grabbed her Smith & Wesson .38 snub nose revolver.

CHAPTER 40

TUBA CITY, NAVAJO RESERVATION, MONDAY 20 AUGUST

It was late afternoon when Rosasharn arrived in Tuba City. For the past four and a half hours, her head had been in a spin as she rehashed every detail, at times wondering if she was mistaken about Scot's reformation at the Big Chino Wash Verde River. The irrational was the rational as far as she was concerned, and she had to focus on the facts which, by their very nature, were inexplicable to the intellectual mind. That's just the way religious experience was.

The battle is with oneself. That was the lesson Scot had learned. What she most wanted to do was to shout it from the rooftops, to explore it.

Rosasharn knew this sounded naive, but she now firmly believed that it was only through disentangling the ambiguities between the world's three monotheistic religions, that justification for antagonism towards the other would be annulled. Ultimately, it would be love with a capital 'L' that acted as the pre-emptive strike for peace.

As much as Rosasharn could explain the past, the future seemed starless. What now, she kept asking herself.

As she drove down the main street of Tuba City, the Warm Springs Bar and Grill caught her attention. 'That's the place where he damaged the parked car,' she said aloud to herself.

She parked her car and went inside. On duty was the bartender who

Chapter 40 *Tuba City, Navajo Reservation, Monday 20 August*

Ishmael had confronted with his objection to the images of the great chiefs of the Indian nations.

'Excuse me, sir. I'm looking for someone called Old Smoke. Have you heard of him?'

'Sure have, ma'am,' replied the bartender. He looked at Rosasharn with such intensity that she wondered if he thought she was a call girl working the reservation. He gave her a big toothless grin. 'Let me introduce myself. I am Little Bird Double Head, born to the Feather people and for the Prairie Chicken Clan.'

'I am very pleased to meet you,' Rosasharn replied, smiling faintly.

'Can I pour you a drink on the house?'

'No, thanks. I'm in a sort of a hurry. Did a man driving a red Ford Escort, average height, light brown complexion, in his early twenties come through here today by any chance?'

The bartender rubbed the stubble under his chin and thought for a moment.

'A man of that description was in here not so long ago, drove the exact same car. Went crazy over the Indian warrior pictures that used to be hanging on the walls. Said it was disrespectful to have them up there for tourists to gawk at.' The bartender pointed to the wall.

Rosasharn looked at the wall, puzzled.

'He was going to knock my lights out. A young man picking on an old guy.' The bartender was becoming indignant. 'Grabbed me by the shirt. I was lucky Grizzly Bear and Flying Tomahawk were in here. One look at those two Muscarlero bikers and he left in one hell of a hurry.' He chuckled.

'Did he hurt you, Mr. Little Bird Double Head?' Rosasharn asked.

'Heck no, but that night I thought about what he said, and you know what ma'am? He was damn right. Those great men of our culture shouldn't be exhibited that way in here, so I took them down. My partner in the saloon wasn't too happy about it, but damn him. I felt good about it. The deputy, young Billy Apple, saw him with Old Smoke. He'd run his car off the road. Followed him and Old Smoke up to Chilchinbito Canyon. They were going to go and arrest him, but I told the sheriff to let it be. I wasn't going to press charges.'

'Well, I'm happy for you Mr. Little Bird Double Head. How do I get to Chilchinbito Canyon?'

'It's about a two-hour drive from Tuba. Stay on one sixty for about fifteen miles, pass Kayenta, then you'll come to the turn-off to Chilchinbito. You'll see Old Smoke's ranch on your right. There's a sign on the side of the road. You can't miss it.'

CHAPTER 41

CHILCHINBITO CANYON, NAVAJO RESERVATION, MONDAY 20 AUGUST

Ishmael wiped his greasy fingers on the back of his pants, stood up and stared in disbelief. 'It's Rosasharn,' he said, astonished. 'Excuse me, Old Smoke. I know who it is.'

Rosasharn pulled up behind Ishmael's car and cut the engine.

Old Smoke stared knowingly at Ishmael and said, 'Time to round up the goats.' He tore off a hank of blackened flesh from the rabbit's thigh, got up and headed over to the windmill. A half-dozen goats were nibbling on shrubs that grew from the sides of the antique generator. Old Smoke called out to them in his native tongue. The goats bleated and made a beeline for the barn.

Ishmael, with bowed head, slowly walked over to Rosasharn's car.

The sight of Ishmael approaching made Rosasharn's blood run cold. She was attacked by an overwhelming fear that she might have got it all wrong. She reached for her gun and gripped it.

Ishmael was just a few yards from her car when he folded his arms, dropped to his knees and prayed aloud in Arabic, giving God thanks that he had been delivered from taking innocent lives. Rosasharn wound down the window, held her breath and listened. She understood what he was saying. All her uncertainties dissolved, she placed the gun in her purse and closed it. Unable to restrain herself any longer, she leapt out of the car, ran over to him, knelt beside him and embraced him.

'You're free, you're free,' Rosasharn whispered in his ear.

Ishmael gently pried her arms loose. He gazed into her tear-filled eyes. 'Yes, I am free. I don't know how to say this, Rosasharn. You see, I came to America to ...' he stopped and pursed his lips, struggled to find the words. 'Rosasharn,' he began, 'I was a terrorist.' His voice cracked like a teenager's. He expected to see revulsion in her face. Instead he saw compassion, understanding and forgiveness. He gazed at her reverentially and thought how brave she was, coming all this way to find him, and confirm those precious moments beside Big Chino Wash Verde River.

He closed his eyes, finished his prayer of thanksgiving and knelt silently, his head bowed to the ground. Rosasharn folded the hem of her dress under her knees, threw back her head and looked up at the sky. The sun had disappeared behind the canyon, leaving a dim afterglow. Old Smoke's echoing cry had ceased. A goat straggled out of the canyon to join its kind in the barn. There had been no rain in this part of the reservation for months. When the wind blew across from Utah, it sent up clouds of fine, black dust that hovered over the canyon for days, a dust that softened all the shapes, creating the effect of an impressionist painting.

Just as they had been at the Big Chino Wash Verde River, they knelt quietly, deep in thought. There were no jejune assumptions. The truth lay as bare and shone as bright as the sun.

Where to go from here? This was the question foremost in their minds.

Ishmael lifted his head and faced Rosasharn, whose attention was absorbed in the peculiar, dusty twilight. She sensed his eyes on her and turned her full attention to him. Beneath the girlish mischief shone an honesty. Now that she knew the truth, he felt an even stronger solidarity with her. Again he struggled to find his voice. Rosasharn looked at him with such intensity that he had to resist shying away.

'My real name is Ishmael Esrom.'

Chapter 41 *Chilchinbito Canyon, Navajo Reservation, Monday 20 August*

Rosasharn repeated his name aloud. 'Ishmael. Well, you can now call me "Isaac", brother.' She winked at him. Ishmael smiled and, for a moment, the grimness of the future lifted.

CHAPTER 42

NEW ORLEANS, LOUISIANA, TUESDAY 7 AUGUST

Canaan parked in front of Jackson Square and walked over to the Mississippi levy. He ran his finger down a placard listing the riverboats and their corresponding berths dotted along the esplanade: the *Natchez* berth 4, the *John James Audubon* berth 5, the *Cajun Queen* berth 6, the *Creole Queen,* the *Mark Twain* berth 7. The *Twain* was the one he was most interested in. From the information he had retrieved from the safety deposit box in San Francisco, Reverend Duvall ran an evangelical ministry on the *Mark Twain.*

The sign also bore a phone number for room bookings and sailing times. Canaan went over to a payphone, called the *Mark Twain* booking office and made a reservation for a three-week stay, which he paid for with his credit card.

He wandered over to Jackson Square where he ate a meal under the marquee in front of Café du Monde. Then he went back to his car and got his suitcase, purposely leaving the keys in the ignition. Most probably the car would be stolen by morning, but he didn't care. He had no more use for it.

He crossed the road without looking back, and made his way to the *Mark Twain* docking berth where he sat on a bench. The boat wasn't due in until six that evening. He closed his eyes and felt the warm wind that blew across the water caressing his face, and silently called out to his mother, telling her that he would soon set her free and fulfill the promise he had made to her so long ago.

Chapter 42 *New Orleans, Louisiana, Tuesday 7 August*

At ten to six a riverboat came around the bend blowing its foghorn. Canaan's heart leapt as the boat drew closer; the name on the side read: *Mark Twain*.

The *Mark Twain* was a fully refurbished, two-paddle steamboat with 105 rooms equivalent in style to those of a five-star hotel. It had been restored to all the former glory of its heydays of 1875 to 1899.

Shortly after docking, the gangway was lowered and passengers began to disembark. Canaan stood watching everybody who got off with intense interest. He looked up to the second deck and there, leaning against the railing talking to an elderly woman, he recognized the Reverend Jonathon Duvall. He was a small, dapper man with steel-grey hair, perfect teeth and a neatly trimmed white beard that gave him the appearance of a wise prophet. Beneath his fleshy Californian veneer was a stratum of myopic predisposition that reached to the very marrow of his bones.

In an instant, time froze like the previous day when he was catapulted back to his mother's death, and Canaan now stood in Duvall's judgment hall back at the Jack Folsom Mission School in India.

CHAPTER 59

BIKANER, RAJASTHAN, INDIA, DECEMBER 1994

The Jack Folsom Mission School, converted from an abandoned Catholic nuns' convent, was in a deplorable state. In resources and essential amenities, the dormitories and classrooms of those who were placed in the care of the mission school were barely adequate. The surrounding tenement slums added to an already depressing sight that was supposed to be an educational beacon for these children, a light that would lead them to better their lives.

Reverend Jonathon Duvall was the spiritual councilor of the Jack Folsom mission school. Duvall did not need his mother's help to lobby Jesus like the mother of Zebedee's boys, who had the audacity to ask the greatest man that ever walked the Earth that her 'two sons may 'sit, the one on thy right hand, and the other on the left, in thy kingdom'. Duvall believed absolutely that he had already been appointed by God Himself. Like Jonah of old, he was in the whale's belly waiting to be spewed out on the shores of the nation of nations, the United States of America.

Reverend Jonathon Duvall had been in the Jack Folsom Mission School for six months and had another two and half years to go. All Duvall had to do now was go through the motions of what was required of a cadet crusader in this God-forsaken land called India. For now he had to do his time in this land of exile, but he knew that eventually he would get back to that blessed land, the United States of America, become the leader of the Jack Folsom Southern States chapters and then

Chapter 59 *Bikaner, Rajasthan, India, December 1994*

run for governor of the state of Louisiana, and after that, run for the presidency of the greatest nation on earth.

It was a blistering Saturday afternoon. Duvall was comfortably seated at his desk, reading aloud from the Bible, gesticulating and putting on a pious air. The exhaust of the portable air-conditioner was facing him. The only other person in the classroom to receive any benefit of its cooling was his interpreter, who sat to the left of the podium. He was a middle-aged, subservient, hollow-eyed, sinewy fellow who translated the Bible stories into Hindi for those who had poor English, which was nearly everyone except Canaan.

' "Nebuchadnezzar the king was astounded, and rose up in haste, and spake, and said unto his counselors: Did not we cast three men bound into the midst of the fire?" ' Duvall paused and glanced up to gauge the degree of attention being paid him, expecting to see the usual pool of brown, wide-eyed faces, all sitting upright on their high-backed wooden chairs apart from Canaan, who generally was always hunched down with his chin on his desk.

Today, to Duvall's utter surprise, Canaan was sitting upright, looking as if he was engrossed in the Bible lesson. It was from the Old Testament, the story of the three Hebrew men — Shadrach, Meshach and Abednego — whom King Nebuchadnezzar had commanded his soldiers to throw into the fiery furnace.

Duvall nodded and gave him an approving smile. Canaan returned a curt shrug, lowered his eyes, picked up his pencil and snapped it in half.

Duvall looked exquisite in his new Valentino suit. The fake Giorgio Armani label stitched to the jacket's lining was what clinched the deal with the greasy-skinned tailor who made perfect, exact-to-the-last-stitch replicas from his exclusive sample of originals. His whole appearance contrasted strikingly with the shabbily dressed, bedraggled-looking, swarthy students.

Positioned on either side of his desk were two mirrors which he used for glancing at his reflection to check out his facial gestures as he parroted the word of God. He constantly straightened his tie, patted down his lapels and combed his hair.

Now and again, his eyes roved over the class to make sure everyone was paying full attention. He never missed an opportunity to wield the wrath of God on anyone who dared to misbehave or who chattered while he preached.

Duvall initially regarded Canaan with reserved compassion, a boy in need of healing, and had passed over him during question time. Every night for the first few weeks before retiring to bed, after spending the greater portion of his prayers on himself, he would briefly petition Jesus to save Canaan's tormented soul, along with the souls of the other defects in his classes.

Waiting for Jesus to save the boy's soul, Duvall's patience eventually wore out, and so he wrote Canaan off to eternal purgatory along with his mother.

Duvall, who openly condemned the practice of Hinduism, used Canaan's tragedy as an object lesson in order to dissuade his students from following Hindu practices and to encourage them to stick to the narrow path of Christianity. As heartless as this was to Canaan, it did have the effect of stamping the fear of God into the minds of the other students.

Duvall continued reading. ' "They answered and said unto the king, True, O king. He answered and said, Lo, I see four men loose, walking in the midst of the fire, and they have no hurt; and the form of the fourth is like the Son of God. Then Nebuchadnezzar came near to the mouth of the burning fiery furnace, and spake, and said, Shadrach,

Chapter 59 *Bikaner, Rajasthan, India, December 1994*

Meshach, and Abed-nego, ye servants of the most high God, come forth, and come hither. Then Shadrach, Meshach, and Abed-nego came forth of the midst of the fire." '

Duvall snapped shut his Bible. The interpreter, who had been translating the story, sat down at once when Duvall waved his hand in a gesture to be silent.

'Unfortunately, someone's mother was left in the furnace and we all know why,' he hollered, staring intently at Canaan.

Rage flared up in Canaan's eyes. He craved for a power that could set the whole world on fire. The story he had just heard spoke volumes to him: the three Hebrew men being thrown into the furnace and emerging unharmed from the inferno. He wished that it could have been that way for his mother. Where was the Son of God on the night his mother was thrown into the fire? Canaan reached under his desk and felt for the piece of wood trim that he had been stealthily pulling away from the underside. The boys sitting either side of him heard the crack and stared at him as he tore the shaft of splintered wood. Canaan shot them a venomous glance.

He stood up. There were no beads of sweat on his brow, nor nervous twitching. Exuding a confidence and conviction that was in stark contrast to his effete reputation, his left hand behind his back clutched the splinter of wood.

'Well, young Canaan, I see you have finally come to the Lord's feast,' Duvall said, raising his voice.

'Reverend Duvall, you might think that I have not been paying attention and learning about the Jesus god,' Canaan retorted.

'Then what are you waiting for? Declare right now in the presence of God and your holy brethren that you have received Jesus the Lord into your heart,' Duvall boomed.

'Why do you always say that my mother is in the fire, like what you said at the end of the story? Momma is in heaven and is right now waiting for me!' Canaan yelled, spraying the boy in front of him with spittle.

'What's holding you back, son?' Duvall muttered under his breath, turning to the interpreter and winking at him. The interpreter returned a nervous smile. 'I've said nothing inappropriate about your poor dear departed mother. May the dear Lord have mercy on her charred soul,' said Duvall mockingly.

'Jesus and my mother have much in common,' Canaan said through clenched teeth.

'Jesus and your mother? A lot in common? Bah!' Duvall jumped up from his chair, raised his Bible above his head and slowly marched down the aisle towards Canaan.

'I adjure thee in the name of Jesus, the Holy Spirit and by the name of our beloved leader, the Very Reverend Jack Folsom. By the holy power that is vested in me, I command the unclean spirits to come out!' Duvall hollered.

'There is no difference between my promise to my mother and the promise by the followers of Jesus to follow him into the next life!' Canaan cried out in a feverish pitch.

Duvall was now standing over him, his cold, dark eyes filled with contempt and indignation. For just a moment, Canaan cowered beneath Duvall's hostile stare.

'How dare you draw parallels with the blessed only Son of God. You blasphemous child. You are vexed with the logic of the devil!' Duvall shouted savagely. 'Your mother is burning, burning, burning,' his voice rose in a crescendo, 'in hell, for when she was on this here God's Earth she had failed to accept Jesus in her heart.' He stamped his right foot on the floor.

'How could she accept the Jesus god when no one told her about him?' Canaan shouted back.

Chapter 59 *Bikaner, Rajasthan, India, December 1994*

'Listen. Listen to me. Listen to me, boy.' Duvall's voice was husky, quieter now. He squatted, grabbed Canaan by the shoulders and shook him violently, jarring the boy's jaw.

'Your salvation is at your very doorstep. Knocking for entry into your life. Be saved, right now, this very moment. Open wide your heart, accept Jesus the Lord of Glory,' Duvall intoned.

Canaan struggled to break free of Duvall's grip. 'No, no, no. I will not be saved without Momma!' he shrieked.

'Sweet Jesus, O Sweet holy Jesus who shed his blood on the accursed cross to save your miserable soul. Repent! Repent from the devil's wiles,' Duvall jabbered. He closed his eyes, tilted his head and stared into his imaginary heaven.

Canaan wrenched himself free and, clutching the shaft of splintered wood, raised his arm and plunged down, aiming to sink his weapon into one of Duvall's eye sockets. In that instant Duvall opened his eyes and saw the wood splinter about to come down on him. He ducked to his right as the splinter of wood whooshed past the side of his head, the point catching on the sleeve of his jacket, ripping a gaping hole in it.

Duvall stared down at his torn jacket. 'You rotten son of a burnt bitch, you done ruined my brand new suit,' Duvall cursed.

Canaan lunged at him, pushing Duvall off balance. Duvall fell backwards and lay sprawled on the floor. Canaan latched his hands around Duvall's throat and began strangling him. Duvall gagged and struggled to throw him off.

'You will take my mother's place in hell!' Canaan screamed. 'Die, die, die!' His eyes blazed with demonic fury.

The interpreter rushed to Duvall's aid. He grabbed Canaan from behind and dragged him off Duvall.

'Duvall, you will take my mother's place in hell!' Canaan shouted, kicking and punching the interpreter.

The interpreter slammed Canaan to the floor, fell upon him and pinned him down. Duvall jumped up and retreated to the front of the room.

The governor of the mission school wrote to the authorities requesting that Canaan be permanently removed from the mission school and placed in a psychiatric institution. He was informed that as soon as a place became available they would come and take him away. In the meantime, they advised the governor to keep Canaan under twenty-four-hour lockdown. A red sandstone, single-room building away from the convent's main dormitory was secured for the purpose.

A devilish pandemonium reigned in Canaan's head as he sat silently in his prison cell. He no longer felt sorry for himself, nor guilty about the broken promise to his mother. He turned his hatred towards the people who came from America, especially towards Reverend Jonathon Duvall, whom he bitterly cursed for sentencing his mother to everlasting damnation. Canaan reasoned that Duvall's life was his to take and that he had to kill Duvall in order to set his mother free the erudite doctrine of eternal punishment for failing to acquaint oneself with Jesus. Only then, and in this way, would he be able to fulfill the promise.

CHAPTER 44

NEW ORLEANS, LOUISIANA, FRIDAY 10 AUGUST

Matteo Silvio Malatesta punched the stop button on the remote control of the VCR, shook his head in disbelief, sighed aloud and got up from the couch. He walked slowly with his head bowed to the tinted plate-glass windows that surrounded his spacious office on the thirty-fifth floor of the Vanderbilt Center on Canal Street. He stood rigid, hands behind his back, rocking on the balls of his feet as he looked out. From here the view was breathtaking: Lake Pontchartrain, the Mississippi winding its way to the delta. On clear days, he could see right out into the Gulf. Matteo loved watching the tiny specks of snowflake-like clouds rise over the Gulf then, within less than an hour, turn into thunderheads, spilling their mass of condensed water onto the crescent city in a deluge of rain that would be accompanied by wind, sheet lightning and thunder.

The clouds would dissipate as quickly as they came, leaving the city steaming in a humid fog. When the fog silhouetted the old town, the French Quarter, which was directly below him, it took on an almost magical, mystical appearance. The rooftop gardens, brimming with pots of bougainvillea, elephants' ears, banana trees and all manner of tropical plants, was an oasis. The canopy created by the rows of oaks that lined the surrounding streets and boulevards acted as a bulwark against the grey, non-descript tenements and the elevated freeway that flanked the inner city.

Today, though, there were other storm clouds on the horizon, clouds that were not going to clear as easily as those in the sky he was looking at now.

In his early fifties, Matteo was trim, fit and youthful looking. His full head of jet-black hair, which he wore slicked back and parted in the middle, hadn't one strand of grey. He was an astute and successful crime boss who never indulged himself in excess; he seldom drank, and then only on rare, convivial occasions. His passions — besides power, fine food and women — were clothes and flowers. Matteo was an extremely well dressed man who always sported in his buttonhole a rose that he personally handpicked every morning from his prize-winning garden.

There were three Malatesta brothers. As well as Matteo, there was Frank, the middle sibling, and Beniamino, the youngest. The two older brothers had their mother's classical, noble Tuscan features — Roman nose, lustrous deep-set brown eyes — and their Sicilian father's olive skin, wide cheekbones and dimpled chin.

Matteo was in the process of changing the décor in his office. He had decided to get rid of a couple of pieces of baroque furniture and move them out to Benny's playroom. Benny was sitting cross-legged, carving his name into the side of his new chest of drawers. Matteo went over to have a look at Benny's handiwork.

'You spelt your name wrong, you imbecile,' Matteo snapped.

Benny spelt the letters out loud: 'B.I.N.N.I. Gee, Matteo I *fink* I left 'Y' out,' he said, wiping dribble from the corner of his mouth on the sleeve his jacket.

'You spelt it right on the side of the cupboard. Ah, what's the use? It doesn't matter. Fuck knows how many times I've told you to use your branding iron when you forget.'

Benny looked up at him. 'I love you, Matteo.'

Matteo gazed down at him with a placid smile. 'Love ya too, Benny boy. Love ya very much.' He patted Benny on the shoulder. 'Now get

Chapter 44 New Orleans, Louisiana, Friday 10 August

your ass over on the other side of the table and go and look at each letter on the cupboard one at a time.'

Matteo couldn't help loving all the crazy things Benny did, his quirky habits and peculiarities. Even the way he dressed. Today, Benny was wearing a three-piece, silver and black pinstripe suit that was two sizes too large and sneakers without socks.

Benny Malatesta, twenty-two years of age and known as Benny the Baby, looked nothing like his older brothers. His mother had contracted rubella while she was pregnant with him. He was a misshapen little imp of a man, with a flat nose and a chin that fell away from a jaw that jutted into his Adam's apple, which caused his mouth to permanently hang partially open. Unable to close his mouth, he dribbled incessantly and his thick tongue hung down over his wet, livid lips which, when he spoke, caused his words to come out strangulated. His dyed chemical orange hair stuck up in tufts and tangles. In his good eye, he had a perpetual look of lunacy and unpredictability; the heavy lid of his right eye drooped half shut.

Benny lived on a different plane than anyone else. Considered a cretin by most, he was a jewel as far as the family business was concerned. His very presence at an interrogation was enough to instill terror, even in the toughest man. In between bouts of taking hold of some unfortunate individual to do with as he liked — to butcher or burn alive — his pyromaniac tendency had to be vigilantly kept in check.

Matteo had poured a large fortune into support groups and charities that helped families with mentally challenged children. The checks were drawn against a trust fund set up for such purposes that didn't have his or the family's name on it. As a result, his philanthropic efforts were never acknowledged, nor were they ever meant to be. Matteo's donations were about looking after his own kind, a lesson he learnt from a few of his Irish friends in Boston.

Things had been going well for the Malatesta brothers. As far as the law was concerned, they were squeaky clean and their deceased father's riverboat ventures were still paying big dividends.

Ever since Balduccio had died peacefully in his sleep at the ripe old age of eighty-six, the family, under Matteo's leadership, had been slowly moving out of drug trafficking and prostitution and concentrating on running the three nineteenth-century paddle wheel steamboats: the *General Sherman*, the *Southern Bell* and the *Mark Twain*. The *General Sherman* was used to smuggle tobacco imported out of the Vuelta Abajo region of north-west Cuba where the world-famous Havana cigars are made. The *Southern Bell* ran legitimate tourist cruises out of Baton Rouge and Memphis. On the *Mark Twain* they ran illegal gambling. Underneath the *Mark Twain's* main dining room was a concealed gambling deck whose only access was through the engine room.

The Malatesta brothers were milking the high end of town. Judges, lawyers, clergymen, businessmen, politicians of all persuasions and from practically all over the country, people who had reputations to protect from their gambling habits who needed a discreet outlet, which left the brothers free to blackmail many a prominent citizen by threatening to hang out his dirty laundry in public. None of the exclusive *Mark Twain* patrons had any idea that the infamous Malatesta brothers were behind the gambling operation. It was purposely rumored that a couple of respectable casino barons from Las Vegas and Atlantic City were behind the operations.

The high-profile presence of Reverend Jonathon Duvall's nondenominational river boat Christian ministry, together with his obstinate stance and outspoken rhetoric on the devil's games, were calculated to deflect any unwanted attention, thereby giving the impression that the boat was the most unlikely floating vessel on the 4,300 mile watercourse to have anything to do with vice.

Chapter 44 *New Orleans, Louisiana, Friday 10 August*

Over time the Sunday service grew to be a major event. The Christian carnival had a twofold effect: first, it attracted people who were genuinely seeking religious expression; second, and most essentially, it attracted the stratospheric high-rolling closet gamblers. While the three-ring circus was playing out on deck, down below, in the bowels of the boat, Sundays were business as usual. The exclusive clientele – sporting and entertainment celebrities, merchant bankers, CEOs of some of the biggest multinational companies in the United States and overseas who needed the diversion on the boat to ease their worried minds of ever being caught out squandering portions of the billions of dollars they owned and controlled – for whom this day was set aside, knew that the minimum bet on all games and tables was twenty-five thousand dollars.

Matteo left Benny hacking away at the chest of drawers with his bowie knife, threw himself into an armchair and punched the rewind button of the VCR remote control.

'Matt, sounds serious,' Frank said as he strolled into the office. He had just flown in from Cuba where he had been organizing a shipment of tobacco. Matteo had briefed him on the phone about what was going down with the FBI and the IRS.

'Sit down and enjoy the show.'

Benny jumped up and bolted over to them, frantically waving his arms about, knife still in his hand.

'Easy. Easy, Benny,' Matteo yelped.

Frank stepped aside as Benny barreled past, then grabbed Benny from behind, spun him around, gripped his wrist and steered the knife safely away. The brothers fell into an embrace.

'I missed you, Frank. I missed you lots and lots, Frank. I thought you were never coming home.' Benny sobbed and buried his head in Frank's chest. Frank patted him on the back, then held him at arm's length and kissed him on the forehead.

'Missed you too, Benny boy. Two and a half days is a long time between hugs and cuddles.'

Frank was the quintessential cool-looking dude. His fingers were bedecked in chunky rings, he was deeply tanned and he wore the latest street wear. His thick mane of long, jet-black hair was plaited in Rastafarian locks. He had none of his father's or older brother's traits, of the kind required for amassing wealth and power. Frank yearned to find his vocation in life. From early boyhood, he had always wanted to carve out his own way in the world. He was always exploring new ways to unearth that special talent he was born with. For a few years in his early twenties, he thought he heard the calling to become a priest. Most recently, paleontology had captured his imagination. Frank wanted to cut loose, go live in Bolivia and immerse himself in the Inca way of life in some remote village high in the Andes.

Matteo pressed the play button of the remote control and clapped his hands. 'Okay, you two lovebirds, the show's starting. Plant your butts on the couch,' he growled.

Frank held out his hand and Benny handed over the knife, blade first. The pair sat down on the couch. Benny's concentration lapsed after about twenty seconds, he stood up and Frank handed him back the knife.

'Don't you leave, Frank,' Benny said, stumbling back to the table, slicing the air.

'No way, Benny boy,' Frank replied.

Using specialized high-tech surveillance equipment that Matteo had got hold of through a firm who had a government contract for research and development meant that most of the audio had been digitally enhanced and filtered of background noise. The tape, already edited down to the essentials, ran for sixteen minutes, ending with Uriah and Salvador leaving the Rio Grande Cantina.

'You've seen the show,' Matteo stated, his demeanor cool.

Chapter 44 New Orleans, Louisiana, Friday 10 August

Frank leant back in the sofa, loosened the buckles of his snakeskin boots and planted both feet on the coffee table. 'So, no one's heard of Mr. Paul South and no one can place him.'

'He's a damn mystery.'

'Must be a lone ranger or working for some minor outfit.'

'I'm gonna have to send someone up north to check out this Locust International firm he's supposed to be working for,' Matteo replied.

'Winning a straight five on the peckers. It's got to be a fix. Crack a rooster's beak before a fight and the next time he appears in public he's on a plate with a sideshow of roast potatoes.'

'I don't know, Frankie. One, two, the max in a round, I can buy that, but Holy Mother of Jesus, five winners? And on top of that he doesn't even collect the winnings.' Matteo grimaced. He loosened his tie and unbuttoned his shirt, picked up the remote control and rewound the tape to where Canaan was walking over to the cock cages.

'You see this, Frankie? Doctor Doolittle talking to the animals. I've seen livelier eyes on a corpse.'

'He's some piece of work. Looks like the kind of guy who gets things done.'

Matteo yanked at the handle of his leather recliner and leant back. 'I don't give a fuck whether he picks winners or losers, whether or not he collects his winnings. Right now he's on the *Mark Twain* for a three-week stay.'

Matteo rewound the tape, this time to when Uriah and Salvador were quietly conversing at the rear of the Rio Grande Cantina's dining room.

'That poor excuse for an FBI agent Stuyvesant is having wet dreams about Paul South, that somehow he's connected to us,' Matteo said. 'Hallucinating that we're responsible for the set up, so now he's poking his nose around the boat.'

'Maybe it's a double sting and the Bureau is setting us up to make a move on this Paul South,' said Frank.

'I wondered the same thing,' Matteo replied. 'But there's one problem with that scenario. Uriah is doing this on his own time. Besides, the local FBI boys should be in on the bird dogging, or at least they should know about it.'

'Coleridge has got his finger on the pulse of the Louisiana branch. Get him to rat fuck him? Force Uriah's hand. Then, we move in on Paul South and start asking some real questions.'

'No.' Matteo shook his head. 'We'd be playing into Uriah's hand if there's a tip-off. He'll know that he's got close to us. At the moment he's just wandering around. He's not 100 per cent, but all it takes is for us to make one wrong move and he could possibly put two and two together.'

'This South dude has fuck all to do with us, yet all his moves in the cantina and on the river point to us,' Frank exclaimed.

'That's about right.'

Frank pulled out a Havana from his shirt pocket, slipped off the cellophane wrapper and lit up. He took several deep puffs and blew out a blue-grey plume of smoke. Matteo looked at his brother with searching eyes. As their eyes locked, Frank grinned. He took another puff of his cigar and flicked the ash into a crystal ashtray on the coffee table.

'This is really eating you, Matteo,' Frank said.

'*Porco Dio*.' Matteo grimaced, got up and went to the fridge for a can of lemonade.

'Pour me a Strega on ice,' Frank said.

'Hey, dopey, you wanna drink?' Matteo shouted.

Benny looked up, startled. 'Yes please, Matteo. A strawberry thick shake and a cheeseburger and a toy.'

'This is a fuckin' office not a fast-food shit hole. Coke or lemonade. Make your choice, retard,' Matteo barked.

'I wanna a strawberry milkshake,' Benny whimpered as he hacked into

Chapter 44 New Orleans, Louisiana, Friday 10 August

the side of the chest of drawers.

'Don't you cry, Benny Boy. We'll go down to McDonald's and get them later.'

'You really mean it, Frank? I love you a lot.'

'I just cannot figure it out,' Frank said. 'This dude comes out of nowhere, gets celebrity status from the FBI and makes his nest on our riverboat.'

Matteo drank the contents of the can in one gulp, flung the empty can across the room, handed Frank his Strega and sat down.

Frank took a sip. 'What's South been up to on the boat?' he asked.

'Nothing out of the ordinary. Rides the boat to Baton Rouge, hangs out in bars on Perkins Street, goes back to the boat a half hour before it leaves for Orleans and goes to listen to Duvall's preaching most nights.'

'What about Uriah?'

'That fuck has been driving back and forth along I-10 like a yoyo.'

'Man, he must have a serious hard-on for this South,' said Frank and snuffed out his cigar.

'Stuyvesant's days are numbered. South checks out on the twenty-ninth. In the meantime we stay in the shadows and watch their every move.'

CHAPTER 45

CHILCHINBITO CANYON, NAVAJO RESERVATION, MONDAY 20 AUGUST

The screech of what sounded like a predatory bird seized Ishmael's and Rosasharn's attention. A chorus of yammering coyotes joined in as if on cue, and from the deepest reaches of the canyon a solo wolf's howl reverberated.

Old Smoke emerged from the shadows. On his head he wore a hollowed-out bear's head, the snout baring its upper teeth. His face and bare chest were streaked with vermilion. A heavy necklace made from wolf's teeth and shards of an eagle's beak hung around his neck. Tied around each arm he wore bands made from a human scalp matted with axle grease. He wore a girdle of wolves' tails, and leggings made from goatskin. He held a live eagle by the neck. Its wings were tied back and its curved talons bound with a leather strap. Its fierce eyes were rolling in its head. Its cries were almost deafening.

Rosasharn frowned, sat back on her heels and pressed her hands to her ears. Ishmael sat watching intently as the figure approached. Old Smoke stood in front of the fire, lifted the eagle above him and called out to his ancestors in his native tongue. He cupped one hand over the eagle's head and with his other twisted its body around and broke its neck. The bird jerked and its wings fanned out to the ground.

An eerie silence befell the entire canyon. Rosasharn and Ishmael remained immobilized, their attention riveted on Old Smoke.

Chapter 45 *Chilchinbito Canyon, Navajo Reservation, Monday 20 August*

Old Smoke picked up a kitchen knife that was next to the ice chest, muttered some barely audible words, cut loose the eagle's talons, and hacked into its breastplate. He pointed the knife at his own heart, threw back his head and shoulders, let out a whoop and slashed into the flesh just below his right nipple. He dropped the knife and prized both thumbs into the eagle's wound, stooped over it and allowed his own blood to drip into the bird's.

He bent down, scooped up a handful of warm ashes and smeared them over his breast, filling the wound and stemming the blood flow.

Taking hold of the bird's wings by the tips, he raised it above his head, imitated a flying motion and began to make squawking sounds.

As if coming out of a trance, Old Smoke looked at Ishmael and Rosasharn, motioning them to come forward. The blood and vermilion on his face and chest glistened in the firelight. Ishmael grabbed Rosasharn by the arm and crawled with her to the opposite side of the fire.

Old Smoke grinned at them; he leapt over the fire and waved the dead eagle in their faces, sprinkling them with blood. He made a motion for them to rise. At the very moment they stood up, as if on cue, the coyotes began their haunting howls.

Old Smoke began to chant and move in slow, intricate steps. Holding the eagle by its wings, he pointed both wings to a torch lying on the ground beside the ice box. Ishmael picked it up.

Old Smoke turned and started back towards the canyon, gracefully flapping the eagle's wings. Ishmael took Rosasharn by the hand and followed, keeping well behind him.

As they moved away from the light of the fire Ishmael flicked on the torch and followed the sound of Old Smoke's chanting while keeping well behind him. They made their way up the steep ascent. The path was rough and strewn with shale and rocks.

As they journeyed into the heart of the canyon Old Smoke's chanting grew louder, as did the coyotes' howling, guiding them to where the eagle was landing. At times, their howls seemed to be only a stone's throw away, at other times, more distant.

Rosasharn held Ishmael's hand. She felt as though she were being lifted above the rugged path, walking on air. She wished that they could go on like this and disappear in the wilderness, never to return to their complicated lives.

They came to a bend. Just up ahead the glow from a fire cast light on the path. Ishmael switched off the torch and headed towards the light. They squeezed through a narrow crevasse which opened into a natural amphitheater.

Old Smoke was standing, head bowed, in front of a stone altar crowned with a buffalo skull. Two trenches encircled the altar. The inner trench was filled with burning wood, the outer trench with water. The rock wall behind the altar was hollowed with niches. In each niche stood a ceramic doll painted and decorated according to the tribe it represented. At the base of each doll was a phial of dirt, a rock and a piece of dried fauna.

Old Smoke had surreptitiously ventured to each tribe's ancestral hunting ground and collected the three elements. Some of these tribes had been bitter enemies of the Hopi nation.

When he was just a boy, Old Smoke had had a vision of the buffalo returning, filling the great prairies, swelling in ever-increasing numbers. He foresaw that, at length, they would begin their stampede over all the European settlements, driving out all whom the Everywhere Spirit had not chosen to be the custodians of the land. As he grew into manhood, the vision had become clearer and his role in it was eventually revealed. In 1989, he began the contentious banding together of all the deceased leaders and chiefs of the Indian nations into the Supreme Spiritual Council. He believed that when every tribe in the Americas was represented in

Chapter 45 Chilchinbito Canyon, Navajo Reservation, Monday 20 August

the council, the buffalo would begin their return.

As Old Smoke turned to face Ishmael and Rosasharn, the coyotes' cries ceased. He motioned them to sit down on a smooth, petrified log on the left side of the altar.

Old Smoke laid the eagle down on the flat stone floor as gently as he would a newborn. He raised a tomahawk above his head, turned his face to the sky and yelled out a deep, guttural whoop. He chopped off the eagle's wings, talons and head, and threw the remainder into the fire. The acrid smell of burning feathers and flesh filled the air.

Old Smoke gingerly placed the head and talons in a leather pouch, then proceeded to pluck the feathers from the wings. With each feather he plucked, he looked up at the sky, summoned a great chief, pointed the feather to the appropriate tribal doll, and placed it upright around the altar.

When Old Smoke finally summoned the last member of the Supreme Spiritual Council, a cacophony of howls, and yelps exploded above them. Falling pieces of shale skidded down the sides of the walls.

The full moon was now directly above the altar, illuminating the sacred space in a yellow glow. Old Smoke threw the plucked bird wings into the fire and sat cross-legged in front of Ishmael and Rosasharn. The yammering above them softened into calm. Old Smoke gave Rosasharn a slight nod. She smiled faintly at him. Old Smoke sat as still as the rocks around him, he looked directly at Ishmael and addressed him firmly.

'The Supreme Spiritual Council calls you to speak from the heart. When I first met you I saw great trouble in your soul. I have spent many nights in preparation, waiting for you, and on this night I have summoned the members of this meeting on your behalf. To evoke the Everywhere Spirit's guidance, you must speak the truth. A blessing awaits you for your noble deed at the Warm Springs Bar and Grill in Tuba City. Feel free to speak whatever you feel.'

Old Smoke paused, spread his arms and then folded them tightly to his chest. Rosasharn, her chin cradled in her hands, divided her attention between Ishmael and Old Smoke.

Ishmael stared at the shadows of the eagle feathers dancing on the rock walls. The ceramic dolls' obsidian eyes glowed in the firelight. He turned to look at Rosasharn. She nodded encouragingly. How many times had he told a fictitious story about himself, stories going as far back as his time working for Raja? Too many times, and he was tired of it. His whole life had been one falsehood after another. He was determined to tell all, knowing he would be judged righteously; of that he was sure. Guilt and lack of acceptance of who he really was no longer terrified him.

Ishmael shifted uncomfortably on the log. He licked his lips and began to speak. As he sat rocking back and forth on the log, his thoughts turned inward. He gesticulated often while he told them his story from as far back as he could remember.

He described how he and Canaan had become soul mates, until death would bring them everlastingly together. He spoke of their time with the contraband dealers and of their imprisonment, and the why of their initial association with the Global Azad Front. And finally, Ishmael concluded with how Rosasharn had untangled the ancient biblical story of Abraham's two sons, speaking, too, of the divine presence that accompanied the telling of the truth.

From the moment Ishmael began to tell his story, Old Smoke, the human ear of the council, went into a trance. Rosasharn gazed at Ishmael, taking in everything, enthralled by this extraordinary story.

CHAPTER 46

BIKANER, RAJASTHAN, INDIA, JANUARY 1995

Two weeks after the earthquake that destroyed the Jack Folsom Mission School, Canaan and Ishmael became friends. At the time, Canaan was still wandering aimlessly through the rubble-strewn streets, lost in his obsession. Like a moth to a flame he gravitated to where fires still burnt out of control. He watched bodies being dragged out, envying the charred remains and cursing Reverend Jonathon Duvall who had barred his entry into the fire. At the end of each day he found himself back at the ruins of the Jack Folsom Mission School. Fragmented recollections of sitting in Duvall's judgment hall relentlessly assaulted him.

Adjacent to the mission school were the ruins of a row of single-story tenement houses. Grieving families lingered around them. Canaan's attention was drawn to a solitary wall, leaning so far that it looked as if it would have toppled had it not been for the support of a splintery, three-legged table propped against it. On top of it was a pile of groceries of some sort. Hunger pains gnawed at Canaan's stomach. He had not eaten for three days.

Just a few yards away from the wall was a boy kneeling on a slab of concrete with his forehead pressed down against it. From what Canaan could make out, he was groping for something underneath it.

Canaan trudged across the road, dodging strewn obstacles. 'Concrete worshipper!' he called out when within earshot.

Ishmael was momentarily startled from his deep sorrow. In recent days, the crushed bodies of Ishmael's father and baby sister had been pulled out from under the rubble. His mother had died from a massive loss of blood from a severed artery in her leg. The three had been buried in a mass grave outside the city.

'Concrete worshipper? Who is he?' he muttered. He raised himself up to see who had called out. As the two boys homed in on one another, their eyes locked, recognition flashing simultaneously.

Canaan stared at the pale-skinned, shirtless figure with the gravel-spangled forehead — Ishmael, the half-breed boy.

'You're Canaan, the one who saw his mother being burnt to death,' Ishmael said sympathetically. 'You tried to kill Reverend Duvall.'

'Yes, and I will try again someday, and succeed,' Canaan replied obstinately. 'Then I will follow my mother into the fire.'

Ishmael shuddered at the thought of being burnt alive. His eyes brimmed with tears that created furrows as they slid down his dusty cheeks.

'Do not dare cry for me,' Canaan snapped, his voice filled with contempt. 'And you are the one whose mother was a whore to some Englishman.'

'She was not. It is a lie. My grandmother was a servant of a man from England, who took advantage of her,' Ishmael said doggedly.

Duvall had singled Ishmael out during one of his sermons. Duvall said it was the fault of someone down the bloodline who was a whore to some fornicating son of a bitch Englishman.

Ishmael's grandmother was certainly not a whore, just a poor peasant girl who had attended laundry duties at the home of Lord Grimsby, an English diplomat in Bombay who had taken advantage of her. When the diplomat was confronted by her father and told that his daughter was carrying his child, the diplomat denied it and had the whole family exiled to Bikaner. The daughter who his grandmother gave birth to was Ishmael's mother. She did not inherit her Caucasian father's fair

Chapter 46 Bikaner, Rajasthan, India, January 1995

complexion; rather, they were passed on to her firstborn son, Ishmael. It was he who was born with the fair skin and endowed with a mop of curly, light-brown hair and vivid green eyes.

'I am not crying for you or your ...' Ishmael hesitated, and then said, 'mother.'

'Make sure you do not, concrete worshipper. Anyway, what do I care who used your grandmother for sex?' Canaan retorted.

'Do not call me concrete worshipper. My name is Ishmael Esrom,' he said proudly.

'Give me some of your food,' Canaan demanded.

Ishmael looked over at the table. On it was a loaf of bread that was being plundered by a squadron of flies, and two tins of baked beans. He had stood in line for three hours early that morning to get it, starting before sunrise.

'Help me move this block of concrete and I will share my food with you.'

'What is it that you are looking for?' Canaan asked.

Ishmael hesitated for a moment, trying to decide whether to tell Canaan about the tin box. He had been desperately sifting through the rubble, looking for the box in which his father kept all their savings, before the bulldozers came and cleared everything away. They had already started on this side of the road.

As if reading his mind Canaan said, 'Whatever valuable thing is under there, I am not interested.'

'Help me if you want food,' Ishmael demanded, trying to hide his surprise at Canaan's inference.

Without further ado Canaan looked around, spotted a wooden beam, picked it up and jammed one end under the concrete slab and levered it up.

Ishmael bent down, peered underneath and pulled out a flattened leather valise. 'It's my mother's!' he cried, flipping it open. The sight of his mother's neatly pressed clothes was too much for him. Ishmael began to wail and moan.

Canaan cringed at Ishmael's display of grief. He eased the pressure off the end of the beam and let the concrete slab drop back to its resting place.

'Join her, if you miss her so much,' Canaan sneered.

Ishmael stared at Canaan through watery eyes for a few moments. 'Holy cows!' Ishmael cried. 'I hate them all. Now the cow lives and my mother is dead, she is dead. She could have been alive. I hate the holy sacred cow, hate them ...' he ranted. Picking up whatever he could lay his hands on — wood, bricks, stones — he hurled them in all directions.

'I do not understand!' Canaan called out to him as he dodged the deadly projectiles. 'The cow lives and your mother is dead?'

Ishmael caught his breath. His voice was low and raspy as he struggled to produce the words. Gesticulating with a piece of wood in one hand, he began to tell his story to Canaan.

'Mother sent me to the market. I was coming back. I felt a little shaking. The shaking was getting bigger. People started running out of the houses and shops into the street yelling that Indra has descended from heaven riding on his giant white elephant, that he is very angry and has come to squash Vrtra the evil dragon. I could feel the footsteps of the great giant elephant getting closer. His feet were making the ground jump up and down. Then it was like my legs and feet were running down a hill, but I was not on a hill. Then I was at the bottom of the hill that I was not on, trying to run up. I was felled to the ground. I rolled and rolled. Then it stopped. All I could think of was my family. I ran back — my legs and feet were really running now — as fast as I could. I kept running. They were over there, Mama and Papa and my baby sister in the kitchen.'

Chapter 46 *Bikaner, Rajasthan, India, January 1995*

He pointed a stick to a pile of tangled beams of iron and wood.

'I heard Mother crying for help. Her leg was stuck, and she was bleeding. I went to find help and found three men in the middle of the road. Two of them had blood all over their clothes. One had a towel wrapped around his head, soaked in blood. I begged them to come and help my mother. They said they would come. Then there was a holy cow, fallen into a big crack in the ground. The men stopped to help the holy cow. When they got it out, they worshipped it and prayed to it. One of the men said my mother would be blessed because it was thanks to her that they were brought down this road. When they finished worshipping the cow they came here, but it was too late. Mother was dead, my father and baby sister were all dead. The men had to save the cow. The holy cow was more important. I hate them ...' Ishmael threw the stick. Canaan ducked as it sailed past his head.

Canaan marveled at what he had heard.

'Stop. Stop, calm down!' Canaan shouted. 'Today is the day of revenge.'

'What? Against Indra's giant elephant for shaking the earth and killing my family?' Ishmael retorted as he tossed a rock and yet another.

Canaan waited patiently until Ishmael had spent all his frustration. Ishmael dropped to his knees and pored over his mother's clothes, holding them close to his cheeks, drying his eyes on them.

'Today we will find that cow that has taken the place of your mother in this world and we will kill it,' Canaan said with verve.

Ishmael's face came alive. 'Kill the cow. Kill the cow. Yes, that's what I will do.'

'Yes, we will find it and kill it,' they said in unison.

They looked furtively at each other. A spark of kinship, of fraternity ignited between the two boys.

'I will burn it alive and watch it run through the streets like a fireball,' Canaan said feverishly.

'No, no. I must be the one to kill it,' Ishmael protested.

Canaan frowned. 'Let us eat first, and then we will look for the cow,' he said. 'Do you remember what it looked like?'

'It was a Brahman cow, yes, a Brahman,' Ishmael replied.

'They are all Brahmans,' Canaan said and rolled his eyes. 'Was it hurt? Did it have a broken leg? Surely you must remember. Think, think.'

Ishmael looked vacantly at Canaan.

'Was it a bull, a cow? Was it old or young? Did it have any black or grey patches …?' Canaan rattled on, despairing at seeing the fire slowly go out in Ishmael's eyes.

'I cannot remember.' Ishmael sighed deeply.

'It does not matter. I will…' Canaan corrected himself, 'You will kill the first one we find.'

'Yes, it doesn't matter which cow. I hate all cows,' Ishmael said eagerly. 'How will we kill it?'

'We need a knife because we must stab it between the ribs to reach the heart,' said Canaan. 'Have you a knife? It has to be long and pointy. Have you got a tin can? I will steal some petrol from a car.'

'There are lots of tin cans around, but a long knife …' Ishmael pointed to a wooden beam. 'Look, there is an axe over there.'

'If that is all you have then you can beat its brains out until your heart is content.'

'Beat its brains out,' parroted Ishmael.

'We have all we need. Come now, let us eat, then we will avenge your mother's death.' Canaan punched the air.

After their meal, Ishmael, with the axe slung over his shoulder, and Canaan, carrying a rusty tin can and a coil of plastic hose, set out to hunt for a sacred cow. They had gotten no further than a few hundred yards down the road when Ishmael said to Canaan, 'Wait,' and ran back to hide his mother's valise and to grab his cigarette lighter.

Chapter 46 *Bikaner, Rajasthan, India, January 1995*

Although Canaan was still smarting over agreeing to let Ishmael kill the cow, he continued fueling Ishmael with a torrent of victory speeches and visions of the great happiness that would follow once he had sunk the axe deep into the cow's skull.

The frequent sightings of the Hindu gods and goddesses who had chosen to live and move in the image and likeness of cows — blocking streets, sheltering at railway stations, loitering under storefront canopies and leisurely going about their sacred business — were nowhere to be seen, if for no other reason than none of these structures they sheltered in were recognizable, all of them having been flattened in the earthquake. Of those incarnated deities that had survived the earthquake, most had been herded out of the city to a tract of land that was free of rubble. Some of them had been transported there on the backs of flatbed trucks by their devout worshippers. It was one of these trucks that the boys tramped behind as it slowly maneuvered through the rubble-littered roads.

An emaciated old man with black, tissue-like skin sat on the cabin roof piping out sacred tunes on his flute, soothing the brindle cow that peered through the wooden slats. When the old engine spluttered and coughed, unable to surmount another obstacle on the road, the men got out and pushed and pulled the royal float.

'Oh no, they're turning back again,' sighed Ishmael, running his thumb over the edge of the axe.

'Let us continue down this road. We do not have to worry about obstacles, unlike those fools,' Canaan said. 'You see those low lying hills?' Canaan pointed. 'We will head for them.'

'There are some green patches there,' Ishmael said, 'I know there are a few wells, too. It has to be where they are taking the brindle cow. We might find the exact one that was more important than my mother,' Ishmael said wistfully.

'I think you are right. Just to be sure, I will go and ask those fools.' Canaan left his tin can and plastic hose with Ishmael. A few minutes later, he was back at Ishmael's side.

'What did they say?' Ishmael asked.

'They are heading for those hills.'

'Do they suspect what we are up to? That old man on the roof is giving us the evil eye.'

'Maybe he is angry that we did not offer help when they stopped to clear the road,' Canaan replied. He picked up his tin can and hose, and they set off towards the hills.

By ten that evening, the pair had homed in on a bull that had ambled away to a hill quite a distance from where the rest of Vishnu's holy herd was congregated. The bull was lying under a mesquite tree, chewing cud. A half moon, hanging over the horizon, bathed the bull's grey hide in a fluorescent tinge.

Canaan was shrouded in a cloak of envy as he watched Ishmael approach his nemesis. In one hand, Canaan held the tin can full of petrol he had siphoned out of a car wreck. In the other, he held Ishmael's lighter, flicking it rhythmically as he waited for his cue to light up the night sky.

Ishmael crept closer to the unsuspecting animal, clenching the axe handle with both hands. The axe itself had taken on a life of its own, infused with the vengeance that coursed through Ishmael's veins. The bull craned its large neck around and gazed at the boy slowly bearing down on him. Ishmael moved closer and stooped over the prostrate bull, his heart hammering. The bull turned its head away from him. With a cruel smile, Ishmael hefted the axe high and centered the back of the cow's head in his line of sight. The edge of the axe shimmered in the moonlight.

Then the axe head wavered. Ishmael's heart fluttered and missed

Chapter 46 *Bikaner, Rajasthan, India, January 1995*

a beat as he recalled the last words his mother had spoken. 'They are the gods' likeness, holy things. They must live, too. If I should die, remember me whenever you see one, and be kind.'

Ishmael froze. He repeated his mother's dying words over and over and, as he did, the lust for revenge drained out of him. He dropped the axe and fell down on his knees, hugged the bull around the neck and started weeping. The bull nudged him and licked the side of his head.

Canaan rushed up to him. 'You do not have to love it before you kill it,' he said sarcastically. 'Get up, swing that axe, sink it deep and kill the bull now. If you cannot, say so and I will do it my way,' he said in one breath.

The bull gazed at Canaan and bellowed a deep-throated moan. Canaan unscrewed the lid of the can of petrol.

'Quick, get out of the way.' Canaan raced around the animal, splashing out a circle of petrol. Ishmael watched, complacent. The bull winced at the petrol vapors.

'You will have to burn me with it. I don't care if I die,' Ishmael sobbed. All of Canaan's talk of revenge and the sweet taste of it had soured in his stomach. He felt the bile rise.

'You really mean that you want to be burnt alive? To die? Oh, how I wish I could join you,' Canaan said, a mixture of joy and sorrow in his voice. 'It is in honor of my mother that I am going to do this. We will meet again. Wait for me on the other side of this life, but first I must kill Duvall. Kill Duvall first then I will follow.' Canaan shook his fist in the air.

'Canaan, I am so sorry. I was about to swing the axe and ...' Ishmael whimpered. 'I just want to die ...'

'No. No, do not be sorry. This is the way it was meant to be. I am happy for you, so happy. You have chosen the right path. May you be blessed, Ishmael.' He felt the cloak of envy wrapping itself even more tightly around him. He continued pouring the petrol. I must not be jealous, Canaan thought. I am honored, yes, honored, to perform this great deed.

'We need wood, lots of wood, anything that will burn.' Canaan placed the tin can down and started ripping branches from the mesquite tree. 'These are too green,' he cursed. 'We need a chain and oil, and naked girls.' Canaan was ecstatic, knowing that this was a foretaste of that great joyful day when he would kill Duvall.

'No, I do not want to wait for oil, and chains and naked girls. Do it now, light the fire, beat my brains out with the axe.' Ishmael spoke in a low voice. 'I was about to swing the axe when I heard my mother's voice ...'

Canaan froze. The words 'mother's voice' tolled in his head.

'What do you mean?' Canaan hissed. He snapped a branch and threw it down. Ishmael nuzzled his head into the bull's flank, breathed in the oily dander and hugged the beast tightly.

'Please,' he moaned, 'there is nothing left for me in this world.'

'Tell me about your mother's voice,' Canaan pleaded.

'Light the fire. I don't want to live another moment,' Ishmael lamented.

'Tell me what your mother's voice said to you,' Canaan demanded. 'I must know before I go any further.'

'Then will you light the fire?'

'Yes.'

'All right.' Ishmael paused and straightened himself up. 'I remembered that I ran back to tell my mother that after the cow was saved, the three men would come to help her. She said, "They are the gods' likeness, they are a holy thing. They must live too. If I should die, remember me whenever you see one and be kind".'

Canaan groaned and gave the can a violent kick, showering them all in petrol. He quickly composed himself, placed his hand on Ishmael's shoulder while the other clasped the bull's horn. The bull brought up some cud and chewed.

Chapter 46 *Bikaner, Rajasthan, India, January 1995*

'Ishmael, you must obey your mother's voice and from now on you are never to hate a cow. Just as I am bound by my promise to my mother, you are bound to your mother's last wish. You must love the beast like it is your own mother,' he said somberly, and squeezed Ishmael's shoulder.

Without another word Canaan trudged off, deep in thought. What business was it of his to aid the concrete worshipper to satisfy his lust for revenge, even worse to help him disobey his dying mother's last command? He was mortified that he had been prepared to help Ishmael disobey his dying mother and her last wish. How could he ever face his own mother in the next world with such a blot on his soul?

In the distance, Ishmael heard the sacred flute melody that he had heard hours before. The bull twitched its ears as it heard the call of the flute summoning him back to Vishnu's holy herd. It raised its bulk and ambled off to rejoin the holy herd.

Ishmael slumped face down onto the ground and shivered as a rush of cold air and petrol vapors enveloped him. He envied Canaan. While he, Ishmael, had to bear the burden of life, Canaan had to bear the deprivation of death.

Ishmael picked himself off the ground and made his way back to the place he had so recently called home. He lit a fire and propped himself against the last remaining wall of his house, pored over his mother's clothes and cursed the holy beast that was more important than his mother. He thrust his bare back against the wall, willing it to fall on him, straining, his heels digging into the ground until he could feel the wall totter and sway ever so slightly. When he couldn't push any longer, he held his mother's clothes against his face and cried into them.

All that night, Canaan wandered aimlessly through the ravaged city, struggling with mixed feelings about the concrete worshipper, emotions that felt alien to him. They made him feel guilty that someone other than his dear, beloved mother was beginning to occupy his thoughts. Someone who might fill the void in his soul.

On his way back from the food shelter early the next morning, carrying his daily ration of one loaf of bread and two tins of baked beans, Ishmael encountered Canaan. There ensued a heated discussion between the pair and before too long, like a truant officer, Canaan led Ishmael by the hand back to the hill they had been on the night before.

By mid-morning, Canaan and Ishmael were sitting under the mesquite tree. A dozen cows were grazing on the sparse tufts of grass that grew on the hill. One of them was the bull they had planned to kill. The axe was still on the ground where Ishmael had dropped it. The vapor of petrol fumes hung faintly in the air.

'Do I have to?' Ishmael whimpered. He picked up a broken branch and started stripping leaves off it.

'You are doing this for your dear mother. You must do what she said to you before she died,' Canaan insisted.

'She didn't say anything about having to feed every dumb cow I see.'

'It is the principle of the matter.' Canaan broke off a piece of bread and ate it.

Ishmael stared fixedly at the axe. 'How about we go and get some more petrol and you burn one of them alive?'

For a fraction of a second Canaan's eyes lit up. 'No. No. No. I have said it a thousand times.'

'That small one over there for the life of my mother.' Ishmael pointed with the branch to a calf suckling on its mother's udder. 'After I beat its brains out then I will be kind all the time I promise.'

'I will not be part of it.' Canaan shook his head fiercely.

'I do not need you. I will kill the cow by myself,' Ishmael said belligerently. 'You put the idea in my head about getting revenge.'

'No, I did not...' Canaan protested.

Chapter 46 *Bikaner, Rajasthan, India, January 1995*

'Yes you did. All that talk when we followed the truck, right up to the minute I was going to crack its skull, of how much happier I was going to be.' Ishmael paused for a few moments, then said, 'My mother's voice came to me when I was about to swing the axe. If it was not for you, I would not have remembered.'

'Yes, you are correct. I did make you remember. I now accept responsibility. I am pleased that my misguided encouragement made you remember your duty to your mother.' He tore off a hunk of bread, got up, looked down on Ishmael and said, 'Mothers always know what is best.' He strolled off.

'Where are you going? Please stay. If you will be my friend, I will not do it.'

Ishmael's need of a friend overrode his craving for revenge. Not just any friend, though he was well acquainted with other boys. Some of them, who had survived the earthquake and had lost loved ones too, had been his friends. They had shared their stories during the long hours they had stood in the food line. However, being a half-breed, he sensed their feeling of superiority and the death of his family as being a just punishment for his grandmother's whoredom.

Canaan was like no other person Ishmael had ever known. Canaan had an aura about him that seemed to subjugate his grief and made his, Ishmael's, burden seem light. He felt it that morning when Canaan confronted him. He was feeling it now.

Canaan stopped in his tracks, faced Ishmael and said, 'I do not need friends.' He shoved a piece of bread in his mouth.

'I will not honour my mother's command. She is dead. Being kind to a cow is never going to bring back my mother. I hate them and always will, until I die.' He threw the branch towards a cow that had wandered close to them. 'You put the idea in my head. I was going to do this because of you, but I will not do it if you'll be my friend. Please would you be my friend?' Ishmael moaned.

Canaan spat the bread out of his mouth. 'Be my friend and you will not do it. That is blackmail. You are again making me responsible for not fulfilling the will of your mother. I told you I will not be responsible!' Canaan shouted.

Ishmael jumped up and grabbed the axe. 'I *will* do it. You watch me.'

Canaan casually strolled back to where Ishmael was standing. Ishmael took a step backwards. Their eyes locked. 'Why won't you admit you need a friend as much as I do? I can see longing for friendship in your eyes,' Ishmael said softly.

Canaan avoided Ishmael's gaze. 'I do not need a friend,' he sneered.

Ishmael looked at him quizzically. 'Is it because you are scared that it would tie you to this world?' Canaan stooped down, scooped up a handful of dirt and sifted it through splayed fingers. He stood up and looked directly into Ishmael's eyes, searching his face for any sign of trickery. 'Will you die with me when I find and kill Duvall?'

Ishmael gazed at the axe in his hands, then over towards the cows. 'Yes, I will,' he said resolutely. Ishmael threw down the axe, got on his haunches, plucked a few tufts of grass and trudged over to the nearest cow to feed it.

Canaan watched Ishmael do his duty. Underneath the bitterness, he felt a sense of pride in what he had done for Ishmael's mother. On the subject of friendship, he decided then and there that he would just use the concrete worshipper until he worked out a way to get to Duvall.

Ishmael and Canaan spent the following days sifting through the rubble of Ishmael's home, searching for the tin of money. On the morning of the third day, the demolition and cleanup crews with their heavy earthmoving equipment reached the row of ruined tenements. The boys had failed to find the tin box.

Chapter 46 *Bikaner, Rajasthan, India, January 1995*

The area was cordoned off, and those who still believed they could make a life among the ruins were ordered to leave. Some took what little of their chattels they were able to salvage. All of them took with them lots of painful memories.

Canaan and Ishmael stood on the other side of the road. A few kitchen utensils and his mother's valise were all that Ishmael took away from the ruins.

Ishmael stared fixedly at the bulldozer, hungrily ladling the rubble and dumping it into a tip truck whose exhaust billowed thick, black, oily smoke. The bulldozer's iron-studded treads pulverized wood, concrete and glass.

Ishmael's heart sank as the bulldozer charged at the last remaining wall of the structure he had called home. Red floral wallpaper, spattered with oil and scuff marks, held the cracked bricks and crumbling mortar together. The three-legged kitchen table that not so long ago had four legs. If only Indra riding on his giant white elephant had delayed his coming at least until he had returned home, he could have died with his family. Before the bulldozer reached the wall, it toppled over and crushed the table.

Ishmael wiped his teary eyes on the back of his hand and turned to Canaan, whose eyes were fixed on the oily black smoke pumping from the bulldozer's exhaust, focused inward and beholding a scene that Ishmael could only imagine. Then, as if awakening to reality, Canaan turned his attention to the ruins of the mission school.

'Do you think they will rebuild the mission school?'

'I heard some talk in the food lines. About how they will have to find another place for the school,' replied Ishmael.

'Whatever they do, surely Duvall will be back,' said Canaan, a glimmer of hope sparkling in his eyes.

By early afternoon, the cleanup crews had moved on. Ishmael tramped up and down the corrugated furrows left by the bulldozer, lamenting over the place he had called home. He kicked over clods of dirt, lifting flattened objects with the toe of his sandal, still hopeful of finding the tin of money. Canaan picked up a stone and threw it over to where Ishmael was rummaging. Ishmael looked at him. Canaan gave him a wave and walked off with an impassive expression.

'Where are you going?' Ishmael called out.

'To find out if the mission school is going to come back!' Canaan called out.

'How are you going to do that?'

Canaan shrugged.

'I will get the food and find a place to stay while you find out if the mission school is going to be rebuilt.'

Canaan paused and considered Ishmael's offer, then nodded his agreement.

Five months after the earthquake, it was officially announced that the Jack Folsom Mission School was not going to be rebuilt and that the land it once stood on was for sale. Ishmael read the article aloud to Canaan, who lay prostrate on a piece of carpet underlay that he used for a mattress, his eyes fixed on the word 'fragile' that was stenciled in red ink across the cardboard ceiling. That which had kept him going all these months was not going to be. Duvall was not coming back. Ishmael had not seen Canaan so withdrawn. He hadn't touched the boiled cabbage cooked on a communal butane burner.

Ishmael folded the paper and placed it neatly next to his mother's valise. 'If Duvall is never going to come back to India,' Ishmael said, 'we then have to go to America and kill him there.'

Canaan snapped out of his reverie. 'Yes!' he exclaimed. 'That's what I'll do.'

Chapter 46 *Bikaner, Rajasthan, India, January 1995*

'America is a long way over the ocean. Somewhere on the other side of the world,' Ishmael said. He drew his knees to his chest and picked at an infected scab on his foot.

CHAPTER 47

CHILCHINBITO CANYON, NAVAJO RESERVATION, MONDAY 20 AUGUST

When Ishmael finally had told all, Old Smoke opened his eyes. His face was expressionless. He rose from the ground, faced the altar and, in his native tongue, sang a song of praise. When he had finished, he said in a loud voice, 'The great fathers of the Indian nations have heard the story and have now passed judgment.'

Ishmael was buoyed by the unburdening of all the radical lies. He saw more clearly that truth, though harder to endure than hiding behind a veil of lies, was infinitely liberating.

'The land of your enemy has shown you a different path. It is the way of the Earth that drinks the blood of all the living. All must go back to it,' said Old Smoke with great gravity.

Old Smoke got down on his haunches, scooped up handfuls of ashes and sifted them through his fingers. The third handful revealed a large June beetle. He dusted its green wing case and then spoke to it.

'Great and Everywhere Spirit, you have heard all that has been said. You were present at Big Chino Wash Verde River, showing your glory to the two witnesses, rebuking the error of human interpretation of your will, manifesting the Truth to the heart and freeing the soul. While still an enemy of the peoples of this land, this man showed reverence to the great leaders of the Indian nations of days long past, whose images were being dishonored in Tuba City. He spoke out against such disrespect.'

Chapter 47 *Chilchinbito Canyon, Navajo Reservation, Monday 20 August*

Old Smoke paused, cupped the beetle in his hand and held it to his ear, listening. He nodded his head a few times, grunted, and placed the beetle on the ground. It scurried away, burying itself in the ash.

Old Smoke threw his head back and lifted his arms. 'Great and Everywhere Spirit we offer you praise and thanksgiving for visiting the human beings!' he shouted.

Old Smoke motioned to Ishmael to speak to the council feathers. Rosasharn touched him on the small of his back as he stood.

'This land is the land of the free, I have learnt,' Ishmael began solemnly. 'The people who think they are in power are of no consequence. I have been judged by the original custodians, for which I am now and will be always grateful. Your people recognize the land as their God-given heritage. It is still yours and remains forever so, though others may inhabit it by force and kill you for it, the *Earth* will not acknowledge them. This is also true for the sacred brotherhood and sisterhood that believe they have been dispossessed. In truth, their God-given heritage forever remains inviolate and sacred.'

He stared into the fire and was rushed back in time. Sudden terrors burnt his brain as the last remnants of Canaan's influence came welling up inside him. Images of his mother's valise burning, the killing of the holy cow, the pact the pair had made under the mesquite tree churned around in his head. He dropped to the ground, held his head between his hands and groaned.

Rosasharn ached to grab hold of Ishmael. Her eyes shot up to Old Smoke. She looked at him pleadingly.

Old Smoke looked sternly at him and spoke in a loud voice. 'The Spiritual Council has pardoned you. But it has not relieved you of your responsibility. A debt has to be paid and now you have the means to pay it.'

Ishmael squirmed and reeled.

It took all of Rosasharn's strength not to fall upon him and offer comfort. She knew this was the way it must be for him. The struggle with oneself is the battle of all battles: holy war.

Old Smoke revelled over the confused and tormented Ishmael, he smiled cruelly down on him and made deep guttural sounds of battle cries, jumped up and down on the spot, threw his arms into the air and yelled out war whoops.

Ishmael got up and staggered out of the alcove, screaming at Canaan to get out of his head. Rosasharn jumped up and raced after him. Old Smoke leapt in front of her and grabbed her by the wrist.

'Please,' she begged Old Smoke, 'let me go.'

'The evil lie must be challenged from within. He has awakened to the duty only he can fulfil. He has received the council's blessing. Now, like all true warriors, he must go to battle.'

Rosasharn slumped onto the stony ground and drew her knees to her chest and wept.

Old Smoke proceeded to gather the eagle feathers and prepare for the end of the meeting. With the utmost care he placed the feathers in a leather pouch, speaking the name of the appropriate council member and pointing to the corresponding ceramic doll before putting each feather away. When the last feather was in the pouch, he extinguished the fire and marched back to the farm. The moon, still high above the canyon, illuminated the path.

Rosasharn followed Old Smoke, her eyes darting in all directions, trying to see Ishmael.

The stirring of horses in the corral caught Rosasharn's attention. She went over and leaned on a fence paling. The buckskin mare trotted over and nuzzled her shoulder, comforting her a little. Old Smoke went over to the woodpile, gathered an armful of wood and rekindled the fire.

'Let's go find him!' Rosasharn called out to Old Smoke. 'He might be

Chapter 47 *Chilchinbito Canyon, Navajo Reservation, Monday 20 August*

lying at the bottom of a ravine, hurt.'

'Accidents are the way of the weak. The Everywhere Spirit will not give him an easy way out,' Old Smoke replied as he positioned the logs under the grate.

Rosasharn sighed, patted the horse on the nose and went over to the fire.

Old Smoke opened the ice chest and grabbed a rattlesnake out of it. With his knife he made two slits under the head, pried his thumb and index finger into the cut and rolled the skin off like a stocking, repeating the procedure with the other snake, and then dropped them onto the hotplate.

Rosasharn stared at the long, slippery coils sizzling on the hotplate.

'That one looks like it's swallowed something big.' She pointed to the rattler that Old Smoke was skinning.

'Baby rabbit.' Old Smoke divided the snake in two, squeezed out a half-digested carcass and threw it into the fire.

Rosasharn grimaced and turned away.

'He is preparing himself to die,' Old Smoke said.

'No!' Rosasharn snapped.

'Yes, I am.'

Rosasharn craned her head and saw Ishmael standing behind her. She jumped up and fell into his arms. 'I don't understand. You're not a terrorist anymore.'

Ishmael held her at arm's length, gazed into her eyes and said, 'There are three members of the cell that have to be stopped. I am going to be a terrorist in the midst of my own people. You see, it would be better for us all to die than be captured by the authorities.'

'You have to live. I want you to live. There must be another way,' Rosasharn cried. 'Just give yourself up, let the authorities stop the others ...'

Ishmael placed his finger to her lips. She took hold of his hand and held it to her cheek.

'It was the purpose of the Spiritual Council meeting to bring out the evil buried in your soul. Evil's heel came crashing down on you to quench the light of good in your soul. This struggle will continue until final victory. Be strong.'

Looking at Old Smoke through tear-filled eyes, he said, 'Thank you, thank you, Old Smoke. Yes. I will be strong.'

Rosasharn and Ishmael sat silently, their faces lit by the flickering campfire. The rattlesnakes were almost cooked. Old Smoke garnished them with spices and herbs and mumbled a blessing over the meal.

'I have to get to Nashville before the other two members of the cell leave for Baton Rouge. I will kill them and then go and meet Canaan. There will be no shedding of innocent blood, I swear,' he said forcefully, clenching his teeth. 'I'll write down names, addresses of sleeper cells, names of those who supply us with weapons. Everything I know about the Azad Front. Once the authorities have this information, they will have no need of us alive.'

'Surely if you offer them such a goldmine of information you could cut a deal with Homeland Security,' Rosasharn said. 'Or you could get on a plane, fly somewhere else and then inform Homeland.'

Old Smoke narrowed his eyes. 'Cutting a deal and running is the coward's way.'

Rosasharn stared unblinking at Ishmael.

Ishmael, seeing the anguish in her face said, 'I wish that you had not found me. It has made it harder for me.'

Rosasharn moaned. 'I had to find you. I know it's going to be much harder for you and for that I am truly sorry.' She began to weep quietly.

Old Smoke diced up the rattlesnake into bite-size pieces, divided the portions onto metal plates and motioned them to eat.

Chapter 47 Chilchinbito Canyon, Navajo Reservation, Monday 20 August

'Thank you, but I couldn't eat anything at the moment,' Rosasharn said, sniffling.

'This is a sacred meal,' Old Smoke said as he handed her a plate. 'We must be one at this meal. It is the custom that we eat together after a meeting of the Supreme Spiritual Council.'

Wiping her eyes on her sleeve, Rosasharn accepted the plate. With a knife and fork she delicately separated the meat from the bones and popped a small portion into her mouth, surprised to find that it tasted a little like chicken.

'Your appreciation of the Indian heritage is respected and acknowledged. You will be welcomed into the burial ground in the sky,' said Old Smoke. He spat out a mouthful of bones and said to Rosasharn, 'The Spiritual Council will guide him. And we two still have an important part to play.'

Rosasharn took a deep breath and replied sadly, 'I am only thinking of myself and my loss, of not having the opportunity to get to know you, Ishmael.'

Ishmael stared into the burning embers, not wanting to make eye contact with her.

When the meal was finished, Old Smoke addressed them.

'Both of you take the trailer. Become one. I must continue my communion with the council alone until sunrise.'

Rosasharn looked straight at Ishmael. She untied her hair, shook it loose, stood up and walked around the campfire to where Ishmael sat and held out her hand to him. Ishmael hesitated for a moment. He stared at Old Smoke with a questioning look in his eyes.

'Go with her, my son, and do not be ashamed of your feeling towards this woman.'

Ishmael, filled with wonder, looked up at her. He took Rosasharn's hand and she led him to the trailer.

Ishmael paused for a moment in front of the trailer door and then pulled it open. Rosasharn jumped back in fright as a rooster darted out of the trailer, crowing and flapping its wings. She leant up against the trailer's side, took a deep breath and let it out slowly. Ishmael held open the door. Rosasharn brushed her hair back from her eyes and stepped into the trailer. She fumbled for a light switch, found it and flicked it on. A low-wattage globe illuminated the musty, cluttered trailer.

With her back to Ishmael, Rosasharn began to unbutton her dress. She wriggled out of it, undid her bra and let her clothes drop to the floor.

Ishmael stood outside the door, staring at her. He stepped up behind her and placed his hands on her hips and eased his fingers under the elastic of her panties. Rosasharn pressed herself against him. He buried his face in her hair and breathed in the smell of her. She reached up, took hold of his head and dug her fingers into the back of his neck.

'Please, just hold me,' Rosasharn whispered in his ear. Ishmael felt all his reserve melt away and allowed himself to want her. He spun her around and looked into her face and kissed her damp eyes, then he kissed her softly on the lips.

Rosasharn maneuvered Ishmael over to the ragged mattress that lay on the floor at the far end of the trailer. They fell onto it.

CHAPTER 48

CHILCHINBITO CANYON, NAVAJO RESERVATION, TUESDAY 21 AUGUST

Rosasharn lay next to Ishmael, drifting in and out of sleep. Ishmael had been awake all night. He had promised Rosasharn he would not leave without saying goodbye. At quarter to five, unable to tolerate waiting for the inevitable any longer, Ishmael leaned over Rosasharn and lightly kissed her on her lips as she slept, and rolled off the mattress.

Stepping out of the trailer he saw Old Smoke, sitting cross-legged in front of the campfire scraping pelts with an ax head, his heavy brow creased in deep thought.

A pot of coffee stood on a hotplate, steam puffing from its spout. He had changed out of his ceremonial clothes into blue jeans and a shirt.

'Time for you to go, my son,' said Old Smoke as Ishmael approached.

'I am honoured to be a son of your people on whose land I walk,' Ishmael replied. He picked up a tin cup and poured himself a cup of coffee.

'Your spirit flows from the same source.'

Old Smoke opened the leather pouch next to him, pulled out an eagle feather and handed it to Ishmael.

'I cannot accept this. It is a hallowed thing.'

'When you reach the other side, the thoughts of the council member it represents will greet you. It is the way and there can be no refusal.'

Ishmael took the feather.

'If, by the grace of the Everywhere Spirit, you make it through and I am nowhere to be found, you must take the feather to the top of Pastora Peak. Follow Highway 160 to Mexican Creek, then go up on foot. When you reach the top, wait until you see three eagles circling above you, then, when the wind blows, release the feather.'

Ishmael brushed the feather against his cheek. For just a brief moment, he experienced the sensation of flight. 'If my time on this land is extended I will place the feather back in the sky.'

Old Smoke rose, placed his hands on the younger man's shoulders and looked deeply into his eyes. Ishmael returned Old Smoke's gaze with the look of a boy eager to hear what his father has to tell him.

'The Truth has set you free from the first error and will continue to set you free until that perfect day when all human beings will stand before the Everywhere Spirit. Our people knew this long before the Spanish missionaries came to show us the way to their Great God.'

Ishmael closed his eyes and prayed to be able to go forward. Old Smoke hugged him and then gathered up the pelts he had been scraping and went over to the corral.

Ishmael finished his coffee and went over to his car, took some paper and a pen from the glove box and began to write a letter to Rosasharn. When he finished writing, he folded the letter, went over to the corral and handed it to Old Smoke.

'Give this to Rosasharn. Tell her I'm so sorry for not waiting for her.'

'I will. Now go. Dawn is breaking.'

Ishmael went back to his car and drove off. What had been revealed at Big Chino Wash and culminated in the confirmation and forgiveness by the Supreme Spiritual Council had made him a new man.

Ishmael was no longer his shadowy self. As with St Paul, formerly known as Saul the persecutor of Christians, the scales over Ishmael's eyes had fallen and he now saw everything clearly.

Ishmael slowly drove out of Chilchinbito Canyon. He turned off the

Chapter 48 *Chilchinbito Canyon, Navajo Reservation, Tuesday 21 August*

access road, pulled up and gazed wanly back at the towering cliffs that bordered Old Smoke's property. The sheer, craggy walls of black mesa were softened by a pall of blue-black haze.

He yearned to go back to Rosasharn, to stay with her for the rest of his life. As much as he wanted her, he knew she wanted him with the same tortured, heartbreaking passion. From the moment they had fallen onto the ragged mattress, there was no more holding back.

He knew she loved him for who he was now, and forgiven him for who he had been. Feeling his resolve to go forward slipping away, he let out a heart-rending cry and gunned the engine in his endeavor to get as far away from Rosasharn as quickly as possible.

CHAPTER 49

BATON ROUGE, LOUISIANA, THURSDAY 23 AUGUST

Ishmael's car broke down ten miles outside of Baton Rouge. He abandoned it and hailed a passing cab.

The taxi pulled up in front of the gangway to the *Mark Twain* at a quarter to seven, fifteen minutes before it was due to depart on its nightly cruise to New Orleans. Ishmael was grabbing his luggage out of the trunk when he heard a call: 'Scot Fall!' He looked towards the boat and saw Canaan leaning over the rail on the quarterdeck, waving. Ishmael returned his wave.

Ishmael was signing the register in the ornate lobby, where a gilt-framed portrait of a young, dapper-looking Mark Twain standing behind a riverboat's steering wheel hung behind the reception desk, when Canaan came up behind him. Ishmael acknowledged him formally, one businessman to another, shaking his hand and exchanging small talk.

'Come on up to my room when you've settled in,' said Canaan. 'I'm in 501.'

'Be there in about half an hour,' Ishmael replied.

'Here's a little present.' Canaan reached into his jacket pocket and pulled out a small package wrapped in yellowed newspaper and handed it to Ishmael.

'What is it?'

'A little token from the past,' Canaan said and winked at him.

Chapter 49 Baton Rouge, Louisiana, Thursday 23 August

Ishmael gazed at the package in his hand, turned around and left Canaan, standing at ease.

Ishmael followed the steward to his room. When they got there, Ishmael thanked the steward and gave him a twenty-dollar tip. The steward graciously took it and headed straight for the captain's quarters. The captain was immediately summoned.

CHAPTER 50

BATON ROUGE, LOUISIANA, THURSDAY 23 AUGUST

Uriah scoffed down the remains of his Captain D fish burger, washing it down with a few gulps of Dr. Pepper. He wiped his mouth on a paper towel, placed all the rubbish in a bag and dropped it on the floor behind the passenger seat of his car. He was parked a couple of spaces back in the lot of the *Mark Twain*'s berth in Baton Rouge. The position gave him a good vantage point to view the gangway. A dozen or so passengers were still queued in front of the gangway, waiting to board. The line was being held up by Alabama Senator Andrew Shadrack and his entourage.

Over the past three weeks, Uriah had been watching the *Mark Twain* come and go between Orleans and Baton Rouge. Uriah was at the end of his tether. If nothing came up by day's end on Sunday, he would have to throw in the towel. He was due back at work on Monday.

Uriah had decided to turn over what little he knew to the local feds. If anything came of it, someone in the New Orleans office would get the credit. All references to his hard work would most probably be omitted because he was on the New Orleans branch's turf with no authority from his boss. That's American law enforcement for you, he thought. If you go strictly by the book, criminals keep walking the streets. He didn't care whose ass was kissed by the bigwigs. What mattered was that Paul South had to be caged up.

What Paul South was doing on the boat had him baffled. He had approached a couple of stewards on the subject, but all had refused to

Chapter 50 *Baton Rouge, Louisiana, Thursday 23 August*

enter into any discussion about passengers. Perhaps it was a meeting place, but from what he could make out, the majority of the passengers were dignitaries and religious fanatics. Where was the link to the Malatestas?

He had been in touch with the Baton Rouge and New Orleans fire departments to see if they'd come across any firebugs with a craving for incinerating domestic pets, but nothing came up, except for a report of a dog burnt on the nose by ash from a crack pipe.

Uriah was puzzled about what had happened to South's car. He last saw it parked by Jackson's Square when South arrived in New Orleans. He had asked a good friend in the New Orleans Police Department if it had been reported stolen, but it hadn't.

The paddleboat's horn blew another last call for departure. Uriah stared up at the leaning column of white smoke billowing from its funnel when his cell phone rang. The caller ID showed Salvador. 'Go away,' Uriah griped.

Knowing that Sal was calling to harangue him about whether he had finished his report on the El Paso assignment, he did not feel like answering it. Sal had been on his back almost daily to get it done.

Salvador was stressed that, when the heads of their departments got together to read it, they would pick up all the inconsistencies in the reports. Whether to include Paul South in it was the sixty-four-thousand-dollar question to which Salvador wanted an immediate answer. While Uriah still had a couple of weeks to hand in his report, Salvador's was overdue. Uriah's planned trip to Oklahoma did not, for obvious reasons, eventuate. He advised Sal to tell his people that he was on holiday, but that didn't solve Sal's overdue problem.

He turned on his car radio. *I'll Buy You Tall Trees* was playing. He whistled along, looking down at his cell phone from time to time. The LCD screen kept flashing. Then it stopped for a moment and started again. He finished his Dr. Pepper and crushed the can with his hands, tore it in two and threw it onto the back seat.

'Persistent, ugly little Mexican.' He flicked off the radio and answered. 'FBI. Uriah Stuyvesant. How can I help?' he said politely.

'Why didn't you answer, you fat piece of shit?' Salvador yelled at him.

'I was outside the car, taking a leak.'

'Bullshit. You were jerking off.'

'Look, Salvy, boy, I'll get the report in. Been working on it all day,' he lied.

'You're gonna have ta tear it up and start again.'

'Why?'

'I got information.'

'What?' There was urgency in his voice.

'It ain't no big thing. Call you later,' Salvador said.

'Stop wasting my time.'

'Say sorry and promise that next time I call while you're jerking off, you'll put your flopper away and answer.'

'Sorry,' Uriah said, gritting his teeth, trying to sound sincere.

'Hey, gringo, you're not sounding too see-ri-uss,' said Salvador in his best Spanish accent.

'That's it. You're telling me now or I'm hanging up. I'll count to five. One ... two ... three ...' he paused, breaking the rhythm, 'four ...'

What Salvador blurted out, in what seemed to be a single breath, left Uriah speechless.

'You're not telling me crap?'

'No, *señor*. I done a search on the Internet.'

'It looks like it's coming together, Salvador. Good work.'

'It was nar-ting, *amigo*.'

As they spoke, Uriah spotted Canaan on the quarterdeck waving to a man standing beside a cab.

Chapter 50 *Baton Rouge, Louisiana, Thursday 23 August*

'You wouldn't believe it, Sal, but this dude has just pulled up in a cab and is waving to Mr. Pyromaniac. I'm on board that tub tonight. Stand by.' He snapped his phone shut.

Uriah sized up the guy who had just collected his bags out of the trunk of the cab, making mental notes about height, complexion, build and facial characteristics. He didn't have a clue how he was going to get on board. From what he knew, one had to have reservations. He had tried a number of times, unsuccessfully, but was told that they were fully booked out up to three months in advance.

Four members of Senator Shadrack's entourage were sorting out luggage beside a limousine. He locked his car and strolled over to them. One of the men, a big, heavy, black man with close-cropped hair who looked as if he might be head of security was giving orders to the much younger men around him.

'Excuse me, sir, may I have a quick word with you?' Uriah called.

The man turned. Uriah flashed his badge.

'So what?' the man said. He picked at his bottom teeth with a gold toothpick.

'So what? Is that all you can say? I must be talking to the wrong guy.' Uriah made like he was going to walk away. He stopped and faced the man and mocked, 'It seems to me that you're not important enough to know why the senator has specifically requested a Bureau representative to be on board.'

'Hey, I resent that,' the security guard said, looking Uriah up and down.

Uriah took a few steps back towards him, cupped his hand to his mouth. 'Look, pal, I am awfully sorry. It's my fault. I shouldn't have let the cat out of the bag. Just act like you don't know a thing, 'cause it's going to be real easy for you.' Uriah paused and then continued, 'Because I'm getting the vibes you fucking don't know a thing. Now you be a good boy and forget I even approached you.'

Uriah stared intently into the security guard's bemused face, his gold toothpick flashing in the sunlight.

'Fuck you, man. You gotta tell me. I make it my habit to know everything that's going down with Senator Shadrack.' He stabbed his thumb into his chest.

'That ain't my problem,' Uriah said a matter-of-factly. He reached into his shirt pocket and pulled out his cell phone.

'Well, you better make it your problem.' The security guard looked at him askance.

Uriah let out a huge sigh. 'Hey buddy, I'm not having a good day. It's this humid heat.' He lifted both arms. 'Lordy, lordy, get a load of these sweat rings on my shirt. They're the size of basketball hoops.'

The security guard shook his head in disgust and mumbled a few obscenities at the FBI man.

Uriah shut his phone. 'Seeing that I am such a good guy, how about you let me make it up to you 'cause I'm to blame for involving you in this very private matter that Senator Shadrack has asked the Bureau to look into. Let's say I, hmm ...' Uriah rasped the stubble under his chin with his cell phone. 'Hey pardner, say if I give you a little piece of the action and if you do your job well I'll guarantee that when the deputy director is standing on the dock in New Orleans debriefing the senator he gets to hear about your cooperation.'

'What've I got to do?' the security guard said through clenched teeth.

Uriah crossed his arms and looked up into the sky. 'How about you ... no. No, I've already assigned that detail to Charlie's capable hands.' After a few moments he smacked his lips and nodded. 'Got just the thing for you, pardner. For starters, get me on board.'

The security guard snatched the toothpick out of his mouth and pointed to the stretch limousine. 'Get the rest of those bags from the

Chapter 50 *Baton Rouge, Louisiana, Thursday 23 August*

trunk of that car, boy, and latch onto us.'

'Yas sir,' Uriah said in a servile tone.

'And I'll tell you this, smartass, if you've been fucking with me, I'm gonna make it my business to find out before that tub docks in Orleans.'

As soon as Uriah was on the deck, he detached himself from the group, ducked into the nearest bar and lay low until the boat set sail. When it finally did, he ordered a drink from a passing waiter. The waiter, along with all the staff on the boat all the way up the chain of command, had been briefed to look out for Uriah.

CHAPTER 51

MISSISSIPPI RIVER, LOUISIANA, THURSDAY 23 AUGUST

Captain Halpin pressed the pager button to summon his head of security to his quarters. After briefing him and ordering him to put all security staff on high alert, he picked up the phone and dialed Matteo Malatesta's cell phone number.

Captain Quincy Halpin was a fourth generation East Texan whose notorious ancestral roots lay deep in the once lawless town of Nacogdoches where most of the men in his blood line had either been hung or shot down. Halpin was a lean, loose-jointed man of sixty-five with an easygoing disposition most of the time. He had long, flowing, snow-white hair and a beard trimmed to a rakish angle. His drinking rivaled Wild Bill Hickock's. The more he drank, the steadier and sharper he was. Captain Quincy Halpin had lived and worked on the Mississippi River for most of his life, except for a five-year spell in the late seventies when his pilot's license was suspended over an incident involving the tugboat under his command, and a barge. He had deliberately collided with the barge to divert the attention of a coastguard patrol boat that was edging up to a freighter for a random inspection. The freighter had been loaded with illegal contraband commissioned by the Malatestas.

'Matteo, it's Captain Halpin.'
'What have you got for me, Halpin?'

Chapter 51 *Mississippi River, Louisiana, Thursday 23 August*

'I just got word that South's got company. Made contact with a passenger who just boarded, a Scot Fall from Arizona.'

A light on the captain's emergency phone flashed red. 'Hold the line, Matteo,' he said and picked up the receiver. As he listened, he shook his head in disbelief. 'Find out who's responsible,' and slammed down the receiver.

'Matteo, I regret to say that there's another tiny problem.'

'What is it, Quincy?' Matteo snapped.

'Stuyvesant is on board.'

'How the fuck did he get on?' Matteo growled.

'I'm working on it,' the captain replied.

'Work fucking harder.'

Halpin heard Matteo take a deep breath. He twirled his pen between his fingers.

'This is it. You know the drill, Halpin.'

Halpin stifled a yawn and recited the drill procedures: 'Close down the gaming room. Put all the staff on red alert. Get word around to our special guests that if they can't control the urge, they have to stay in their cabins and play with Monopoly money.'

As Matteo turned into the oak-lined driveway of the family's palatial lakeside antebellum mansion in Barataria, he cupped in his palm the diamond-studded cross hanging from his rear-view mirror, held it tightly and then said in a calmer tone, 'Maybe it's because of this new guy, that Stuyvesant is moving in. If, for whatever reason, he arrests them on the boat, it's either going to be swamped by the feds or they're going to be waiting for them when you dock in Orleans in the morning.'

'My hunch is that they're going to wait until Orleans.' Halpin rolled back on his swivel chair and, with the toe of his boot, jimmied open the bottom drawer of his desk and grabbed a bottle of bourbon.

'Even better. I'll have a watch posted there. I want to know everything that goes down the shitter before the *Mark Twain* docks.'

'I'll keep you posted around the clock,' the captain replied and twisted the cap off the bottle with his teeth.

'Tell your men I'm counting on them. When this blows over, there's a bonus waiting for them, but those responsible for letting Uriah on board are going to get their asses kicked.' Matteo snapped shut his cell phone, pulled up in front of the portico, stepped out of his car and made his way over to the rose garden to turn on the sprinkler.

With the exception of the captain, whose fidelity had long ago been confirmed way beyond the call of duty, the whole crew of the *Mark Twain*, right down to the kitchen hand, the lavatory attendant and the senior officers, had been handpicked. All of them were highly trained in the skills of running a boat and an illegal gambling venue. Most of the crew were recruited from Las Vegas or poached from illegal gambling venues run by other crime syndicates. The lavish salaries and perks, a tradition the Malatesta family was renowned for, ensured the absolute loyalty of just about anyone who was motivated by nothing other than money.

CHAPTER 52

MISSISSIPPI RIVER, LOUISIANA, THURSDAY 23 AUGUST

Ishmael locked the door of his cabin and pulled the small package from his pocket. He studied the type on the faded yellow newspaper. It was Hindi. He ripped it open and gasped at the sight of the brass buckle from his mother's valise. He couldn't believe what he was holding. He closed his eyes and clutched the buckle to his chest. He longed to be in his mother's loving embrace. Long-forgotten memories of his childhood overcame him. He dropped to his knees and started a downward spiral into his past.

The present intervened; Ishmael opened his eyes and stared at the buckle. The thought that Canaan was going to have his way in the final hour horrified him more than death. He stood up, tossed the buckle over to the other side of and stripped down to his waist and donned his bomb belt.

Ishmael firmly pressed the Velcro together and looked at the ceiling, relieved to see that the cabin was fitted out with sprinklers. He assumed that Canaan's cabin was much like his own, and that it would be devastated by the blast. With only the two of them in the room, he was certain there would be no other casualties. Then again, there were the adjoining rooms. Surely these would suffer damage, though to what extent it was hard to say.

He walked over to the full-length mirror a little stiffly, having strapped the bomb too tight. He could feel it press against his ribs. Ishmael laughed with exasperation. 'It will all come off very soon.' He studied himself. It felt a lot less cumbersome with the reduced RDX and circuitry. Under a loose-fitting shirt, no one would notice it.

He went to his suitcase, selected a shirt and put it on. He pulled from the pouch the envelope with all the information on the Global Azad Front that he had prepared for Homeland Security and the eagle feather. He picked up the buckle from his mother's valise, kissed it and placed it on the bedside table next to the envelope. Finally, he slid the eagle feather into the Velcro strap, buttoned up his shirt, and left his cabin.

He made his way along the walkway to his self-imposed destiny and gazed out onto the river. He took in the great span of water, the scenic shoreline dense with trees and the state capitol looming high above them, silhouetted against a blue sky.

As he slowly climbed the stairs and approached Canaan's cabin, a stillness washed over him. Ishmael paused for a moment in front of Canaan's cabin door.

The temptation to throw himself over the side and let the mighty Mississippi have its way with him was overwhelming. Ishmael knocked on the door.

CHAPTER 53

MISSISSIPPI RIVER, LOUISIANA, THURSDAY 23 AUGUST

Canaan was sprawled on the couch thumbing through a pictorial anthology on the masters of delta blues, listening to Robert Johnson singing, *'When you got a good friend'*.

From the moment Ezra Willy Bill Appaloosa had first introduced him to this music, Canaan had become hooked. It spoke to him of pain, regret, hardship and loss. Immersing himself in it alleviated the unrelenting need to go on a fire-lighting rampage. It reached right into the core of his being, evoking a mixture of pleasure and pain.

Canaan checked his watch. The boat was just about due to depart. He was not overly concerned that the other two members of the terrorist cell hadn't shown up. If they had missed the departure from Baton Rouge, they would head for New Orleans. Ishmael was on board; that was all that mattered. With Khalil and Amon out of the way, tonight could be the night. He would have to wait until long after midnight when the decks were clear to retrieve the RDX and bomb-making gear hidden in a lifeboat.

There was a knock on the door. Canaan sprang to his feet and opened it. He stepped back and looked Ishmael up and down. Canaan's eyes lit up, he smiled broadly and embraced him, running both his hands up and down Ishmael's sides, pressing the small of his back. He buried his head into the crook of Ishmael's neck for what seemed a long time and held him close. Ishmael could feel tears rolling down the nape of his neck.

'Ishmael, Ishmael, my only friend. You have come prepared,' Canaan whispered in Hindi into Ishmael's ear.

'Yes, I have,' Ishmael replied, also in Hindi.

'I thought I had to …' Canaan's voice broke and he couldn't continue. He dropped his arms to his side, head bowed. He took a few steps backwards.

Ishmael stepped into the room and shut the door. The boat lurched as it pulled from the dock.

Canaan lifted his head, his composure fully restored, and for a moment, as Ishmael stared at his friend, he seriously wondered whether he had imagined the last minute. He touched the back of his neck. It was damp.

'We are a little late setting sail this evening. Soon we will be smoothly sailing all the way to New Orleans.' He motioned towards the porthole. 'Did you know that the proper way to pronounce it is "Noo-or-lins", not New Or-leans?' Canaan planted himself on the couch and stretched his arms across the back.

'Is that so?' Ishmael replied, steadying himself as the boat pitched forward.

'Yes, my brother. A black man I met in a bar taught me.'

'I see this place has been getting to you.' Ishmael cast his eyes around the room. It was much bigger than his cabin. It looked like a luxury suite. All the better, he thought. To his left was a large bathroom, to the right a walk-in wardrobe. The impact of the blast to the adjoining cabins would be lessened considerably.

'Believe me, Ishmael, I have got Duvall just where I want him. It is only a matter of moments,' he said, his flippancy segueing into a more serious mood.

Chapter 53 *Mississippi River, Louisiana, Thursday 23 August*

The music coming from the CD player caught Ishmael's attention. He cocked his ear and listened.

'They call it the blues,' Canaan said. He picked up the remote and selected another CD. 'Listen to Bukka White.' A grating guitar, accompanied by a low, guttural voice moaning in a syncopated rhythm, blared out of the speakers. It started off with a choking, melodic drone from a national steel guitar:

I'm lookin' funny in my eyes,
I believe I'm fixin' to die, believe I'm fixin' to die.
I'm lookin' funny in my eyes and I believe I'm fixin' to die.
I know I was born to die ...

'He is playing our song,' Canaan roared and punched the air. The song finished with an ear-piercing slide to the guitar's bridge. Canaan switched off the player.

'Since when have you been interested in music?'

'Ezra Willy Bill Appaloosa Junior introduced me to it.'

Canaan reached under the coffee table and grabbed a tattered, cloth-bound booklet and threw it on the table. Ishmael picked it up and read the title.

'Jack Folsom and I have something in common,' Canaan said, and proceeded to explain the final episode in Jack Folsom's life.

CHAPTER 54

MISSISSIPPI RIVER, LOUISIANA, THURSDAY 23 AUGUST

'I want to know minute by minute where that FBI man is lurking around the boat,' Captain Halpin said, then hung up. He turned his attention to the closed circuit TV monitors covering Canaan's cabin. Two of his senior officers were manning the control panel.

Under Matteo's orders, Canaan's room had been bugged with pin-sized, wireless security cameras and microphones that were being monitored in the captain's quarters.

'These two must be from the Middle East. Can't understand a bloody word they're saying,' said the first mate as he handed the headset to the captain who listened for a moment, bewildered, then handed the headphones back. He picked up the phone and dialed Matteo's cell phone.

'Matteo, Captain Halpin here.'

Matteo was pacing up and down the corridor, stepping in and out of rooms, slamming doors behind him as he anxiously awaited news from the *Mark Twain*.

'What's happened? They let the cat out of the bag?' Matteo snarled.

'I can't say,' Halpin answered.

'Why not?'

'Need an interpreter. These guys are ... I don't know ... must be Middle Eastern.'

'What? You mean raghead mumbo jumbo?'

Chapter 54 *Mississippi River, Louisiana, Thursday 23 August*

'Maybe,' Halpin replied.

Matteo paused and tried to make sense of the situation. He stepped into the lounge and called across the room to Frank. He was engrossed in the NBL game on the 250 cm LCD TV screen. The New Orleans Giants were playing the Wisconsin Whalers.

'Hey, Frankie, our friends are talking some towelhead lingo.'

Frank turned down the volume on the television. 'What was that?'

'Our friends on the *Mark Twain* are talking in some foreign language,' Matteo said in a slow, sharp voice.

Frank stared at him, his expression blank. 'If they're feds, it's totally out of left field.' He turned up the volume and continued watching the game. Matteo shook his fist at Frank.

'Where's Uriah?'

'Drinking in the Tom Sawyer Bar.'

'This is not good, Halpin. That fuck Uriah is on board and this guy South is talking in tongues to the new kid on the block.'

'Your call, Matteo. Let it play out or what?'

'What's the action in South's room?'

Halpin turned to the monitor and described the scene.

'South is sitting on the couch and his friend is standing. South seems to be doing all the talking.'

The second mate removed his headset and handed it to the captain. 'I can make out the name "Jack Folsom" in their conversation,' the officer said.

The first mate switched the live feed to playback. Halpin listened for a few moments and handed the headset back.

'Matteo, it seems that they're talking about Jack Folsom. South keeps dropping his name in the middle of the mumbo jumbo.'

The first mate interrupted again. 'Excuse me, Captain. Duvall's name has just come up again.'

'Also they're dropping Duvall's name.'

Matteo put the two names together and came up with a partial picture. He had worked hand in hand with his father setting up the riverboat gambling venture. Maybe there had been an oversight that neither he nor his father had picked up on. He wished his father was still alive.

'Papa would've gotten to the bottom of this, Quincy. Weeks ago.'

'Honestly, Matteo. I figure your papa wouldn't have done anything different.'

'Thanks, Quincy. I needed to hear that.'

'Look at it this way. It could be that these two have got a score to settle with Duvall.'

'Yeah, I'm thinking along the same lines. Get that piece of unholy shit up there. Who knows? Maybe he can identify the new man.'

CHAPTER 55

MISSISSIPPI RIVER, LOUISIANA, THURSDAY 23 AUGUST

Reverend Jonathon Duvall was at the lectern in the boat's whitewashed chapel humming a hymn while marking citations in his most prized possession, his family bible. It had been passed on to him from his own father's deathbed. He was especially excited about Senator Andrew Shadrack attending this evening's service. The senator had personally phoned Duvall for a private meeting. After the senator had poured out his soul, he would direct the conversation to getting his candidacy nomination secured for the next Louisianan state election. Shadrack's brother was a prime mover in the state Democratic Party.

The political and business personalities who attended his non-denominational Evangelical ministry on the *Mark Twain* were of all persuasions. Duvall welcomed them all with open arms.

Just as Duvall completed marking his final citation from the Book of Job, he was interrupted by a steward who walked into the chapel without knocking.

'Duvall, you're wanted in the captain's quarters, ASAP.'

'What in the name of Christ Jesus and the blessed virgin mother of God gives you the right to barge into the sanctuary of God's anointed, you insolent fool?' Duvall protested.

'Sorry, Rev.' The steward looked over his shoulder in a comic gesture and then turned to Duvall and cupped his hand over his mouth. 'He's on the phone to Matteo Malatesta,' the steward said in a low voice. At the mention of Matteo, Duvall baulked.

'Ah. Well then, we must not keep the good man waiting.' He grabbed his walking stick and hobbled out of the chapel.

CHAPTER 56

MISSISSIPPI RIVER, LOUISIANA, THURSDAY 23 AUGUST

'Incredible. Jack Folsom died trying to save the girl from the funeral pyre,' Ishmael exclaimed. He placed the booklet on the coffee table. 'There was no one to save your mother.'

Canaan glared at Ishmael and balled his fists.

'No, Canaan, please don't get me wrong. I wasn't saying that you didn't attempt to save your mother. You were only a little boy. You were without help.'

Ishmael stared wide-eyed into Canaan's eyes and, for the first time in his life, he saw them flinch.

Canaan leant forward and propped his elbows on his knees and rubbed his forehead. 'Oh, my brother in death, I wish that I had at least tried to save my mother. If I had, our lives would have been different.' He sighed.

Ishmael was astonished. He couldn't believe what he had just heard, Canaan contemplating a scenario different to the one that had occurred all those years ago.

Canaan lifted up his head. 'It is time to die,' he said in a low voice.

'No ... I mean yes, it is time to die, but I must talk first ... I have to tell you ...' Ishmael's words came out strangulated.

Canaan raised his eyebrows and gave him a thin smile. 'All your pain will soon be over.' He got up from the couch and slowly walked over to Ishmael.

'Listen to what I have to say,' Ishmael pleaded.

Canaan stopped a few feet away from him and burst into a fit of maniacal laughter. 'Okay, Ishy boy.' He retreated to the couch, sat and folded his arms across his chest, his expression softened.

Ishmael walked over to the porthole on the opposite side of the room and looked wanly out onto the river. A barge glided past, its gunwale almost submerged. He faced Canaan, swallowed dryly. 'You were right about religion. So much has happened in the last couple of days.'

'Was that you who called on Saturday night?'

Ishmael nodded.

'Whatever has happened is not important now. You are here and Duvall is here.'

'It is important,' Ishmael snapped. 'Canaan, we have been wrong in following Akmid's plan and joining the Azad Front.'

'We have been wrong? No, my friend, you have been wrong. I never bought into that terrorist bullshit.' Canaan sniggered.

'Okay, I've been wrong.'

'Do not waste your breath. Our hour is at hand.' Canaan looked at his watch. 'In forty-five minutes Duvall will be saying his last prayers.'

'No!' Ishmael stamped his foot. 'I didn't come here with the bomb belt to go and blow up Duvall.'

'How many kilos of RDX have you got?'

'Three kilos. Just enough for us, here and now.' Ishmael gasped for air. He was feeling asphyxiated.

'Three kilos of RDX will be more than enough for the three of us. I am sorry to say that you are not going to be able to take a lot of Americans to God with you.'

'I don't intend to kill innocent people. I am through with my faith,' Ishmael retorted.

'Are you back to worshipping something a bit more solid, concrete

Chapter 56 *Mississippi River, Louisiana, Thursday 23 August*

worshipper?' Canaan said mockingly.

'No. I mean the wrong teaching of it.'

'Wisely spoken, my good friend.' Canaan stood and slowly walked over to Ishmael and held his gaze. He reached out with both hands and grabbed hold of Ishmael's hand.

'Let us go. We are ready for the other side. Mother calls. She will be free,' Canaan said in a thin, reedy voice.

Ishmael groaned and shuddered. His hand in Canaan's went limp. He had the strangest feeling that he was becoming one with Canaan. Without his religion, all his defenses fell away.

'Be still, my friend in death. The time has come for you to help carry the burden.' He whispered into Ishmael's ear, 'It will be only for a short time. The fire will extinguish all.'

CHAPTER 57

MISSISSIPPI RIVER, LOUISIANA, THURSDAY 23 AUGUST

'Blessings and salutations from our Lord Jesus,' Duvall bellowed as he limped into the captain's stateroom, pushing the door shut behind him with the end of his cane. The first and second mates rolled their eyes.

'Duvall's here. Hold the line.' The captain waved the receiver at Duvall. 'It's the big boss man.'

Duvall's eyes darted to the captain, who looked at him inquiringly.

The captain briefed Duvall on the crisis taking place, including Uriah's presence on board.

'Why y'all losing sleep over that Paul South? What's he up to now?'

Duvall had been ordered to keep a watch on Canaan during his church meetings. He had spotted Canaan in the back pew during services, muttering to himself, apparently immersed in a trance. He wrote him off as another tormented soul with a guilty past. His assessment of Canaan to the captain was nondescript.

As for being informed about Uriah's stakeout of the boat, Duvall was somewhat concerned. For whatever reasons the FBI man was hanging around, Duvall was confident it had absolutely nothing to do with him. He pulled up a chair and let out a sigh as he took the weight off his gammy leg.

'Take a look at the monitor,' said the first mate.

Duvall folded both hands over his walking cane and leant forward.

Chapter 57 *Mississippi River, Louisiana, Thursday 23 August*

'Mmm, that's Senator Shadrack in the Aunt Polly Dining Room. My dear Captain, make sure that the senator samples the Mississippi Delta wine collection during dinner. It's a winner every time.'

'Forget the fucking senator,' Captain Halpin said sharply. 'Look at the screen on the right.'

Duvall squinted at the monitor. 'I ... I see, captain. Yes, yes, I see,' he muttered.

'Do you recognize South's roommate?' The captain pointed with the telephone receiver.

'May the Lord God be my judge. I have never seen him before.'

'You see that little book on the coffee table?'

'What in the Holy Father's name am I supposed to be looking at?' Duvall sighed.

'The little book,' snarled the captain.

'The book ... oh, yes, the little book. What about it?'

'It's *The Jack Folsom Story*,' said the first mate.

Duvall froze, his eyes glazed over with fear. 'What are they doing with it? They're not spreading lies about me, are they? Where's the volume for that damn thing?'

The second officer slapped a set of headphones on Duvall's head.

'Turn it up,' the captain ordered the second mate. 'Loud.'

Duvall listened intently, nodding his head slightly. 'By Jesus, they're talking in Hindi, an Indian dialect from up north. Rajasthan. I haven't heard that in years,' exclaimed Duvall as he took off the headphones.

'What are they saying?' the captain snapped.

'I don't have a clue,' Duvall replied nervously.

'Duvall says it's Indian, Bollywood and curry, all that stuff.' Halpin spoke into the phone.

'What are they talking about?' Matteo snapped.

'Duvall recognizes it but doesn't understand it.'

A momentary silence ensued. The captain stared at the monitor. 'These two might be gay. They're holding hands.'

'What's that around his waist? Some type of back support?' Duvall said.

'What the hell is going on?' Matteo yelled into his cell phone.

'Things are looking like they're getting out of hand.' The captain spoke into the receiver, his eyes riveted on the monitor.

'What do you mean?' Matteo snapped.

'The new guy looks like he is wearing something lethal around his torso. We're going to have to do something about this right now Matteo.'

'Ok Halpin start clearing the surrounding cabins of all passengers. Have security stationed in the cabins adjoining Paul South's. Seal off all corridors and put stewards at both ends, barring wandering passengers.'

The captain relayed the orders to the first mate.

CHAPTER 58

MISSISSIPPI RIVER, LOUISIANA, THURSDAY 23 AUGUST

'I will wear the belt,' said Canaan as he began unbuttoning Ishmael's shirt.

Ishmael could feel his resolve weakening.

The eagle feather tucked into the Velcro strip caught Canaan's attention. He pulled it out and held it up. With half-closed eyes, Ishmael stared at the feather. Recollection's of Old Smoke and Rosasharn came flooding into his drowning consciousness, buoying him up. He snatched the feather out of Canaan's hand and pushed Canaan back, toppling him over the coffee table. Canaan shook his head as if coming out of a trance. He picked himself up off the floor.

'What's with the feather?' he growled, pointing at it.

'It's an eagle's feather. It represents those who really own America.'

'What is that to me? Take off the belt.'

'I'm sorry, Canaan, I am so sorry.' Ishmael reached down and cupped the dangling detonation button in his palm.

'You are not going to press it.'

'Yes I am.' Ishmael's voice quivered. He held up the eagle feather and earnestly implored the Spiritual Council for strength.

'The promise, concrete worshipper, the promise,' Canaan insisted vehemently. 'It cannot be broken, you know that. The belt buckle to your mother's valise, has it not jolted your memory?'

'The promise, the promise.' Ishmael's blood ran cold. He felt the energy flow out of him.

Canaan smiled cruelly and nodded. 'Yes, it is the promise that binds us.'

Canaan and Ishmael's eyes locked.

'What did this promise mean?' Ishmael said. A realization swept over him. 'Canaan, please listen. The whole religious doctrine of a person being damned for not receiving Jesus in their heart is wrong, just like the radicalized ideals Werter von Stumpf and Akmid had me believe. Understand that Duvall has no authority, neither on Earth nor in heaven, to condemn your mother for not knowing Jesus.'

Canaan clasped his hands over his ears and violently shook his head, biting down on his bottom lip until he drew blood. He sucked hungrily on his wound and spat saliva and blood in Ishmael's direction.

'Take off the belt.' He gritted his teeth. Blood trickled down his chin.

'I'm going to detonate now,' said Ishmael doggedly.

'You do not have it in you to press it, concrete worshipper.'

'Yes, I do. Yes, I do,' Ishmael protested.

CHAPTER 59

MISSISSIPPI RIVER, LOUISIANA, THURSDAY 23 AUGUST

Uriah wolfed down a bag of roasted cashews and washed them down with a beer. He checked his watch. It was just after eight.

Salvador's information, being in the right place at the right time, seeing the firefly make contact with a new man, it all jelled to make Uriah feel somewhat triumphant.

After being told about South stopping at the Southern Mormon and Latter Day Saints Tabernacle, Salvador messed around on the Internet. He typed in the tabernacle's address, the *Mark Twain* and Paul South. The search engine generated newspaper stories from the *Washington Post*, the *New York Times* and a dozen or so southern papers about the demise of the Jack Folsom Crusaders and how Reverend Jonathon Duvall had been embroiled in exposing the scandal. The Malatesta brothers had been linked to the murder of Reverend Doctor Cecil Wiltshire, chairman of the board and presiding minister of the Sunday morning services.

'Excuse me, do you know what time the Reverend Duvall starts his service?' he asked.

'Eight o'clock,' the waiter replied. He placed the bill face down on the table and walked off.

'Whereabouts on the boat does he conduct the service?' Uriah called after him.

'Fifth deck, portside,' the waiter replied. He hurried back behind the bar and relayed the information he had just gleaned up the chain of command.

Uriah left ten dollars on the table and strolled out. With a little luck, he just might run into Paul South and his new friend.

Uriah wandered from deck to deck. He was in awe over the paddle steamer's opulence. It was straight out of Mark Twain's book — Life on the Mississippi. Elaborately furnished bars and restaurants, hand-carved mahogany balustrades, colossal crystal chandeliers, plush carpets, and the crew and other personnel dressed in period costumes.

On the third deck he came across half a dozen stewards hovering around the corridor; they were big, heavy-set men who looked as if they were pumped with steroids. As they escorted passengers away to other cabins, Uriah walked nonchalantly up the corridor, peering into the cabins that were being evacuated.

CHAPTER 60

MISSISSIPPI RIVER, LOUISIANA, THURSDAY 23 AUGUST

Canaan heard the sound of a key being inserted into the lock. He faced to see the doorknob turning slowly, then the door burst open and eight heavily-armed security guards stormed into the cabin.

'Nobody move and nobody will get hurt,' the captain said evenly.

Ishmael froze, his finger on the button. He defied the impulse to press it and threw up his hands. Canaan's mind was racing. He scanned the faces around him, recognizing only the captain, who was standing inside the door.

A sound, as if someone was tapping a stick on a wall, could be heard. A voice outside the corridor called, 'Got to have a closer look at these two,' Canaan instantly recognized the voice. It was Duvall. Canaan whirled around, astonished, his eyes bulging as Duvall entered the cabin supporting himself on his cane.

'Freeze,' a security guard growled at Canaan.

'Duvall, I told you to fucking stay outside!' yelled the captain.

An explosion of hope surged through Canaan. His eyes darted around the armed men, who were momentarily distracted by Duvall's presence. Ishmael was about an arm's length from him with his back against the wall. Canaan could see the detonator clearly.

This was it, the supreme moment Canaan had been waiting for, Ishmael, Duvall and himself in one place. Only one question coursed through his mind: were the three kilos of RDX in Ishmael's bomb belt enough? It was enough to kill everyone in the cabin. He shot a glance at Ishmael. Their eyes locked and said all there was to say.

Canaan lunged at Ishmael, knocking him to the floor. Ishmael struggled to keep Canaan's hand off the detonator. Four guards jumped upon the scrambling pair. They seized Canaan by the legs and shoulders and dragged him back across the room.

'Push the button!' Canaan shouted to Ishmael. They pinned him onto the floor, he fought like a raging lunatic, writhing, twisting, half flinging them off. Another two guards came to their aid. This time there was no contest.

On the other side of the room Ishmael offered no resistance. 'Not innocent lives!' Ishmael shouted back. 'Not innocent lives. I'm sorry, so sorry.'

In a matter of moments, Ishmael and Canaan were tied up, their mouths and eyes bound with duct tape.

The captain stared down at the hogtied prisoners. Despite the fact that Canaan was gagged and tied, he was wriggling like a worm. His cell phone rang. Someone on the other end of the line informed him that Uriah had been inquiring about Reverend Duvall's services. He turned around and glared at Duvall.

'Duvall, I don't know what the fuck these two are up to, but your name keeps popping up. Uriah Stuyvesant is now looking for you.'

'Maybe the man needs some religious succor. I am here to do the Lord's work.' He stamped his walking cane on the floor.

'The only work you do is worm your way through life,' one of the security men commented.

'I assure you, Captain, that I have never seen these two miscreants in my entire life.' Duvall's attention hovered between the captain and the two captives on the floor. 'I commend you, Captain, and your men, on a fine job.'

Chapter 60 *Mississippi River, Louisiana, Thursday 23 August*

'Spare me the bullshit, Duvall,' the captain said.

'If they came to destroy God's anointed, their plan has been foiled.' Duvall prayed aloud. 'Oh, thank you, sweet Jesus, for saving thy humble servant.'

Wearily, the captain shook his head.

One of the guards, who happened to be a former US Navy SEAL, was inspecting Ishmael's bomb belt. 'Captain!' he called out, 'this is the real McCoy. US Army RDX.'

'Oh, man, this is insane.' The captain went over to take a closer look.

Duvall looked at his watch. 'I'm late,' he exclaimed. 'I'll bid you gentlemen a good night. I have my religious duties to attend to and an appointment with the senator from Alabama. As for these two rogues, may God have mercy on their miserable souls when Matteo gets hold of them.'

Duvall snatched up the Jack Folsom booklet from the coffee table. 'I am the innocent here,' Duvall said aloud to himself as he hobbled out of the cabin. 'How my good name got embroiled, heaven only knows. All this is surely a deceitful conspiracy to tarnish my good name.'

One of the guards, who had his knee pressed down on Canaan's head, called out, 'Hey, Cap, Duvall's walked out with the book.'

'Forget him. He's going to have to answer to Matteo.'

'I wonder if his God will help him?' another guard remarked.

Grave questions were now flying through the captain's head but, with all the pressing issues to be dealt with, he had no time to think them through. He still had to get a briefing from Matteo about what to do with the prisoners, keep Uriah at bay, and get to dinner with the senator.

'No. Fuck the senator.' He turned to one of the stewards. 'Go and tell the senator that I am tied up with some urgent maintenance work and apologize for missing dinner.'

CHAPTER 61

MISSISSIPPI RIVER, LOUISIANA, THURSDAY 23 AUGUST

'Excuse me, sir, is your cabin in this corridor?' a steward with an eye patch inquired.

'Looking for a friend of mine,' Uriah replied.

'I'm sorry, sir, but I have to ask you to leave this part of the boat.'

'What's happened? Some kind of emergency?' asked Uriah.

'One of the cabins has been flooded by a broken water pipe, so we've had to turn off the water supply in this area.'

'Is that Reverend Duvall?' Uriah asked the steward, pointing down the corridor at a preacher man hobbling towards them.

'Yes. Now please, would you leave this area,' he said forcefully.

Duvall hobbled past them. Uriah called out, 'Reverend Duvall!'

'I'm in hurry, son. I have a church service to conduct.'

Uriah followed him up the stairwell. 'Just got a couple of questions. Allow me to introduce myself, sir. Jeff Evans. I'm a reporter from the *Atlanta Tribute*.'

Duvall stopped, clutched the stair railing and stared disbelievingly at the FBI man. 'Sorry, got no time for the press.' He continued up the stairs.

'I know you're a busy man, but I just want to talk to you about animal welfare and how your church feels about animal rights,' Uriah said.

Duvall paused on the landing of the fourth deck. He looked directly

Chapter 61 *Mississippi River, Louisiana, Thursday 23 August*

at Uriah, rubbed his chin, pursed his lips and nodded. 'I am always happy to talk about animal welfare.' He looked at his watch. 'Come up to my office. I can spare you ten minutes.'

'Why, thank you, Mr. Duvall.'

Duvall looked at him sternly. 'Please, sir, when addressing me would you kindly refer to me as Reverend Jonathon Duvall?'

'I'm sorry, Reverend Jonathon Duvall. I do apologize.'

'See that you get it right when writing for your newspaper.'

They reached the fifth deck where Duvall's chapel and office were located. As they turned into the corridor, Duvall halted. Standing outside his office were Senator Shadrack and his wife.

'Look here, my fine fellow,' Duvall said to Uriah, 'on second thought, you'd better come around later this evening. The senator is waiting to see me.'

Uriah looked towards the senator and nodded. 'Not a problem. Say, around ten?'

'Yes, yes, that's fine. Senator Shadrack,' Duvall called, waving his cane.

CHAPTER 62

MISSISSIPPI RIVER, LOUISIANA, THURSDAY 23 AUGUST

Reverend Jonathon Duvall was in his study, anxiously waiting for Uriah. He had just spent the last couple of hours with Senator Andrew Shadrack. As no one had attended his service and the captain had been unable to dine with the senator that evening, the Shadracks had made themselves comfortable in Duvall's office. They had had dinner brought up to them.

He racked his brain, trying to come up with a reason why the FBI man wanted to talk to him. Eventually, one thought coursed through Duvall's mind. It had to be about the murder of Conway Lascelles, or of Wiltshire, both of whose deaths, to this very day, had not been solved.

The more he thought about the episode with Paul South and his partner, the graver it appeared to be. The Army RDX, whatever that was, the Jack Folsom booklet. What were those two men doing with it? Why were they bandying his name around? And why were they speaking Hindi? He was adamant about what should be done. They should be given over to the proper authorities.

He looked at his watch: five minutes past ten. He buffed the glass of his diamond-studded Rolex with his jacket sleeve. When he had first received the watch, he had been thrilled and couldn't wait to get rid of his fake one. Now it reminded him of a past he didn't particularly care to remember, a past that kept creeping closer.

Chapter 62 *Mississippi River, Louisiana, Thursday 23 August*

It was time to move on and enjoy the sweet fruits of his forbearance. Duvall would give the Rolex back to Matteo. He did not care to own any mementos that had been obtained from the proceeds of crime. They could be used as evidence against him. He had done his second stint in the wilderness with the influential people who came on board the *Mark Twain* to secretly gamble away their fortunes, many of whom he had become intimately acquainted with. Now, the way was clear. They would rally behind him. They had no choice.

There comes a time, a rare moment of decision in the life of every humble minister of the gospel, when it is expedient to break the oath of divine confidentiality. Suffer it to be so now for the achievement of a nobler good. Yes. Yes. It was time that the hand of justice got a hold of the Malatesta brothers and set the records straight as far as his minuscule involvement in the demise of the Jack Folsom Southern Baptist Revival Crusade of Louisiana was concerned. The Democratic nominations were only six weeks away. He would milk Uriah for what he was worth, then he would cut a deal. There was a knock on the door.

'Enter.'

Uriah stepped into the room.

CHAPTER 63

MISSISSIPPI RIVER, LOUISIANA, FRIDAY 23 AUGUST

'It can't be. This is not happening,' Captain Halpin kept muttering to himself. His face was a ghostly grey. For the first time for as far back as he could remember, he felt that not even a case of the finest bourbon in the country could make the slightest difference to the way he felt.

He stared nervously at the four items on his desk. An eagle feather, a suicide bomb belt, an envelope addressed to Homeland Security, and a brass buckle. After he'd finished reading the contents of the envelope, his natural patriotic inclination was to call the CIA, the navy, the marines, anybody in authority who could deal with what he had discovered.

Any other type of crazed lunatic who decided to do away with himself on the boat, he wouldn't give a damn. But these two were terrorists. The whole damn weight of every law enforcement agency in the country would come crashing down on his boat.

Captain Halpin just wanted to curl up in a corner and go to sleep in the hope that when he woke up he would find that the whole thing had been a bad dream. The captain picked up the phone with a trembling hand, sucked in a deep breath, held it and let it out slowly as he dialed his commander in chief.

CHAPTER 64

BARATARIA, LOUISIANA, FRIDAY 23 AUGUST

Matteo was pacing the floor, hands clasped behind his neck, anxiously waiting for Halpin to call. Matteo had tried ringing him numerous times but had been unable to get through.

'They're the best. They know how to handle a crisis,' Frank assured Matteo.

'Why the fuck hasn't Halpin answered his phone? Something's going down the shit hole and I want to know about it now!' Matteo slammed his fist on the dining room table.

'Give it another hour. If no word comes, I'll take the cruiser up river to have a look,' said Frank.

'No more waiting. Get your ass on that river now!'

'Whatever you say, big brother.'

The direct line from the *Mark Twain* rang. Both brothers stared at the phone and, for just a moment, Matteo hesitated, as if trying to fortify himself against what he expected to be told. Frank patted him on the shoulder. Matteo squeezed his brother's hand and snatched up the phone.

'What the fuck is going on?' he thundered down the receiver.

'Everything is under control for now,' Halpin replied solemnly.

'What do you mean "for now"? It is, or it isn't.'

'It's best if I don't say anything over the phone.'

Matteo launched into a tirade of Italian abuse and profanity.

Captain Halpin held the receiver away from his ear and, for a moment, he pictured Nunzio on the other end.

'Jesus Christ, these lines are secured! Quit jerking me off!' Matteo was yelling.

'Matteo, cool it!' Halpin yelled back.

'I didn't hear that, Halpin,' Matteo said, his tone threatening.

There was a deathly silence between the two men.

'Are you still there? Talk to me. Your job, your fuckin' life, is on the line.'

'Listen here, Matteo. At this very moment my life isn't worth living. I don't even care for having a drink.'

Matteo dropped the receiver to his side. 'Hey, Frankie, Quincy just said he doesn't care for a drink.'

Frank threw back his head and laughed, making a jerking motion with his hand.

'Halpin, start spilling your guts.'

'South and his friend are hogtied in the engine room's store bunker. I want them off this boat ASAP. Send Frank to collect them. I'll have a complete report ready for you. At the present moment, I assure you, everything is under control, for how long I can't guarantee.'

'Since when the fuck do you make decisions?'

'Matteo, just do what I say.'

'Damn you, Halpin.'

Matteo rubbed his chin with the end of the receiver. He had known Halpin ever since he could remember. Papa had regarded him in high esteem; not once had there been any sign of insubordination. 'Okay, Halpin. The show's in your hands. How far down river are you?'

'About three miles below Bayou Goula.'

'Frank will meet you north of Burnside, adjacent to the Rudolf plantation.'

Matteo turned to Frank. 'You heard. Get going.'

'Yeah, yeah, I heard.' Frank turned to Benny who had just entered the

Chapter 64 *Barataria, Louisiana, Friday 23 August*

room. 'C'mon Benny, get your clothes on. We're going on a midnight boat ride.'

Benny's glazed eyes came to life. For the past hour, he had been languidly wandering around the house in his green day glow Incredible Hulk pajamas, sucking milk from a baby's bottle.

'Can I drive? Please, please, Frank? Can I?' he shrilled.

'Pirates on the high seas time.' Frank did his best rendition of a buccaneer's voice.

'Okay, you two fuck knuckles, not another word,' Matteo growled. Frank held his finger to his lips and Benny hushed up. He tossed the bottle aside, hitched up his pajama bottoms and ran out of the room.

'Can I ask where that meat-head Uriah is?'

'We put him under house arrest for not having a ticket,' Halpin said coolly.

'You should have consulted me before you did that too.'

Halpin took a deep breath. 'Matteo, I am sorry, sorry for you, for me, for all of us. From what I figure if the FBI had any inkling about what South and his friend were really up to ... I'll tell you the truth. I wouldn't be here talking to you, and you would not be there talking to me.'

For a moment, Matteo considered what he had just heard. Halpin was not a man who wore his heart on his sleeve. The effect of what Halpin just told him hit the spot where even the toughest men realize their weakness and helplessness to control a situation in which they are supposed to have ultimate authority. The smart ones take notice.

'Okay,' Matteo said, a little calmer now.

Halpin continued, 'We picked him up having a heart-to-heart with Duvall.'

'Duvall. I'd forgotten about that son-of-a-bitch preacher. What's he doing spilling his guts to that fuck? Don't bother to explain. Just get me the facts by sunrise.' Matteo slammed down the phone and roared like a chained lion.

Benny came back into the room wearing his pirate costume, complete with eye patch, a steel hook mounted on his left arm and a pirate's hat on top of which sat a plastic orange parrot.

'Benny, I'm not taking you anywhere if you don't strap the leather muzzle on that hook,' Frank said.

Benny swiped his hook. 'Love you, Frank,' he said and raced out the door to get the muzzle. Frank slipped out after him, leaving Matteo deep in his own thoughts.

CHAPTER 65

MISSISSIPPI RIVER, LOUISIANA, SATURDAY 25 AUGUST

It was three in the morning when the two-and-half-million-dollar Malatesta cabin cruiser came around the second bend in the river opposite the Rudolf plantation. Frank spotted the *Mark Twain* slowly drifting down river and radioed the bridge to get clearance to come alongside.

Benny had been incessantly pestering Frank to let him drive the boat. Frank promised him that after they dropped off the cargo, he would let him go for a cruise in the Gulf.

Within ten minutes of radio contact, Ishmael, Canaan, Halpin's report, and the envelope addressed to Homeland Security locked in a briefcase were on board the cruiser, heading down river to the Gulf of Mexico. Their destination: Vermilion Bay, twenty-five miles south of New Iberia. The Malatestas ran fishing boats, charter cruises and half a dozen speedboats that they used to pick up drug consignments dropped overboard from container ships. When Frank got them there, the two captives would be taken deep into the swamplands to a safe house.

CHAPTER 66

CHILCHINBITO CANYON, NAVAJO RESERVATION, TUESDAY 21 AUGUST

The sun was beginning to rise over the canyon ridges when Rosasharn opened her eyes. The light streaming in the trailer windows was thick with dust motes. It took her a moment to work out where she was. Then, as it all came back to her, she reached across the mattress only to discover that Ishmael was not there. Rosasharn got up and quickly dressed. She stepped outside, looking around the yard, and saw that Ishmael's car was gone.

'Where's Ishmael?' she called out to Old Smoke, who was in the corral, saddling his horse.

'He has left,' Old Smoke called back.

'No. No, he can't be gone.' Her voice trembled. 'He could've waited for …' she moaned, dropping to her knees. Then she cupped her face in her hands and wept.

Old Smoke fastened the straps around the horse's belly, then slowly walked over to her, bent down and gently placed his hand on her shoulder.

Rosasharn raised her head and brushed her tangled hair from her face. She stared into Old Smoke's weather-beaten face. He removed a piece of folded paper from his shirt pocket and handed it to her. She grabbed it and wiped her face on her sleeve.

'I will leave you to read,' said Old Smoke.

'No, please stay. There's no one I can share it with but you.'

Chapter 66 Chilchinbito Canyon, Navajo Reservation, Tuesday 21 August

She unfolded the paper and began to read:

Rosasharn, just a matter of days ago I could never imagine myself being or even allowing myself to become attracted to you. You know why, I don't need to explain. Thank you for opening my eyes to a higher and humane way. To ask for more would be ungrateful.

I must get to Nashville to take care of two members of the cell, then I will go to Baton Rouge to meet Canaan. I will take all necessary precautions to cover my tracks, so you and Old Smoke will not be implicated.

Please get on with your life and, if you can, tell the world that there is hope if one fights with reason, understanding, and truth. These are the great weapons of your America, in fact all of humankind, that will secure everlasting peace.

Goodbye, my dearest beloved never to be forgotten and always to be remembered, new friend.

Rosasharn folded the paper and looked at Old Smoke. He was staring solemnly into the canyon.

'We must keep the way clear for Ishmael.' Old Smoke faced her. 'Tell me, have you told anyone about him?'

'The only one who really might know something about him is my mother. It was through her and my brother that I came into contact with him. I also called an old college professor of mine. I think he consults for Homeland Security on Middle Eastern history. Asked him the spelling of a couple of words from the prayer I heard Ishmael say, which turned out to be a prayer used by suicide bombers.' She went on and recounted what had happened the night of her niece's birthday party.

She also told Old Smoke that she had inquired about Ishmael at the Warm Springs Bar and Bistro, and how she had learnt from the bartender about Ishmael's confrontation with him over the images of the great leaders of the Indian nations of America.

'I described Ishmael to the bar tender and he told me that someone of that description came in and started making trouble over the pictures of the great leaders of the Indian nations.'

'Do not give it anymore thought, I am in possession of a fingernail and a tuft of hair that belongs to that bar tender. His name is Little Bird Double Head.'

She gave him an inquisitive look.

The sound of an approaching vehicle caught their attention. A column of dust was rising up behind the foothills of Old Smoke's property. Rosasharn's heart leapt. 'Look, a car! He's coming back! It's Ishmael!'

Old Smoke fixed his gaze on the rise. Rosasharn ran towards it, hope welling inside her. Old Smoke called her to come back.

When the car came over the crest, she stopped, stunned. She spun on her heels and dashed back to Old Smoke and fell into his arms. Her breath came in gasps. Old Smoke embraced her, snatched the letter out of her hand, crumpled it up and slipped it into his back pocket.

Deputy Billy Apple, born to the Red River Clan and for the Red Sandstone people, parked his Toyota Land Cruiser next to the pair, wound down his window and turned off the engine.

'Hey, Smokin' Joe, your female company expecting somebody?' He grinned. 'Maybe her pimp,' he muttered under his breath.

Billy Apple reached over to the back seat and grabbed his felt hat with the Navajo tribal police emblem on it. He slapped it on his head, adjusted his gold-rimmed sunglasses and inspected himself in the side mirror. He tilted the hat a fraction to the left, nodded into the mirror, stepped out of the car, and stood with his arms akimbo.

Deputy Billy Apple was just over six feet tall. He had an athletic build, chiseled Indian features with cheeks that were deeply mottled with scars. A braid with a single turkey feather hung from the back of his head. His shirt and trousers were pressed and his black leather boots had a high sheen. His uniform was bedecked with just about every piece of police issue accoutrement: badge, brass eagles on each epaulet, tie clasp, cufflinks and chains of various thicknesses. Medallions awarded for excellence and bravery hung from colored ribbons pinned to his shirt pockets.

Apple eyed Rosasharn and Old Smoke. Rosasharn glanced at the deputy. He flashed an enameled smile and nodded nonchalantly at her. She turned away.

'You're a shy, pretty thing,' he said and swaggered over to the corral and stood by the trough where Old Smoke's horse was drinking.

Old Smoke kept his hawk-like eyes on the deputy.

Deputy Billy Apple took note of Old Smoke's bear scalp and necklace half-hanging from one of the saddlebags.

'I see you're fixin' for a bit of mountaineering. Pastora Peak's nice this time of year,' he called out, not looking back.

He reached down and pulled a clump of grass from the base of the water trough and held it out to the animal. The horse raised its head, snatched it out of the deputy's hand and chomped on it. The horse whinnied, reared high on his hind legs and came down on its front legs in a puddle and splattered the front of the deputy's shirt in a spray of mud.

'What the hell you done a thing like that for? Goddamn you!' the deputy yelled at the horse. He pulled out his revolver, cocked the trigger and aimed at the horse's head. 'Come near me again and I'll put a bullet between your eyes.'

The horse snorted, turned and galloped to the far side of the corral. Billy Apple holstered his gun, pulled out a handkerchief, and attempted to clean the mud off his shirt as he marched back to where Old Smoke and Rosasharn were standing.

'You'd better learn to control that dumb animal, Smokin'. He done soiled my clean shirt and freshly ironed shirt. This here's Navajo tribal police property he's interfered with. I's got a good mind to run you in.'

Old Smoke took a couple of steps backwards and drew Rosasharn to him. He glared at the towering Billy Apple.

'Smokin', we had some complaints last night that the wildlife has gone crazy across these parts of the reservation. This morning, my brother rings me and he tells me he couldn't get his goats to step out to graze. They was all cowering in the corner of the barn, like there's a bear outside.'

Rosasharn looked up at Old Smoke. He gave her a slight grin.

'If I find any remains of a dead eagle or any burnt feathers up at your Supreme Spiritual Council meeting pad, I'm gonna call Joseph Aaron Jasper from the FBI Gallop office to get on down here immediately and charge you with killing a protected species, which is a federal offence.'

Rosasharn turned around to face the lawman. Deputy Billy Apple produced one of his charming smiles and tipped his hat to her.

The leather pouch with the eagle talons engraved on the flap around Old Smoke's waist seized the deputy's attention. He removed his shades, nodded and forced a smile.

'Well, what do we have here? A feather pouch. Surely that wouldn't be stuffed with feathers of a particular breed of protected fowl.'

Old Smoke's face remained passive.

The deputy lunged at Old Smoke, attempting to tear the pouch from him. Old Smoke flung Rosasharn out of his way, stuck out his foot and tripped up the deputy. He stumbled and fell, sliding across the gravel.

'I want to see a search warrant, Deputy,' Old Smoke said, grinning.

The deputy got up and dusted off. His trousers had tears in the knees and some of the metal he was wearing had become grazed.

'Goddamn you, man!' the deputy shouted. His eyes flared with rage. 'You're done for, Smokin'. You got eagle feathers in that pouch and I'm going to hunt you down dead. I know where you're going to take them, too. I'll be on Pastora Peak, just waiting.'

Deputy Billy Apple marched back to his car, got in and gunned the engine and drove back up to the highway.

Old Smoke mounted his horse. Rosasharn stood next to it, stroking the side of its head. Old Smoke opened his pouch and handed her an eagle feather. He gave her the same instructions he'd given to Ishmael on how to dispose of it. From a leather bag hanging off the pommel he took out an animal pelt, pulled a whisker off the snout, and placed it on Rosasharn's head. He mumbled an incantation and blew it off. 'When the sign of the rat appears it will be the time to tell the truth so it will be believed, yet not perceived.'

Rosasharn looked up at him quizzically. Old Smoke raised both arms and let out a war whoop, turned his horse, and galloped off without looking back, his destination Pastora Peak.

Rosasharn combed the tangles from her hair, tied it back, and left Chilchinbito. Old Smoke's words — "When the sign of the rat appears it will be the time to tell the truth in a way that it will be believed, yet not perceived" — kept coming back to her. It was a way out for her, she knew that, but out of what? The events of the past seventy-two hours had taken a heavy toll on her nerves.

Still, if she were to have these past days over again, she wouldn't have done anything different. In the faint glow of the trailer's dim light, as Ishmael lay on top off her, she had lifted his head and stared for what seemed a very long time into his eyes. She could see into the depths of his soul. She knew he wasn't a stranger and that he loved her.

During the long drive back to her home town, she managed to convince herself that she committed no wrong and had not been unpatriotic. She would tattoo the American flag on her face for her country if called upon. Sure, she had information about a terrorist cell, but that was all going to be taken care of in a way that would yield no more intelligence than they could gather by detaining Ishmael.

CHAPTER 67

LAKE HAVASU CITY, ARIZONA, TUESDAY 21 AUGUST

Rosasharn had her finger on the rewind button of the cassette player, rewinding her *Black and Blue* Rolling Stones tape for the ninth consecutive time to the start of the song *Memory Motel*. Its haunting melody, along with Jagger's heart-rending melancholy vocals, soothed the void in her heart. Then she saw, in her rear-vision mirror, the flashing lights of a state trooper's squad car closing in behind her and the trooper signaling her to pull over.

Rosasharn stopped the car along the side of the road. As the trooper pulled up, a helicopter appeared overhead, vibrating the dash. It landed in a clearing next to the road. A team of heavily-armed men immediately jumped out and made a beeline towards her car.

CHAPTER 68

SAN FRANCISCO, CALIFORNIA, MONDAY 20 AUGUST

Professor Joseph Rand at Stanford, renowned for his scholarly achievements, an authority on Arabic literature and respected in all the great learning centers of America, was a humble, easygoing, grandfatherly figure. Though bookish by nature, he was not one to put on airs. He had written extensively on all the ancient texts, and had been appointed as a consultant by Homeland Security for his expertise in Middle Eastern and Ancient Persian culture.

Late that morning while he was tidying his desk, he noticed the Arabic words he'd written on the corner of his desk blotter from his conversation with Rosasharn.

Rand cross-referenced the words; it took him about five minutes to work out their meaning and context. They were from an ancient tribal prayer that had been discovered on a cliff face in the Wadi Musa (Valley of Moses).

Professor Rand stood up from his desk, grabbed his walking cane and hobbled over to his bookshelf. He reached behind his 1899 leather-bound copy of *Smith's Bible Dictionary* and grabbed a bottle of gin. He filled his coffee mug, returned the bottle to its hiding place and went back to his desk.

Rand was deeply concerned by where Rosasharn might have gotten the ancient words and why she needed to learn their meaning. He had

Chapter 68 San Francisco, California, Monday 20 August

been briefed by Homeland Security that the ancient prayer was the signature call of the Global Azad Front. People who had survived terrorist attacks recalled these words being recited just before the terrorist blew himself up, attacks that the Global Azad Front had claimed responsibility for. It was obvious that she had not found them in a textbook. If she had, she wouldn't have called him. Had she overheard someone saying them? Was this someone a possible terrorist?

Rand had first met Rosasharn when he gave a series of lectures on the development of ancient language at the Arizona State University. He was impressed with the caliber of the questions she asked after the lecture. Rosasharn gave the professor her thesis on the Battle of Tours in 789 AD, which her Arabic history lecturer had graded poorly, disapproving her creative interpretation of this historical event.

Professor Rand regarded her views on the battle as being well put and thoughtfully argued. He wrote to the head of the history faculty, asking to have Rosasharn's thesis reviewed and upgraded. His request was accepted, resulting in Rosasharn receiving a high distinction.

Rand was in an awkward position. Being a historical consultant to the Department of Homeland Security, he was under oath to report Rosasharn's inquiry. He knew all too well what Homeland Security would do with his report. It would be reviewed, scrutinized and, most probably, Rosasharn would be detained and interrogated, her whole life put under a microscope. Her views on the Middle East would certainly put her under suspicion as being a sympathizer to the radical cause. This was exactly the kind of incident he was under oath to report.

He sat on his leather swivel chair, deep in thought, sipping from his coffee mug. He hated what his country had become since the attacks on the World Trade Center. Then again, the American people were not strangers to a government over-protective about national security.

He rotated the mug in his hand and thought about how it was all happening again. Homeland Security had used him on a number of occasions to infiltrate a dozen or so extreme religious factions and mainstream groups on and off campuses throughout the country.

No matter how trivial he believed the information, he was required to pass it up the chain of command. He was sorry to do this to Rosasharn. Whether he was under surveillance or his phone tapped, he did not know, but he suspected he might be. Homeland Security officers frequently swaggered into his office, unannounced as always, and demanded answers to whatever wild goose chase they were assigned to.

Just the other day, two Homeland officers barged into his office and threw a book written by a Palestinian refugee that had been brought to the attention of Homeland Security by the South Carolina Council for Jewish Faith. They ordered him to dig out anything that they could use to arrest the author, and if there wasn't anything contentious, then conjure something that would stick.

'How had she come across the words? One thing was certain: the words were not part of the everyday Arabic lexicon. He stared at what he had written on the corner of his desk blotter. 'Got it. She heard them on some talkback show on TV or radio.'

He picked up the receiver and phoned the Homeland Security hotline. Just as he was about to dial the last number he paused, and thought about warning Rosasharn.

Immediately after the professor hung up the phone, he left his office and headed down to the Golden Gate Cafe on Fisherman's Wharf where he ordered a drink, tipped the waiter handsomely, borrowed the waiter's mobile phone and made a call to an old friend who had access to some of the biggest media outlets in the country. This was the second time in his life that he felt it was his civic duty to inform the press. The first was during the Hoover witch-hunt years in the early 1960s, when the FBI

Chapter 68 San Francisco, California, Monday 20 August

was flexing its muscles against teachers and academics, and along with other American institutions, their unions, who were being ferociously undermined by informers to weed out teachers and lecturers who had different political opinions than the government's.

He knew that what he had to tell his friend would make national news — free-speech activist arrested, undermining the freedom of expression as outlined in the First Amendment.

CHAPTER 69

LANGLEY, VIRGINIA, WEDNESDAY 30 AUGUST

Special Operations Manager of the Interrogation Department, Hank Yoakum, had just finished reading Harvey Spender's report for the third time. In all his years of sifting the chaff from the wheat in various capacities in just about every law enforcement agency of his country's government, he had never been so perplexed by an investigation of something that seemed so petty yet at the same time somewhat disturbing.

At just a tad over forty, Hank wondered where the past twenty years of his life had gone and, more crucially, where the next twenty were going to take him. He still had the youthful good looks and build of a Californian lifesaver: bushy, bleached blond hair, cleft chin, angular profile and a set of straight gleaming white teeth that were the real thing. One's first impression of Hank, who had never spent so much as a summer by any ocean, was that he was a surfer dude from way out west. But when he opened his mouth, his accent was pure Georgia. He was the type of man who always had a smile on his face, his eyes that told you if he was happy or not.

Yoakum opened the first page of the report, ran his thumb along the contents list, picked up his pen and jotted down a couple of question marks. He thought about the heated argument he'd had with Harvey Spender. In retrospect, he wished that the director had followed Spender's advice and just waited for Rosasharn's second call to Rand, but when it came to terrorist matters, government policy was to treat everything, no matter how insignificant it seemed, with the utmost urgency. In his short tenure with the Department of Homeland Security, Hank Yoakum learnt that he

Chapter 69 *Langley, Virginia, Wednesday 30 August*

was not paid to express opinions, just to collect the facts and pass them on to the director. These pithy jobs that kept landing on his desk made him seriously consider if it was time to move on, maybe go over to the corporate world where he would get paid to think.

He closed the report and checked his watch: 10:30 p.m. He pressed a button on the intercom.

'Sonia, would you please bring forward my flight to Langley by about an hour? And also, sweetie, have Harvey Spender come up and see me ASAP.'

Senior Interrogation Officer for The Department of Homeland Security Special Agent Harvey Spender stood at attention, stone faced, in front of his boss's desk. He brushed his hands over his mop of snow-white hair and then felt his heartbeat.

A former CIA agent with thirty-five years under his belt, he had often reproached himself for defecting to Homeland Security. Spender had been much happier working for less money with the old guard. Just a few more years and then he was out and Homeland could kiss his ass goodbye. There would be no more coming out of retirement for him. He had given his all to the country and that was all they were going to get. Hank placed the phone back in its cradle and looked up at Spender, smiling. 'At ease, soldier. You're relieved from guard duty. Relax, have a chair. Pour yourself some sparkling mountain water.' He motioned towards the water cooler. 'Or if you like, I can have the lovely Sonia brew you up a mean cup of coffee, guaranteed to put lead in your pencil.'

Spender gave his boss a crooked smile as he sat down awkwardly on the edge of his chair.

'Hey, by the way, congratulations on your fortieth wedding anniversary.' Hank extended his hand across the table and pumped Spender's hand.

'Thanks, Hank.'

'Doing anything special?'

'Usual romantic bullshit that women love. Candle light Dinner on Saturday night, get-together with the extended family at the house on Sunday.'

'Make sure you give the lovely lady my warmest.'

'Yeah.' Spender unrolled the newspaper and placed it in front of his boss.

Hank glanced over the front page with feigned interest, then looked up at Spender. 'I've read the paper.'

'Why the hell did the director have to hold a press conference,' Harvey grumbled as he pulled the chair closer to the desk. 'Compromised the whole investigation. It's not half obvious how Rayner is going to use the media circus that's setting up tent at Fort Apache Military Base.'

'To my knowledge, Harvey, the leak was already out way before the director was briefed. The media demanded a press conference with him after the leak.' Hank cleared his throat. 'Anyway, compromised or not, it doesn't really change anything as long as the Department of Homeland Security is seen to be following every lead, however great or small.'

'And however absolutely ridiculous,' Harvey interjected. 'Great and minuscule.'

'Ultimately, it's the way to go.' Hank cocked his head and gave Harvey a slight grin. 'Homeland has got to be seen to have its tentacles spread across the globe and in its own backyard. That's what we're all about. The director, I hear, is going to milk it for all it's worth.'

'I'll tell you what it's worth: jack shit. We arrested her on two flimsy something-or-other charges.' He waved his hand. 'A phone call to Rand inquiring about the suicidal prayer and her files and teacher's reports from Arizona State University. I've looked at the Patriot Act until I was blue in the face and for the life of me, and I am getting closer to

Chapter 69 *Langley, Virginia, Wednesday 30 August*

my "use by" date, I still can't work out what law of conspiracy she has broken or if there is anything in the slightest applicable. As much as I detested Hoover, at least everyone knew where they stood when he was running the show.'

'Her file reports show her to be a bona fide radical. The paper she wrote on the 789 Battle of Tours, she argues that it didn't matter who won,' said Hank. He paused to align his desk blotter before looking up at Spender again. 'The way it gets interpreted affects people's perception. Maybe that's not such a bad thing.' Hank shrugged.

'It's not a good thing when people get the facts wrong.'

'What are you getting at?'

'Ask yourself this, Hank. Who makes history?'

Hank was about to answer, but Spender held up his hand.

'People at a given time and a given place who interpret what went on before.'

'Yes.' Hank nodded. 'We interpret a few ancient Arabic words that some smart girl wants to know the meaning of and they turn out to be a bomber's suicidal prayer. Whether she's a terrorist threat is for us to interpret. You see, my good man, we're paid to find out what's whizzing around in people's heads.'

Spender stared at his boss with unblinking eyes. 'Yeah, yeah, it's the story of my life.' He leaned back in his chair, threw one arm over the back and crossed his legs.

'I know where you're coming from, Spender, but the prayer isn't your run-of-the-mill petition to the almighty God. It's the signature calling card of the Global Azad Front. Yes, the prayer is widely known, but more so in its modern Arabic translation. You know damn well that MI6 and Interpol have uncovered quite a number of the Azad Front's operatives and busted cells in Europe. Some of those men who were arrested had it tattooed on their chests. Remember that decapitated, limbless torso in that restaurant bombing in Brussels, where a group of bigwigs from the Justice Department were killed? The prayer tattooed on the guy's chest was the only thing that identified him as the bomber.'

'I hear what you're saying, Hank.' Spender nodded solemnly. 'From the moment I got assigned to this case my mind jumped to quite a few uneasy conclusions. Look, I've thought about it long and hard, but the book she claims she got the English version from, the *Archaeological Discoveries in the Wadsa Valley*, was sitting on the coffee table in her apartment. She went on about how she was attempting to work backwards from the English to the original. It had to do with the importance of authenticity and getting all that bullshit right for the book she's writing. Swears she didn't have the faintest notion of its relation to the Azad Front. And as far as her knowing whether Rand was consulting for us, I still haven't made up my mind.'

'You reckon she knew?' Hank reached across his desk and picked up his pencil sharpener.

'I figure she had an inkling that he was supposed to have his finger on the pulse of religious student groups and societies inside the walls of American academia for us.' Spender paused for a moment and rubbed his chin. 'She swears that she just wanted to save herself a bit of leg work. Got a feeling that Professor Rand's version of Rayner's phone conversation with him is partial.'

'What do you mean?'

'My first talk with Rand was brief. I got the impression from him that she wasn't sure about what she was asking him. My second chat with him, he played down what he said initially. He went on about how she'd been working on her book and it wasn't the first time she'd called up to be pointed in the right direction.' Spender leant forward and placed both hands on the edge of the desk. 'Hell, I respect the old fart, but what can I say? Between you and me he just wasn't his usual stoic self. Now don't

Chapter 69   Langley, Virginia, Wednesday 30 August

get me wrong Hank, I love my drink, maybe a little too much, but after the working day's done. Not before it starts.'

'I reckon his the one responsible for leaking her story to the media, but we got no proof,' said Hank. He slowly rotated the end of his pen in the pencil sharpener, staring intently at a slither of plastic unraveling from the blade.

Spender nodded agreeably.

'So the professor has helped her out on a number of occasions on this book she's writing?'

'Yeah, way before he was with us.' Spender sat back in his chair and rubbed the back of his neck. 'We turned her apartment upside down. Not one scrap of forbidden literature there, none of the usual handbooks and manuals on how to make bombs, waging terrorism, extreme religious propaganda. Nothing like that. About this book she's writing, well, there it was in a cardboard box. I reckon there were up to two thousand plus pages of handwritten and computer printout notes. The handwritten stuff was in the smallest scrawl I've ever seen, and believe me, I've seen plenty. We had to enlarge it by photocopying it. Then there was the printed material that we had a heck of a time deciphering. It was formatted in a mishmash of typefaces, type sizes, color and shading. Her cross-referencing, filing system and indexing were yet another jumble. She told us she uses this type of quantum leaping, time-warped calendar. Fuck knows where she got it from.'

'What do you mean?'

'Pages were dated with calendar months having over forty days assigned to them. As far as we could make out, it dated back to when she was in her first year at Arizona State. From what we have managed to piece together, there are notes on every religion on the planet, cross-referenced and traced back to this author or that prophet from some other religion that she had discovered was plagiarized either from Greek mythology, pagan Rome, Babylon ... it just goes on and on. There are a lot of contentious assumptions and hypotheses in it. In my professional opinion, from what Professor Rand said about it, I figure it pales into insignificance when you look at her stuff on the Battle of Tours. We attempted to reconcile what she told us in the interview with her manuscript, which, from what we have read, is non-fiction.'

'So how did she explain it?' Hank asked.

'She went on and on about St Paul's road to Damascus,' Spender explained. 'It's a curious story, mixture of myth and reality. She said what's written in the manuscript is the backbone of all the unwritten stuff in her head which, in her own words, is "the flesh and the life of all her academic research". Some of it is based on actual stuff about her mother's psychic abilities. We talked to the brother and sister-in-law. They were well aware of the book she was writing, but she guarded its content as if it were a national secret.'

'How did they react when they heard that she was taken into custody?'

'Stunned, utterly speechless, but like her brother said, it's a mystery half the time what goes on in her head. He played down his mother's psychic abilities in a sort of nice way.' Spender paused for a moment, then went on, 'Her mother did run a New Age crystal healing practice, reading minds, until she had a stroke and wound up at Big River Nursing Home.'

'The mother, a psychic from Sedona who can read terrorists' minds.' Hank chuckled.

'If she ever recovers she could come out of retirement and get a job as an air marshal,' Spender joked. 'Homeland could use little old ladies like her. All she'd have to do is look at them.'

'What about friends, work colleagues? There's not much about them in the report.' Hank motioned towards Spender's report on his desk. He smiled, but his eyes were deadly serious.

'Her work colleagues were astonished over her arrest. From what they

Chapter 69 Langley, Virginia, Wednesday 30 August

told us, she was social person around the office but kept her private life out of the workplace.'

'Did she ever mention anything about radicalized prayers to her friends?'

'No, nothing at all along religious lines. Her girlfriends didn't strike me as the philosophical kind or even the intellectual kind. They also, like the brother, didn't have a clue about what was whirling in Rayner's head.'

'Did they know about her involvement with Concho Thomas Paintrock, alias Old Smoke?

'No.'

Hank flipped through the report to review the suicide death of Old Smoke. He nodded and smacked his lips. 'This Old Smoke fellow. Things are a little sketchy about him in the report,

'I rang up the American Indian Movement. They emailed a few pics of Old Smoke standing in a group shot with Marlon Brando in front of the church at Wounded Knee.'

'Was he an extra in a Hollywood western?

'No. A police report from back in 1973 stated that he was a member of the two hundred headstrong Indian war party that had that seventy-one-day stand-off with the federal marshals at Wounded Knee. It had something to do with declaring the place an independent Oglala Sioux nation. The story goes is that Brando refused to accept his Academy Award for Best Actor for his role in *The Godfather*. In protest against Hollywood's inaccurate depiction of the American Indian's. A few day after the awards Brando shows up in support for the standoff.'

'Did you dig up anything else of interest?'

'Old Smoke's got virtually nothing in his rap sheet except a charge for having an illegal firearm.'

'Old Smoke.' Hank repeated it to himself a couple of times. 'Now where have I heard that name?'

'Probably in some John Wayne movie,' Spender replied.

'No. There was a book I read a while back ... It'll come to me. He's a type of medicine man?'

'It's funny you mention medicine man, Hank. Some interesting stuff I learnt about Old Smoke from Joseph Aaron Jasper from the FBI office in Gallop, Arizona. It's not in the report.'

'Do tell, Harvey.'

'Jasper told us that Old Smoke is an enigma. He's got a reputation as big as Texas for his supernatural exploits that either cause uproar or calm among the people around the reservations spread across that neck of the woods. The guy was renowned for crossing sacred tribal taboos. All his practices seem to be derivatives and a mixture of just about every tribe on US soil. On the Ute res, for instance, he's known as your run-of-the-mill medicine man, on Laguna res, a conjurer, and on the Mescalero res, listen to this, a hand trembler.'

'Must help the locals get over their jitters,' Hank quipped.

'The list goes on.'

'Sounds like he ought to be in the pantheon of Marvel Comics' super-heroes and villains,' Hank commented wryly.

'As far as our investigation is concerned, we refer to him in this report as a Hopi Skinwalker, which is really a solecism because in Navajo folk-lore they class their witches as Skinwalkers. Old Smoke is a full-blood Hopi, and they have their own terminology. It slips my mind right now.'

'A Skinwalker. That's a new one on me.'

'Skinwalkers are supposed to have power to transform themselves into any animal that they take a fancy to. They do it by draping, say, a wolf pelt or bear's hide over their body so as to metamorphose into the real thing.'

'Sounds like a shape shifter. Dean and Sam from that Supernatural TV series used to shank those beasts. Interesting.' Hank thumbed through

Chapter 69 Langley, Virginia, Wednesday 30 August

the report until he found what he was looking for. 'This is the bit that puzzles me. I want to know more about this Old Smoke's death. Again it's incomplete.'

'I've come up with a few interesting things about his supposed suicide. From what I've been told, it's got jack shit to do with our investigation. Besides, it's an internal matter for the reservation police.'

Hank stared at Spender and grinned. 'Harvey, believe me when I tell you I understand where you're coming from. Those days are gone. It's all about being a team player. No more "us" and "them". Things have changed since September 11.'

'Yeah, yeah, we're all one big happy law enforcement family sharing all our secrets,' Spender said.

'Talk to me about it. Let me decide if I should bore the director with it.'

Spender reached over the desk to grab a paperclip and bent it out of shape. 'You asked for it. How about I pick up the thread where it starts in relation to Rayner?'

'Put it anyway you like.'

'Okay. What we learnt about the eagle feather found in Rayner's glove compartment was that the tip of it was cut in a V-shape, which had all the signs of being done by a Native American. The day Rayner was picked up, the FBI office in Gallop got an anonymous call reporting that someone on the Navajo res over by Chilchinbito Canyon was butchering eagles for ritual purposes. The office is always being inundated with such calls, so they put them in the "not now" basket.'

'When it overflows it gets emptied into the wastebasket?' Hank cut in.

'They just stopped sending their people if it ain't something major. You've worked in the Indian Affairs Bureau. You know what it's like.'

'Soon as they set foot on the res, a cold wall of silence descends.'

'Yeah, Hank. Anyway, we stuck our noses in, rang Chief Archie Rosedale from the Navajo Reservation Tribal Police. He knew of only one man at Chilchinbito who had a reputation for trapping eagles for ritual purposes: Old Smoke.

'Some of this stuff I'm telling you will be in Rosedale's report, which, by the way, should've been in days ago. He's been dragging his heels on it,' Spender paused and uncrossed his legs, 'which is why it's not in the report on your desk now. And, putting it frankly, when it finally does arrive, it will be immaterial,' Spender said firmly. He placed the bent paperclip on the edge of the table.

'I'll get someone a bit higher up to put the thumbscrews on the guy.' Hank made a note on a legal pad.

'Higher up? Hah.' Spender guffawed. 'That fat feather-brain couldn't be inspired to move any faster to open his front door if the president were knocking on it. So, according to Jasper, Deputy Billy Apple's brothers ...'

'Apple is the deputy who was dispatched to bring in Old Smoke?'

'He's some piece of work, this Apple,' said Spender. 'His uniform is like those banana republic generals with their decorations plastered over every square inch. There's a tribal turf war going on. Apple and his brothers have been itching to get their hands on Old Smoke's property, he being the only Hopi who had claims around Chilchinbito. Old Smoke's property has got a natural spring. The Apples have to truck their water in.'

'Whenever Old Smoke performs his Spiritual Council get-together ritual, the local wildlife gets a little stressed.'

'The wildlife gets stressed!?' Hank leaned back in his chair.

'Hear me out,' Spender replied. 'This is where it gets strangely exciting. Apple was out at Old Smoke's ranch investigating the animal disturbance. From what Apple told us, his brother, who lives on the west side of the canyon, called him up to complain that his goats wouldn't go out to pasture.'

'That's mighty serious stuff, the goats not going out to graze.'

Chapter 69 *Langley, Virginia, Wednesday 30 August*

Spender ignored the jibe and continued. 'Jasper's hunch is that it was, in all probability, Apple's brother who put in the anonymous call that morning to his office.'

'Director's sure going to love hearing about goats not going out to graze. I can just picture him briefing the president,' Hank said, grinning.

'It's an Indian reservation,' said Spender, stifling a yawn. He stood up and went over to the water cooler and poured himself a drink, took a couple of sips and leant against the wall. 'That morning Apple was over at Old Smoke's ranch giving him a hard time over his brother's goat troubles, he finds Rosasharn and the old Indian exchanging intimate cuddles by the camp fire.'

'It puts Rayner at Chilchinbito Canyon. So, they were having some type of affair.

'Billy Apple figured that she was a whore working the reservation.'

'How long has Rosasharn known Old Smoke?'

'These were her exact words: "How long does a woman need to know a man before she sleeps with him?"'

'Only a woman can answer that,' Hank replied.

'Deepens on how much he pays her,' Spender quipped.

'Okay, tell me more of what I don't know.'

'Well, Hank, you asked for it. Here's another feather to put in your hat for the director. While over there that morning Apple noted that Old Smoke was wearing a leather pouch around his waist. Apple alleges it was stuffed with eagle feathers. It seems that there was some type of scuffle. Rayner's account was that Apple lunged at Old Smoke in an attempt to yank the leather pouch from his waist and in the process Apple tripped over and tore his pants or something. According to Rayner, Apple was mighty pissed off at Old Smoke and threatened him.

'In hindsight, it was bad timing to dispatch Apple to bring in Old Smoke. According to Jasper, things have been coming to a head between

Old Smoke and the Apple clan for quite a while. Jasper's take on the way it played out was that Apple was pursuing Old Smoke up Pastora Peak.'

'And I can guess the rest,' Hank cut in. 'Billy and the rest of his posse help the bird man over the side, Billy files a report and calls it suicide.'

'Yep, I figured the same. What with all those feathers and Old Smoke being in a bird frame of mind,' Spender paused. 'But according to the final act in the ritual, he's not supposed to turn himself into an eagle with the feathers. He's meant to just let them flutter away.'

'Any witness to verify Apple's version?'

'There were a couple of old toothless Navajo women tending their sheep herd. One of them is a distant relation to the Apples.'

'Jesus Christ, what a subplot to the Rayner investigation,' Hank said.

'Wait. There's still more. Late yesterday I called the Indian Affairs Bureau and learnt that the Apple brothers have lodged a claim for Old Smoke's estate.' Spender went back to his chair and sat on the edge.

'I see what you mean,' said Hank. He picked up his pen and made a few notes in the margin of the report.

'That's what's been bugging me from the start. Apprehending Rayner before she made the second call to Rand and not having one of our people with Apple's war party to pick up Old Smoke. We moved in too fast.'

Hank drummed his fingers on the edge of the table. 'So, what was Rayner's reaction when she heard Old Smoke was dead?' Hank asked.

'She burst into tears. After she settled down, she sort of opened up. She was still clearly distressed, but all her vague answers and that cackling and giggling had stopped. I'll tell you this, Hank, over the years, in this line of work, you get to the point where you feel like putting a bullet between the eyes of some spy's head. This was the first time I wanted to strangle someone with my bare hands. Worse still, I felt I could derive pleasure from it. Old Smoke knew something. If we had the two of them

Chapter 69 Langley, Virginia, Wednesday 30 August

I'd be able to pull together all the threads of what she told us. Whatever secret they had between them ... well, it's now under lock and key,' Spender replied.

'It just seems odd that Old Smoke would go to such great lengths to have a Spiritual Council meeting for a phoney terrorist. Then again, if he is a charlatan, it doesn't matter. So tell me, Harvey, why include Native American spirituality in the story?'

'She wanted to have a type of alternative jurisdiction to pass judgement and it's Native Americans who were on this land way before any European settlement. She believes they are the legitimate custodians of this land and didn't want to identify forgiveness with any of the mainstream religions.'

'I got to admit, it's original. Why go to the trouble of re-enacting the ritual? Hell, it cost the life of Old Smoke. Most writers put it down on their PCs in the comfort of their own homes.'

'It's got to do with all that authenticity crap. Getting the details right and actually going through the motions, which she reckons gives her an insight and untainted first-hand impressions.'

Hank closed the report and leant forward on his chair. He stared at the Confederate flag punctured with bullet holes encased in a glass frame mounted on the wall of his office.

'The Spiritual Council meeting is a type of celestial courtroom. The Skinwalker is the medium between the celestial beings and the terrestrial.' Harvey explained the significance of the eagle feathers. Hank listened with intense interest.

'The Supreme Spiritual Council is made up of warriors and leaders of the Indian nations. They were the ones who passed judgment on a fictional terrorist who had seen the error of his ways,' Harvey continued.

'Did the council find him guilty?' Hank asked.

'No.'

'I don't think the deputy director is going to lose any sleep over the death of Old Smoke,' Hank replied. 'Okay, let's say he was going to share in the spoils of Rayner's success as a novelist. That brings me back to my first question. If he did it for money, why commit suicide? Then again, from what Jasper told you, he did not commit suicide, it was murder.'

'That's about it in a nutshell,' said Spender.

'Was a third person in on the act, someone to play the suppositional terrorist?'

'That part she denies. We have an eyewitness that Rosasharn stopped at the Warm Springs Bar and Bistro. Went in and had a word to the bartender on duty, who is also a part owner of the place, a little old fellah goes by the name of Little Bird Double Head. We tried to get in touch with Double Head by phone, but his brother said he was laid up with a fever. So we didn't waste any time and sent that new young buck, Liam Kinsey, ex-naval intelligence guy, with Dave to have a chat to him and get a signed statement.'

'What did they come up with?'

'Double Head's place was in some rocky, godforsaken valley. When they finally got there, it was just on sunrise. There were people standing around together, crying on each other's shoulders, old women lamenting and cutting their chins with sharp stones. A dozen or so men were punching a hole in a dwelling the Navajo call a hogan on the north or east side. I don't remember which. It's got to do with dragging the corpse out of the house according to tribal customs.'

'You mean literally, with their fists?'

'No. Sledgehammers. Anyway, after they identified themselves to a teenage girl, she pointed out Double Head's brother. They chatted briefly with him. He told them that just after midnight a wolf-like ghost appeared on top of the hill the hogan backed onto. For about ten or so minutes, the ghost danced and whooped and recited Navajo prayers so

Chapter 69 Langley, Virginia, Wednesday 30 August

loud that it was like he was standing in front of a P.A. At the end of the final prayer, which was really the beginning.'

'What you mean it was the beginning?'

'The ghost was reciting them backwards. It's supposed to put a malevolent spin on them. Turning the blessing into a curse. At the end of it the ghost vanished, and then he heard his brother scream out a death cry. What you make of that, Hank?'

'Old Smoke the Skinwalker must have worked his juju on Double Head,' said Hank.

'Problem with that scenario is that Old Smoke had committed suicide twenty-four hours prior to Double Head's death.'

Hank nodded.

'That reminds me. It's probably irrelevant as far as our investigation is concerned, a few weeks ago, some hot-headed Indian enthusiast made a scene in the Warm Springs Bar and Grill about the pictures hanging on the wall. He had a beef about it being disrespectful and manhandled Double Head. It was reported, and guess who was dispatched?'

'Deputy Bad Apple.'

'Apple noted that he witnessed Old Smoke with the mystery man later that day helping the guy with his car.'

'Did Apple get the registration?'

'No. He told us no charges were being filed so he didn't bother.'

'So that brings us back to Indian war games they play on the reservations,' said Hank.

'We got two deaths, one definitely suspicious, the other maybe a medical. Who knows? Still waiting for the autopsy. It'll be in Rosedale's report.'

'It's just way too coincidental. Sounds like the stuff conspiracy theories are forged from,' Hank said. He flipped open the report to the summary of Rosasharn's whereabouts during the days preceding her arrest. 'Sunday, she told us she drove out to Prescott to drop some books at a friend's house. The friend wasn't there but she left them on the doorstep with a card. Saturday, picking up her mother and going to her niece's birthday party at her brother's house.' Hank stared at the question mark next to a name in the 'Persons of Interest' section of the report.

'Hold it there, Hank.' Spender shifted uncomfortably in his seat. 'I know what you're getting at. It's about that guy from the aqueduct plant who works with her brother. She gave him a lift home from the party.'

Hank looked at Spender. 'Scot Fall. How is it that you haven't talked to him?'

'Percy Owens, the personnel manager, said he had to make a lightning trip back to Canada to visit a sick relative. Said he would be back early next week. Owens is going to ring me the minute Fall sets foot back in the office.'

'You learn anything about him?'

'Owens spoke very highly of him. He's supposed to be some whiz kid from the Canadian water authority.'

'What about finding out where he's staying and sending someone over to have a chat? Get his cell phone number.'

'We've called his cell phone,' Spender replied, 'but we just keep getting a recorded message that he will be available when he's back at work. Look, Hank, of all the people we needed to talk to, I slotted him at the bottom of the list. Everyone's so tied up on more pressing assignments. As soon as someone's free I'll send them up to Canada to talk to him. But frankly, all he's going to tell us is that he had a romp with her in the back seat of her car after they dropped off the mother.'

'It depends how long she had known him.'

'I'll pay that one,' replied Spender.

'Don't you reckon it's another convenient coincidence that this Scot Fall, who has a brief dalliance with Rayner, suddenly heads up north?'

Chapter 69 *Langley, Virginia, Wednesday 30 August*

Spender sighed, thought for a few moments and then shrugged. 'When you put it like that, what can I say? Let's jump on him. I'll get on the next plane to wherever he is.'

Hank leant back in his chair and rubbed his chin. 'You can't do that.'

'And why not?'

'You got an anniversary this weekend.'

'It won't be the first I missed.'

'With Rosedale's report still pending, hang loose. Wait for the call from Owens then get back to me,' Hank said with an ominous tone in his voice. 'I just want to know if he's still alive and kicking. If this Scot Fall does some type of disappearing trick or turns up dead, then it's a threesome on this investigation.'

'Whatever you say, big boss man.'

Hank closed the report and placed a palm on the front cover. 'Look, Harvey, as you've probably already figured, I got you here to explain why the things we've talked about are not in your report. After what you've told me I have revised my poor opinion of it. But how does it all tie in with Rayner's call to Rand and how she came to being privy to an obscure prayer? Seriously, where do you begin to join the dots? I have to agree with you that the circumstances leading to Old Smoke's death are immaterial.'

'I appreciate what you just said and that you let me air my grievances. Now that I've gone over it with you, I'm starting to have second thoughts. Don't get me wrong. I still think it's been a storm in a teacup, but everything is just a little too neat and tidy. Expedient for all parties involved.' Spender removed his glasses, pulled a handkerchief from his shirt pocket, buffed the lenses, and then put his glasses back on. 'We've got two deaths. Deputy Billy Apple is embroiled up to his neck and has been not in the least conducive to the investigation from the outset, and his motives are clearly not in the interest of national security. And there is Professor

Rand. I'll put him in the same basket, and then there's a question mark hanging over Scot Fall's head. All of it only makes me feel I want to start again.'

'I get your drift, Harvey.' Hank looked at his watch. 'In a couple of hours I have to brief the director. My hunch is that the director is going to whitewash the whole thing and let her walk.'

Spender stood up and made his way to the door, paused, then said, 'I know I left a few details out and it's not too late in the day to fill in the gaps. I'll get to work on it now and by way of apology, I'll throw in the Chief Rosedale stuff at no extra charge. I'll email it to you in time to read before you walk into the director's office.'

'You got a deal there, Harvey.'

'No sweat, Hank.'

'One more thing. Did she tell you how her story ends?'

'The way she tells it, the reformed terrorist, wearing his suicide bomb belt, goes back for a final meeting with the cell, tells them they haven't got a fucking clue about doing Gods will and dispatches himself along with his cell mate to hell without a dead American credited to their names.'

'Some imagination. What's the book called?'

'*Radical Lies.*'

CHAPTER 70

VERMILLION BAY, LOUISIANA, FRIDAY 31 AUGUST

The Malatesta luxury cruiser was anchored 150 yards from the shore on the eastern end of Vermilion Bay. Frank and Benny had been living on the boat since rendezvousing with the *Mark Twain*. Frank and Matteo had been commuting back and forth to the prison house, questioning Ishmael and debating long into the night.

Matteo Malatesta had been to hell and believed with all his heart that, after reading the contents of the envelope addressed to the Department of Homeland Security, he was going to stay there indefinitely. He was so overcome with anxiety that he was reduced to extreme physical weakness. Not even retreating to his much loved rose gardens or pottering around his glasshouses to lovingly spray a rose gave him any calm from the calamitous and potentially fatal visitation of two terrorists to the *Mark Twain*. Matteo didn't see the delicate petals and exquisite blooms. All he could focus on were the barbed stems. How was he going to extricate himself from what he now knew, even though the terrorist attack had been unwittingly thwarted?

In his long career in the underworld, Matteo had seen it all. He was no patriot, but now he was firmly on the side of American law and justice. More than anything else in the world, he wanted to wash his hands of this intractable crisis and would gladly place the whole matter into the more than capable hands of the Department of Homeland Security, telling them all he knew. But there was a problem. He was, after all, on the wrong side of the law.

Matteo spent two days in sackcloth and ashes, attending Mass, and rendering his soul bare before the Virgin Mary, imploring her for succor and wisdom on how to go forward. On the third day, he flung himself into damage control. First, with Uriah still fresh on Paul South's heels, he indefinitely suspended all gambling on the *Mark Twain*. Second, as for the eight security guards and the steward who were present during the siege in Canaan's room, Matteo individually and collectively, debriefed them all.

After delicately questioning Duvall in order to find out how much he knew, Matteo ascertained that the preacher was completely ignorant of the terrorists' plot. He seemed to believe that all the goings-on had to do with the murder of Conway Lascelles and Wiltshire. Matteo set him straight and allayed his fears that he might be in any way to blame.

Matteo was slouched in a deckchair, dangling a fishing line over the side of the boat, his face awash in meditative contemplation. He was wearing a pork pie hat perched at a rakish angle and a tropical shirt. Beside him, along the edge of the gunwale, was a row of the proudest looking potted roses.

Frank, stripped to his waist, was sitting on an ice chest opposite him, swatting at mosquitoes with a rolled-up newspaper, desperately trying to keep them off his freshly drawn tattoo: a band of razor wire that circled his upper left bicep.

Benny, on a treasure hunt, was traipsing along the shore with a shovel slung over his shoulder. To keep him off their backs and from interrupting his older brother's deliberation, Frank had buried a cooler full of ice cream and oysters in the sand.

A dozen or so of Malatesta's men were on the shore, camped next to the petrified boardwalk, built by Portuguese slave traders, that led to the prison house a couple of miles inland. Apart from a small, narrow beachhead on the western end of the bay, their prison house was inaccessible by

Chapter 70 *Vermillion Bay, Louisiana, Friday 31 August*

land and water. The demarcation between land and water was defined by a dense line of cypresses, magnolias and water gums that pushed for miles inland, beyond them were endless fields of maize, sorghum and corn that stretched out beneath the firmament.

Marshes and swamps infested with alligators, blood-sucking leeches and bottomless mud pits were the Malatestas' natural security against unwelcome intruders. The western end of the beachhead, a state wildlife sanctuary was also secured. Wildlife officials and park rangers who patrolled the coastal wetland were on the Malatesta payroll.

Except for Benny's occasional outbursts, the sound of schools of fish bobbing to the surface to snap at insects and the distant drone of commercial fishing boats trawling the shoreline, Vermilion Bay was as tranquil as heaven.

Frank slapped at a mosquito on the gunwale.

'Use the repellent,' said Matteo.

'Tattoo Tony says no chemicals until the scabs fall off,' Frank replied, belligerent. Out of the sheer boredom of waiting around for his brother to arrive, he had gone up to Abbeville and had gotten the tattoo. He swiped at another mosquito as it hovered above his arm. The edge of the rolled up newspaper sliced off part of the scab, causing it to bleed.

'Damn it,' he growled. He tossed the paper over the side of the boat and inspected the wound. 'Oh shit, look what that flying pinhead made me do.' The tattooed band of razor wire now looked like it had a breach.

Matteo threw him the can of repellent. Frank caught it and lightly sprayed his arm, attempting to keep clear of the tattooed area. He averted Matteo's gaze by staring over the side at the floating newspaper.

The front page of the *Daily Iberia* carried a picture of Rosasharn. The headline read: 'Public outcry against Homeland's Hoover-style tactics.' The brothers had been closely following the Rosasharn Rayner story as it unfolded in the media with intense interest.

Frank brushed a flaking scab from his arm and let out a groan of utter frustration. He wished with all his heart that both of the terrorists had fallen into the water when Benny had decided to play pirates on the open seas.

It was just before sunrise when the cruiser arrived at Vermilion Bay. While Canaan was being lifted into the rubber dinghy by two of the cabin cruiser's crew, Benny, who had been pestering Frank to let him 'sail the pirate ship', jumped behind the wheel and started playing captain, swinging his hooked hand around as he commandeered in ghastly merriment his imaginary crew. He switched on the engine and, before anyone could stop him, put the boat in gear. As the boat lurched forward the two members of the crew, who had been about to haul Canaan into the rubber dinghy, lost their footing and dropped him in the water. Hearing the 'Man overboard!' calls, Benny panicked and put the boat into reverse and, in the process, everyone present believed that Canaan was sheared by the propeller. The boat's spotlight had been played all over the water, but no body was recovered.

Matteo had posted a $75,000 reward among the wildlife officers on his payroll for the recovery of Canaan's body.

Frank's face flushed red with anger as he thought about it all. 'Look, Matteo, how many more times do we have to trek through that jungle before we wipe him off the face of the earth, burn the fuckin' envelope and flush the ashes down the commode?' he snapped. He pounded the deck with his left foot in rhythm with his frazzling nerves. He was ready to bury his head in a bucket of Colombian cocaine and then go and put a bullet in the back of Ishmael's head.

'Today was the last time. Tonight we're pulling up anchor.' Matteo's answer was sharp.

'Well, all right. It's show time.' Frank grabbed the two-way radio from the deck. 'I'll tell Gaetano — the Coffee Grinder — to mix the concrete

Chapter 70 *Vermillion Bay, Louisiana, Friday 31 August*

down at the luxury suite in the swamp and to pull a few espressos,' said Frank eagerly.

Matteo narrowed his eyes and shook his head.

Frank sighed loudly and stared glumly at the pulsating LED on the handset. 'I'm still trying to come to terms with how Paul South, Canaan, whatever his name was, was all set to sink the *Mark Twain*,' Frank said, sounding almost like a frightened child. 'Can't get it out of my head. It's like a movie reel.'

'The curtains are down on Canaan. He's history,' Matteo retorted.

'Yeah.'

'Look, Frankie, if Uriah hadn't been snooping around, we wouldn't have been alerted to Canaan's presence. Sure, the consequences would've been disastrous, but it didn't happen, little brother. Get that through your head. So why cry over beer that ain't on the floor?'

Frank shrugged and forced a smile. 'I suppose you're right, as usual.'

Matteo's fishing line flexed. 'I think I caught something. Throw me the net. It feels like something big.' Matteo frantically reeled in the line.

Frank leant over and grabbed the net next to his foot and threw it to his brother. As Matteo scrambled for it, the line slackened.

'Damn you, Frank. Look what you made me do.' Matteo reeled in the line and threaded the hook through a shrimp. 'If you ain't gonna fish, don't come up,' and he cast the line back into the water. Turning his attention back to Frank, he said, 'Frankie, we've been in and out of tight squeezes before. This one is no different.'

'No different? Are you fuckin' crazy? He's a terrorist, for Christ's sake.'

'That's in the past. His brain has been rewired. He's seen the light. A man who tells the truth, not out of fear or for gain but for the truth's sake, deserves respect,' said Matteo.

'Bullshit. There's no honor, maybe in Papa's days, but not these days. It's about looking after number one. Exterminate him and let's get on with what we do best,' Frank pleaded. 'Hell, we would be doing the guy a favor. He's been begging us to put him out of his misery.'

Matteo nodded and smacked his lips. 'Frankie, Frankie. It warms my heart to hear you taking a real interest in the family business. This has got to be a first. All your life you've been searching for that special vocation. Mother Mary knows how many times Papa and me have been telling you that it's right before your eyes and now you're saying you want us to go back and do what we do best.'

'You know what I mean,' Frank said sheepishly.

'Yes. Yes I do, Frankie. Look, let's not get sidetracked. How am I going to get it through that dreadlocked head of yours that it did not happen? So quit breaking my balls over it.' Matteo cupped his groin.

'But Matteo ...' Frank whined.

'Shut the fuck up and listen, Frank. You're starting to sound like Benny. You're talking about looking after number one. Well, kiddo, let me tell you something. It's all about decision making and thinking it through.' Matteo tapped the side of his head. 'Because when you learn how to think and you apply that thinking to the business at hand, you'll be a winner every time.'

Matteo grinned at his younger brother. 'Papa done it pushing wheelbarrows full of horse and chicken shit up and down the vegetable patch for days at a time, thinking. I got my roses.' He motioned towards the pots. 'And now I'm starting to see the flowers again. The thinking is done. Time for action.'

'Matteo, while I was here waiting to get word from you, I ...' Frank stopped and held Matteo's gaze for a moment, then turned away and looked towards the shoreline. Benny was up to his waist in a sandpit, madly shoveling.

Matteo reeled in his line a few notches, cleared his throat.

'Being one step ahead of your opponent gives you the edge. Look at

Chapter 70 Vermillion Bay, Louisiana, Friday 31 August

it this way. We're there in El Paso, keeping an eye on our FBI and IRA friends. You know that a lot of our money goes across the Rio Grande, which is a weak link in our operations. That's why I keep this little pinkie on the pulse there.' Matteo cracked his knuckles and wiggled his little finger. 'Paul South shows up out of the blue and that fuck Uriah gets a hard-on over him, hoping South will lead him to our door.' Matteo reeled in his line. 'Pass me that bait bucket. I've got to find something meatier. The fish are stealing my bait.'

Frank kicked over the bucket.

'Grab yourself a line and let's try to get some relaxation time. It's not every day we go out fishing together.'

'It's not every day we wind up in the middle of a fucking terrorist plot either. Geez, get real, bro.'

Matteo gazed at the setting sun on the horizon. The Spanish moss hanging over the limbs of the cypress and oaks glowed an iridescent orange.

'Man, look at that sunset,' Matteo sighed.

Frank stared at the sunset. A downcast expression crept over his face. He went below to get a beer and a fishing rod.

'Hey, you want a drink?'

'Grab me a Coke.'

Frank climbed back on deck, threw a couple of handfuls of bait into the water, baited his rod and cast it over the side.

'You're only a kid, but what you say is right.'

'Just trying to work it out, Matteo.'

'Now that you've settled yourself down, you're going to listen to me and look at the process that goes into making the right decision.' Matteo grinned at his younger brother.

'I'll tell you this, Frankie. When I learnt that we had a couple of terrorists on our hands my bowels turned to water.' Matteo leant over and placed his hand on Frank's knee. 'I was sitting on the crapper emptying them out while I read the report addressed to the Homeland Security. I know that I shouldn't have kept you in the dark for three days about the watery shit going down.' Matteo sighed. 'Hell, Frankie, I really believed with my whole heart that the thing was a curse and that it was the beginning of the end for us all.'

His voice quivered. He stared across the water at the exposed sandbars. 'You know what it's like when a thick fog settles over the French quarter? How you can't tell if you're heading up Bourbon or down Royal? Then a wind whips up from the gulf, you blink and everything is where it should be. You know what I am saying?'

'Yeah.' Frank placed his hand over his brother's hand and gently squeezed it. 'Sure do.'

'Whatever was going to happen? I had you and Benny ready to head south to Havana in this tub at the drop of the hat.'

Frank nodded and motioned him to talk on.

'I was driving home from St Augustine after pouring my heart out in front of the altar. Fuck knows how long I was there. I knew it was way past closing time because cranky Father Ugo Albino was leaning against the light switch box, twirling his key ring and chain. On my way home, as I was coming over the rise down to the house ... you know, that spot where you can practically see the whole lake?'

Frank nodded.

'I pulled over by the side of the road, stared out at the water for a long time, again for how long I can't fuckin' remember. After a while I began to feel not so alone on this problem. I felt that Papa was in the car, sitting in the back seat chewing on the end of an unlit cigar with the heel of his shoe jammed between the console and front seat. Just like when he used to listen to Gaetano or Sammy sitting opposite him when one of them had just brought him bad news. And I swear, Frankie, I heard Papa's

Chapter 70 *Vermillion Bay, Louisiana, Friday 31 August*

voice loud and clear saying to me, "Piece of cake to fix. We get over this like having a shit." Frankie! Believe me when I tell you. I knew then and there in my heart,' he pounded his chest a couple times, 'a solution was there for the taking. Didn't know what the fuck it was, but it was there.'

Frank stared at his brother, wide-eyed, open-mouthed for a few moments. 'The solution is to mash the guy in the mud and you have to disturb the fuckin' dead to clear the fog in your head. Come on, Matteo, get real,' Frank growled.

'It's not about the bullet in the back of the head. Why we need him alive is clear, and boy, I thought this out through and through.' Matteo grimaced, stood up and urinated over the side.

'They're going to start biting now,' Frank quipped.

'Trying to get through to you is as hard as pissing in the wind and trying not to get your pants wet. If you don't want to hear me out, fine! End of fuckin' story.'

'Hey, Matteo.' Frank was serious now. 'You know I've never lost any sleep over whatever was going down in the past. But I've been knocking down sleeping pills and stress tabs like a junkie over this one.'

Matteo sat back down, grabbed his rod and took up the slack in the line. 'I know you got to know. Thank God I don't have to explain it to Benny. Where is he by the way?'

They looked towards the land. Benny was pounding the back of the shovel on what appeared to be some unfortunate sea turtle the size of a rubber exercise ball.

'It looks like Benny has found the turtle's soft spot,' Matteo exclaimed.

'Benny boy ought to be hacking the edge of that fuckin' shovel across that terrorist's neck,' Frank blurted.

'When we first got hold of Scot Fall alias Ishmael-the-terrorist, I was going to let the retarded monster loose on him. It would've given me a hard-on to send one of those motherfucker suicide bombers to their maker with no slave trophies. Benny has already dispatched one to his maker empty-handed.

'But after today's interrogation and what I read in the paper this morning, that broad Rosasharn is deflecting the heat.' Matteo motioned to a pile of newspapers. 'She's plastered on the front pages of right-wing papers as an extreme sympathizer of the radical cause. Others are saying she's an insightful intellectual. It's all got to do with the ideas she expressed in a couple of papers she wrote during her days at school. Everyone has read them and made up their mind. Honestly, I don't give a shit. What the fuck they picked her up for, so far it's not clear, but whatever she mouthed off to her professor friend was enough to warrant him ratting her to Homeland.'

'That's what they pay him for. She just rang the wrong person, is all,' Frank said as he trimmed his line.

'Read between the lines in the interview with the old professor in yesterday's paper and I bet a hundred grand he is of the mind that Homeland shouldn't have taken such drastic measures on the poor bitch. Where the hell she got the harebrained idea that they picked her up because of some book she was writing, I'll never know, and I don't want to know.'

'Hey, Matteo, she actually is writing a book. Her brother and sister-in-law confirmed it.'

'Whatever she's singing to Homeland, I figure it's going to get her out of the shit hole she's fallen in. What little we know from the papers and the television I figure it backs up that Ishmael is not fucking with us.'

'You think so?'

Matteo nodded thoughtfully. 'The interview on NBC with the officer from the Navajo police department assigned to bring in the old Indian alive goes by the name of ... Billy Plum, or Peach ... some fruit ...'

'The one wearing all the medals that Homeland is grilling?'

'That's him. The Navajo cop knows something, but he ain't coming to

Chapter 70 *Vermillion Bay, Louisiana, Friday 31 August*

the powwow with Homeland. Whatever for, I figure he's got his reasons. I'm going to make it my business to find out.'

Frank frowned and shook his head.

'The old Indian is dead. The bartender they wanted to question is dead. So that leaves only Ishmael for them to question.'

Frank stared aghast at his brother. 'What the fuck has he got to do with Homeland's investigation?' he snapped.

'Cool it, Frankie. You'll scare the fish. Now hear me out. The papers give a fairly detailed account of her movements over the past few days, before she got herself arrested. Ishmael told us that he left the party with her and her mother on Saturday night — there were a lot of witnesses — but the papers say she went to a friend's house alone to drop some books off in Prescott on Sunday. We,' Matteo pointed to Frank and himself, 'know for a fact she was accompanied by Ishmael. He has his eureka moment — Santo Paolo, hallelujah bless me sweet Jesus, I've seen the light — to whatever that place is called.'

'Damascus, Matteo. The capital of Syria.'

'Yeah, Damascus and — shazam — he's not a terrorist anymore.'

Matteo paused for a moment. 'Frankie, I caught something.' He madly reeled in his line, an expression of anticipation on his face, but the line broke and, in his frustration, he threw his rod into the water. 'Fuckin' cheap rods,' he cursed.

'Cheap rods? Pig's ass. That's $750 worth of tackle you threw overboard, bro.'

'Forget the rod. Now, where was I?'

'Ishmael has just seen the light.' Frank leant over the side and lunged in vain at the sinking rod.

'Okay.' Matteo took a long drink of his Coke and belched. 'This is the gamble. We don't know for sure whether the boys from Homeland want a word with our man or not, ask him a few questions, if he had sex with her when she gave him a lift home from the party and if he did, how good was she.'

'Just good old routine detective work so the boys in the office can have a laugh over the whore,' Frank added.

Matteo nodded agreeably and continued. 'It's about crossing the Ts and dotting the Is. As long as they do it everything's copasetic. Now, his boss from the Colorado Aqueduct, or whoever is in charge of talking to the boys from Homeland, tells them that Scot Fall, our prisoner down in the swamp, had to make an urgent trip back to Canada because of that sick relative stuff he used for an excuse to get time off work. So they send a couple of their men to have a talk with him while he's playing nursemaid to his aunty. They get there and discover he's played some hoax on his boss to get time off work. That's fine. They aren't truant officers, so they shut the fuck up about it, but they still want to talk to him, but he's nowhere to be found. Now, for the very reason that he was with Rosasharn who, according to Homeland, is a possible threat to national peace and security, Homeland might find the vanishing act a little bit too hard to swallow. If they didn't give a flying fuck about him in the first instance, they sure as hell are going to get hot flashes for him now. So they get some sex-starved nerd in the department to look into it. This guy leaves no stone unturned is how he gets his rocks off.

'Now they're going down a road that wasn't on their map. Ishmael is completely decked out in the forged Scot Fall identity kit, which might be watertight on paper – getting through customs, passport, getting a green card ... From what Ishmael has told us, if Homeland gets around to doing a little door knocking and starts talking to Hagar Rinehart, CEO of the industrial engineering faculty at the University of Montréal, I figure leaks are bound to spring up. Maybe they get Interpol on board to look into her boyfriend, that Nazi kraut Akmid, who masterminded the scholarship scam. Who the fuck knows? Only Jesus Christ himself.'

Chapter 70 *Vermillion Bay, Louisiana, Friday 31 August*

Matteo threw his arms into the air. 'What's in that black hole? If they start shining a torch down it, something is bound to show up to tickle their fancy. Hey, maybe Paul South, who was way out of focus, suddenly comes into focus.'

Frank sighed. 'What the hell are you getting at, Matteo? It sounds to me like when you make minestrone soup. You don't know when to stop tossing diced vegetables into the pot. When it's cooked it's so fuckin' thick, you have to carve it to eat it.'

'Keep your ears pricked, little brother, because it's going to get even thicker and you are going to need a chain saw to cut it.'

Frank rolled his eyes and motioned him to talk on.

'Now, if there's one thing this fuckin' terrorist crap has made me realize,' Matteo said, 'it's that being one step ahead is not enough. You've got to get some mega mileage behind you. Those Homeland heavies aren't looking for hard evidence to switch into overdrive. What it is that I'm trying to get through to you, Frankie, is that as long as the file is open on Scot Fall, sooner or later something is bound to surface.'

'Hey, Matteo, that reminds me. You heard anything more about the body that was recovered from the western end of the bay?'

'Kramer rang me a few hours ago and told me it had breasts. I realise that the chances of South getting a mention are remote, but if he does,' Matteo shook his head, 'it's going to jog that meat-head Uriah's memory big-time. You following what I'm saying, Frankie? From the look on your face I know you're still thinking to yourself that I'm running at the mouth.'

'Correct,' replied Frank.

'I still got more to say,' Matteo said, raising his voice.

Frank motioned him on as he trimmed the slack on his line.

'For whatever reasons, they may decide to wait until Scot Fall gets back to work. There'll be a note waiting for him on his desk to ring so-and-so from the Homeland office who wants to take him out for coffee. Let's say he doesn't turn up back at the Colorado Aqueduct. Well, the same shit is going to hit the fan.'

'I suppose so, Matteo.'

'Whatever way the cat falls, it's going to land on its feet. Eventually, they go back and have a talk to the Rayner girl who, by the way, was the last person to see Scot Fall alive, which was on Saturday night. And now, for argument's sake, let's say they discover she was with him on Sunday on her mission from God. They are going to sort out the facts from the fiction from the story she told them the last time they had the pleasure of her company.'

Frank swallowed hard a couple of times. 'For all we know, they could be hunting for the guy at this very minute,' he said.

'Good point.' Matteo nodded approvingly at his brother. 'So why don't we pull up anchor and scoot off to Havana? I'll tell you why. There's nothing in the news about looking for a missing person who's wanted for questioning. For how long, we don't know. When there is, it'll be a nationwide hunt, maybe even international.

'Okay, we know Uriah can definitely link Paul South to the *Mark Twain*. If he recognises Scot Fall on the wanted posters, he's going to instantly place him talking to South on the *Twain*. That's why he snuck on board. Sure, our name is clear, but Uriah learns that he was tracking a possible terrorist. Homeland heavies are going to ask questions about why those guys were on the *Mark Twain*. And then, we not only have the FBI but also Homeland on our backs. Homeland's heavies are not going to pussyfoot around. They'll go for the jugular. That's a scenario I do not want to deal with.'

'Hey, Matteo, the solution is easy. Let's bump off Uriah. He's the only link to us.'

'Killing Uriah could turn the heat on us even higher, even though

Chapter 70 *Vermillion Bay, Louisiana, Friday 31 August*

Uriah is not around anymore to place Ishmael boarding the *Mark Twain*. Salvador would then get drawn into the picture. We then have to bump him off. So, one murdered FBI agent and his partner from the IRS, and they were assigned to our tail. Who killed them would need solving. The big brass assume they found some dirt on us because where has Uriah been hanging out the past three weeks?'

'The *Mark Twain*.'

'Correct. So we're their first port of call. It's a problem we can handle, no sweat. You know that, Frankie. As long as it involves local law enforcement officers who have to stick by the rules to make their cases stand up in court.'

'So, what are we waiting for? The tide to come in?'

'Because even though we think we've covered all bases I figure it still leaves us open. Homeland would then seriously hunt down our reformed terrorist friend. For how long, who knows? We'll be forever looking over our shoulders, not for the FBI, or some smartass rookie cop wanting to kick start his career by solving some misdemeanour that leads to our doorstep, or a budding district attorney who, with a stroke of luck, stumbles on some finer point of the law that eventually catches us out. No, no, no,' Matteo said forcefully. 'It's more than all of that. This stuff is worse. It has a lifespan equal to spent radioactive isotopes.'

'Matteo, we just do an insurance job on the *Mark Twain*. Sink it to the bottom of the river and collect. Halpin is more than capable of doing it.'

'If the *Mark Twain* ever gets onto the Homeland's hit list they'll dredge up every piece of wood from the bottom of the river. Okay, they don't find any gambling chips or even a rusted-out roulette wheel, but when they start looking into every owner of that boat since it rolled out of the Memphis dry dock, who knows where the paper trail is going to lead? Papa is dead. We don't know where he landed his signature or who he swindled to get a hold of the river tub. Now, Frankie that may not be of interest to Homeland, but it might spark the attention of someone who might know someone who is interested in the intelligence.'

'You think of everything, Matteo. Looking at it that way, it just gets messy,' said Frank.

'All I know is that we've got to get Ishmael back to his Scot Fall routine at the Colorado Aqueduct and mop up everything down here. Uriah is being taken care of. Halpin is pressing charges against him for boarding the boat under false pretenses. He's got Senator Shadrack's security man coming to the party and a statement from the senator himself, and from what I've been told, Uriah's sorry fat ass is in boiling oil.'

'Can we trust Ishmael, say, if he eventually gets picked up and Homeland finds out the truth? He's going to spill his guts.'

Matteo looked at Frank as if he were considering his question thoughtfully. 'You tell me. Will he or won't he? What's that to us? He can say what the fuck he likes once he's out of our hands alive.'

'It's not like he's going to cut a deal with the DA and get put in a witness protection program,' said Frank, nodding agreeably.

'Precisely,' said Matteo. 'He's not in the least bit interested in taking anyone down with him. As far as dying is concerned, I never knew anyone who ever begged to bring it on, other than Jesus Christ himself.'

'And Plato,' Frank added.

'Who the fuck's he?'

'Some other time.'

There ensued a few moments of silence between the brothers. Matteo picked up a paper and started thumbing through it. Frank stood up, reeled in his line and re-baited the hook. As he was about to cast his rod, he abruptly halted as a disturbing thought came to mind. He was momentarily frozen, the baited line and sinker swinging like a pendulum above his head. He stood there, motionless. Then his knees started to weaken. He eased himself down on the ice chest and looked over at his

Chapter 70 *Vermillion Bay, Louisiana, Friday 31 August*

brother, who had his head buried in the newspaper.

'Something just occurred to me about Rayner telling Homeland a whole mess of believable bullshit,' Frank said, his voice trembling.

Matteo folded the paper. 'What's the matter, Frank? You see a ghost? Is it papa?'

Frank shook his head. 'Look, Matteo, I've followed what you said and I believed at first that killing was the way to go, but after listening to the way you explained it, why we need him alive makes a lot of sense.'

'So what's causing you grief, Frankie?'

'The Rayner girl at this very moment is not crafting her story to Homeland thinking that when she gets out her reformed boy wonder is back at his desk at the Colorado Aqueduct. All she knows is he's heading down south to end it all with his boyhood bum chum and that he's going to leave behind the envelope addressed to the Homeland.'

Matteo's concern for his brother turned into amusement. There was a twinkle in his eye. 'Bingo! You got it. The penny finally dropped.'

'What's so funny? I just put a fuckin' pin in the balloon you've been pumping up my ass to float us to safety, and you're happy?' He threw the fishing rod down and held his head between his hands. 'Where is that bucket of cocaine?'

'Because that's what's been busting my balls. Look, Frankie, everything about this guy in the swamp defies logic. Remember what cranky Father Ugo Albino used to say in Sunday school? That the Virgin Mary, her Son and all the Saints work in mysterious ways and we little boys are not to try and scientifically work it out like they try to do in the Christian Science Church down the road from St Augustine. We "are required only to have faith".'

Frank gazed mournfully at his brother.

'You heard it from the man himself that it was God that gave him a new heart and that the girl was an instrument of God. He told us that on three occasions he was going to press the button to end it all. His suicide bomb belt packs it in on the Greyhound bus. Finally, when he's got the nerve and the bomb is working properly, well, you know what happened on the *Mark Twain*. If God gives a man a new heart because the old one is corrupted, then you've got to say to yourself that God wants that man alive on earth, not dead.

'Somebody up there,' Matteo raised his hand, 'has got a finger on Santo Paolo down in the swamps and strings are being pulled, left, right and center on all of us puppets down below.

'You got the comanchero dead along with the bartender. Billy Apple's tight lipped. The professor is batting for her and only God Himself knows who is getting pressure from on high to do His bidding. And we, my dear brother, are part of that divine holy plan.'

Frank was dumbstruck. He picked up a fishing knife from off the deck and pared his thumbnail. Finally, he said, 'So, all that's left to do is burn the report addressed to Homeland.'

Matteo leant over, plucked a rose stem and brought it up to his nose, closed his eyes and breathed in its heavenly scent.

'Dear little brother of mine, I think it's time for the underworld to do its bit to protect the homeland.'

Frank felt his heart lurch up in his chest. He violently harpooned the knife into the deck. Just then, their attention was diverted by an ear-piercing shriek.

'Looks like Benny's hit pay dirt,' said Matteo.

CHAPTER 71

OKLAHOMA CITY, OKLAHOMA, MONDAY 3 SEPTEMBER

Uriah had been pacing the floor in reception, outside his boss's office, for the past thirty minutes. Inside, his boss, Iceum Parks was on the phone to Senator Shadrack, apologizing profusely on behalf of his wayward man who had been poking his nose where he had no business to poke it. Shadrack was threatening to lodge a formal complaint to the director's office to have Uriah disciplined and Iceum's office investigated.

Uriah knew that someone on the *Mark Twain* had tipped off the captain that he was on board without a ticket: he guessed it had to have been Senator Shadrack's head of security. It seemed strange that it wouldn't have been more than two minutes after he entered Duvall's office, seated himself and exchanged a little small talk with the preacher that security burst into the office and arrested him for boarding the riverboat without a ticket.

What captured his imagination was the fear he'd seen on Duvall's face, the guilt too, when he saw one of the guards nodding slightly to Duvall. It had given him the impression that Duvall had been caught out at something, although he couldn't be sure what. All that Uriah could come up with was that someone did not want him talking to Duvall.

If Uriah still wanted to pursue the firebug, he would have to divulge all he knew to the New Orleans Branch and what he knew wasn't much. He sat down and picked up the newspaper from the coffee table and read the headline — HOMELAND SAYS SORRY. Accompanying the story was a photo of Rosasharn being escorted out of the Fort Apache Military Base in Arizona, surrounded by her family and friends.

Iceum Parks stuck his head out of his office door and growled at Uriah to get inside. Uriah threw down the paper, stood up and paused for a fraction to fortify himself against the onslaught of his boss's wrath.

CHAPTER 72

PASTORA PEAK, NAVAJO RESERVATION, SATURDAY 8 SEPTEMBER

Ishmael and Rosasharn sat on a flat rock on the summit of Pastora Peak gazing up at the clear blue sky. Other than a couple of condors gliding low in the valley, there were no other birds of prey to be seen.

The rock face fell away gently for about fifty feet and then to a sheer drop of more than a thousand feet. This was the spot where Old Smoke had supposedly plummeted into the maze of narrow crevices among the splintered boulders below. Old Smoke's body had not been recovered. It had rained very heavily the day Old Smoke died, all traces of blood were washed away. After four days, the search was called off.

What had happened beside the bridge surrounded by ancient cottonwoods at Big Chino Wash Verde River? The trial and passing of judgment on Ishmael by the Supreme Indian Spiritual Council, presided over by Old Smoke, had culminated in each of them being released from their captors: Rosasharn walking free from Fort Apache Military Base and Ishmael from the clutches of the Malatesta brothers. The only thing they intuitively knew was that a power not their own had brought them together. Now, in this moment, sitting on the summit of Pastora Peak, all that mattered was waiting for the three eagles to appear and fly in a circle.

They had left the car at Mexican Water and hiked up the sacred mountain, bringing along provisions to spend the night on the summit, prepared to stay there as long as it took to dispose of the eagle feathers according to Old Smoke's instructions.

Ishmael's repatriation into the land of the living as Scot Fall had been seamless. Matteo had taken care of every detail, motivated, of course, by his own need for self-preservation and the conviction that to have done so was the divine will. Ishmael had incessantly begged Matteo to kill him, to no avail. Finally, he succumbed to the way things had to play out. When Ishmael got back to the Colorado Aqueduct, a memo was waiting on his desk to ring the Homeland office. He had had a brief talk with Spender concerning whether Rosasharn had mentioned to him anything that might be of interest to them. He replied in the negative.

As much as he wanted to believe that Canaan was dead, deep down in his soul he felt that his lifelong friend was still alive somewhere. Canaan had an incredible capacity to hold his breath under water, an ability he had acquired during his days in the Uttar Pradesh Juvenile Prison, when the jailers manacled him and strung him up by his feet and lowered his head in a barrel of water, leaving him submerge for minutes at a time, before throwing him into solitary confinement.

'You know, Ishmael,' Rosasharn pointed in a north-easterly direction, 'over to the right is Colorado, to the left Utah, New Mexico is that way, and this here is sweet Arizona.' She slapped her hand on the rock she was perched on and pulled her knees to her chest. 'I'm imagining that I am not looking across the borders into four states, but way, way back into the past.'

'What do you mean?'

'I'm thinking of the real custodians of this land. To the south, Pueblo and Apache, to the north, Ute, Shoshoni, to the east, Kiowa, Wichita.' She swept her hand towards the horizon and pointed out to the plain.

'The people from the time before the rocks were hard,' replied Ishmael with a warm smile.

Chapter 72 Pastora Peak, Navajo Reservation, Saturday 8 September

Ishmael bowed his head and stared at the leather pouch with the eagle talons engraved on the flap, the two eagle feathers tucked inside. A few feet away was a wreath of withered flowers, wild flowers of all kinds, and cactus buds, crudely woven, held together by duct tape. The wreath rested on a stone that had an inscription: *Old Smoke, born to the Rocks people, and for the Salt of the Earth clan.*

'It should have been me, not Old Smoke.' Ishmael sighed and picked up the wreath. 'I've tried to make sense of it.'

'You've tried to make sense of it? I don't even know where to begin. At least you've started,' said Rosasharn, pulling a water bottle from the top of her backpack.

'If Old Smoke wasn't murdered and Little Bird Double Head hadn't died, you wouldn't have made up the story to tell what actually happened as if it were fiction, and Matteo wouldn't have believed anything I had said.'

'And you wouldn't be here.' Rosasharn cut him off. She took a sip of water.

'How did you know that I was still alive?' Ishmael scraped some flaking moss off a rock with the heel of his boot.

'After I was told that Old Smoke had ...' she stopped, craned her neck and looked down the craggy chasm. 'That wanker Billy Apple murdered Old Smoke.' She told Ishmael how the deputy had come to be at Old Smoke's property and how he had threatened him.

'They read me the memorandum, dressed me in orange cover-alls, and locked me up. I didn't know what was going on in the outside world, whether you had done all those things you said you would, if they had Old Smoke or if they'd talked to that bartender from the Warm Spring Bar and Bistro. I asked the bartender if you had passed through, and got directions to Old Smoke's ranch. God knows what he would have said to the Homeland people if he hadn't died. Everything was just going to snowball and the snowball would have rolled you over.

'I was getting the third degree by this junior officer, who was giving me a hard time. Throwing questions left, right and center about my college days and what groups of people I associated with. Finally, he got onto the subject of what I was doing at Old Smoke's place the morning I was picked up. I couldn't deny it. Billy Apple had seen me there that morning.

'When he told me about Old Smoke committing suicide, I burst into tears. He went out to get some tissues and I was left alone for what seemed like ages. Eventually, I pulled myself together, dried my tears on my sleeve. Then this weird thing happened. I felt something run over my shoe. I looked down and I saw a rat. It arched up on its hind legs and stared up at me, nodding its head and twitching its nose as if trying to communicate to me. Can you believe it?'

Ishmael gave her a knowing smile. 'Yes, I can. Have you ever heard of the Karni Mata Hindu Temple at Deshnok in India?'

'No, but do tell me about it.'

'It is dedicated to the worship of holy rats.'

Ishmael told her that when he was a boy, he had spent hours at the Karni Mata Temple trying to spot the rare white rat eating — *Prasad* —, holy food offerings, amid the plague of holy rats that roam freely in and out of its silver doors, along its tessellated corridors and around carved marble columns. Legend had it that it brings good luck if one beholds this rare repast. Minor blessings are available if rats scamper over one's feet.

'Well I certainly spotted a rare rat scampering over my foot in that Fort Apache interrogation room. And it wasn't a minor blessing it bestowed on me. Just moments later, I heard the door open and this older guy came in. Later he introduced himself. It was Harvey Spender, the one you talked to. I looked up at him and then down to the floor, but the rat had vanished. Harvey Spender said, "You better tell us the whole story." Out of the blue I suddenly remembered what Old Smoke

Chapter 72 *The End*

had said to me before he mounted his horse: "When the sign of the rat appears it will be the time to tell the truth so it will be believed, yet not perceived." I knew then and there what I had to tell them, I just let my imagination run wild and they swallowed it all.'

'That is amazing. I don't know what to say.'

'Praise God,' Rosasharn replied.

'Yes,' Ishmael said in a low voice.

They closed their eyes and prayed in silence.

The squawk of an eagle broke the trance and, for a moment, they were back at Old Smoke's place, staring at him as he emerged from the canyon holding the eagle.

Ishmael looked up and saw three eagles circling not too high above them.

'Look!' Ishmael cried, pointing to the birds.

Rosasharn looked up and gazed wondrously at the majestic birds gliding in perfect circles. She reached out her hand and encircled Ishmael's wrist. 'You know, Ishmael, it's like we've found another reality.'

Ishmael smiled. 'All I know is that this is a taste of heaven.'

A gust of wind swept through the valley. Ishmael opened the leather pouch, removed the eagle feathers, and handed one to Rosasharn. They raised their arms and let the swirling breeze lift the dark feathers from their open palms. Higher and higher they rose, gyrating into the azure sky.

THE END

EPILOGUE

Canaan crouched low on the rooftop of a building in the French quarter. His face shone with hatred; his lips were drawn back tightly across his teeth as he sighted Duvall in the crosshairs of the telescope of his high-powered hunting rifle with a silencer. Duvall was sitting at a table in front of a café sipping coffee and chatting gaily to an elegantly dressed elderly woman. Canaan had been poised there for the past ten minutes, his finger resting lightly on the trigger. He had followed with keen interest the events of the past few weeks. When he had been fortuitously dropped into the water, he had managed to free himself and wade to shore where he had stayed until dawn, all the while spying on the Malatesta boat. At sunrise Ishmael was on shore, being escorted at gunpoint by Matteo's men to the safe house. At the time Canaan believed it was the way things were going to be and had planned to wait until Ishmael was killed by these people. Then he would go and find Duvall by himself. Much to his disappointment, it was not to be.

On an adjacent ridge overlooking the top of Pastora Peak, Deputy Billy Apple was standing next to his horse looking through a pair of binoculars at Rosasharn and Ishmael. Concealed behind a rock, not too far away from where Billy Apple stood, was Gaetano the Coffee Grinder, relaying what he was observing into his cell phone to Matteo.